The House of New Beginnings

Lucy Diamond

The HOUSE of New BEGINNINGS

MACMILLAN

First published 2017 by Macmillan
an imprint of Pan Macmillan
20 New Wharf Road, London N1 9RR
Associated companies throughout the world
www.panmacmillan.com

ISBN 978-1-4472-9911-0

Typeset by Ellipsis Digital Limited, Glasgow
Printed and bound by CPI Group (UK) Ltd, Croydon, CR0 4YY

Visit **www.panmacmillan.com** to read more about all our books
and to buy them. You will also find features, author interviews and
news of any author events, and you can sign up for e-newsletters
so that you're always first to hear about our new releases.

For Martin, with love
Here's to many happy years
in House Number Three

Acknowledgements

It seems apt to be writing my thank-yous for *The House of New Beginnings* amidst a sea of boxes and packing tape – as we too are soon to be moving to a different home, for our own new beginning. Here's hoping my next set of neighbours are as lovely as some of the characters in this book . . .

New beginnings are all well and good but you can't beat the satisfaction that comes from working with a great group of people over a number of years . . . and I couldn't have a better team at Pan Macmillan. Thanks must go especially to Caroline Hogg, champion cheerleader and inspirational editor, who adds so much to every book of mine. Grateful thanks are also due to Anna Bond, Katie James, Alex Saunders, Jeremy Trevathan, Stuart Dwyer, Jo Thomson, Emma Bravo, Kate Bullows, Kate Tolley, Nicole Foster and the whole lovely lot of you.

A huge round of applause for the whip-smart and fabulous Lizzy Kremer at David Higham Associates. Thank you for your creativity and insight, and for always telling it like it is. You're a star.

Massive thanks to Jo White and Kate Harrison for the Brighton love, pub tips and excellent nights out. Special thanks to the audience at Gateshead Library who were the first people to hear a section of this book and responded just as I'd hoped – thanks also for your title suggestions, which were greatly appreciated!

Thanks and love to Martin, Hannah, Tom and Holly for constant support and their willingness to brainstorm plot ideas over the dinner table at the drop of a hat.

Finally, thanks as ever to you for picking up this book to read. I really hope you enjoy it.

SeaView House Noticeboard:

POLITE REMINDER
To All Residents

PLEASE pick up post as it arrives and sort it into the appropriate pigeonholes. Please do NOT leave it lying around. It is unsightly and a fire risk. For sorting purposes, residents' details are as follows.

Flat 1 – Rosa Dashwood
Flat 2 – Joanna and Beatrice Spires
Flat 3 – ~~Michael Donovan and Dominic Sanders~~
Flat 4 – Charlotte Winters
Flat 5 – Margot Favager

Angela Morrison-Hulme
Property Manager

Prologue

Charlotte was dreaming about Kate again. This time, they were in a beautiful garden, just the two of them, with magnolia trees in full bloom, and birdsong, a host of pink tulips nearby, swaying gently in a whispering spring breeze. *Oh, Charlotte was thinking in surprise, here you are, Kate! I must have got it wrong. Wrong all this time, and nobody told me!*

She couldn't stop looking at Kate's face. Those rosebud lips, the rounded apple cheeks, the dark downy hair on her head. 'I thought I'd lost you,' she said in wonder, holding her close, breathing in the warm soapy scent of her. She wasn't sure whether to laugh or sob at the relief of it all, the feeling of Kate's soft face against her own. It was the best feeling in the world. 'But you were here this whole time. Why did nobody tell me you were here?'

'And the headlines at seven o'clock this morning,' a stern voice said just then, interrupting the moment, and everything seemed to shimmer, the sun passing behind a cloud.

Charlotte took no notice. *Not interested*, she thought, arms tightening around her daughter.

'A forty-nine-year-old man is being questioned about the murder of a police officer,' the voice went on, and a cold wind blew through the dream-garden in the next second, silken petals dropping from the tulip heads. When Charlotte looked down, Kate had vanished.

'No,' Charlotte said, whirling around in distress. 'Kate!'

'Pope Francis is due to make a speech today about—'

'*No*,' Charlotte cried again, the dream splintering around her in shining fragments. If she could just get back there, she thought frantically, pulling the duvet up over her head to muffle the sound of the radio. Back to the moment when they'd been together, just her and Kate, the moment when everything had been all right again. *Happy*.

'The Prime Minster is under fire this morning, due to—'

Go away. She reached out a hand and thumped the snooze button on her alarm, not wanting thoughts of the Prime Minister to crawl into bed with her. Because of course, she *was* in bed, and not in a garden. She was thirty-eight years old and waking up all alone in a small quiet flat, as she did every morning these days.

As for Kate . . . well, she was most definitely gone, and not coming back. Not ever.

Chapter One

Georgie Taylor pulled on the handbrake, turned off the engine and caught the eye of the small green-haired gonk that spent its life hanging from her driver's mirror. 'So here we are in Brighton,' she said to it, lifting one aching shoulder then another, in a vague approximation of a yoga class she had once been to. 'A long way from home, right?'

The gonk, unsurprisingly, didn't respond. Georgie's boyfriend Simon would have snorted if he could have seen her conversing like this with a small inanimate creature with seriously bad hair, but Georgie had come to feel rather fond of the gonk's benevolently smiling face, its wide plastic eyes never judging her atrocious parallel parking or wonky reversing. Sometimes she would glance over at it after a terrible overtaking manoeuvre and it was as if they had shared a little moment, never to be confessed to Simon. What happens in the car, stays in the car. Or something. Maybe she was over-thinking this, on second thoughts.

Anyway – here she was: Dukes Square, her new address,

her new city, her new life! *Hello, Brighton*, she thought, clambering out of the car, legs stiff and heavy after the five-hour drive south. *So this is what you look like.* She gazed down past the busy road at the bottom of the square to the beach beyond, where the warm April sunshine was bouncing off the sea like a thousand glittering sequins. She'd driven past the Palace Pier a few minutes earlier, with its roller coasters and souvenir stalls, and there below was the promenade with ornate Victorian lamp posts and duck-egg-blue railings. She could smell chips and seaweed and diesel, so different from the clean wet grassy air she was used to in the Dales. Despite the trepidation she'd felt about packing up their life in Yorkshire for the move, she couldn't help feeling the merest flicker of excitement too all of a sudden. Living by the *sea*! They were actually going to be living by the sea, just the two of them, in a cosy little love nest together. A new adventure. A new chapter. Fun times ahead!

Hi! she texted Simon. *I'm here! Are you on your way?*

She scanned the horizon while waiting for his reply, smiling to herself as she imagined him pelting up the hill towards her and then the two of them in a slow-motion run, arms outstretched. Two whole weeks they'd been apart, after all. Two weeks of her lying awake at night listening to all the weird noises their house made in the dark and worrying that she'd left a window open somewhere. Two weeks of him living it up in a posh hotel down here while he got stuck into his new job. It felt like the longest time when you had spent your entire adult life with the same person, which they had.

Georgie and Simon had dated the whole way through sixth-form, then gone to Liverpool university together, before returning to Stonefield upon graduation. There they'd both found local jobs – her as a librarian, him as an architect. And while she was a mediocre sort of librarian if she was honest, preferring rainy days when the library was quiet and she could sit sucking boiled sweets and reading detective novels, he, by contrast, had turned out to be really good at his job. Within five years, his distinctive style had become sought after by all manner of people around the north – and now a former boss had requested his input for this new project down in ruddy *Brighton*: transforming a vast derelict Victorian mansion just out of the city into a state-of-the-art hotel. It was to be the biggest project he'd worked on, and he'd been thrilled to have his designs chosen out of the many who'd tendered for the job. 'They want me to project manage the whole thing, I'd be mad to turn it down,' he'd said, eyes shining. 'It's only going to be for six months or so, and this could really put me on the map, George. This could be the big time.'

Because she was a nice, generous-hearted sort of girl-friend, Georgie had been pleased for him, and proud too. Of *course* she wanted him to earn his place 'on the map', of *course* she hoped he would hit this mystical big time. But because she was also a human being who couldn't quite square his new career development with the happy-ever-after *she'd* always envisaged for the pair of them – the dog, the kids, the lovely big house up in Yorkshire, maybe another dog for good measure – she also felt kind of unsettled. 'So what am I meant to do if you're down there for six months?' she'd asked, trying to keep the petulance she felt from her voice. 'Twiddle my toes the whole time?'

He'd looked a bit pained at her question. He'd actually pulled this 'Search me' face where he didn't meet her in the eye, as if the question of her, his beloved, hadn't particularly crossed his mind in the whole decision. As if he didn't care! 'We can talk on the phone, Skype each other . . . ?' he'd replied haltingly.

'For six *months*?' She'd stared at him, horrified by how nonchalant he seemed at the prospect of so long apart. Meanwhile in Stonefield, her best friend Amelia had recently got engaged (Valentine's Day, the lucky cow) and was already talking about wedding dresses. Their friends Jade and Sam were due to get married in summer, too. When Simon had told her he had something to say that evening, Georgie had assumed that it was her turn – finally! – to have that question popped, and she'd gone all quivery inside. In the past, she had wondered (many times) how she might react to this moment: a scream of joy, her arms flung around his neck, an exuberant dance on the spot, maybe even a spontaneous double-fist air-punch. It looked as if she was going to have to wait a bit longer yet to find that out, clearly.

There had been a too-long pause where he'd frowned uncertainly, as if trying to work out the right thing to say. 'You could . . . come with me?' he had suggested in the end.

She didn't *want* to have to go with him, that was the thing. Especially when the offer had been made so half-heartedly, like an afterthought rather than a serious proposition. She would have much preferred for both of them to stay right there in Stonefield, playing house in their tiny terrace with its cosy wood-burning stove, going to the pub with their mates every Friday night, hearing the bells ring in the old stone church every Sunday morning. (Okay, so maybe not the church bells on second thoughts. They were actually a pain in the neck waking you up so early, and brutal if you had a hangover.) Venture somewhere new where she didn't know anyone, where she didn't have a job or any friends? It sounded awful. But then again, whenever she had imagined her boyfriend down in Brighton on his own for six long months, surrounded by all kinds of temptations, while she was stuck up north, she wasn't sure that that was any better an alternative.

'You should keep an eye on him,' Amelia had pronounced ominously, sucking her teeth and twiddling the engagement ring on her finger. She'd been to her cousin's hen do in Brighton the year before and now considered herself an expert on the place. 'It's like the Wild West down there on a Saturday night, I'm telling you. Hen parties. Stag parties. Bare bums and bad behaviour everywhere. There's no way I'd let Jason out of my sight for five *minutes* there, let alone six frigging months, George.'

Georgie was the first to admit that her boyfriend was extremely fanciable to other women, with his broad rugby-player shoulders, sandy hair and easy smile, and thus it was the vision of him surrounded by sex-crazed hens, maybe even lassoed by a raunchily dressed cowgirl, that finally sealed the deal. It wasn't that she didn't *trust* Simon, she told herself. She was making the move with him because she was a loyal, supportive girlfriend, that was all. And he'd do the same for her, wouldn't he, follow her to the end of the country, if their positions were reversed? Of course he would.

Anyway. They were taking the plunge and that was that. He'd moved down a fortnight ago, while she handed in her notice at the library, put a load of their stuff in storage – well, her parents' garage, same thing – and arranged for tenants to rent their house for six months. In that time, Simon had found them a place to live and now here she was, in the centre of debauchery, apparently, although the genteel surroundings where she now found herself seemed infinitely more respectable than she'd imagined.

She gazed around at the large square which sloped up from the seafront, bordered on three sides by white and cream-painted bow-windowed Regency houses, with a huge communal lawn in its centre. Which, she wondered, was her new front door? ('Seriously? You're letting him choose your *flat*, without you even seeing it first?' Amelia had screeched, hand clutched to throat – she had always been the dramatic sort. 'That's very . . . trusting of you,' she said, although Georgie could tell from her expression that she meant 'completely mad' instead of 'very trusting'.)

Georgie felt quietly confident, though. She had given Simon very specific instructions about what she wanted in their new home: a sea view, for starters, or at the very least, huge windows through which she could nosey out at the rest of the world passing by. A lovely big living area, in which to entertain friends (not that they knew anyone here yet but she had always been the sort of person who could make new pals in the ladies' loos, on a bus, in the Debenhams lift once, even). A bedroom large enough to house her books. ('You don't need to bring all your books,' he'd told her. 'Of *course* I do!' she'd told him right back, astonished that he could suggest otherwise.) A living room with an open fireplace. ('For roasting chestnuts,' she'd said dreamily. 'In *April?*' he'd replied, disbelieving. 'All right, to have sex in front of then,' she'd said instead, which she knew would do more to convince him.) Oh yes, and a garden, just in case they decided to get a dog, was her final request. ('We're not getting a dog,' he'd said, flat-out, but Georgie, who adored dogs, and could think of nothing that would make a place more homely than a bouncing bright-eyed mutt of some description, had ignored this last statement. Simon just needed to warm up to an idea sometimes, that was all.)

There was still no sign of her boyfriend so she began walking up the hill to seek out their new home, number eleven, apparently. ('Ooh, the eleventh house, that's very lucky,' Amelia had said immediately when Georgie passed on the address. Amelia was into astrology in a big way, and took the whole thing extremely seriously. Astral Amelia, they'd called her at school. 'The eleventh house in astrology is the house of friends, hopes and wishes, goals and ideals. Couldn't be better!')

Seven . . . nine . . . eleven. There it was. An imposing black front door, three storeys, that gorgeous curving bow window at ground level – the sort of elegant old house, in short, where you could imagine Victorian ladies emerging, long petticoats rustling on the white-painted steps. *So there, Amelia,* she felt like texting, and held up her phone to snap a photo of it, just as a huge dusty Land Rover with tinted windows swerved up from the main road below, obscuring the view. The driver flung the vehicle into a parking space (with enviable panache, it had to be said; no need for any gonk-commiserations in *that* car) then swung herself down from the vehicle: a brassy-haired woman in sunglasses and a black asymmetric dress, heaving a massive zebra-print handbag over one shoulder whilst apparently bollocking someone on the phone. 'Don't say I didn't warn you,' she said tartly as she marched over the road.

Georgie gulped as the woman strode up the steps of number eleven. 'Well, that's not my problem, is it?' she snapped into the phone before hanging up abruptly. Then she glanced at her watch, pursed her lips and stood waiting, arms folded expectantly.

If Georgie wasn't very much mistaken, this somewhat intimidating woman might well be her new landlady. And seeing as Simon still hadn't replied to her text – or made any kind of sprinting appearance – it seemed there was only one way to find out.

'Perfect timing!' the woman declared with a wide red-lipsticked smile when Georgie approached and tentatively introduced herself. Her eyes were as blue and sparkling as the sea but there was a keenness about them too, a sharp sort of interest as they rested on Georgie. 'Hello, I'm Angela Morrison-Hulme, the owner of the apartment block. Nice to meet you.'

Georgie wished she was wearing something a bit more glamorous than faded blue jeans, a striped T-shirt and her naff old trainers that had seemed like a good idea when facing a 250-mile drive. She probably didn't smell all that fresh either, come to think of it. 'You too,' she replied, her voice emerging in a nervous sort of bleat. 'I'm not sure where Simon – my boyfriend – is, but he should be here any minute. I'm Georgie Taylor anyway. Hi.'

'Well, then, Georgie Taylor,' said Angela, who, unlike her grubby newest tenant, gave off a waft of heavy perfume that had probably cost more than Georgie's car. 'I can't wait around all day for this boyfriend of yours, so let me give you these.' She unhooked two sets of keys from the vast jingling collection that emerged from her handbag. 'This key is for the front door, okay? And this smaller one is for your flat. If you lose them, there's a twenty-pound charge for replacement, plus you run the risk of triggering my notoriously explosive temper, so try not to do that, all right?' She gave a loud laugh to show that she was joking. At least, Georgie hoped she was. 'Shall we go in?'

After a last searching glance each way down the seafront to check that Simon wasn't panting towards them – unfortunately not – Georgie heaved a suitcase and sports bag out of her car boot and followed her new landlady through the front door of the house. 'Wow,' she murmured, stepping into the entrance hall. It had a cavernous ceiling and a wide red-carpeted staircase winding up and back on itself, the oak banister polished smooth by hundreds of hands over the years, while the wrought-iron sides of the staircase somehow gave off a Parisian sort of glamour.

Mrs Morrison-Hulme looked pleased. 'You like it?'

Georgie nodded. 'It's amazing,' she said, unable to help comparing it to the narrow staircase of their Stonefield home where you could touch both sides of the wall with your elbows if you stuck them out at right angles.

They went up the stairs to the first-floor landing and Mrs Morrison-Hulme unlocked the door marked '3'. 'Welcome!' she said, holding it open so that Georgie could step inside.

Georgie found she was holding her breath as she walked into a narrow hall, off which another door led to the living room. Setting down her case and bag and gazing around, her heart sank down to her festering trainers. There were no two ways around it, her first impression was . . . disappointment. Back in Stonefield, she had worked hard to create a cosy, luxurious-feeling living room with dark varnish on the floorboards, a soft white rug, a big squishy leather sofa with fluffy cushions, and the wood-burner which chucked out tons of heat on a frosty evening. By way of complete contrast, this room was small and musty-smelling with an ageing navy blue sofa that sagged in the middle and dusty velvet curtains which even the most generous person couldn't fail to describe as 'shit-brown'. Despite the filthiness of the sash window, there was no disguising the fact that their 'view' was one of a tiny back courtyard and a pair of wheelie bins rather than any grand vistas featuring the sea. *Oh, Simon*, she thought in dismay. No wonder he hadn't shown up on time.

Too embarrassed to face her in light of this Not-Ideal-Home situation.

'So . . . this is obviously the living room,' Mrs Morrison-Hulme said, walking briskly into the room beside Georgie and waving an arm around as if showing off an opulent space.

'Yes,' Georgie replied faintly, unable to dredge up any further comment, let alone enthusiasm. She should have listened to Amelia. She should have insisted on Simon Skyping her through every flat-hunting session. What had he been *thinking*?

'Your bathroom is along here . . .' the landlady went on, retreating back to the corridor and indicating the next white-painted door. 'The kitchen's obviously here' – she gestured to a blue-tiled galley space with a sink, fridge and cooker and two small cupboards, then demonstrated how to adjust the thermostat and use the greasy-looking hob. 'And the bedroom's down at the end. Okay? I think that's everything, other than to remind you – no smoking, no sub-renting, no pets, no parties, no music after eleven o'clock at night.'

'Right,' said Georgie, her voice a croak. No fun, basically. No enjoyment. And definitely no gorgeous, funny dog, bumping his nose against her hand and lolloping after tennis balls on the grassy square outside.

Angela pulled a business card from her handbag and pressed it into Georgie's palm. 'Anything else, give me a call

– here's my mobile number. My son Paul helps out with the business, so you'll have either me or him at the other end.' She winked a turquoise-shaded eyelid and leaned closer. 'He's very good-looking by the way, my Paul. If it all goes pear-shaped with the unreliable boyfriend – where *is* he, anyway? – then a nice girl like you could do a lot worse. Just saying!'

Georgie tried to smile but it was an effort when panic was crashing through her like the waves down on the beach. Oh God. What had she done? What had she agreed to? And why on earth had Simon chosen this dump of a flat? Call himself a great architect, a designer of beautiful buildings? Why hadn't that artistic vision extended to their new love nest? 'Thank you,' she managed to say, as the questions beat about her head like midges, and then, feeling belatedly defensive about her relationship, added, 'He's probably got tied up with something at work.'

'Of course he has,' replied Mrs Morrison-Hulme with another meaningful wink that said she didn't believe it for a minute. 'Anyway, I'd better be off.' Her heels left small indentations on the carpet as she took the few steps back to the front door. 'All the best. Welcome to SeaView House!'

The door closed after her, and then it was just Georgie on her own, completely overwhelmed with the awfulness of this new situation. *SeaView House, my arse*, she thought indignantly, remembering the 'view' of the dustbins out the back.

She could smell the pong of something rotten in the kitchen and there was a damp patch on the ceiling. What would Amelia say if she could see her now? *Oh my God, George. Total nightmare! What the actual frig?* Tears pricked her eyes at the thought of her best friend's shocked voice, and she had to fight the impulse to dash out to her car again and drive straight home. 'Big mistake,' she imagined herself telling the gonk as she made a wheel-spinning U-turn. 'Disaster!'

But then her phone rang: Simon. 'Hi,' she said warily. 'Where are you? I'm in the flat.' *Please tell me there's been a mistake and this is not our actual new home,* she thought, poking a toe at a dustball on the carpet.

'Sorry,' he said. She could hear conversation in the background, another person laughing. 'Something came up here. You met the landlady all right, though?'

'Yeah. She's been and gone.' Georgie raked a hand through her hair and leaned against the wall. Now that she was finally in the same city as him, she no longer knew quite what to say. *I hate the flat!* she wanted to wail. *I can't live here!* But she knew he hated her making a fuss. And besides, she didn't want to be the clingy sort of girlfriend who made fusses. Gritting her teeth, she made a gigantic effort to banish the lump in her throat and pull herself together.

'Bit of a character, isn't she? And I know the flat is kind of spartan but I just loved how light it was – and it's a great location, right? Couldn't be nearer the beach! We can go for early-morning swims together.'

She gave a hollow laugh. 'Yeah.' Er, *no*. Was he mad? What about the list she had given him? Had he even *listened* to a single word she'd said? 'So are you on your way over now?' she asked. Everything would feel better once he was there too, she reminded herself. They could laugh about the decor, she could tease him about his terrible lack of taste, they could test out the double bed. (Well. Maybe after she'd hoovered it for bed-bugs and sprayed it with several gallons of Febreze, anyway.)

'I can't really get away right now but I'll make sure to leave at five, all right?' he said and her spirits sank all over again. 'We can get fish and chips and a few beers, sit on the beach and toast our new start, yeah?' There was another burst of laughter behind his voice and Georgie had to press the phone to her ear in order to hear him. 'I'd better go anyway. See you later!'

'See you.' She hung up and took a deep breath, trying not to give in to dejection. Fish and chips and beers with Simon later, she reminded herself. The beach. Their new start. *Come on, George, chin up, it'll be fine.*

Wandering into the poky living room, she peered out of the window to see two gulls tussling over a chip wrapper in the courtyard, wings beating, beaks lunging. She was not a quitter, she reminded herself, as one eventually flew off, victorious. Definitely not. She had once queued all night in Leeds to be near the front of the queue for the Kate Moss collection at H&M, hadn't she? She had stuck out a Saturday job at the hairdressers for two years as a teenager as well, even though the endless hair-washing had made the skin on her fingers crack and weep pus. And she had taken her driving test three times before passing, so determined was she to succeed. She didn't give up on things, that was the point. And there was no way she'd give up this time either, and slink back to Yorkshire only to endure all the pitying looks that her friends, however well-meaning, would give her. Absolutely not.

So that was settled. She would unpack and make the best of it. It wasn't all bad, was it? There was the sea right there, just a few hundred metres from her front door, blue and shimmering, with its percussion of pebbles in every wave – plus there was a whole new city for her to explore too. Adventures to be had! Fun to seek out! Maybe even new friends and a bit of work here and there. She could do it. She could cope. She would go and write her and Simon's names on that flat listing downstairs for starters.

'Right then,' she said aloud. 'Let's do this.'

Chapter Two

There was something zen about preparing onions, Rosa had always thought, fingers plucking another papery bulb from the pile and getting stuck in. A slice off the top, a slice off the bottom, and then the burrowing of one's fingers under the coppery curling skin to peel it away, revealing the naked white bauble beneath, smooth as an egg. Plunge the knife down to split it through the middle, slice into translucent rainbows ('Fingers like bear-claws!' as Liz, her favourite teacher on the catering course, had instructed) then chop, chop, chop until you had a mountain of pale watery rectangles on the chopping board, a thousand miniature opaque windows.

'Would you hurry up with those fecking onions there now, Dorothy,' barked Brendan in a distinctly un-zen-like way just then, shattering her trance. Brendan was the sous-chef at the Hotel Zanzibar, a belligerent Dubliner with a thick neck and an even thicker moustache, who took it upon himself to bellow out orders as if marshalling troops in bloody combat. He was also the sort of person who didn't bother learning the actual names of his staff, calling them whatever he felt like on that particular day, and so it took Rosa a second to realize he was addressing her.

'Won't be long,' she mumbled, bending lower and chopping faster.

In the next moment he was looming over her, the smell of garlic and last night's beer oozing from his pores. 'Won't be long, WHAT?'

'Won't be long, *chef.*'

'And don't you forget it, girl. Courgettes and peppers next. You're not in Kansas now, Dorothy. Plenty more where you came from.'

'Yes, chef,' she muttered, whacking her knife down on the board with extra force. She was thirty-five years old and had once been 'someone' in advertising, even winning an award for her 'witty and innovative' Betty's Butter campaign, but here she was a nobody; lowly kitchen staff on a pittance of a wage, where she was expected not only to graft like a slave but also to be grateful for the dubious honour of her employment. And to put up with shite round the clock from the likes of Brendan, moreover. She glanced through her eyelashes to see him now berating poor pasty Natalya, the Russian apprentice, whose hands were permanently covered in blue plasters from knife slips. Rosa gave it two weeks, possibly three, before the girl quit for an easier life. She'd only been working there a few months herself but it was enough to know that apprentices came and went like buses.

Hotel Zanzibar was situated on Brighton seafront, built around the turn of the century; a classical stucco-fronted building with five-star luxury accommodation, its own private wine cellar and an opulent penthouse suite up at the top where all sorts of famous people were rumoured to have stayed in times gone by. There was a glass lift, and a fountain in the reception and a doorman with a burgundy uniform who the kitchen staff enjoyed taking the mick out of whenever possible. Rosa knew that upstairs in the hotel there were beautiful tasteful bedrooms with sea views and balconies, monsoon showers and posh toiletries, with white fluffy bathrobes folded just so in the wardrobe, and a minibar stuffed with temptations. She knew this, of course, because it wasn't all that long ago since she'd been staying in places like this herself – for conferences and meetings with work, in chichi suits and high heels, or for dirty weekends away with Max, with sexy lingerie and room service on the king-size bed, no expense spared. Obviously she hadn't given a thought to the kitchen staff or cleaners backstage, scurrying like ants behind the scenes, chopping, basting, scrubbing, scouring. Why would she?

Sometimes she wondered how Brendan would react if he could see a previous incarnation of Rosa, a year ago, say, groomed and toned, addressing a conference hall in a suit, her long dark hair obediently glossy post-blow-dry, rather than scraped up beneath a smelly kitchen hairnet. Would he even recognize this version of the quiet, humble Rosa who slaved in his kitchen today, the Rosa who wanted nothing more than to blend into the background?

'*Onions*, Dorothy! For crying out loud!'

Speak of the devil. 'Coming right up, chef,' she replied, hacking through another onion, imagining as she did so that the blade was cleaving right through Max's beautiful lying head.

Whoever had designed the shift pattern at the Zanzibar must have had a sadistic streak running through them like the pink lettering on all the seafront sticks of rock, because nobody could have kidded themselves that their kitchen rota was an easy ride. Some days Rosa would have to work a split shift – from ten in the morning until two in the afternoon, and then go back to the hotel from five in the afternoon until midnight. Some days she'd start at five-thirty to cover the breakfast orders, and finish after the lunch session, others she might be on evenings only. It was hell if you wanted a social life, but then again in Rosa's case, she barely knew a soul in Brighton other than her equally overworked colleagues, and when she wasn't here at the hotel, she was generally sleeping off her most recent shift, dead to the world. That suited her just fine right now anyway. In her experience, it was only when you let other people into your life that problems started. Going solo, keeping herself to herself, constructing a fence around her small quiet life – it was self-preservation, nothing less.

Today she had been on an early and had the entire afternoon and evening to herself. Not only that but tomorrow – Friday – was also a short shift, finishing after lunch. She planned to spend her time off in a gloriously lazy fashion: a leisurely saunter around her new city (she was still making discoveries after four months), a slow, people-watching coffee in one of the many fabulous cafés, and then perhaps she would try a new recipe in her own kitchen.

Cooking had always been her thing. When she'd been a student, she'd been known for her magnificent Sunday roasts with the best gravy and fluffiest Yorkshire puddings. In her twenties, she would lay on great Indian banquets for her friends on a Friday night – curries fragrant with cardamom and cumin, steaming jasmine rice, and bowls of smoky dhal. She loved throwing sumptuous, hangover-obliterating weekend brunches for her best girlfriends too – *huevos rancheros* or stacks of golden pancakes studded with shiny blueberries – and of course, when Max was home, she'd enjoyed cooking seductive dinners for two – seabass with almonds, paprika chicken, steak and dauphinoise potatoes . . .

'You should do this professionally,' her friends had always swooned, asking for seconds and thirds, scraping the last crumbs from their plates. However many times they said it, though, Rosa knew, as they had done, that there was no chance of leaving her prestigious and extremely well-paid job in advertising to go and grub about in a sweaty kitchen for a living. And yet that was exactly what had happened.

'My goodness, I wasn't expecting this,' her human resources director, Colin, had said, startled, when she'd sat down in his office and handed over the crisp white envelope containing her resignation letter. He'd stared at it for several seconds with the air of a man eyeing an unexploded bomb, before pushing up his round glasses and raising his gaze to hers. 'Can we persuade you to stay? A pay rise, or some other kind of financial incentive?' he asked coaxingly. 'An extra week's holiday, how about that?'

'I don't think so,' she said, folding her hands in her lap. Having discovered the shattering truth about Max the night before, she had barely slept, but she did know, with great certainty, that she wanted to run away. Anywhere. And even though it felt right now as if she was standing at the edge of a precipice with the safety of office life behind her while ahead was a gaping chasm of emptiness where the land completely dropped away, she knew that whatever Colin might offer her, it wouldn't be enough to keep her in this office, right under Max's nose.

And so she had come to Brighton pretty much on a whim that same afternoon, a mad rush of adrenalin and anger and hurt. The city was lit up for Christmas and it had been like driving into a fairy world, where nothing mattered, where nobody would judge her. As soon as she'd moved into her new flat, one of the first things she'd done to christen the place was to go out and buy cake tins and ingredients, queuing up with all the frazzled Christmas shoppers, perspiring in their big coats and scarves. A Victoria sponge was a guaranteed short-cut to making a place feel more like home, she had figured. A Victoria sponge, then a round of mince pies (well, it *was* nearly Christmas) and then some home-made gingerbread and a Christmas cake to soften up her mum for when Rosa had to drive up to Derby on Christmas Eve, and face the difficult conversations she knew lay ahead. ('He what? You're kidding. And then you . . . Oh, you didn't, love, tell me you didn't!')

If in doubt, bake, she told herself through those first few grim days where she kept wondering what the hell her game-plan would be now, what on earth she was going to do next. But that was when it had occurred to her: that *this* was what had always made her feel better – the weighing and whisking and baking. Forget her years of advertising experience, forget her knack for brilliant jingles and creative flair. With a pinny on and her hands floured, all felt temporarily bearable in her world. Maybe it was time for a total sea-change, she had thought, and where better place than right down here by the sea?

Her mum and sister, of course, thought she had totally gone lala. Her friends too couldn't quite believe she'd gone through with it. ('I know you're upset,' a couple of them had said in talking-to-a-mad-person voices, 'but don't you think this is a little . . . extreme?') Admittedly, there had been a few occasions during Rosa's six-week intensive cookery course in the new year at the local college when she'd had what felt like out-of-body experiences, and stared at herself making a *vichyssoise* or tartare sauce in a starched white apron, and thought, what the hell . . . ? Maybe everyone was right, maybe she *had* lost the plot, she had worried each time. Here she was, after all: miles from her friends and family, pursuing this whim which had no guarantees of work, security, decent pay . . .

At moments like this, she'd find herself flashing back to something one of her teachers had once written in a school report: *Rosa is a rather emotional girl with a tendency to over-react.* A cold-eyed biology teacher, she seemed to remember, who had taken umbrage when Rosa refused to dissect a dead frog in a lesson, due to reasons of squeamishness. Was that what was happening here? Had she over-reacted again, been too emotional; the pale nauseous one heaving over a rubbish bin at the side of the lab, while the rest of the class got stuck in with their scalpels?

Well, if she had, so be it, she kept having to reassure herself. Better to be emotional than unfeeling, surely. And, okay, so perhaps she *did* have a tendency to over-react, but she also had a streak of sheer determination that acted as a counter-balance. She would see this through, come what may. She would take the gruelling shifts and physical exhaustion on the chin, she wouldn't let other people's doubts eat away at her. Besides, she only had to taste whatever she had cooked that day – a Thai green curry with home-made puffy naans, a damp rhubarb cake with just a hint of ginger, a seared tuna steak with tongue-zinging salsa verde – and she would feel her equilibrium return.

A change is as good as a holiday, her gran had always been fond of saying. And even though working for Brendan did not quite equate to holiday bliss, Rosa just had to keep cling-ing on to the thought that she was doing the right thing.

It was a twenty-minute walk along the front from the hotel to her flat and there was a stiff breeze, whipping the sea into frothy white peaks, flapping at the striped awnings of the souvenir shops and sending the postcard racks spinning diz-zily in a blur of colour. Rosa freed her hair from its ponytail and shook it loose around her shoulders, breathing in appre-ciatively as she passed a fish and chip restaurant. Hot chips and beer and ice cream, the rush and suck of the waves – those were the smells and sounds of her adopted city, and they already felt like home.

Aside from the fact that her heart had been ripped in two,

and that everyone clearly thought she was having a break-down, starting again had turned out to be the best kind of distraction. Her new home was a stone's throw from the seafront, on a Regency square with a large grassy lawn in the middle. The rent wasn't cheap and the landlady seemed rather overbearing (and kept going on about her handsome son in a heavy-handedly suggestive sort of way) but Rosa loved the house's proximity to the city centre and the prom, plus her new kitchen was a generous size and well equipped. What was more, the shabby grandeur of the old building felt a million miles from Max's sleek modern Islington bachelor pad that she'd moved into far too quickly – which could only be a good thing. Rooms of her own; Virginia Woolf would definitely have approved.

Turning off the promenade and up the slight hill towards the house, she could see a family having a picnic on the long sloping grass in the middle of the square, a golden Labrador flopped beside them, keeping a close eye out for dropped crusts or stray crisps. A safe distance away were two stu-denty types lying in each other's arms, 'canoodling' as her mum would have said, all pale angular limbs and tousled hair. She felt the familiar tightening in her throat that still came when she thought about Max and hurried on. The last time she'd spoken to him was after she'd done her flit; he must have come back to the flat and discovered her gone. *I can explain*, he'd grovelled and her fingers had trembled on the phone at his voice. *I fell in love with you and things got out of hand. I'm sorry.* She was on the pier, of all places, and the December wind was lashing, raw and merciless, in her face, making her eyes stream. *So you bloody well should be,* she'd replied, then promptly hurled the phone out into the sea, a flash of silver arcing against the gunmetal sky, before it dropped like a stone beneath the surface.

Her mind would turn to that phone sometimes, on the bottom of the seabed, gradually becoming buried by the sand and silt. Maybe one day it would wash up on the shore. Maybe it had been pulled further out to sea and was now halfway to France, tumbling silently along the soft muddy sand at the mercy of the undertow. She wondered how many times Max had tried calling again, if he'd left a series of apologetic messages, or if he'd just deleted her number, his bluff called, giving her up as a bad job. Maybe he was on to his next conquest already, who knew?

Lost in her thoughts, it was only as she reached her building that she noticed there was an ambulance parked outside and that the front door was wide open. What on earth . . . ? With a jolt of alarm, she hurried up the front steps, just in time to see her neighbour Jo emerge from her flat, supported by two paramedics, one male, one female.

'Jo!' Rosa cried in shock. The other woman's face was deathly pale against her vibrant crimson hair and her eyes were glazed. 'What's happening? Are you all right?'

'Rosa,' Jo said, her voice gasping and weak, her eyes rolling back in her head as she spoke. Rosa didn't really know her, as they both worked shifts – Jo as a cancer nurse, she seemed to remember – although she had seen her a couple of times, accompanied by a sullen-faced girl with a lot of messy red hair she guessed was Jo's daughter. 'Rosa, I need . . .' she gasped.

'Yes?' cried Rosa anxiously. Christ, what was *wrong* with her? 'What is it?'

'I need . . . Bea. Can you look after Bea?' Jo panted, sagging like a rag doll against the paramedic, as if it had taken every ounce of strength left in her to get out the words. 'Please?'

Bea? That must be the scowling teenage daughter. 'Um . . .' Rosa said uncertainly, wondering what this would entail, not to mention whether she was up to the job. But Jo's eyes were pleading, her face desperate. 'Sure,' she mumbled eventually, because how could she reply otherwise when the poor woman in front of her appeared on the verge of death? 'Where is she?' she asked, glancing about as if Bea might be lurking, kohl-eyed and mutinous in a doorway.

'School.' Jo's eyelids were falling like blinds, the words puffing out slower and fainter. 'Back at . . . three-thirty.'

'Come on, love, we need to get you out of here,' the male paramedic said, hauling Jo up so that her thin bare legs dangled over his arm. One of her pink flip-flops swung away from her foot as if trying to make a break for it and Rosa darted forward and slotted it back on. 'We're going to the Royal Sussex,' the paramedic told her, bundling his limp human charge away towards the front door.

'Right,' Rosa said, hurrying after him. The second paramedic was already flinging open the back doors of the ambulance and Rosa felt a lurch of panic. Jo *would* be coming back, wouldn't she? 'What's wrong, anyway? What's happened?' she blurted out. Her neighbour looked so poorly, her eyes were no longer even open. 'Will she be all right?'

'We'll know more at the hospital,' the female paramedic replied without looking round, which sounded worryingly vague and not remotely reassuring. And then they were loading her into the back and slamming the doors, and Rosa stood there dumbly on the dusty pavement as, seconds later, the ambulance started up, complete with siren wailing *woo-woo-woo-woo* as it accelerated down the road. Even the canoodlers paused mid-smooch to look up and watch it go.

Rosa went back inside the house, the lobby cool and dark after the bright sunshine outside, and she blinked dazedly before heading towards her flat. That had all been a bit dramatic, she thought, frowning as she slotted her key into its lock. What had happened to Jo? When would she be back? And – shit. How was Rosa going to cope with Jo's silent, surly daughter in the meantime?

Chapter Three

Georgie had been in Brighton for a week now and in that time had flung herself wholeheartedly into her new city, pounding the streets like the most hardcore of tourists. The weather had been unseasonably warm – more like summer than spring – and she loved the way the place crackled with energy, the streets teeming with life. Every café and pub worth its salt set up pavement tables, there were buskers and street performers on each corner, and music floated out from open windows. Georgie enjoyed getting lost in the warren of alleyways known as the Lanes, browsing in one funky boutique after another, eyeing up the many gorgeous clothes she couldn't afford, and breathing in the scents of the artisan bakeries, the Vietnamese restaurant, the retro ice-cream parlour and all the rest. It was a city bursting with flavours and experiences, and she felt by turns dazzled and delighted, seduced by its charms.

But then, inevitably, she would return to the flat – the small, dingy flat which still looked depressingly bleak, however hard she worked to make it feel homely – and the emptiness of her life would enclose her again. It was lonely and quiet – too lonely and too quiet – even when she had the radio on and sang along in an attempt to cheer herself up. By the time Simon came home, she would be desperate for company, practically wagging her tail like a dog as she heard him clumping up the stairs. She was not a shy person, Georgie, but chatting to friendly baristas in cafés when she ventured out for a coffee or sandwich had so far been the extent of her socializing here in her new home. It didn't feel like nearly enough.

Lucky you!!!! her friends Amelia and Jade replied whenever she posted sunset beach photos on Facebook, and updates about how much she was enjoying being a lady of leisure. (Well, come on. She was hardly going to tell the truth and confess to feeling bored and lonely on social media.) *JEALOUS!!!* they sighed as she photographed a cool pair of shoes she'd spotted or a quirky interior design shop.

The words might lift her for a few seconds each time she saw their cheery messages but then she'd end up feeling sick inside with deceit. Especially as Amelia and Jade were both busily posting photos of wedding venues and bridesmaid dresses, or nights out down the Shepherd's Crook, and actually it was all Georgie could do to stop herself from replying *Lucky you!!!! JEALOUS!!!* in reply to *them*. She would just have to make the best of it, she told herself whenever homesickness stole in. Six months wasn't *that* long, was it?

The most discomfiting thing, though, was how the move had changed her relationship with Simon. She'd always viewed the two of them as equal partners in a team – both independent and free with their own friends and routines, yet committed to one another at the same time. Now the dynamic had completely shifted. Simon had people to see, a job to go out to every day, appointments and meetings and a whole other life outside the flat. Georgie, by comparison, had nothing. There was only so long you could kill time wandering around shops taking photos of burnished jewellery and arty lampshades before the assistants started to eye you as a potential shoplifter. Similarly, there was only so long you could eke out a coffee in a café before the waiting staff began pointedly scrubbing the table.

Thank goodness for the weekend when they had two whole days together and she felt, for the first time, as if they were a couple again. They'd started with a proper Saturday brunch in the nearest greasy spoon diner, before driving out to a local beauty spot, Devil's Dyke, where they watched people leaping off the steep side of the hill to paraglide. That evening they'd gone to an amazing Indian restaurant near the seafront and ended up in a cocktail bar, getting completely hammered on mojitos and laughing themselves senseless. Sunday had seen them hiring bikes and heading out along the seafront to blow away their hangovers before stopping for lunch in a pub and a leisurely browse through a pile of newspapers. It had all been perfect. *This is more like it*, she'd thought happily, feeling the wind in her hair as they pedalled home. He'd glanced over his shoulder to grin back at her, his sandy hair flopping about, his body pleasingly muscular under his T-shirt, and she'd felt a burst of joy, as hot and pure as the sun above their heads.

But then had come Monday morning with Simon slipping out of the flat before Georgie had even opened her eyes, and the week had yawned ahead of her all over again with absolutely nothing on the horizon. Back to square one and the long lonely silences.

Simon had not been terribly sympathetic when she voiced her feelings a few evenings later, telling him how she felt like a housewife all of a sudden. He'd not specifically said the words 'Well, why did you come here, then? What did you expect?' but she suspected an equivalent response might be fairly near the tip of his tongue. She had ended up laughing and making a joke of the situation – 'I'll have your slippers warming by the fire and dinner on the table when you get home at this rate!' – so that he wouldn't think she was complaining. Because she wasn't complaining, obviously. Well, okay, maybe just a little bit.

So much for Amelia telling her that the eleventh house was one of friendship and all the rest of it; she hadn't met a single one of their neighbours yet although she had seen a few letters arriving for a Ms Charlotte Winters in Flat 4, and a Jo Spires in Flat 2, and she'd heard some grungey music coming from one of the lower-floor flats too. And then, the other day, after having forced herself out for a jog along the seafront, she came back to the house and caught a fleeting glimpse of a much older woman vanishing up the stairs ahead. The woman was dressed in a tailored black dress and a boxy cerise jacket, her hair cut in a neat silvery bob, with a trail of jasmine perfume in her wake. First appearances: impressively glamorous, especially compared to Georgie, who was there with sweat patches under her arms, her blonde hair falling out of its messy bunches and a shiny red face. Still, she couldn't pass up on the opportunity to intro-duce herself after all those days of silence.

'Hi!' she'd called, hurrying after the woman. She hoped she didn't smell too ripe. 'I just moved into number—' Then she realized the woman was in the middle of a call on her phone and oblivious to the scarlet-faced jogger behind her.

'Well, I don't care, I don't *want* to see this doctor,' the older woman was saying imperiously, a trace of a foreign accent audible in her voice, and Georgie stopped short, not wanting to interrupt. Maybe another time, she told herself, crestfallen.

A job. That was what she needed: something to get her up and out of the flat, something to chat about with Simon in the evening other than how *his* day had gone; a purpose in life again, where she could hopefully make a friend or two as well. That wasn't too much to ask, was it?

'What do you think you'll do?' Simon said, poking a fork rather dubiously into his pork chop as she told him her idea over dinner that night. (Georgie had experimented with a mustard sauce for their chops and it hadn't been an over-whelming success.) 'Look for another library job?'

'Maybe,' she said, although without any real conviction. Since leaving her old place of work she'd come to realize that her favourite thing about it – aside from the quiet days of boiled sweets and paperback thrillers – had been compil-ing the monthly newsletter that she sent out to all the library members. It was her own creation, born out of sheer bore-dom one particularly dreary afternoon, but she had come to love writing it each time: detailing new arrivals on the shelves, occasional author events, book group meetings and a chatty little intro that often strayed into observations about the weather, whatever she might be reading herself that week, and sometimes, if she was desperate to fill up the space, photos of her parents' cockapoo Reggie and his latest exploits. 'Maybe I'll get some kind of writing job,' she replied impulsively, as much in the hope of impressing Simon as anything else.

Unfortunately his phone beeped in that moment and he stopped to scrutinize the new message – yes, at the table;

yes, even though they were still eating – but she went doggedly on, embellishing as she spoke. 'Yeah, I could set myself up as a freelancer,' she said, trying to drag his attention away. 'Roving reporter, that kind of thing. I've always quite fancied it, to be honest. Or maybe I'll just be an astronaut. *Simon.*'

'Yeah,' he said, finally putting his phone down. 'Good idea.'

She rolled her eyes in frustration. Well, she'd show him. With or without his encouragement, she'd make him see he wasn't the only one who could nab himself an interesting job. So there.

The writing idea might have floated out of her brain on a whim but the more she thought about it, the more she fancied giving it a crack. Why not? She was a good writer, people had always said so. Her hit rate on the library newsletter had been impressive and she always got lots of chatty emails in reply, which had been very pleasing. (Even if half of them *were* from dog-lovers requesting more pictures of Reggie.) As a kid, she'd written little newspapers for her mum and dad: *The Stonefield Times* and *The Hemlington Road Gazette*, filled with scintillating items about her pet rabbits, her brother's most recent telling-off at school or whatever gossip she'd overheard her mum discussing with the neighbours. Later, as a teenager, she'd been offered work experience at the local newspaper during the first summer of sixth-form, and had enjoyed it so much she'd flirted for a while with taking on an apprenticeship there after her A-levels. This plan had lasted right until Simon had announced he was applying to Liverpool University – at which point Georgie had promptly applied there too, plumping for an English degree instead.

She sighed as she lay in bed that night, thinking about this and its parallel with her current situation: how she'd followed her boyfriend to Liverpool, and how she'd followed him to Brighton. Was that all she was good for, tagging along, being the subordinate sidekick? Was it enough? Was *she* enough? 'Simon,' she whispered, suddenly needing reassurance but he was fast asleep and unresponsive beside her. What would she have said to him anyway, she thought glumly, turning over and trying to get comfortable. *Hey, sorry to wake you up, just wondering, how do you see our roles in this relationship? Because I'm feeling a bit uncertain of mine right now.*

Listening to his deep, even breathing failed to soothe her. In fact, it only made her feel more awake than ever. It wasn't as if she hadn't enjoyed her English degree, she reasoned, finding herself on the defensive now. She'd loved it, actually, all those books to devour, whole days swallowed up prone on her bed with a play or novel, as well as the occasional midnight essay to scrawl. Still, every now and then she would read a particularly good newspaper or magazine article that stirred something inside her, and she'd remember again that fleeting teenage dream of being a journalist herself, writing sparky, spiky copy in a busy, exciting newsroom with occasional trips out to interview film stars or politicians. The power of words; the bricks with which you could construct a story.

Well, then, she told herself firmly, wrangling with the pillow one last time. There was her answer. She might have followed Simon to Brighton, but maybe now was the time to revisit an unfulfilled ambition, to take the tiller of her own life and steer it in a brand-new direction, wherever she wanted to go. Hell, yeah.

It went without saying that Georgie didn't have her head *completely* in the clouds. She knew that writing jobs did not grow on trees – you had to go out and pitch for them, and what was more, you had to prove yourself against hordes of other talented writers, all of whom would have far more journalistic experience than a small chatty library newsletter to show for themselves. But then again, she'd also once heard Mary Portas giving an interview where she had described being so determined to work for Harrods, she had phoned up their human resources department every single day until they eventually offered her a post. Tenacity, that was the name of the game. Bloody-mindedness. Refusing to take no for an answer. And if that approach had worked for Mary Portas then who was to say it couldn't work for Georgie Taylor too?

The very next morning, she got stuck in, researching all the local-ish publications she could find as well as the big glossies, and jotting down their contact details. She who dares wins, she reminded herself, before compiling a list of potential articles she could tailor for each one. Now she just needed to convince someone to take a chance on a newbie, she thought, dialling the first number on the list.

Her initial round of speculative calls didn't go brilliantly well, to be honest. *Brighton Life* magazine flatly rejected her suggestion of a 'New Girl In Town' column, based on her experiences since moving to the area. 'I'm straight out of the Yorkshire Dales, throwing myself into the delights of the city,' she'd pitched. 'The highlife, the lowlife, the people I meet, the—'

The features editor politely interrupted her before she could get much further. 'We've done that before,' she replied, before adding that she had to go to a meeting and hanging up.

Sussex Now magazine were equally lukewarm when she ran a different feature idea past them, inspired by her Sunday cycle ride, about bike trails across the county. 'We're covering something similar in next month's edition,' the bored-sounding editor told her. He too seemed in a hurry to get off the phone and Georgie let out a little sigh as she said good-bye and hung up. Thanks but no thanks. On that bike of yours, love, in other words, and pedal off.

Undeterred, and using the last of the milk to make herself a motivating coffee, Georgie next tried a smaller indie magazine, called *Brighton Rocks* which seemed witty and vibrant, and was stuffed full of articles about the city, as well as pages of What's On listings at the back. With her most confident voice, Georgie pitched the same 'New Girl In Town' idea, only to be told by this third editor, Viv, that they too had already covered similar ground. Hmm. Maybe she wasn't quite as original as she'd thought. Still, she hadn't actually been hung up on this time, which was progress at least. Taking this as encouragement, Georgie quickly suggested an 'Action Girl' column instead – basically her, trying a new activity around the city every week. ('Roller-blading along the pier, tandem-riding, zorbing . . . I'll do anything!' she'd declared, crossing her fingers that Viv wouldn't ask her what 'zorbing' actually was. Or decide to send her to the bondage dungeon featured in last week's edition.)

'Hmm,' Viv replied. She had a throaty London accent and it sounded as if she was breathing out a plume of smoke as she spoke. 'Got anything else?'

Georgie swallowed. 'Got anything else' was by far the most positive response so far. It was practically an open door compared to the previous two calls! Heart pounding, she scanned her list of ideas and pitched a 'Brighton and Hove Through the Keyhole' idea instead, where she set out to explore behind the scenes of some of the city's most iconic places. 'I was thinking, the Royal Pavilion, the Palace Pier, um . . . Zoe Ball's house?' she finished up.

Viv gave a little snort and Georgie cursed herself for mentioning Zoe Ball's house. Now she sounded like some kind of weird stalker. 'Look, darling, I appreciate you ringing with all these ideas,' the editor began, 'but—'

Oh God. No. Not the 'but'. The 'but' was almost certainly a precursor to 'Jog on' and then 'Goodbye'. Before Georgie could stop herself, she was hauling out the Big Gun of Pleading. 'I'll write anything!' she blurted out desperately. 'And I've got loads of other ideas. Dogs of Brighton – people's pets,' she said randomly, remembering how popular her Reggie updates had been in the library newsletter. 'Um . . . Lunch with Georgie – a restaurant column. Undercover Shopper – me, checking out the latest new boutiques. I could have a hidden camera, maybe. I'm very discreet!'

There was a pause from Viv and for a moment Georgie thought the other woman had put the phone down on her. She could have kicked herself for letting her mouth run away with her. Dogs of Brighton indeed. Why on earth had she come out with *that*? Maybe she was wasting her own time here, as well as that of all these long-suffering editors. Perhaps she should just swallow her pride and go out and find a café job or something to keep her busy while she was here instead. Like anyone would be interested in her lame ideas anyway!

But then, to her surprise, she heard Viv say, 'Well . . . Actually there is something we've been considering. Why don't you come in and we can chat it through? This would be freelance, mind, and I'm telling you now, the pay isn't brilliant.'

'I'll do it,' Georgie said, quick as a shot. 'Whatever it is, I'll do it.'

Half an hour later, she'd put on a proper face of make-up, her smartest jeans and her favourite white shirt with a big pointy collar, plus a silver star necklace for good luck. *I'm going to be a writer*, she thought with a burst of butterflies in her stomach. *I might actually be able to pull this off.* Then she headed into town to find the *Brighton Rocks* office, which was situated above an antique-glass shop in the Lanes. 'We're what you call a shoestring operation,' Viv had told her, dead-pan.

When she found it, the small office up two flights of stairs in an old Victorian building was not exactly the buzzy newsroom of her imagination; more, a cramped room with two desks, one sloping skylight and a heap of unopened post on a chair. It was not what you would call minimalist either: there were folders and books piled on shelves, a life-size cardboard cut-out of Steve Coogan as Alan Partridge leaning lopsidedly in one corner, a huddle of plants in varying stages of death, and a fridge in another corner, with a note on the front saying 'STOP STEALING THE SOYA MILK'. Still, she reminded herself, it made a change from the mummifying quiet of her own flat, at least.

Viv was about thirty, Georgie guessed, with a lot of dark eye make-up and a crumpled salmon-coloured T-shirt that read BITCH SAYS YES. Her dark red nail varnish was chipped and she smelled of cigarettes and last night's wine. In fact, there was a half-open bottle of claret on one of the filing cabinets, Georgie noticed. And was that a sleeping bag folded messily in the far corner of the office? 'So,' Viv said, hauling the pile of post off the chair and into a perilously full in-tray, so that Georgie could take a seat, 'you want to be a writer. Join the club, darling. You can't walk down the street in this city without tripping over them. Coffee?'

'Um . . .' Out of the corner of her eye, Georgie could see a collection of unwashed mugs by a small sink and decided not to play e-coli roulette. 'I'm fine, thanks.'

'As you can see, we're a tiny set-up here,' said Viv, perching on the edge of a desk. 'It's just me and another part-timer, Danny, doing everything ourselves: writing, design, accounts, advertising, you name it.'

Cleaning? thought Georgie although decided to keep such facetiousness to herself.

'We've been running on adrenalin and sleepless nights for the last six months, and it's all a bit hand-to-mouth – so, like I said, don't get your hopes up in terms of cash because we've barely got a pot to piss in. But Danny's about to get hitched and is insisting on taking a honeymoon, the selfish bastard, so we're a bit short-handed this month. That's where you come in.'

'Fantastic,' said Georgie eagerly. 'I'm game for anything.'

'Good, because I'm looking for someone to do us an agony column. Only not one of your typical ones, with whingey letters and mumsy replies. *My boyfriend's been unfaithful, boo hoo, I'm really insecure,*' she said contemptuously, and Georgie felt obliged to give a short disparaging laugh, even though she personally could see nothing wrong with someone worrying about their unfaithful boyfriend. Who *wouldn't* feel insecure?

'We want something edgy, funny, modern – and very Brighton-centred,' Viv went on, ticking off each adjective on her fingers. 'Don't be afraid to dish out a sharp reply if it's warranted, or take a letter-writer to task when they're feeling sorry for themselves. Our agony aunt should be waspish and sassy; all about the tough love. Above all, we want this to be something that people talk about. *Have you seen this week's reply? Classic!*' She raised an eyebrow. 'What do you reckon?'

Georgie felt a swelling sense of excitement. Her own column – this was absolutely perfect! And advice too – fabulous. Georgie loved giving people advice, whether they wanted it or not. Back in the library, her customers were frequently pouring their hearts out to her, and her friends did too. 'And what will it be called? "Dear Georgie"?' she suggested eagerly. '"Ask Georgie"?' Her head spun. '"Doctor Georgie Will See You Now"?'

Viv frowned, as if inwardly debating whether or not her newest freelancer was completely sane. 'Er, no,' she said bluntly. 'We were thinking something more current – something to distinguish us from every other boring old advice column. Perhaps "Hey Em".'

Georgie thought for a moment that she'd misheard. 'Hey M?'

'Yes, it's a bit more casual. Like, *Hey Em, I've got this problem. Hey Em, I don't know what to do. Hey Em, I need some help.*'

Now it was Georgie's turn to be politely doubtful. It sounded crap to her but maybe that was because she was an out-of-towner, too parochial. *Hey Em, your column name sucks, mate.* 'Right. So it's like . . . M for . . . er . . . Mystery Agony Aunt?'

Viv gave her an *are you kidding?* look. 'No, E-M, short for Emily or Emma,' she explained, and Georgie blushed, feeling like the village idiot. 'We think it sounds friendly, approachable. I see Em as a twenty-something girl about town. Feisty, cheeky; she tells it like it is, no punches pulled.' Viv pulled out a sheaf of printed pages. 'Here are some problems. We've been running an ad for the last few weeks trailing the new column and asking for letters. Take a look through, choose the one that appeals to you most and give me your reply. Bring Em to life for us. I'm looking for four hundred words for the whole thing, including the actual problem. By tomorrow?'

Flicking through the print-outs, Georgie glimpsed the following phrases in quick succession – *anal sex, mother-in-law, infected piercing, wedding, very shy, custody of the cat* – and tried to swallow back the gulp of nerves she suddenly felt. Blimey. This was a far cry from listening to the woes of Mrs Harris at the library on her grandson's misdemeanours, or her friend Mel's trauma over a colleague at work buying the same shoes as her. A pinch of doubt took hold. Who was she to start dishing out advice to strangers, anyway? What did *she* know? She hadn't been married or divorced, she didn't have kids, she didn't even feel equipped to pass comment on the cat custody problem, because as far as she was concerned, dogs were better anyway.

Not that she was about to admit to any crisis of confidence now that she was on the verge of getting some actual paid writing work, of course. Hell, no. 'Absolutely,' she said breezily, giving Viv her bravest and best smile. 'Thanks very much. Leave it with me.'

One handshake later, she was out of there, the spring sunshine warm and bright on her face, feeling as if she'd just been presented with a key to a whole new door – a whole new land, even. Talk about a stroke of luck. Talk about landing on her feet! If Viv liked the piece she handed in then the magazine would run the column and give her a trial period of a month – four letters in total, in order to gauge the public response – although, as Viv had warned, the pay she would receive for each one was pretty diabolical. But it was a start, wasn't it? Experience. Something to fill the hours.

Now all she had to do was choose a letter and write the perfect dynamite reply. *Hey Em, I need to make a good impression here*, she thought, grinning moronically to herself as she strode back through town, past a group of drama students with pastel wigs who were engaged in some kind of outdoor performance, past the vegetarian kebab stall that always smelled so tantalizing, past a busker giving it his best Bob Dylan on the street corner. *Hey Em, I really want this to work out, you know. I've got to totally nail it.*

A vision swam up in her head, of the eponymous Em herself: a woman with big hair and loads of eyeliner, a wide lipsticked mouth and a husky laugh. And then, almost immediately she could hear the reply, loud and clear, drawling from the woman's red lips. *You go for it, girl. Do yourself justice. Show the world what you're made of!*

Chapter Four

Charlotte Winters was in a meeting. This was nothing new; working as part of the conveyancing team at Dunwoody and Harbottle meant that her week was taken up with many, many meetings but this one was a company-wide affair, with the entire workforce gathered, rather uncomfortably, in the boardroom that smelled faintly of cheese and onion crisps. Maybe that was just the man standing next to her, though; they were all packed in together so tightly, she could actually hear him breathing.

Dunwoody and Harbottle was a medium-sized legal firm, for whom Charlotte had worked first in her home town of Reading, before making the move to the Brighton office three months ago. She had assumed law firms everywhere would have the same safe greyness about them, the lack of surprises, the steady, busy pile of work to tackle, one case at a time, but it hadn't taken her long to realize that they did things differently in Brighton. There had been the company team running the half marathon dressed as zombies, for instance; the away-day to Rye in February for new employees where they'd been forced to compete in sack races and a karaoke sing-off to 'get to know one another'. Then on Maundy Thursday last month, an actual Easter bunny – well, some poor sweating trainee in a rabbit costume, presumably – had come lolloping around with a basket of Easter eggs, bouncing from desk to desk to distribute them amongst the staff. For Charlotte, who had come to the new office precisely with the intention of keeping her head down and getting on with the job, all this enforced jollity was kind of discombobulating. Camaraderie could be over-rated.

'. . . And so, as we are keen to really *engage* with our community, to play a valuable *part* within our city, not just in the excellent work we do for its residents, but also to add something *extra*, something more *meaningful* . . .' Anthony, the oily-haired shiny-suited PA to the company director, was going to run out of breath any second, Charlotte thought to herself. 'I am delighted to welcome Janet Thompson from Sunset Years to talk to you all about a new project we will be running together. Thank you, Janet. Take it away.'

There was a round of dutiful clapping and then a small energetic-looking woman in a pale pink suit stood up with a smile, pressing a clicker that activated a PowerPoint presentation. The first slide read SUNSET YEARS – AND YOU, and Charlotte felt a weary sense of apprehension, along with a pang for the Reading office where nobody expected you to do anything for your community, apart from perhaps chip in a few quid once a year for a local hospital collection.

'Hello, everyone, thank you so much for having me,' said Janet. She was in her late forties, Charlotte guessed, with bright blonde hair cut in a chin-length bob, and beady bird-like eyes that swept around the room as she spoke. 'I'm here today to talk about loneliness and what can be done about it. First of all, I'd like to ask – does anyone here ever feel lonely?'

Oh God. Of all the questions. Charlotte did her best to keep her expression impassive but could feel heat rising to her face. Did she feel lonely? Living here in a city where she knew nobody, in a tiny, over-priced flat overlooking the beach where at the weekend you could hardly walk down the street for laughing throngs of friends and family get-togethers? Did she feel lonely? Only every single day. Sometimes it felt as if this whole city was one gigantic raucous party to which nobody had thought to invite her. Not that she would dare to put her hand up in front of her colleagues and admit as much. No way.

Nobody had put their hand up in answer to Janet's question in fact, and she nodded with a knowing smile. 'Of course you're not lonely!' she cried. 'You're all busy with your social lives and work and parties and dinners, you're all so happy happy happy, posting hilarious updates on social media every night – look at me, having fun, not lonely at all . . . yes, I know.' She paused, her eyes narrowing a fraction. 'And even if you *did* secretly feel lonely, there's something about admitting it, isn't there, a terrible stigma attached to loneliness that makes even the most confident-seeming person refuse to dare confess. Right?'

There was a longer pause this time, her words hanging in the air, and Charlotte felt her face grow even hotter. It was as if Janet was talking about *her*, as if, any minute now, she would shoot a finger out at Charlotte and tell the room, 'There's one. Her with the chubby face and brown swishy hair. *She's* lonely.' Even the landlady of the flat she was renting had tried to fix Charlotte up with her apparently gorgeous son; that was how obvious her aloneness was to the rest of the world.

Shuffling her feet, she glanced despairingly at the tightly sealed windows – was it her imagination or was it getting clammier by the second in this boardroom? Her face was already doing a good impression of a red traffic light, and she could feel her back becoming sweaty too under her cheap white blouse. If anyone happened to look round at her now, they would surely see her visible awkwardness, her sense of being rumbled. *Gotcha!* If they even recognized her, that was. Charlotte had done her best to stay under the radar here, making apologies when it came to the out-of-hours activities the management team seemed hell-bent on organizing, claiming she had casework to finish whenever someone suggested going to the pub at the end of the day. They didn't know her. They probably had zero interest in her either, frumpy shy Charlotte who never had much to say for herself. One guy in the team, Zack, had called her Catherine for three weeks before she plucked up the courage to correct him.

'It's funny, you know,' Janet went on, with a stagey little laugh, 'I always start off my speeches this way and nobody ever puts their hand up. Never. Not once! But I know *I've* been lonely in the past. Oh goodness, yes. I remember when I started at university, feeling dreadfully homesick and wondering if I'd get to make any friends. Similarly when my first daughter was born and I felt house-bound with her for a while, my social life closing off like a door shutting . . . I felt lonely then, too.' She looked around the room, making eye contact with anyone who dared look back, although Charlotte gazed hurriedly down at her feet. 'I'm pretty sure that everyone else here will have felt lonely at some point as well. We can all remember those days, however much we'd like to forget them. They are hard, painful times. They make us unhappy and uncertain, they make us question ourselves and whether we've got what it takes.'

There were a few other bowed heads in the room and Charlotte could feel a crumpling sensation inside. *Oh Christ, Janet, give it a rest*, she thought dismally. This was not exactly the most motivational speech she'd ever heard.

'As for elderly people, who can find it difficult to get out of their homes, who might have lost their loved ones, who perhaps no longer work or have a reason to leave the house . . . Loneliness can be a real problem. They call it the silent killer because it can be every bit as deadly as cancer, eating away at a person, day after empty day, destroying every last bit of their confidence.' She paused for dramatic effect, the atmosphere in the room now well and truly subdued. 'But that's where we come in. And hopefully that's how you're going to help too.' She beamed and pressed a clicker in her hand and a new slide appeared with the words BEFRIENDING THE ELDERLY; rays of golden sunshine emerging above the lettering.

Cheese and Onion man had slumped beside Charlotte. She knew how he felt.

'We are thrilled that your company has chosen to partner us in a community project,' Janet went on. 'We work closely with the elderly population here in Brighton to ensure that as many people as possible have a friendly face popping in every now and then – whether it's for a cup of tea and a chat, or to run little errands for them, to help with any computer or technical problems they may encounter, even to accompany them to a doctor's or hospital appointment. Some of these people have nobody else,' she said, her smile fading momentarily. 'I can't tell you how much a visit from our befriending team can lift their spirits. Between us we can make a real difference to our elderly neighbours. So welcome on board! I hope you'll really enjoy the project. I know our clients will.'

'Thank you, Janet,' Anthony said with a respectful nod, and led the room in a smattering of applause. His hands were pink and smooth, and came together politely in light claps as if they didn't know each other very well. Then he turned to address the rest of the staff. 'So you're probably all wondering how this is going to work,' he said, to some furtive eye-rolling and shuffling at the back of the room. 'Over the next week, we will either assign you an elderly person local to you, or you can find your own willing victim – I mean, participant, ha ha. And then, from next Friday, we're going to finish work an hour early every week for the next three months, so that you can spend some time with this person. Build a relationship.' He beamed insincerely. 'I, for one, am really looking forward to this wonderful new venture.'

'Simpering prick,' muttered Cheese and Onion man under his breath.

'I'll put a sign-up sheet on the shared drive,' Anthony went on, 'with full details of the partnership. Thanks again for coming in, Janet. The rest of you can get back to work now. Thank you.'

'Great,' groaned a woman ahead of Charlotte as everyone made their way back towards their desks. 'Pensionerbothering. Why can't they just let us get on with our sodding jobs?'

'I don't even *know* any oldies,' another woman said, tossing her hair and not noticing as it almost whipped Charlotte in the face. 'And are senior management going to be doing this too, I ask myself? Are they bollocks.'

Charlotte sat back down at her desk and refreshed her computer, sipping on the coffee she'd left there which was now stone-cold. Everyone else seemed to be whinging about the new directive and moaning that they couldn't spare the time. She, on the other hand, was almost looking forward to it. How would her colleagues react, she wondered, if she admitted to them that a weekly one-hour meeting with an elderly person would be the sole social encounter of her sad solitary life?

Imagining the looks of horrified pity, she said nothing, though, as usual, and buried herself in work instead.

It had been a sunny spring day and the air still felt warm as Charlotte made her way back towards the flat that evening, some salad and halloumi in a carrier bag swinging from one hand, plus a Waitrose New York cheesecake just in case she was still hungry afterwards. (Let's face it, she was always hungry afterwards.) Her gaze was caught by the sea ahead, a tranquil blue today with a scattering of yellow flashes where the sun fell on the water. *Ssssh*, said the waves, as if keeping a secret. *Ssssh*.

Let's see; Thursday, she thought to herself, approaching Dukes Square. Thursday meant ironing and dusting, the recycling to put out, that new Channel 4 drama starting on telly. Busy, busy! She had taken to ironing everything since she moved house, she found it relaxing and it was a good way of filling her time. As for the dusting – you'd be surprised how much could accumulate on a single potted plant and the television set over a week. Plus she would definitely fit in the bracing post-dinner stroll along the seafront that she kept vowing to add to her routine. She had bought some trainers especially but they were still in their box, and now pushed under her bed out of sight. Once upon a time she had been the sort of person who went to aerobics classes and rode a bike and thought nothing of swimming fifty lengths in the pool before work. These days, a soft layer of fat encased her body and her cheekbones had all but disappeared. She'd gone up a whole size in trousers. But so what? she thought bitterly whenever she had to suck her stomach in to do up a button. Who cared anyway?

As she neared SeaView House, Charlotte saw a small, rather hunched woman with silvery hair and a black raincoat at the front door, turning a key in the lock. Hurrying the last few steps towards her to catch the door, Charlotte felt a prickle of curiosity. Despite living at 11 Dukes Square for three months, she'd only ever seen a single other resident there, a scarlet-haired woman called Jo from one of the downstairs flats, who had asked her in for coffee both times they'd met. Unfortunately Charlotte had been on her way out each time – first en route to the dreadful 'Fun Day' in Rye and already late, and the second, dashing to catch the train back to Reading for her mum's birthday – and she'd had to make her apologies and flee on both occasions. Although Jo seemed perfectly nice, Charlotte had shied away from knocking on her door and taking her up on the offer of coffee since then because . . . well, she didn't know, really, other than she had lost her nerve when it came to things like knocking on people's doors these days and making conversation. Conversation always seemed to lead to awkward questions and somehow it just felt easier to get along on her own.

She hung back now, shyness creeping in, but the woman who was pushing open the heavy wooden door with some effort must have noticed her, because she held it open, waiting for Charlotte to catch up. 'Hello there,' she said, a trace of a foreign accent – French? – just detectable in her voice. She was so small and slender she looked as if she might blow away in a sea breeze, Charlotte thought. 'Do you live here or are you just hoping to take advantage of a feeble old lady and break in?'

Charlotte smiled tentatively, hoping that this was a joke. 'I live here,' she replied. 'Charlotte Winters, from Flat 4.' She held up her keys, as if that proved anything.

'Ahh, then you'd better come in,' the woman said. Once they were both inside and the door had shut with a muffled thud, she extended a slim hand with a lot of fine gold bangles clinking at the wrist. 'Margot Favager,' she went on. 'Flat 5. Right at the top. All those stairs, my God!' She had a lined face but her silvered hair was cut in a stylish jaw-length bob with a cool short fringe, and her eyelids were dusted with lilac eyeshadow that brought out the blue in her eyes. As well as her black belted raincoat she wore a Liberty print scarf at her neck and small black ankle boots, and carried a large shiny handbag with an old-fashioned clasp fastening on top.

Charlotte shook the hand of tiny Margot Favager, feeling lumpier and frumpier than ever. If even a woman the age of her grandmother looked more stylish than she did, then what hope was there? She doubted Madame Favager had ever consumed an entire Waitrose cheesecake alone, either with or without tears dripping silently down her cheeks; she probably lived off China tea and delicate petits fours, approximately one a year, to be nibbled at now and then. 'Hello,' she said politely as they both walked through the entrance hall, 'it's nice to meet you.'

Given the choice, she would have hurried up the stairs and away, bad as she was at chit-chat nowadays, but of course that would have been rude, and Charlotte's mother had brought her up to be well mannered. And so they walked up side by side, with Charlotte making a tactful swerve to Margot's right so that the older woman could take the banister if need be. 'Do you want me to . . . um . . . carry any of your shopping?' she asked, remembering in the next moment the Befriending project at work.

'That is very kind of you, but I'm fine, thank you. I am not dead just yet. Not today,' Margot replied, as they plodded slowly up the stairs. 'Tell me about yourself then. Charlotte, did you say? How are you finding SeaView House?'

'Very nice, thank you. I've been here a few months now. It's . . . lovely,' Charlotte answered gamely, trying not to think of the house she and Jim had owned back in Reading, with its long leafy garden and the all-mod-cons kitchen and Kate's tiny room upstairs, hopefully decorated with the Winnie the Pooh frieze around the wall, the brand-new Moses basket she'd never even slept in. *Don't think about that now.* 'Really lovely,' she repeated, more forcefully.

'I am glad to hear it,' Margot said. 'I have lived here for twenty years now, can you believe it, and I have seen many people come and go from this house. They wash up with the tide, some of them, it seems.' Her eyes were shrewd as she considered Charlotte. 'But then they find their life again – is that the saying? – and they leave, somewhere nicer, that is what usually happens. Apart from me, of course, and I'm not going anywhere now – until I am carried out in my . . . how do you say it? Box.'

'Er . . . Coffin?' Charlotte hazarded, hoping she hadn't misunderstood horribly.

'*Coffin!* Exactly. Yes. In my coffin. Ha! It will be hard work down these stairs, eh? They will be complaining about me, *non?*'

Charlotte ventured a smile, not certain of the etiquette, how best to reply when an older woman joked about being carted off in a coffin. 'Well . . .' she began hesitantly, then decided to give a polite laugh instead. 'I'm sure it's all part of the job. For the . . . um . . . funeral people. I mean . . .' She broke off, wishing she had kept quiet after all.

'Yes. Part of the job. Not a very *nice* job, I think.'

'No.' *God, how had they ended up talking about this?* Charlotte thought, her face growing hot with the awkwardness. Thank goodness they were almost at the first-floor landing now and she'd be able to make her escape.

Margot's sharp eyes were on her again, though. 'And you have made a lot of friends here?' she asked. 'You are happy, enjoying life by the sea?'

'Oh! Well . . . You know, I've met people at work, and . . .' Charlotte's voice trailed into nothing and she looked down at the carpet as she took the last step up. *No, she thought in embarrassment. No, I wouldn't say I was happy. But then again, I wasn't exactly happy in Reading either, was I?*

'I see.' Margot's face softened as they both stood on the landing and Charlotte delved in her bag for her keys, thankful that this ordeal was almost over. She would not insult stylish, self-assured Margot by asking if she needed befriending for the Sunset Years project, she decided; the older woman would probably take great offence at the question. She might even wallop her with that gigantic handbag.

'Anyway, nice to—' Charlotte began saying again, but Margot spoke at the same time.

'You must come for tea,' she announced. 'Perhaps at the weekend, when you are not so busy.'

Charlotte could feel herself turning pinker at the thought. It was as if her neighbour knew full well that Charlotte filled every evening with cleaning and eating and the watching of terrible TV programmes.

'Thank you,' she said. 'That would be very nice.' She smiled politely. 'Well, better be off. Bye now.'

'Before you go,' said Margot, and now she was sliding a hand into her own handbag and withdrawing a small black leather purse. 'Here,' she said, unzipping it and taking out a pound coin. 'For you. It was nice to meet you.'

'Oh,' said Charlotte nonplussed, looking down at the pound coin in her palm. It was like going to visit an elderly relative and being given some pocket money. Maybe Margot wasn't quite as with it as she'd first thought. 'Are you sure?

No, I couldn't . . .' she began saying, but Margot waved away her protestations.

'I insist,' she said, briskly walking across the landing to the next flight of stairs. 'Goodbye.'

'Oh,' Charlotte said again, still faintly bamboozled. 'Well, thank you. That's very kind.' She hesitated before slipping it into her pocket. 'I'll spend it wisely!'

Margot turned and smiled. She must have been beautiful back in her day because the smile lit up her whole face. 'I know you will,' she said. 'Until next time.'

And then she was gone, leaving Charlotte fumbling to get her key in the lock before escaping into the quiet sanctuary of her small flat.

There. Safe. Private. She leaned against the door, eyes shut and trying not to think about the fact that an elderly neighbour had just taken pity and attempted to befriend *her*, rather than the other way round. Then she took a deep breath, hung up her jacket, stowed her shoes neatly in their place by the door, and went to assemble that evening's meal. Busy, busy. Just keep busy.

She was fine, she reminded herself with all the conviction she could muster. This was all fine. Whatever Margot Favager might think, Charlotte Winters was definitely, one hundred per cent, *fine*.

Chapter Five

Rosa sifted flour into the bowl, watching it fall like fine snowflakes onto the creamy yellow mixture beneath before folding them gently together. Baking a cake was her favourite kind of magic: the alchemy of ingredients, the soothing processes of measuring and mixing, the scent of something delicious in the oven. She added a tablespoonful of milk and then a teaspoonful of vanilla extract, and after one final stir, decanted the contents of the bowl into two greased tins and slid them into the oven. Setting the timer on her phone, she saw that Jo's daughter Bea would be home in less than an hour. Rosa might not have the first clue about teenage girls and how to look after them, but she did know at least that a slice of home-made cake could prove a great comfort in times of adversity.

Cook it better; she should really get it printed on a T-shirt. When her first teenage boyfriend Jon (floppy hair, bad poetry) dumped her, she had baked for two weeks solid: brownies, pies, bread, sponge cake, like her life depended on it. After her grandma died, she'd gone home to her mum's for a week and made lasagne and casseroles, hearty comforting family food to help them through their sadness. Following the split with boyfriend number two, Peter the cheater, she'd thrown herself into more cheffy things, home-made pasta and flaky pastry. Croissants, even. And now look at her – working with food full-time after the most devastating heartbreak of all. It helped, though. It made her feel better. And nobody could fail to be cheered by sponge and buttercream, right?

As she washed up, Rosa heard the quick light footsteps above her head that meant someone was home up there. She hadn't yet met the new people living in the flat upstairs but had heard them: furniture being moved around, a piping treble voice singing along to the radio, an explosive argument one day, and some very loud sex that same evening. Today the female voice was singing 'I Feel Pretty' loudly and quite badly over the roaring of the Hoover. She smiled briefly, tightly, remembering how Max's neighbour in Islington had been a semi-professional soprano; how they'd been able to hear her practising her arias on summer evenings when the windows were open. Was he still keeping up pretences and living there? she wondered for the hundredth time, picturing his long lean body as he . . .

The wet ceramic mixing bowl slipped in her fingers suddenly, clattering against the draining board. *No*, she told herself. *Forget him.*

Once the sponge cakes had been baked and were cooling on a tray, Rosa still had twenty minutes left before Bea was due home, and found herself drawn towards her laptop, as if it carried a powerful magnet she was unable to resist. Just a quick look, she told herself. Five minutes. Her guilty little secret.

The Facebook page came up as her most-visited site now, more so even than her email and Netflix. It wasn't stalking, she kept telling herself. Could she help it if Ann-Marie was so clueless as to leave her page unprotected by privacy settings? It was as if she *wanted* the world to see her smug, happy life, as if she positively welcomed onlookers to inspect the glorious honour of being lucky Ann-Marie Chandler. *Come in, roll up, take a look, try your hardest not to envy me! Tricky, huh! Shucks.*

Beautiful, wholesome Ann-Marie was thirty-seven, which meant she was actually two years older than Rosa – although annoyingly, she looked younger, happier and way more photogenic. Maybe that was what having a wonderful life did for you: it magically airbrushed away those pesky worry lines and eyebags, ensured those hands remained soft and pretty, as if they'd never washed a dish or peeled a potato in their blessed life. Perhaps your body simply aged differently when you lived in a picture-perfect Cotswold village with a massive garden and your own Land Rover Discovery, and you had two blonde beaming children, Josh and Mae (also known as 'my little man' and 'my little princess'). Yeah, it must be great, living in a real-life Boden catalogue; all those coffee mornings with friends, and their picturesque children, and the rolling green countryside, and . . .

Jesus, stop it, Rosa, she thought, suddenly sickened by her own bitterness. Spying on Ann-Marie sometimes seemed counter-productive, more agony than it was worth. With every click on the woman's timeline, it was as if her insides were curdling, her sanity shrivelling – and for what? Ten minutes of juicy sneering? A new shot of rage to fuel the inner furnace? Somehow Rosa had turned into the horrible, vindictive sort of person who found herself hoping that Ann-Marie would choke to death on one of her home-baked cookies (Hashtag-yummy!), or that precious Josh and cutesy Mae would be found face-down in that idyllic stream that pranced along at the bottom of the Chandlers' garden. No, she didn't hope that, she reprimanded herself severely. Of course she didn't. She wasn't a total psychopath. Not yet, anyway.

So how were things in Ann-Marie world this week? Oh, sweet, she had taken Mae to a teddy bears' picnic. Bless. Photos, of course, of Mae in a cute pink sundress and matching cardigan (designer, no doubt) and sparkly trainers that almost certainly cost as much as Rosa's own Nike Airs. Hashtag-sucker, thought Rosa, nose wrinkling as she scrolled down.

Look, there was precocious Joshie, Ann-Marie's 'little man' aged seven, in hideous prep school uniform with a cap as well, for goodness' sake. Only the best for Ann-Marie's family though, eh? He'd be running the country in thirty years, just wait, she thought, reading on.

Ahh. Wasn't that nice? A romantic weekend away planned for Ann-Marie and her husband David! Handsome, square-jawed David, or 'hubby' as she termed him. Well, how lovely. Lucky Ann-Marie! Rosa hoped she and David wouldn't accidentally suffer terrible food poisoning from their room service dinner. Shame they weren't coming to the Zanzibar really, wasn't it? Wouldn't that have been a coincidence!

Rosa was startled from her nasty little dreams just then by a knock on the door and she shut the laptop hurriedly. Her heart was actually pounding, she realized, putting up a hand to her chest, and feeling it thumping there. Steady on, love. It's only a stupid Facebook page. How ironic would it be, after all her nasty secret murderous thoughts, if it was her who ended up dropping dead of a heart attack, killed by her own dastardly body?

'Coming,' she called. Goodness, yes, that would be Bea, Jo's daughter, and she needed to pull herself together and deal with this new drama. 'Hi,' she said apprehensively, as she opened the door. 'Bea, isn't it? I'm Rosa.'

'I got your note,' the girl said, chin wobbling as Rosa let her in. Her fox-coloured hair looked wilder and tanglier than ever, falling over one eye, and she had on chipped mauve nail varnish and about twenty badges pinned to the lapels of her school blazer. *Normal People Frighten Me*, said one. *Zombie Outbreak Response Team*, said another. 'What's going on? What do you mean, Mum's in hospital? What happened, was it her asthma, or . . . ?'

'She . . . to be honest, I don't really know,' Rosa replied wretchedly, realizing far too late that she should have phoned the hospital by now in order to have gleaned some proper information for the girl; hard facts in answer to the questions Bea was always going to ask. Instead she'd been too busy sneering over another woman's life to actually deal with a real-world situation. She was a terrible person, basically. 'I got here just as the paramedics were taking her away, it was all a bit of a rush. She asked me to look after you, so . . .'

'What, and you didn't even bother to find out why she was ill? What had happened? Fucksake!' Bea cried, staring angrily at her, that foxy mane practically bristling with indignation.

'I'm sorry,' Rosa said with a stab of guilt. Having been in her solitary bubble for so long, she felt out of practice when it came to social situations and had absolutely no idea how to speak to this belligerent girl-woman, she thought, biting her lip. It was like having a wild animal on her doorstep, glaring and unpredictable. 'Look, come in a minute. Let me ring the hospital right now and find out. I'll see if we can go and visit her.'

Bea deflated a little as Rosa went to retrieve her phone. ''Kay,' she mumbled, gnawing at one of her mauve nails.

Three minutes later, Rosa had spoken to a sister on a ward at the hospital and been told that Jo was now apparently 'comfortable' but would definitely be staying in overnight. They were welcome to go and see her, and visiting hours went on until eight that evening.

'Right,' said Bea at once, turning as if to leave. 'I'll be off then.'

'Oh, but—' Rosa began, taken aback as the girl hoisted up her enormous bag of school books and started walking away. There was something about the set of her shoulders – high and hunched, radiating tension – that made her seem vulnerable all of a sudden, more little girl than teenager. *I don't need anyone!* Except of course she did.

Rosa thought of the two pale yellow sponge discs that would be cool by now, the bag of icing sugar ready on the side. But she'd told Jo she'd take care of this girl, and so the cake would have to wait. 'I'll give you a lift,' she said, grabbing her car keys and hurrying after her.

Jo was up in one of the wards, at the end of a long echoing corridor. Appendicitis, a nurse told them as they arrived in the reception area, with surgery needed urgently. That didn't sound good, Rosa thought to herself, trying to remember back to biology lessons at school. She wasn't even completely sure where the appendix *was* but knew that burst ones could cause a lot of pain. Surgery too, poor Jo. How long would it take a person to recover from that anyway? she wondered, casting a doubtful eye at the glowering Bea. Looking after someone else's kid you didn't know for a few hours was one thing, but overnight – and possibly longer still – was something different altogether. She had a feeling it would take more than a slice of Victoria sponge to win over this particular home guest.

'Can we see her?' Bea was saying, squaring up to the nurse, voice hostile, as if prepared to argue, very hard, that she *had* to see her mum.

'Of course you can,' the nurse said, not reacting to the combative posture of the girl. The nurse was younger than Rosa, with brown curly hair and a generous sprinkling of freckles. 'We've had to give her some fairly strong painkillers, so she might be groggy, but we're keeping her comfortable until she can go into theatre. Follow me.'

Jo was asleep when they edged around the curtain, her complexion greenish white, her crimson hair startling against the pillow.

'Mum,' Bea said quietly, edging towards the bed. 'Mum?'

Jo stirred and made a mumbling sound in her throat but her eyes remained closed. A tear rolled down Bea's face and dripped onto the white starched sheets, leaving a wet blotch.

'Mum, it's me, wake up,' she said, her voice tremulous, but still Jo didn't move.

'Do you want a tissue? I've probably got one in my—' Rosa said, ferreting around in her bag but Bea merely glared at her again, slumping into a chair nearby.

Rosa hovered awkwardly. Now what? She remembered with a pang her plans for today's free time – treating herself to a coffee at one of the pavement cafés, mooching about the shops in the sunshine with the luxury of nothing to do. By moving to Brighton she'd deliberately cut herself off socially and that was how she wanted it, being on her own, with only herself to have to think about. Meanwhile, here she was on this ward, the smell of sanitizing hand-gel stinging her nostrils, the sound of someone crying softly in the next bed along – plus there was Bea, this girl for whom she'd unexpectedly become responsible. Cast out of her comfort zone, Rosa didn't have a clue what to do next. *Come on*, she reminded herself. *You're the adult here. Take control.*

'Should I leave you two together for a bit?' she asked after a few moments had passed.

'What, so we can have a private conversation? Er . . . not sure that's exactly gonna happen right now,' Bea said caustically, gesturing at the motionless form of her mother.

Rosa felt herself flush. *Look, I don't have to be here, kid*, she felt like retorting. *This was my afternoon off, thanks, and I've got things I'd much rather be doing than hanging around a hospital, chaperoning you and your sarcasm.*

But just then, as if to be contrary, Jo did crack one eye open and murmur, 'Bea?' and Bea was up and leaning over her in the next second. 'Mum?'

Rosa took that as a sign to give them both some privacy. 'I'll wait outside,' she said, slipping out through the curtain.

Jo had not really come round, save for that brief moment of consciousness, and so after twenty minutes or so, Bea admitted defeat, and shuffled out to find Rosa. 'Should I call your grandparents, do you think, or your dad?' Rosa asked as they made their way back through the warren of corridors and out towards the car park. Admittedly, Jo had asked her to look after the girl but that was due to simple timing alone, Rosa's appearance on the scene just as Jo was being taken away. There had to be someone better equipped to deal with Bea, surely. Someone, moreover, that Bea would rather be with too. And, without wanting to sound uncharitable, the sooner Rosa could return to her solitary, fuss-free world, the better, frankly.

Bea's head whipped round in alarm. 'Why, do you think she's going to die or something?'

'No! I meant, to help out, to look after you,' Rosa replied. 'To go and visit her too.'

'Oh,' the girl said and shrugged. 'Well, my dad's a tosser,

his parents are both in New Zealand, and my other grand-parents hate us,' she went on bluntly. 'So no, basically.'

'Right,' said Rosa, chastened. They had reached the car park now and she peered about, trying to remember where she'd parked. 'What about aunties, then? Other relatives? Friends?'

Bea shoved her hands into her pockets. 'I just want to go home,' she muttered. 'I'll be fine on my own. I *am* fourteen.'

'Well . . . .' Rosa began weakly, but Bea's face was so mutinous she found herself trailing off. 'We'll talk about it later,' she fudged in the end, feeling out of her depth. This is what happened when you got involved with other people, she thought glumly, spotting the car at last and heading towards it. Confrontation, difficulty, stress . . . Oh, why hadn't she walked a longer way home that afternoon, and avoided all of this? Why couldn't the rest of the world just leave her be?

The atmosphere as they drove back was strained and largely silent. Bea scrubbed her eyes now and then and turned away from Rosa so that she faced the passenger window, in order, Rosa suspected, to try and hide her tears. A sudden shower of rain made the colours outside seem smeary and Rosa switched on her wipers, headlights and the fan heater, one after another, her mind straying to a memory of how much Max loved the rain, thunderstorms in particular; how he was the sort of man who'd throw his head back and laugh if they were ever caught in a downpour, rather than scurry to the nearest café (Rosa's preference). Headstrong, that was Max. Reckless and impulsive, the type who was all about the big gestures, the passion, the expensive presents. But of course Rosa knew by now that this was just his sleight of hand, a dextrous illusion to distract you from the shallows within.

I thought I saw Max today in the King's Road, Catherine had said that time, eyebrows lifting in her guileless way. She had been smiling, as if this was great news, as if she was happy for Rosa. *Is he back early from Amsterdam?* And Rosa hadn't twigged for a second. *I wish!* she'd said, grimacing in reply. They'd been in the Pitcher and Piano down the road from work, and were perched on a slouchy leather sofa together, the sort that was just a bit too low to be fully comfortable, sipping gin cocktails and catching up. *He's back tomorrow night*, she'd said, twirling her straw around the ice cubes to mix her drink. *Can't wait!*

Stupid Rosa. Stupid, trusting Rosa. She braked for the traffic lights now, the windscreen wipers hissing and sliding through the rain, just as Bea banged a clenched fist down on her seat and said, 'I don't want to go to my dad's. I just don't. You're not going to make me go, are you? He's such a prick.'

Rosa, indicating to turn right into the square, said nothing for a moment. She didn't want to start having to lay down the law with this girl she barely knew, especially as she

could see Bea was fragile beneath all the scowling and bra-
vado – but at the same time, as the adult in the situation, it
was down to her to make the decisions. 'What happened
with your grandparents?' she asked, avoiding directly answering the question for now. *They hate us*, the girl had said on
the way to the car but Rosa guessed this was mere teenage
melodrama, exaggeration for effect. Surely Bea's words
couldn't be true?

'They don't get on with Mum,' Bea mumbled, lip curling.
'First of all because she came out and dumped Dad for a
woman, and they're like really super-religious, the sort who
try and convert you all the time and make you pray with
them and shit. They call themselves Christians but they don't
like gay people . . . I mean, how does that even work? I
thought Christians were all about love and forgiveness, that's
what our RS teacher said.'

'God,' Rosa said, without thinking, then pulled a face as
she heard her own accidental blasphemy. 'I mean—'

'Oh, I don't care. They're awful. God can't possibly think
they're okay when they're so mean all the time anyway.'
Her fingers clenched and unclenched in her lap as the rain
drummed on the roof of the car. 'The second reason they
hate Mum is because we ran off to India, but then I nearly
died, and we had to come back, and then they had a massive
go at Mum and said she was a bad mother, and not fit to
look after me.'

The crack in Bea's voice belied her vulnerability, however scornful her tone. 'That sounds kind of harsh,' Rosa commented warily.

'Yeah. They're praying for us though, so that's all right.' Bea pulled a ferocious face. 'And they send us things now and then, like a cushion cover that Granny made with "Repent and you will be saved" embroidered on it.'

'Jesus Christ,' said Rosa, accidentally blaspheming again. She reversed into a space, pulled on the handbrake and said, deadpan, 'Well, they sound delightful. Are you *sure* you don't want to go and stay with them?'

'No, I d—' Bea began to snap, right up until she realized that Rosa was joking. 'Oh, ha ha,' she said, rolling her eyes. Was it Rosa's imagination or did she seem a fraction less angry?

'Well, in that case, I guess you'll be staying with me tonight,' Rosa said, trying to suppress her sigh. The thought of having another person in her flat made her feel uncomfortable but she couldn't see any other way around it. 'Let's go in.' She switched off the engine, doing her best to sound upbeat. 'I baked a cake, by the way. Do you like cake?'

Bea shrugged as if she couldn't care less about cake and got out of the car. 'S'pose so,' she muttered, but then relented. 'Yeah,' she admitted, lifting her gaze and giving a tiny nod. 'Actually I do.'

Chapter Six

'Let's go out for dinner!' Georgie cried when Simon got home from work. 'I have news!'

Simon, who had purple bags under his eyes after a series of six a.m. starts, made an exasperated sort of noise at her words. 'You're paying, are you?' he asked, shrugging off his jacket and loosening his hated tie in a distinctly going-nowhere sort of way. With his broad frame and neck like a prop-forward, he was one of those men who couldn't bear the tight collar of a shirt. 'We can't keep eating out all the time just because you can't be arsed to cook. The prices round here are ridiculous, and this flat is costing me an arm and a leg for starters.'

His words took her breath away. Oh God. Listen to him. He'd turned into Bitter Breadwinner already, after only a few weeks of her coming down here. He'd always been a bit on the tight side and now every conversation seemed to find a way around to the fact that you could get things for half the price back in Yorkshire, they could live in a palace in

Stonefield for the rent they were paying down here, he was sick of Brighton mugging him off every time he got his wallet out. To be honest, all the moaning was getting right on Georgie's nerves.

'I *am* paying, actually,' she replied tartly just to shut him up, although the finances of dinner had not occurred to her until now. Sod it, she bloody well *would* pay too, even if it sent her plunging into the red. No way was she a sponger. No way was she going to put up with barbed comments about how much the flat was costing *him* and subsequent implications that she was not contributing. 'Because I've just been given a *job*, thank you very much. But I'll go out and celebrate on my own if you're not bothered. Suits me.'

This little speech had the desired effect because he turned round at once, his expression a mix of apology and surprise. 'You've got a *job*? George, that's brilliant. Sorry, I just thought . . . So what is it?'

'Writing for a magazine,' she replied with an air of studied nonchalance. She wouldn't let on that it was only one measly column, she had decided. Nor would she confess how paltry the pay. He didn't need to know boring details like that – and anyway, this was merely the start of her glorious new career, wasn't it? 'I went along to meet the editor today – Viv,' she went on, pretending to examine her nails, even though she knew they were already perfect. (Yes, she *had* treated herself to a manicure on the way home from the office. Yes, she probably *had* blown her first paypacket in the process.) 'She's really cool. So, yeah, dinner on me. Journalist's treat. If you want it.'

His mouth was still slightly open in a classic village-idiot-style gape but then he ran a hand through his sandy hair and grinned. He had a good grin, Simon – generous and genuine – and at last he was looking a bit more like her boyfriend again. He'd been so uptight lately, so stressed about having to prove himself at work, especially as the redevelopment had already run into local opposition. 'Wow, George. That's really cool,' he said. 'How did you swing that?'

'Er . . .' She *definitely* wasn't about to tell him she had basically begged for it. (All in all, there was quite a lot she wasn't telling her boyfriend about this new career path, she thought guiltily.) 'Well, I just phoned up and pitched some ideas, she asked me in for a chat and then gave me the commission, basically.' She jokingly flexed her bicep. 'Georgie power!'

He was looking at her with what could only be described as respect. Respect and – yes, she was certain of it – admiration, too. Overall, the combination was a powerful one, leaving her more than a little giddy to be basking in such approval. It had been some time since he'd looked at her like that, as if she was worth anything. 'Cool,' he said again. 'What magazine is it? Anything I'd have heard of?'

'It's this local one – *Brighton Rocks*,' she replied, bubbling over with pride at her own success. 'It's really good: funny, irreverent, contemporary . . .'

But somehow she had lost him. 'Oh, right,' he said, and just like that, the respect and admiration seemed to be dimming. 'What, one of the freebies? I thought you meant . . .'

She felt herself flush. He thought she meant a proper magazine, in other words. A big fat glossy one sold in train stations and WH Smith. 'Well, yeah, it *is* one of the freebies,' she admitted, 'but it's still good. It still counts!'

'Sure,' he said appeasingly, although she could tell his interest had waned, and he was no longer so impressed. Oh God, he was even looking a bit sorrowful, a bit patronizing, as if she was an idiot for being pleased. 'And they're actually paying you, are they?'

'Yes!' She glared at him. Why did he have to be such a wanker about it? This was what she'd been dreading: him being half-hearted in his congratulations, dismissive, even. As if she'd dare ask if *his* employers were paying him properly. 'Look, do you want to go out or not? Because any second now, I'm going to withdraw my offer and you'll have to fend for yourself.'

'Sorry,' he said. 'I'd love to go for dinner. And I *am* pleased for you, of course I am. That's brilliant news.'

Yeah, she thought, her buoyant mood souring as she went to put on some lipstick and perfume. Well, it *had* been brilliant news in her mind, anyway – right until she told him about it, that was. And now she felt as if he had written her off, not taken her seriously. Her hackles rose as she blotted her lipstick and she realized she was scowling at her own reflection. Well, she'd show him, she thought crossly. She'd show him when she was nominated for some prestigious writing award and accidentally-on-purpose forgot to thank him in her winner's speech. Ha!

Hey Em,
    I've got this terrible problem. I . . .

Sitting cross-legged on the bed the next morning, Georgie got straight to work. That had been her intention anyway, but having read through the letters from Viv three times now, she didn't feel inspired. They were all too daunting, too out-there for her to know how best to reply. Still, she was not one to be easily defeated, no way, and so she had taken the executive decision to make up a letter of her own, one she thought she could actually answer. With a bit of luck, Viv wouldn't spot it wasn't genuine, especially if she came up with something absolutely brilliant.

Now all she had to do was come up with said piece of brilliance. Unfortunately this appeared to be the downside of the plan. Shit. She read through the existing eight words she'd typed so far – three hundred and ninety-two to go! –

and bit her lip, fingers hovering over the laptop as she waited for further inspiration to strike. Hmm.

She drank the last of her coffee, wincing at how pokey it was. She'd made herself a really strong one, hoping it would blast away the remnants of her hangover but so far it was only making her jittery. God knows how Simon was managing at work when he'd been even more rat-arsed than her last night.

Sighing, she fell backwards against the pillows, pulling ugly faces at the ceiling. Ugh! It was hugely unfair, feeling so morning-after-ish when she hadn't even enjoyed a very good evening out. They'd gone to Mexica, this fancy restaurant on the seafront – fancy but not cheap – and she'd nearly had a coronary when the bill arrived at the end. Yes, all right, so she *had* said 'Money's no object!' in a grand sort of a way as they sat down, but he could have chipped in a bit, couldn't he, when he had ordered the steak, the most expensive thing on the menu? He could at least have slipped in a tenner for the tip rather than leaving her to ferret around for the last coins in her purse, feeling stressed about the fact that she might just have bankrupted herself in a single vain act of showing off. That would teach her.

Worse, Simon hadn't been in a very good mood. He'd yawned a lot and checked his emails as they came in, and moaned on the whole time about all the problems they were facing at work, and how a group of protestors were threatening a sit-in at the hotel site. ('But why?' Georgie had asked, to which he grumbled, 'Because they're a bunch of sanctimonious twats with nothing better to do, that's why.') To be honest, it was kind of annoying after a while, especially as this was supposed to be a celebratory dinner. Georgie had almost been put off her very expensive food by how irritated she was becoming. 'It's not all about you, you know,' she felt like saying. 'Get over yourself!'

Heaving another deep sigh at the memory, she hauled herself upright again and focused back on her laptop screen. As for this, her exciting big break, it was turning out to be a bit pants as well, so far. When she really needed to pull something fabulous out of the bag to impress Viv, too! Deleting her opening sentence, she decided to just start typing, pouring out her heart and seeing how she got on. In the past, when she'd written the library newsletters, she had found that she always needed to warm up first; splurge a bit, then polish. Time to get splurging, she thought, putting her fingers back on the keyboard.

> *Hey Em,* she typed,
>> *Do you know what, my boyfriend is being a real arse. He's got this hot-shot new job and now thinks he's like this super-amazing professional. We've moved down all the way from Yorkshire so that he can indulge his wet dream, I mean, take up this wowzers*

*job, and I feel a bit insignificant to him all of a
sudden. I'm trying my best – I've gone out and found
my own new job – but it's like everything's changed in
our relationship. He acts like he's the important one,
while I'm just tagging along for the ride. Maybe I am
just tagging along for the ride. Maybe I should get off
the sodding ride and leave him to it!*

She stopped typing, horrified at where her train of thought had taken her. Leave Simon? What was she saying? That was the last thing she wanted. The hangover had sent her mental, she thought, hands flying up from the keyboard as if she'd just touched something dirty. Leaving was not an option, not when she'd made such a big deal about moving in the first place, and especially not when she was still boasting to all her friends on social media about what a great time she was having down here!

Get a grip, love, she imagined Em saying, adjusting her beehive and touching up her smoky eyeliner. *Have a frigging chill pill and take a look at yourself, willya?*

Em was right. And actually, talking of social media, that might be just the place to seek inspiration, Georgie thought, clicking away from her own moany document and onto Facebook. What problems did her friends have right now? Maybe she could appropriate one for the newspaper. They'd never have to know. She scrolled down her timeline to see.

Amelia Noble: OMG, like NIGHTMARE!!! Trying to finalize guest list – somehow need to get it down to 200!!! – but Jason's aunty isn't speaking to his mum's best friend and we don't know whether to invite them and hope they've sorted things out by then, or just leave them both off the list. Heeeeeelp!

Georgie snorted. She loved her friend dearly but this Bridezilla act was starting to get right on her wick. Unlike her fictitious agony-aunt alter ego, she was not a person to go in for tough love, though. *Nightmare!* she typed sympathetically underneath instead. *I prescribe wine!*

She scrolled down to read what other friends were up to.

Jade Hamilton: Looking at honeymoons. Maldives or Bahamas?! Am I allowed to choose both?!!!!

Mel Batley: Did anyone pick up my coat on Sat night? Think I left it in the Greyhound??

Nora Taylor: Reggie enjoying a walk in the sunshine!

Christ, they were a boring lot, Georgie thought crossly, scrolling further down and seeing baby photos, lunch photos, new dress photos plus about twenty almost identical photos of Reggie poddling about in the Dales, his tongue hanging out in a doggy sort of grin. A boringly contented lot, at that, the selfish so-and-sos. This was no good for a foraging agony aunt. She needed more . . . well, *agony*, frankly.

About to close the laptop, she was unable to resist a tiny bit of boasting before she left. *So, guess who's been asked to start work as agony aunt on a local magazine??* she typed as her status update and added a row of beaming faces. That would impress them all. Librarian Georgie and her dazzling new career trajectory. Yeah! Even if the word 'career' *was* pushing it a bit, they didn't have to know that, did they?

Logging off, she got to her feet, stomach rumbling as she brushed her hair and put on some mascara. She'd take the laptop to the café down the road and try again over some food, she thought, and maybe – idea! – she could eavesdrop on other people there, tune in on somebody who was having a whinge and use that as the basis of her problem. Genius!

Spirits already lifted, she set off. Now to hope for some loud-voiced miserable people out there. Mission Whingers was go.

The nearest café to Dukes Square was called Sea Blue Sky and Georgie had been in a couple of times already, mostly as a break from the flat whenever cabin fever became too stifling. There was a big terrace at the front where smokers and dog walkers tended to congregate, and inside it was all dark wood and dove-grey walls, with a hissing monster of a coffee machine and a brunchy kind of menu chalked up on a blackboard behind the counter.

Having ordered poached eggs on toast, an espresso and a

full-fat Coke – that should see off the hangover – Georgie cast her eye around for the table with the best eavesdropping potential. There was a group of students in one corner – the perfect demographic for the magazine, she reckoned, but unfortunately they were all laughing and seemed far too happy to have any problems. There were two older women at a table near the back who looked promisingly gossipy, leaning over conspiratorially as they talked. Some young mums too, each with grizzling babies in their arms and pallid expressions. They looked fed-up, admittedly, but as Georgie wandered slowly past, they appeared to be discussing the colour of their babies' poo. Maybe not.

The older ladies it was, decision made, Georgie thought, plonking herself down within earshot. Then she opened her laptop which brought up her document from earlier. Start again.

Hey Em, she typed then sipped her Coke, tuned in and waited.

Eavesdropping was fun! Way better than listening to her own boring thoughts. Savouring her food, she listened avidly as Older Lady 1 (green fleece) let rip about her son-in-law's useless ways (with particular uselessness around child-rearing apparently) and then Older Lady 2 (lavender cardigan) confided, amid snorts of laughter, a story about Him at number 23, 'you know, the one I told you about, with all the tattoos', who had been taken to A and E the night before because – 'and I'm not lying, this is what Barbara told me, and she knows *everything*' – he'd got a champagne cork stuck up his bum.

It was all Georgie could do not to join in as both women started cackling. Green Fleece and Lavender Cardi were ace, she thought, quite wishing she could be a member of their little gang. Then she remembered the point of her being there and stared at her laptop, which had put itself on standby through lack of attention. Hmm. Entertaining as Green Fleece and Lavender Cardi had turned out to be, unfortunately she wasn't sure a Hey-Em letter about a useless son-in-law – or even a useless son-in-law with a champagne cork up his jacksie – was the exact problem she was looking for. And what would waspish Em have to say about such a situation, anyway?

> *For Christ's sake, have you never heard of lube?*
> *Don't waste NHS resources on your sexual*
> *incompetence, darling! And, for the love of God,*
> *read your daughter a bedtime story once in a while,*
> *will you? Or are you illiterate as well as stupid?*

She choked back a laugh – better not – just as the guy who seemed to run the place came over and cleared away her empty plate and cutlery. 'Everything all right?' he asked.

He had such an open friendly face, Georgie couldn't help smiling back up at him. 'Lovely, thanks. Top poached eggs.'

'Great, cheers, I'll tell our chef.' Then he raised an eyebrow. 'Is that a Yorkshire accent I hear, by the way?'

'It certainly is,' Georgie replied in delight. 'Excellent observation skills. Is that where you're from too?'

'Not me, but my mum's from Bradford,' he said. 'That's how I guessed. Not that I'm saying you're anything like my mum.' Bless him, he was actually blushing.

'Er, good?' said Georgie, raising an eyebrow. 'No offence to your mum, obviously.'

He grinned. 'Can I get you anything else?' he asked. 'Another coffee? A second round of eggs?'

She eyed her laptop and then glanced around. The café was starting to thin out now and her gossipy neighbours were getting to their feet. Eavesdropping time was over. 'No, thanks, I'd better shoot off. But . . .' She hesitated, not wanting to leave the café without a single juicy problem for her column. 'Erm, I know this might sound weird, but humour me, will you?' she blurted out. 'I was just wondering, if you were going to write a letter to a problem page, what might it be about?' He looked at her, confused, and she felt she had to explain further. 'I'm an agony aunt,' she said. 'Or rather, an agony aunt in training. Without any actual problems to write about yet.'

'Ahh, I see.' He twisted his mouth while he thought. 'I'm

not sure my problems would be all that interesting for anyone else, seeing as they basically revolve around trying to pay the bills and take care of my kids,' he said, 'but I can send over Shamira, if you want, one of our waitresses. I happen to know she's got some drama going on in her life right now.'

'Really? And you think she wouldn't mind?' Georgie could see the woman he was pointing out, a waitress with brown spiral curls and freckles, and a tiny cobalt blue nose stud.

The man rolled his eyes. 'Between you and me, she talks about nothing else,' he said conspiratorially. 'She's been bending our ears non-stop.' He called over. 'Shamira? Could you come here a second?' Then he winked at Georgie. 'All the best with it.'

Hey Em, she typed once she was back home,

> *My sister was with this guy – let's call him John – for six years and the two of them seemed really happy together. I always thought John was the bee's knees. He's gorgeous, sexy, funny . . . and seemed madly in love with her too. I even quite envied her for a while – and joked to her that I wished I could find someone so lovely myself.*
>
> *The problem is, they've just split up and then two days ago he turned up at my door telling me*

*that he thought he was in love with me. I must
confess, I felt flattered at first – I mean, this was
perfect John, after all! – but confused too. What do I
say to my sister? She would be devastated if
anything happened between us – it wasn't so long
ago she thought she and John were going to be
married with babies, together forever sort of thing.*

*I don't know what to do. If I go for it with John,
my sister would never forgive me. But if I turn John
down then I might be giving up the best guy I've
ever met.*

Help!

Freckles

Georgie had all but run home in order to type up the
waitress's problem. She had hardly been able to believe it
when this complete stranger had provided her with such a
humdinger of a juicy real-life dilemma. 'Bloody hell,' she'd
said at the end of it. 'What are you going to do?'

'I dunno,' the waitress had replied, pulling a face. 'Because
I love my sister, but . . . you know. What if he's The One?'

'God,' said Georgie, feeling her agony. She was a big
believer in The One, after all. Everyone had their one true
love, didn't they? 'Well, good luck,' she said eventually,
squeezing the waitress's hand. 'It's a big decision. I hope it all
turns out okay.'

Back at the flat, letter typed, Georgie shut her eyes and put aside the real her, the her that squeezed strangers' hands, and believed in true love, and didn't want anyone to be upset. Instead, in accordance with Viv's instructions, she did her best to channel the fictitious Em: big hair, big lipstick and big opinions – got it. Em wouldn't mince her words about this situation, no way.

> *Dear Freckles,* she typed,
>
> *Stop right there. Are you seriously telling me, hand on your heart, that you don't know what you should do? Listen to yourself, darling. You say in your own words that your sister will be 'devastated', that she'll 'never forgive' you. Er . . . hello? Why are you even considering letting these things happen? This is your own flesh and blood we're talking about, Freckles – family. You go on about this John being 'perfect' and 'thoughtful' but – newsflash! – he's hardly been either of those things to your poor sister recently. He sounds a total chancer if you ask me. As for you saying he 'thinks' he's in love with you . . . Is that the sound of somebody hedging their bets, by any chance?*
>
> *Sorry, Freckles, but you know what you should do. We all know what you should do. Bin John for the sake of the sisterhood. There are plenty of other*

guys out there – and you and your sister both
deserve way better than this creep.
    Love Em

She sat back and read the piece aloud to herself, tweaking a few words here and there. Too glib? Too unsympathetic? She wasn't completely certain that she even liked this Em character, she thought worriedly. Still, tough and no-nonsense was what Viv had asked for, she reminded herself. Maybe this was just how things were in a city – people were that bit brasher with you, less inclined to actually give a shit.

Perhaps she should add something extra to the piece, though, she thought, reading it yet again. She wanted this to be perfect, after all, and she definitely didn't want her new boss to regret hiring her. Plus it never hurt to show willing and make a good first impression, did it?

Thinking back to how the conversation had gone over at the magazine office the day before, she remembered Viv saying she wanted the column to be a talking point, to engage readers. Well, what better way to engage them than by asking for their feedback directly?

An idea came to her and she began typing again.

Did Em get it right? What do you think Freckles
should do in this situation? Take part in our online
poll and have your say!

Freckles should:
DUMP HIM? He's no good! Steer clear!
HUMP HIM? Sod it, he sounds hot, shag him
anyway!

She smiled to herself, reading it all back. An online poll was dead easy to set up and they could show the result the following week to get people coming back. It could even become a regular aspect of the column. Yes!

She saved the document – Agony1, the first of many, she hoped – and was just about to email it straight off to Viv when she realized with a little shriek that her rant about Simon was still lurking at the top of the page. Yikes! How unprofessional would that have looked? Quickly deleting it and saving the document again – AgonyOne – she composed an email to Viv. Blah blah blah, hope you like it, blah blah, happy to make any amendments, or . . . Wait a minute. Her fingers froze as it occurred to her that she was missing a trick here. This was a golden opportunity for her to pitch for some more work, now that she had the editor's attention. Why send off one thing when you could also be angling for a second?

Abandoning the email momentarily, she opened a brand-new document and pulled out her original list of feature ideas. She would develop the best three, she decided, and condense each idea into two fantastic, tantalizing sentences that Viv would be unable to resist. This wouldn't be her blathering on desperately about 'Dogs of Brighton' or other moronic ideas on the phone either, these would be carefully considered, painstakingly crafted pitches. Hey, with a bit of luck, she'd have a second commission by the end of the day and then even *Simon* would have to be impressed by her entrepreneurial spirit.

Muttering out loud as the ideas took shape in her head, her fingers began flying over the keyboard again. *I can do this*, she told herself. *I can do it!*

Chapter Seven

The rain had now stopped but the pavements around Dukes Square still gleamed wet as the streetlights began coming on, the beaded droplets on car bonnets and windscreens glistening like shiny sequins. The dusky sky was darkening, the sea a navy band on the horizon; lamps were being lit inside houses and curtains pulled across the windows. Inside Rosa's flat, she and Bea had put away the most comforting dinner she could conjure up – macaroni cheese, all bubbling and golden, with cake for dessert – and although Bea had been largely uncommunicative, hiding behind that sheaf of bushy red hair and contributing little to Rosa's conversational attempts, she did at least seem less combative than earlier. That was the power of cheesy pasta for you. And actually, thought Rosa, licking icing off her finger, it had been surprisingly nice to cook for another person again. She had forgotten how pleasurable it was, seeing someone else enjoying her food.

'So,' she said, stacking their empty plates, 'do you have

any homework, or stuff you need to do for school tomorrow?'

Bea thought for a moment then gave a theatrical groan. 'Shit, I'm meant to be doing an *essay*. On the most boring play *ever*. And it needs to be in tomorrow.' She sighed with world-weariness. 'I'd better get some books from our place.'

'Sure.' Rosa hesitated, her thoughts flashing ahead to sleeping arrangements. Seeing as Bea had failed to provide her with a single other person who could care for her overnight, the responsibility was most definitely Rosa's, like it or not. 'Listen, what do you want to do about tonight, by the way?' she asked. 'Do you want to stay here at mine, or . . . ?'

Bea's eyes slid away and she gave an awkward shrug. 'You could stay at ours?' she said gruffly after a moment, tugging her school jumper sleeves low over her hands. 'You could sleep in Mum's bed.'

It seemed the most practical way around things and so, a few minutes later, once Rosa had finished the washing-up, she followed her teenage neighbour across the hallway and into Jo's flat. 'Wow,' she said, blinking as she gazed around. Compared to her own rather plain living quarters, Jo's place came as an assault on the senses with candyfloss-pink walls in the kitchen, a turquoise living room with Indian-style rosewood furniture, fat vibrantly coloured cushions of mirrored fabric on the golden-sari draped sofa, and a faint smell of incense in the air. There was a collection of flowering orchids along one window ledge, shelves of books piled higgledy-piggledy, travel guides and novels and poetry all randomly heaped in together, and an eye-popping Andy Warhol print on one wall.

'It's a bit of a mess,' Bea conceded, looking rather defensive as Rosa stood staring.

'It's lovely,' Rosa found herself saying. 'So homely.' Her eyes couldn't register everything quickly enough: framed prints of Bea and Jo on the wall, the two of them tanned and laughing in sombreros, Bea as a toddler in a red mac and wellies, Jo with blonde hair, black hair and pink hair, depending on which picture you looked at. There was a pile of school exercise books on the coffee table, a pair of navy blue woolly slippers, a vase of bright daffodils on the mantelpiece, a nurse's uniform on the ironing board. The rooms were bursting with colour and personality, exactly the way a home should be. And exactly how her place *wasn't*, a voice in her head pointed out.

'Wow, is that you two on an elephant?' Rosa asked, peering at a framed photo on the bookcase.

'Yep,' Bea said. 'And that's Mum bungee-jumping off a cliff. Live for today! That's what she always says,' she added, rolling her eyes. 'Apart from when she's, like, semi-conscious in a hospital bed, that is, looking as if she's about to die.' Her chin wobbled, betraying her bold words, and she swung her face away abruptly.

For the sake of Bea's dignity, Rosa pretended she hadn't noticed and went on gazing at the photos. Elephant-riding and bungee-jumping and child-rearing . . . it all seemed so vivid and colourful. She felt as if her own life had shrunk to a very small sphere in comparison, consisting only of the hotel kitchen and her drab little flat. Would she ever feel like embarking on exciting new adventures again?

'Mum's room is through here,' Bea said, leading her along to a small sea-green-painted bedroom with white linen on the bed. The floorboards were bare with a conker-brown varnish and there was a nubbly cream rug in the centre of the room, plus a big mirror above a chest of drawers, draped with scarves and fairy lights. It was a personal, feminine space with Jo's antique perfume bottles and a big powder puff on display, her silky sky-blue kimono hanging on the back of the door. Rosa had a flashback to her old bedroom in the Bloomsbury flat, the rose-pink wrap Max had bought her on one of his trips abroad. *Take all your clothes off immediately*, he had said mock-sternly, putting the robe into her arms. *And model this for me.* She could still remember how the silk felt on her bare shoulders, how he'd slid his hands inside and then peeled it off as if unwrapping a present.

She dragged herself back to the moment. 'Are you sure this is okay?' she asked doubtfully, feeling like an intruder as she saw a pair of purple knickers sticking out of the top of one of Jo's drawers. 'I don't mind sleeping on the sofa if that's easiest.'

Bea didn't reply. She seemed very subdued, as if being here without Jo had brought the reality of her mum's absence crashing back in. She went to shut the curtains against the darkening sky and picked up a small wooden elephant on Jo's bedside table. Standing there, turning it between her fingers, her voice was low when she eventually spoke. 'Do you think she's going to be all right?' she asked.

'Your mum? Absolutely,' Rosa replied as staunchly as she knew how.

'We got this in India,' Bea said, still turning the elephant in her hand. Its tusks and eyes were painted a bright gold. 'We went there two years ago. It's Mum's favourite place.' Her voice wobbled for a moment and she hunched her shoulders as if she was about to cry.

'It'll be all right,' Rosa said and, before she could wonder if it was the right thing to do, was over at the girl's side, one arm around her. Bea felt as rigid as a block of wood but didn't wrench herself away at least. 'Try not to worry. I'm sure she'll be okay.'

'She just looked so . . . *ill*.' Bea's voice was almost a whisper. 'Didn't she? Really horribly ill, like she was going to die or something.' She twisted a ring round and round on her finger, her eyes haunted. 'I don't know what I'd do if she died.'

'She's not going to die,' Rosa said firmly although she was starting to feel uncertain herself by this point. The day had started in such an ordinary way, too – and now here she was, sucked right into a family drama with two relative strangers. *I don't feel qualified to deal with this*, she said to the universe in her head, hoping that some celestial rearranging might take place accordingly if she thought it loud enough. *Did you hear that? I can't do this, I don't know how. HELP.*

Rosa hadn't been sure if she would be able to sleep in Jo's bed at first. She could smell the other woman's mimosa perfume on the pillows, plus there was a gap at the top of the bedroom curtains which let in a strip of orange streetlight. More pressingly, the events of the afternoon and evening kept replaying in her head, looping over and over, and she couldn't help worrying about both Jo and Bea. Earlier, she had called the hospital for an update but there hadn't been much news, other than that Jo was currently in surgery. Despite Rosa's best attempts at positivity, Bea had sloped off to her room claiming to be doing her homework, but really, Rosa suspected, in order to play thrashy music and have a private cry. When she did finally manage to drop off, Rosa fell into an anxious recurring dream about Max: that she was on a flight to Amsterdam and he had just sat down next to her on the plane, easing his long legs into the seat and putting a hand on her thigh. 'Hello, darling,' he said in a low, amused-sounding voice and she woke up in a sweat, the bed sheets tangled around her body, the green numerals of Jo's bedside clock telling her that it was 3.08: insomniacs' hour.

Rolling onto her back, she stared up at the ceiling, where she could make out the shape of the silvery pendant light in the gauzy darkness. Stop bloody thinking about him, for God's sake, she ordered her subconscious, wishing for the thousandth time that there was a delete function in the brain, some kind of mental shredder to dispose of unwanted memories and people. But when you'd been with someone for eight wildly happy months, when you'd slept beside them, shared your most private thoughts with them, seen each other drunk, naked, hungover, happy, sad, ill . . . there was a lot to untangle; there could be no neat scissoring out of a lover from your head, as from a photograph. The way he smelled so good, even when he'd been out running. Those long eyelashes of his, the cheekbones she liked to trace with a finger, the Nordic-blue of his eyes . . . *You were definitely a Danish prince in another lifetime*, she had told him once, her imagination furnishing him with a crown and cape, on a Viking ship, on a galloping horse . . . oh, so many fantasies, in fact.

Scissor, scissor, scissor, she reminded herself, scissor him away. Well, she was doing her best to remove him but he was not a person to be so easily discarded. Especially after what he'd done.

I thought I saw Max today in the King's Road! Is he back early from Amsterdam?

No, actually. Turned out he was a lying bastard. I know! Men, eh?

She'd met him in a hipster bar in Shoreditch of all places. Her three best friends had forced her to come out and drink sickly cocktails with them, because she'd been, as they put it, 'moping about with a face like a slapped arse' since getting dumped by Graham, the sensible pharmacist she'd been trying and failing to convince herself she was in love with. (Secretly it was a relief. Graham, although a catch on paper, had a nervous habit of making gross swallowing noises whenever they began foreplay and all she could think about was saliva in his mouth, gallons of saliva sloshing about in there. Yes, she *was* a shallow person. No, she probably didn't deserve any kind of happy-ever-after because of such meanness.)

Rosa didn't even like hipster bars, especially not ones with random vintage items whimsically bolted to the walls (a penny-farthing bicycle, a grandfather clock, something that looked like a spinning wheel, for crying out loud). On that particular evening, she didn't like men full stop, either, even though her friends kept badgering her about getting back in the saddle and getting out there again. Any minute now, they'd be whipping out a pair of bolt-cutters and removing the sodding penny-farthing for her to clamber onto, she thought, rolling her eyes. Her friend Catherine, who became very loud and pointy-fingered after a few cocktails, was already scouring the pub for suitable pharmacist replacements. 'How about him?' she'd blared, indicating a bearded guy in a red Fred Perry top and jeans who was holding court on the next table. 'He looks fun.'

'I hate men with beards,' Rosa had replied balefully. 'And I hate fun people.'

'Him, then,' another friend, Alexa, had suggested, picking out a man with a bleached buzz-cut and piercings. 'He looks sexy. I bet he's got tattoos as well. Dare me to ask him?'

'I hate pierced noses,' came Rosa's damning reply, even if it wasn't strictly true. 'Definitely not.'

Undeterred, they went on searching. 'Well, what about him at the bar? He's gorgeous,' Catherine said, loud enough for the elegant, square-jawed man to turn his – okay then, admittedly gorgeous – head their way, and eye them in amusement. 'Yeah, *you*,' Catherine confirmed, emboldened after her fifth cocktail of the night. She was a liability when she got started. 'I was just telling my friend she should go and chat you up.'

'*Catherine!*' Rosa exploded, throwing her hands up in mortification, but the man merely laughed and raised an eyebrow.

'What can I say, I agree,' he said, a smile playing on his lips. 'You really should.'

Catherine had cheered, the others had laughed and Rosa had turned bright red. 'Ha ha,' she had said witheringly.

'I'm serious,' he said, picking up his glass of red wine and strolling over to their table. He winked. 'Go on, what are your best lines? Seduce me. I'm game.'

Oh, he'd been game, all right. It had *been* a game to him, more like. And now here she was, wide awake in the middle of the night because she was starting to feel angry with him all over again and even angrier with her own naive self for falling for his shit in the first place. Punching the pillow, she tried to find a comfortable position in Jo's bed but it seemed impossible now that her head was full of him, Max, bloody Max, and his terrible lies. If only she could go back in time and put up more resistance to Catherine and the others when they had nagged her about coming out with them on that fateful night! *Sorry, I'm washing my hair; sorry, I'm sorting out my tights drawer; sorry, I'm single-handedly resolving world peace.* There should be some kind of danger sign that came with men like Max, an alarm that was triggered in a woman's head the moment he approached, eyes glittering. *Get lost,* she'd have said, if she'd known. *Do one.*

I didn't like to say at the time but I did think he was too good to be true, you know, her mum sighed inside her ear for the millionth time, and Rosa groaned. 'And you can sod off and all,' she snarled, pulling the covers over her head.

★

She must have fallen asleep soon afterwards because the next thing she knew was a blast of grungey music from the bedroom next to hers and it took her a moment to orient herself. Mimosa perfume. The wooden elephant with golden eyes. Jo's room, she thought, blinking and pulling herself upright. The events of the day before all seemed like a weird dream now but she rubbed her eyes and shambled through to the kitchen to make coffee and phone the hospital again for news.

When Bea emerged in a grubby pink towelling dressing gown, her hair a bird's nest of tangles, face pouchy and grey, Rosa took a deep breath and poured her a coffee before gently giving her the update. Unfortunately Jo continued to be quite poorly, according to the nurse Rosa had spoken to. Although the emergency operation had been successful, they would still need to monitor her for at least another twenty-four hours, probably longer, in case of infection, or any other post-operative problems.

Bea sagged into a chair at the small scrubbed pine table and put her head in her hands. 'Infection, they mean that MRSA thing, I bet,' she said. 'People die of that, don't they?'

'It's not necessarily MRSA,' Rosa tried saying but Bea was on a roll and not listening.

'I googled "burst appendix" last night and there's this thing, peritonitis, where basically your blood gets poisoned, and you die. What if she's got that?'

'She's not going to d—'

'But she *might*! You can't say for sure. Fuck! I can't believe this!' She wiped her eyes with the sleeve of her dressing gown. 'Do I have to go to school?' she pleaded, slumping over the table. 'Please? Can you write me a note to say I'm stressed out and, like, too *ill* with worrying to go in?'

'I've got to go to work,' Rosa said helplessly. She had been hoping that this morning would mark a neat separation, the return to their individual lives, but Bea's neediness was impossible to ignore. She sighed. 'But I finish early today so I'll be here when you get back from school,' she added reluctantly, 'and we could visit your mum again then, I suppose. Decide what's best.' Bea was still motionless, her head on the table, a hank of her rust-coloured hair gently draped across the sugar bowl. It was all very dramatic being a teenager, Rosa couldn't help thinking. 'Come on, have some breakfast,' she urged. 'Do you like porridge? I can make us some, if you want.'

'Yes, please,' Bea mumbled, unmoving.

'Fine. Why don't you wash your face and get dressed, and I'll sort that out,' Rosa said, conscious of the time, and her own need to get on. Porridge and one more hospital visit, she could manage that much, she thought, hunting in Jo's cupboards for the right sort of pan. By this evening, it would all be over, and she could retreat into solitude once more, job done.

★

'You should sneak her into hotel. She could stay there,' said Natalya when Rose told her of the situation. The two of them were taking a break outside the back of the Zanzibar, Natalya with one of her noxious-smelling Russian cigarettes, Rosa with coffee in a chipped mug. 'What?' she asked, shrugging, when Rosa pulled an I-don't-think-so face. 'I do it before, with my friend Svetlana. Nobody notice. I just sneak her through the back.'

'She's only fourteen,' Rosa said, her mouth puckering at the coffee. She'd made it extra-strong, feeling the need for caffeine, but every sip was making her head pound. 'And she's all prickly and cross, there's no way she'd be able to blag it if anyone questioned her.' She turned her head to avoid Natalya's smoke. 'I'm going to have to get in touch with her dad.'

'The bad dad? But she hates him!' Natalya protested with a frown.

'I know, but . . .' Rosa shrugged. 'I'm working here all weekend. What else can I do?'

'Nothing else,' Natalya agreed morosely then, after one last hard pull on the cigarette, she dropped it and stamped it out. 'I wonder why she hates him that bad?' she mused as they turned to go back to the kitchen. 'Is he like criminal, maybe? Hitman?' She wiggled one bushy eyebrow. 'The mafia?'

'It's a good question,' said Rosa. 'I've been wondering the same.'

'Gareth? Hi, my name is Rosa. I live next door to Jo and Bea. I'm just—'

'Who?' There was music in the background and the sound of voices. Was he in a pub? she wondered.

'Jo and Bea?' she repeated while Bea made a gun shape with one hand and pretended to shoot herself in the head. It was early evening that same day, and following a visit to the hospital after school, where the nurses had informed them that Jo would be staying in for at least another forty-eight hours, Rosa was now on the phone to Gareth, Bea's dad, although judging by his confused response, she was starting to think she might have the wrong number. Unless the guy was so clueless as to have forgotten the names of his own daughter and ex-wife, she thought, remembering her conversation with Natalya. Surely nobody could be that crap though, could they?

'Oh sorry, love, didn't hear what you said. Jo and Bea, got it. What about them?' He had a low husky voice that had a laugh in it, a southern accent. There was the sound of cheering in the background and a football chant. Definitely a pub, Rosa thought.

'Well, Jo's not well, she's gone into hospital,' she told him. 'She's going to be in for another few days too – and I've looked after Bea here until now but I've got to work tomor-row and so . . .' She was talking too fast, the words rushing out of her. 'So Jo was wondering if Bea could come to yours then.'

She glanced across at Bea who was now pretending to hang herself, and felt wretched about the whole situation. Poor kid. Jo had still been pale and wan when they saw her earlier but at least this time she was awake and able to speak, insisting that Bea would have to go to her dad's. 'Come on, love,' she'd urged. 'It's been so long. This could be your chance to put everything behind you, start again.'

'Huh, right,' Bea had snarled but her protests had fallen on deaf ears. Jo was resolute.

'Sure,' Gareth said now, over a gale of blokish laughter in the background. 'No problem. I'm over in Kemp Town, Essex Street. She knows where it is.'

'Okay, so should I just . . . drop her with you tomorrow morning? Around nine o'clock?' This was all turning out to be easier than she'd expected, even if Bea *was* shaking her head darkly and pulling sick faces.

'Er . . . yeah,' he replied after a brief hesitation. 'Nine it is. Tell her I'm looking forward to it.'

'He's looking forward to it,' Rosa duly repeated after hanging up but Bea just made a scornful sound in her throat and stared pointedly at the ceiling. 'I'm sorry, there's not really any way around it,' she went on. And there wasn't! She couldn't look after the girl the whole time, could she? This was nothing to do with her, not her problem. So why on earth was she feeling so guilty about Bea's unhappy face all of a sudden? 'Look,' she blurted out before she could stop herself, 'I finish my shift on Sunday after lunch so how about you come back here then, and I'll make us a slap-up Sunday roast?'

Lips tightly pressed together, Bea did at least give a small grudging nod. 'I suppose so,' she growled.

Rosa, you ridiculous pushover, she thought in the next moment, cross with her own weakness. Since when did you turn into such an utter sap? 'Right,' she said with a sigh. 'So that's settled.'

Chapter Eight

A small white envelope had been slipped under Charlotte's door when she returned from work on Friday. Her name was written on the front in black cursive handwriting and she knew instantly who had left it there.

Sighing a little, she put it on the side in the kitchen unopened while she hung up her jacket, tidied her shoes into their usual place and then set about making her tea. Well, all right, opening the plastic pot of Marks and Spencer Mediterranean pasta salad and decanting it onto a plate anyway, and then pouring herself a glass of Chilean cabernet sauvignon. The chocolate eclairs she slid into the fridge, just in case she might feel like one later. Both, even. If you couldn't treat yourself on a Friday night, when could you? she thought defensively.

Fridays were always a bit hard to get through, to be honest. Kate had been born on a Friday. She'd died on a Friday too, after just two short weeks of life. You wouldn't think that a grown woman's very best and very worst moments could be experienced in such a limited time period, but Charlotte had discovered, unfortunately, that this was entirely possible. Three little words: congenital heart defect. That was all it took to shatter your entire world, as it turned out.

So yes, Fridays tended to be particularly tough. Everyone else always seemed in a carefree, weekend-starts-here sort of mood which made things worse. The only time she ever felt like reconnecting to her ex-husband Jim was on a Friday although she was trying not to ring him any more. 'We've got to stop this,' he'd said gently the last time, when she was drunk and incoherent, her face dripping with tears. The kindness in his voice had pulled her up short; the pity, with the merest hint of irritation in the background. The next time he might tell her to eff off, she had realized with a shock.

Since moving to Brighton she often worked late on Fridays now, prolonging the inevitable moment when she'd be back here alone, doing her best to avoid getting out the shoe-box of memories at the bottom of the wardrobe. You had to ration yourself with the sadness, sometimes. If you could just distract yourself, keep busy, keep active, then the hours would eventually drag by until you could turn the lights off and go to sleep. And so Friday nights were often the busiest of her week: she would get all her paperwork done, bill-paying and shopping-ordering and accounts. She would clean out the fridge and scrub the salad drawer, descale the kettle, mop the kitchen floor, disinfect the bin and slosh a capful of bleach down the sink. She would sort out the week's dry-cleaning to take in the next morning, hanging it tidily by the front door in readiness, and then she'd clear out any receipts or unwanted bits and pieces from her handbag. There was barely a moment left in which to feel sad. That was the plan anyway. Unless she ended up getting drunk and maudlin again. You could never really predict which way it would go.

Once she'd eaten her tea – on her lap, on the sofa (the kitchen was barely big enough for a cooker, let alone a luxury like a dining table) – she remembered again the small white envelope with the elegant handwriting that had been pushed under her door. Opening it revealed a folded sheet of paper with the following words:

> *Dear Charlotte,*
>   *It was very nice to meet you. Would you be free to come to tea with me on Saturday at four o'clock?*
>   *Best wishes*
>   *Margot Favager*

It was rather like being summoned by the queen. Was she supposed to reply? she wondered, draining her glass of wine. RSVP a scented note, slip it under the door of Flat 5, or just turn up, knock on the door with a bunch of tulips and a bashful smile?

She poured herself another glass of wine. That was if she even decided to go, of course. She was just going to have to sleep on it.

The next day was Saturday, which meant she had the bed linen to strip and wash, the hoovering and dry-cleaning to tackle and the . . . Ahh. She found herself remembering the unworn trainers still under her bed, taunting her with their newness. *Here we are, still box-fresh! Hey, but we look good, right? Like we never left the shop!*

Yes, all right, then, there probably *was* time for a healthy walk along the seafront today, she supposed. And then, of course, the afternoon tea upstairs with Margot. Awkward silences over the bone-china tea set, her spilling biscuit crumbs down herself no doubt. She was still half considering sneaking up there on Sunday with an apologetic note in reply – *So sorry, have been away, having an amazing time with all my many friends, just so busy, you see, and received your note too late, alas.* But whenever she thought of Margot's shrewd eyes on her, sussing Charlotte right out for the liar she was, she found herself cringing at her own deceit. Perhaps not.

She busied herself with her chores and headed out to the dry-cleaners a few streets away where she dropped off her work clothes as usual. Afterwards she was about to go home again when she found herself hesitating on the street corner, feet unmoving, the world around her coming into sudden sharp focus. It was another lovely spring morning, she realized; the sun shining, a balmy benevolence about the air. The sea was a serene, luminous blue, and there were hordes of people out, making the most of the good weather: down on the beach, cycling and roller skating along the front, piling onto the Palace Pier. There were even a couple of hardy souls in the sea, although it must have been freezing.

You are happy? Margot had asked the other day as they made their way up the stairs, and Charlotte had blushed and stammered in response. But there was something about today – the breeze tugging at her hair, the smell of candyfloss and hot dogs and fried onions, the sound of the seagulls calling overhead in the wide blue sky – that lifted her spirits just a fraction. And then, before she even really knew what she was doing, she found herself turning in the opposite direction and heading towards the pier.

I went to the pier, she imagined herself telling her parents tomorrow when they rang for their weekly chat. You could always detect the anxiety in her mum's voice as she asked how Charlotte was doing, gauge how worried she was in the careful listening silence as Charlotte mumbled that she was fine, work was fine, there was nothing really to report, before switching the subject to them. You could hear too the unspoken questions lurking just below the surface of the conversation: *Are you coping? Promise me you haven't been trying to steal any more babies? You will tell me, won't you, if you need me to book an appointment with Doctor Giles again . . . ?*

They worried about her, she knew, and yet she felt unable to say anything to assuage their worries. But *I went to the pier* might be a start. She pictured her parents exchanging a pleased glance back home. *She went to the pier! Did you hear that? Sounds like progress to me!*

She rolled her eyes at her own lame self as she trudged along. Oh God, calm down, Charlotte, you're not exactly Ranulph Fiennes, she thought. Ten minutes along the road to a tourist attraction . . . it was hardly a big deal in anyone's book. *And* she hadn't remembered to put on her new trainers so this didn't even count as a proper fitness mission. Never mind. She'd wander to the end of the pier and back, see what all the fuss was about, have something positive lined up to report to her parents and then go home and have a nice cup of tea. Job done.

Once at the pier's entrance, she found herself part of a slow-moving mass of people, all apparently with the same idea as her. Charlotte had existed in a numb sort of paralysis for some time now – a year, three months and sixteen days, actually – but even she could feel the palpable buzz of excitement as she made her way down the old wooden boards, past slot machines and arcade games and blue-rinse grannies nursing hot drinks in the sheltered area. Now and then a strong breeze would whisk up from the sea and everyone would clutch at their baseball caps and headscarves; balloons tied to pram handles would bob and dance, children ran along with their arms stretched wide as if hoping to be lifted up like birds on the wind.

I am alive, thought Charlotte, feeling a surprised sort of thrill as she leaned against the eau-de-nil ironwork of the pier's side. Her coat flapped and her hair streamed around her face and she could smell the sea below, briny and pungent, clumps of seaweed drifting in dark shapes through the water. *I am alive.* She lifted her face up to the sky and shut her eyes for a moment, marvelling at it all. And then there was a soft thump against her jeaned legs and someone was pulling at her sleeve.

'Mrs Johnson? Will you help me find Daddy?'

Charlotte looked down in surprise to see a little girl in a pink raincoat and tufty blonde bunches, a gap in her front teeth. 'Um . . .' she said.

'Oh,' said the girl in dismay. She could only have been five or six, and her nose was running from the wind. Her small pink fingers unwound themselves from Charlotte's coat and she took an uncertain step backwards. 'I fort you was Mrs Johnson.'

'I'm not Mrs Johnson,' Charlotte said. Her heart was pounding all of a sudden and she glanced around, wondering where this child's mother was. Parents could be so negligent. So thoughtless! 'Where's your mummy?'

'I lost Daddy,' the girl said, wiping her nose on her sleeve. Tears swelled in her blue eyes and she turned her face up to Charlotte, stricken. 'I *losted* him.'

Charlotte wasn't sure what to do. The woman from the park in Reading was in her head all of a sudden, that angry, shrill red-faced woman, screaming *Get away from my baby! What do you think you're doing? Get your hand off her this minute!* and she felt her throat swell up at the memory. 'I . . . Where did you last see him?' she asked, glancing round again. Any second now, some furious parent would run towards her, accusing horrible things, she thought in a panic. Been there, done that, had the breakdown. 'What does he look like?'

'He looks like *Daddy*,' the girl said unhelpfully. She had a faint dusting of freckles across the bridge of her nose and her lips were chapped at one corner. 'We was at the hot dogs bit cos Amber was hungry and then I wanted to go on the teacups but he said no and then Amber needed a wee and he said wait there, and I *did* wait there but then I saw a seagull and I fort it was hurted so I followed it for a bit and then I couldn't see him no more.' Her face crumpled suddenly and new tears spurted from her eyes. 'I just want my daddy!' she howled.

People were turning to look at them wonderingly and

Charlotte felt her agitation grow. Taking care not to actually touch the child or get too close – she had made that mistake before – she bent down and said, 'Don't worry, I'll help you find him. What's your name?'

'Lily,' sniffed the little girl and then she took two sideways steps over and put her hand in Charlotte's. 'Fank you,' she added trustingly.

Oh God. Oh God. The girl's hand felt so warm in hers, so solid, it was all Charlotte could do not to start sniffling herself. She dreamed sometimes that Kate was alive, growing up, a toddler now in stripy tights and tiny shoes, a hand in hers, just like this. For a second she wondered if she was hallucinating, dreaming while wide awake, and that she'd look down and the girl would be gone, and then she would know for sure that she'd completely lost the plot. But no, there was Lily in snot-smeared real life, holding tight to Charlotte's fingers, and cheering up almost immediately as they set off, hopping from foot to foot, telling Charlotte about how they'd lost Amber's teddy and how she'd got her shoes and socks wet where the sea had come in too quick, and that Daddy had been a bit cross and said, *Oh,* Lily, *not again.*

She was *adorable*, thought Charlotte with a pang, her earlier caution vanishing like a sea mist burning away. She was so sweet with her little round face and those tears clinging damply to her lashes, her incessant chatter, the way her coat was slightly too big and bunching on her arms. And there it was, the temptation, as strong and pulling as the tide itself; the temptation that whispered to her to just turn around with the girl and take her home, clutching that small clammy hand, she could do it. *I'll look after you, Lily, you can be my little girl now. Would you like that?*

But no, she mustn't. She wouldn't. Would she?

Just then there was a man bearing down on them anyway, a man pushing a buggy with another small girl strapped inside, a man with rumpled hair and glasses and a panicked set to his mouth, shouting, 'Lily! For heaven's sake! Where have you *been*?'

And before Charlotte could snatch her hand away from the girl's – I was *not* stealing your daughter, I was *not* – Lily had released her grasp and the spell was broken as she went pelting across the wooden boards of the pier – 'Daddy!' – all the way over to the man who threw his arms around her and squeezed her and kissed her blonde head, his big arms wrapped around her doll-like body.

Charlotte's hands felt emptier than ever and her adrenalin leaked away like a punctured balloon as she stood there dumbly watching the heart-warming scene. *Idiot. You didn't really think you could keep her, did you?*

'Thank you.' Standing upright again, still holding on to Lily, the man had noticed her at last, standing there like a spare part. 'Thank you so much,' he gasped, relief evident in every syllable. 'I was just taking my youngest daughter to the loo – I must have been two *minutes* – when . . .'

Charlotte's lip curled. She didn't want to listen. Nothing made her angrier – nothing! – than parents who couldn't be bothered to look after their own children. Parents who had no idea how bloody lucky they were. 'You should take better care of her,' she said coldly, biting down the rage she could feel swirling up inside like the beginning of a violent tornado.

'I fort she was Mrs Johnson,' Lily said, tugging at her dad who didn't seem to notice. 'Daddy? I fort she was Mrs *Johnson*.'

But the man was staring open-mouthed at Charlotte, looking taken aback. Hurt, even. 'Take better care . . . ?' he echoed, colour rushing to his face. 'I *do* take good care of them. Not that it's anything to do with *you*.'

'It *is* my business when I find your child wandering around, lost and crying, because you can't be bothered to keep tabs on her,' Charlotte said, anger spiking through her. Even as she was saying the words she knew she was being unfair but she just couldn't help it. Weekend dads like this guy were the worst too – not a clue, most of them, more interested in peering at their smartphones than any interaction with their poor children.

'Daddy! I fort the lady was Mrs *Johnson*!' Lily said again, banging their entwined hands against the man's leg to make him pay attention.

The man's face was screwed up as if he was about to yell something rude back at Charlotte but at his daughter's words, he turned away, his body like a shield for both children. *I'll protect you from the crazy angry lady. Daddy's got you.* 'Yes, I heard, darling,' he said to the girl, crouching down and putting his arm around her. He leaned his head against hers in a tender, weary sort of way. 'Come on, let's get home now,' he said in a gentler voice, and in the next moment, the rage had left Charlotte and she was filled with mortification in its place.

'I'm sorry,' she blurted out. 'I didn't mean to – I'm sorry,' she said, and then whirled around, unable to control her emotions a moment longer, and marched back along the pier, tears pouring down her cheeks. *Fool. Idiot. Madwoman. Go home and calm the hell down, Charlotte.*

The spring sunshine seemed to mock her now. People made indignant noises as she barged blindly through them, but she barely heard as they called 'Oi!' and 'Watch it!' after her. What was wrong with her? What had she become?

Yeah, I went to the pier, Mum, she thought, still smarting from the encounter and wrapped her arms around herself as she picked up speed. *It was great. Had a lovely trip out. No problem at all.*

★

It wasn't as if she had ever really been going to *steal* the woman's baby, back in the park in Reading anyway. She had only gone over because the baby was crying in the pram and nobody seemed to be paying her any attention. 'Hello, sweetheart,' Charlotte had breathed, gazing down at the soft round face, the single tooth visible in the pink lower gum, the dark curls mussed up where the baby had been twisting her head. Breath catching in her throat, Charlotte had put one gloved hand on the knitted coverlet – only to soothe her! Not to take her! – and had felt the warmth of the infant's body through the wool, so alive, so real. Her heart had ached with sheer longing, and without knowing what she was doing, her other hand reached in automatically. Just for that contact, the warm, baby contact again. Just because it was impossible not to.

But then had come the commotion, running footsteps, the ugly accusing screeching, the woman's red shouting face. *What the hell do you think you're doing? Get your hands off her!* It was as if a spell had been broken, and Charlotte had had to scuttle away, face burning, with all the other mothers looking scandalized in her wake. *Weirdo. Baby-snatcher. Paedo.* 'I was a mother once too, you know,' she wanted to shout in her defence, but she had clamped her jaw shut and run out instead, the child-proof gate clanging behind her. *Keep out and stay out.* It was pretty much the moment Charlotte decided she needed to leave town, just get away, anywhere, to start over.

I was a mother once too, you know. That was one of the hardest things: that there seemed no adequate term to describe the devastating enormity of Charlotte's situation. She was a woman who had once traced the rounded curve of her newborn baby's cheek and marvelled at her delicate pink ears, pressed her nose into the soft whorls of hair on her baby's head, but whose hands now hung empty. An ex-mum. A former parent. Christ, these were surely the worst words in the world. The sort of the words that stripped away your reasoning in children's playgrounds, that sent you screaming at strangers on Brighton pier. Good one, Char. There's a reason why you don't spend much time interacting with the public, remember. She should have known by now to grit her teeth and walk away but that small hand in hers had unlocked the madness all over again.

Are you sure I shouldn't give Doctor Giles a call? her mother asked tentatively in her head and Charlotte felt a sob build-ing in the back of her throat, tight and painful. No, she did not want to go back to Doctor Giles and take any more of his pharmaceutical cosh pills which left her feeling so dis-connected from the world. Oh, her mum thought she had all the answers: pills, counselling, meditation, cakes. *Plant a tree in Kate's name,* she had urged. *Put together a memory book.* All things she'd read in her Grief and Bereavement leaflets;

all things which Charlotte rejected angrily, one after another.

You don't understand, she told her mother. Nobody did. How would planting a sodding tree help, when her baby had died?

Back at the apartment block, she raced up the stairs, desperate to get inside her flat where it was calm and safe. Just as she was nearing the landing, though, the door of the flat next to hers opened and out came more neighbours she hadn't yet met. It was a twenty-something couple – him tall and sandy-haired in a trendy T-shirt and jeans with gel in his hair, one of those 'good-looking and I know it' type of men who had always looked straight through Charlotte. The woman had blonde hair up in a jaunty ponytail, and a wide smiling mouth, and wore a cherry-red skater skirt, grey Converse and a silky navy bomber jacket. Charlotte had heard them through the wall a few times – laughter and music and the shower running at six-thirty every morning – but it was the first time she'd actually seen them in real life. Of all the moments, too, when she was flustered and on edge. She scrubbed her face furtively, trying to wipe away her tears, and forced a smile as the woman caught her eye.

'Hello! Do you live here? I'm Georgie and this is Simon, we're in flat number three,' the woman said as they met on the stairs. 'We've been here nearly two weeks and I haven't met anyone yet. I was starting to think I was living amongst a bunch of hermits, ha ha.'

'I'm Charlotte. Flat number four,' she said weakly, feeling frumpy and middle-aged; a loser in life compared to this bright shining young couple.

'Oh, so we're next door to each other! Excellent. I've been meaning to pop round. Great to meet you, we're just on our way out but we should definitely catch up some time. Have a drink.' She mimed pouring one down her throat and her boyfriend rolled his eyes affectionately for the benefit of Charlotte.

'Lovely,' squeaked Charlotte. 'I'd better get on, but it's good to meet you.'

'You too! Fab. And I love your shoes. They're so cool,' Georgie called after her, leaving Charlotte to stare down at the clumpy brogues she'd had for about ten years as she tramped up the last few steps to the landing.

She unlocked her door and slid to the floor in the small hallway, trying to catch her breath. *You're all right. You're all right*, she said to herself. And actually, as her heart slowed and her breathing returned to normal again, she realized that the brief one-minute exchange with her neighbour had somehow taken the sting out of the pier encounter, made her feel more normal again. Forget the man and his little girls, forget her mortifying burst of misplaced emotions. She was home now and she was safe.

★

Once, when she was twenty-one and far bolder than she was these days, Charlotte had taken part in a charity tandem sky-dive at university. She couldn't even remember what they were raising money for now, but she did remember being up in that tiny plane, with the world spread out, yellow and green in miniature below; sitting on the floor, knees up, har-nessed to the instructor behind her; the deafening rush of air when the door was opened, and that heart-stopping sensa-tion of plunging down through the blue, moments later. Freefalling, the breath snatched from her lungs, the ground rushing up closer with every microsecond, adrenalin going berserk. *Open the parachute*, she had thought frantically. *Why isn't he opening the parachute?* . . . right up until she had felt a sudden sharp swing upwards, and seen the parachute filling with air above them.

Ever since Kate had died, Charlotte's thoughts had returned frequently to the dizzying terror of that twenty-second freefall, and an anxiety would seize hold of her so that her lungs felt too shallow to breathe. Life seemed to have become one permanent freefall these days: the lack of control, the powerlessness, the awful uncertainty about when it would end. *Open the parachute*, she screamed in her dreams as the ground hurtled up towards her again and again. *Why aren't you opening the parachute?*

'These feelings will pass,' the counsellor she'd seen had said when Charlotte told her of this recurring thought pattern. 'Try to acknowledge that you are feeling grief and travelling through a period of mourning. Remind yourself that you do have control over many other aspects of your life. It's up to you how you choose to react.'

The words had been a small parachute of their own, guiding Charlotte down in times of need. She thought of them again at precisely one minute to four that afternoon, as she heaved a deep nervous breath and gave herself a last look in the mirror. *I have choices*, she remembered. *I have control.*

Having seesawed this way and that about whether to accept Margot's invitation, the decision had eventually been made when Charlotte noticed the date – 23 April – and realized that it would have been her grandmother's birthday, had she still been alive. Her kind, twinkly-eyed nana, who would also have invited an unhappy young woman into her house for afternoon tea in the same circumstances – and who would have been hurt and disappointed if that young woman hadn't turned up without so much as a word of explanation. 'I'm doing this for you, Nan,' she muttered under her breath as she straightened her denim shirt-dress, added a pale pink ballerina cardigan that knotted at the front and picked up the bunch of white tulips she'd bought earlier.

Afternoon tea and a chat. Charlotte was a polite sort of person and had always loved spending time with her grandparents; she could do this. It might even be enjoyable. With these brave thoughts in mind, she walked the twelve carpeted steps up to Margot Favager's flat, a pleasant smile fixed firmly in place. She was just about to knock, though, when she became aware of an impassioned voice from within: Margot herself, having some kind of argument all in French. Charlotte might have done a GCSE in the subject back in the day but the rapid-fire dialogue she could hear now was all but impossible to comprehend. The only word she recognized – repeated several times in varying degrees of volume – was '*Non*'.

Her hand dropped down by her side and she shifted from foot to foot, feeling as if she was eavesdropping, which was clearly ridiculous when she could barely understand a word being said. '*Non!*' Margot cried again with new vehemence, and then there came a small crashing sound. Charlotte couldn't help imagining a phone being flung at a wall and took an involuntary step backwards. Maybe she should just go, come back in ten minutes. She moistened her lips, trying to decide what was best to do. She didn't even know this Margot woman after all. What might she be getting herself into here? Her grandmother had been soft of voice and soft of lap, prone to giving ticklish kisses all over one's face. Her mother, too, was a woman who showed kindness with a hug, a cup of tea when you hadn't asked for one, clean bed linen and comfort food when you were having a nervous breakdown, and then a new lipstick once you started coming through the other side.

Meanwhile, an uneasy sort of silence had fallen inside Flat 5. Her fingers now a little clammy around the tulips, Charlotte lifted her other hand and knocked. 'It's Charlotte,' she called, just in case her elderly neighbour was at all anxious about that sort of thing.

Margot answered the door looking ruffled, her eyes red-rimmed and somewhat wild. She was wearing a grey jersey dress with a gold locket at her throat, plus a number of gold rings on her fingers, and Charlotte felt instantly dowdy in her denim dress, which somehow seemed more creased than it had done in front of her mirror. 'Charlotte!' Margot cried, smiling, but then pulled a rueful face almost immediately. 'I think you hear the argument, no?' she said, seemingly reading Charlotte's fearful expression. 'It was my son Michel. He think he know everything but . . .' She rolled her eyes melodramatically. 'Pah. He does not.'

'Are you all right?' Charlotte asked tentatively.

Margot gave a very French sort of shrug then held the door wide so that Charlotte could enter the flat. 'Come,' she ordered. 'Well, you see, that is the story. Am I all right? *Non.* I am dying.'

Charlotte gulped. 'Oh my gosh. I'm so sorry. I—'

Margot waved a hand. They were in her narrow hallway but whereas Charlotte's hallway was as bland and anodyne as a budget hotel, Margot's was covered in ornate wallpaper, striped fuchsia and gold. There was a huge gilt-edged mirror just behind them and a grand old iron sconce with a fat white candle wedged into its cup. 'We all die,' she said. 'And I am an old woman, *hein*? But Michel, he wants me to come back to France, he say I should die at home.' She gave a haughty sort of sniff. 'I say I will die where I please. And this *is* my home. So there. But come, let me make some tea. I have macarons and pastries, we will have a nice time. And I will stop talking about dying, okay? Come, this way.'

Feeling rather dumbstruck, Charlotte followed her hostess into a grand living space, the walls papered a rich midnight blue, the ceilings high with white mouldings patterned in leaves and flowers and fruit, and a glittering chandelier at the centre. 'Oh wow, this is lovely,' she breathed, gazing around at the oil paintings clustered on the walls, the thick soft grey carpet, the original cast-iron fireplace and the generous windows, through which the spring sunshine fell.

'You like? I am glad,' Margot said graciously, waving her into one of the chocolate-brown armchairs just as a ringing started up. The sound appeared to be coming from the direction of the skirting board and Margot's eyes narrowed. 'We will ignore that,' she decreed, before bending rather stiffly to retrieve the phone from the ground and jabbing an imperious finger at the keypad. 'There. He is gone,' she said with a flourish. 'And now I will make tea. Sit. Sit!'

Charlotte sat, and then promptly got up again, proffering the tulips which she had quite forgotten about with all the drama. 'These are for you,' she said, hoping they weren't too vanilla for her neighbour's taste. Now that she was here amidst such opulent surroundings, she wished she had plumped for something more exotic: hothouse orchids or some spiky-leaved birds of paradise flowers.

'How kind! White flowers are so elegant. Thank you,' Margot said with gratifyingly authentic-sounding pleasure. 'One moment, please.'

She bustled out of the room and Charlotte was left to gather her thoughts. So far the conversation had not exactly proceeded how she had expected it to. This wasn't, for instance, the cosy sort of chit-chat she had formerly enjoyed with her grandmother. 'Can I help?' she called, remembering her manners. 'Can I do anything, Margot?'

But Margot had already re-emerged with a plate of dainty little pastries and colourful macarons. 'Thank you, no,' she said, setting them on a small walnut coffee table between the two armchairs. 'Please – be my guest. Take one,' she said, putting down two small side plates. 'They are from Julien Plumart on Queens Road, do you know the place? The best patisserie in this city.'

'Thank you,' said Charlotte, feeling all thumbs as she plucked a tiny lemon macaron and nibbled the edge. They were very good, it was true. She would definitely put those trainers on and go for a proper walk later, she vowed. Although perhaps not in the direction of the pier, for obvious reasons. 'Mmm. Delicious.' She licked a crumb off her finger. 'So when did you come to Brighton, then?' she asked as Margot poured tea from a tarnished silver pot.

'Twenty years ago,' Margot said. 'My husband, he died, I took a lover and we came here.' She raised an eyebrow in a naughty, conspiratorial sort of way. 'An *English* lover. Better than I expect, I must tell you. Better than my husband if I am honest with you . . .'

Charlotte spluttered on her macaron, hoping her eyes weren't boggling. 'Um . . .'

'My sons, they did not approve,' Margot went on. 'We had big argument. Many argument. We did not speak for a long time – I am stubborn, you see. They are stubborn too. But then my lover, Andrew, he died, since three years. And the boys, they forgive me at last. We are a family again. Although . . .' She gestured at the phone. 'Now they ring me. Maman, you must come home. Maman, you cannot stay there alone. Maman, you must see the doctor.' Setting the teapot back on the table, she passed Charlotte's cup and saucer to her. 'But I say no. I do not like the doctor. I do not want to travel. I will die here in my chair, with a glass of good cognac and a smile on my face. And that is that.'

All this talk of dying and arguing and passion, Charlotte didn't quite know how to respond. She poured milk from a small silver jug into her tea and stirred. 'Sounds good,' she said, then could have bitten off her tongue. Margot dying in that chair sounded *good*? So much for manners.

Thankfully Margot seemed unperturbed. 'Yes,' she agreed. 'But that is dull anyway, it is not what you want to speak of, I am sure. You are here for a nice time and I am being a miserable old woman. Enough! Let us celebrate a new friendship.' She raised her teacup. 'As we say in France – *santé*. Your health. And to us!'

Charlotte raised her teacup. '*Santé*,' she echoed faintly.

Chapter Nine

SeaView House Noticeboard:

POLITE NOTICE
To All Residents

May I please remind you that communal lights
should be turned OFF when not in use.
Think of the planet!
Think of my electricity bill!!

Angela Morrison-Hulme
Property Manager

The house on Essex Street had all its curtains closed and
responded to Rosa's knocking with utter indifference. 'This
is definitely the right number, isn't it?' she asked, after they
had been standing there for a few long seconds, met only

with silence from the front door. A stiff breeze was funnelling up the street from the sea, and a Coke can bounced tinnily along the gutter. Somewhere in the distance a dog was barking with increasing volume.

Bea nodded grimly. 'Definitely the right number.' She pressed her face against the bubbled glass pane of the front door, then curled a hand into a fist and thumped it against the white-painted frame three times. A lithe black cat perched on the windowsill of the house next door watched them intently through golden slit eyes, as if it was a diligent Neighbourhood Watch Scheme member, on the lookout for possible intruders.

Rosa looked at her watch and bit her lip. She was meant to be starting her shift in twenty-five minutes and Brendan felt very strongly about punctuality. He had hurled a stainless-steel ladle at Natalya's head the other morning when she came in ten minutes late, mumbling apologetically that her bus had broken down. 'Do you think I give a shite about *buses*?' their boss had roared, the ladle clattering to the floor (luckily Natalya had the reflexes of a ninja). 'I couldn't give a flying fuck if your *spaceship* broke down, is that clear? I just want my staff here on time, and doing their job, do you hear what I'm saying?'

Yes, it had been resoundingly clear. Yes, they had all heard what he was saying. Even people down on the beach listening to music with noise-cancelling headphones on had probably heard what he was saying. And no, Rosa didn't want to find out if her ducking reflexes were as swift as her colleague's, if it was all the same to Bea's elusive father.

She shifted from foot to foot, wondering whether it was too soon to knock again. 'Maybe we should give him a ring?' she suggested, just as they heard a faint thud of footsteps from within. At last. 'This must be him,' she said, seeing a shadowy figure approach, distorted by the patterned glass.

It took the unshaven, bleary-eyed man a moment or two to register who they were and why they were knocking at his door at nine in the morning. As he shrugged on a knackered-looking navy fleece dressing gown, Rosa caught a flash of black boxers and pale muscular thighs and looked away, disconcerted, before turning her eyes up to his face. Handsome, of course, even when dishevelled and recently awoken, with rumpled dark hair, just starting to speckle with grey at the sides, and golden brown eyes, like caramel. The handsome ones were the worst, as she knew. Not to be trusted.

In the next second, the man blinked, focused and smiled, taking a step towards his daughter. 'Bea-Bea! Good to see you, kiddo. A sight for fatherly eyes, if ever there was one. How are you doing?'

'It's Gareth, isn't it? Hi, I'm Rosa,' she said, fairly pointlessly, as Gareth held out his arms to his daughter and Bea, with visible reluctance, shuffled forward into them.

'Ugh, God, Dad, you stink,' the girl said, wrinkling her nose.

Another voice, female, sleepy, wafted through from the depths of the house. 'Who is it, Gar?'

'Just a minute,' he yelled back, tugging his dressing gown more firmly around himself. Then he clapped Bea on the back. 'So how's school? And just look at you! You get taller every time I see you.'

Bea rolled her eyes. 'Yeah. It's this phenomenon called "growing", Dad? It happens to most teenagers, believe it or not.'

He put his hands up in mock-protest. 'Whoa, whoa! Give a bloke a chance, love. You're not in the door yet and you're having a pop at me. Pace yourself, why don't you?' He laughed, giving Rosa a conspiratorial *Kids!* sort of look.

Bea was not laughing along. 'I knew this was a bad idea,' she growled, folding her arms across her chest.

Rosa glanced from one to the other, aware of Brendan's beady eye on the clock, and all the utensils he might be lining up to use as missiles if she hung about much longer. Time to take her leave and get back to real life. 'Um . . . So I'll be off, then,' she said. 'I've got to go to work now, but I'll be around tomorrow afternoon, from about four if . . .'

'And I can come over then? For our roast dinner?' Bea interrupted.

'Sure. You can come over then. Bye, Gareth.'

★

143

'Be receptive to joy,' a fortune teller had once said to Rosa. This was a cheap-as-chips fortune teller down in Margate many years ago, mind, when she and a group of mates had gone there for a girls' weekend, back in their early twenties. 'What a load of bollocks,' Rosa had grumbled as her friends dragged her towards the small office – above a hairdressers! That was mystic for you – where Madame Zara, or whatever she called herself, did her readings.

Typically, everyone else in the group – Catherine, Alexa, Meg – all received wonderful predictions for their patronage. Exciting travel opportunities, fabulous partners ('I don't quite know how to put this, darling, but my spirits are telling me that this particular guy in your future . . . well, he's built like a tin of *Pledge*, if you get my drift'), stellar careers . . . all were foreseen in Zara's tarot cards, apparently, and delivered theatrically with much wiggling of the old charlatan's dark eyebrows and even more gesturing with her scarlet-nailed hands.

Then it was Rosa's turn and Zara's dark-lipsticked mouth had pursed for rather too long as she dealt out the cards. 'Hmm,' she said, ominously, at which point Alexa started giggling and Rosa shot her a look and mouthed 'Cobblers' at her.

There were no exciting travel opportunities, or well-hung men for Rosa, according to old Zara. Oh, no. Instead, she kept going on about Rosa earning a lot of money (rubbing

her thumb and forefinger together in an unpleasantly lascivi-
ous way), as well as various guesses at dead relatives. 'Someone beginning with J, I think? Or maybe . . . K?'

'Nope,' Rosa said flatly, quite glad to prove to the others
just what a faker this headscarf-draped Zara really was.

'My advice to you – be receptive to joy,' the fortune teller
ended the reading. 'It will not always be so easy to see. Open
yourself up to it, I beg you.'

Right. Brilliant. Was that it?

'Well, that was a load of old shite,' Rosa had said loudly,
the moment they were walking out of the door.

'Not for me,' Meg had grinned. 'I'm meeting a man with
an enormous penis, apparently. I'm definitely going to be
receptive to *that*.'

For some reason – and quite annoyingly, as it turned out
– Zara's parting phrase had stuck with them all. Whenever
Rosa was bitching about a neighbour, a colleague, the unreli-
ability of the 43 bus, her friends would cock their heads
and say demurely, 'But are you being receptive to joy, Rosa?
Maybe if you could just open yourself up to it . . .' before
dodging away as she tried to swipe them with the nearest
object. (At least none of them had dared trot it out when
they heard the news about Max. Small mercies.)

The words returned to her again, as she walked back from
work along the seafront on Sunday afternoon. She had been
more than ready to hang up her apron and trudge home,

footsore and weary after two gruelling weekend shifts, including slogging through the rowdiest, messiest wedding the hotel had ever witnessed, according to Brendan. ('And as an Irishman in me prime, I've seen a few, I can tell youse.') Knackered as Rosa was, though, even she was able to appreciate the sun's warm golden rays on her face, the soaring arc of a seagull in flight high overhead, the delicious smell of frying onions wafting from a nearby hot-dog van.

I am receptive to joy, she told herself, feeling surprised by how apt the previously mocked phrase was right now. Because, actually, being aware of beautiful things around you, however tiny, made a person feel better. Happier. Not exactly punching the air and jumping up and down, but sending enough sparkles of gladness through her to recognize that she felt good during that single moment.

Hark at her, getting all mindful! She imagined Madame Zara giving a satisfied nod to herself over in Margate, telepathically receiving the psychic update that Rosa had finally taken her advice on board ('About time too!') and her lips twitched in a smile. Oh, whatever, Madame Z. You got me. Rosa was definitely, one hundred per cent receptive to the joy of getting home and having nothing to do, perhaps even taking a mug of good strong coffee and a book out to the lawn in the middle of the square in order to lazily soak up some sunshine and vitamin D. Yep, bring on all of the joy because she was totally ready for it now.

Plans made, she'd only just walked into the hallway of SeaView House, though, blinking as her eyes adjusted to its cool quiet dimness, when she heard Jo's front door creak open and then Bea emerged, looking kind of sullen and mutinous. Ahh.

'Hello,' Rosa said. So much for peace and solitude, then. So much for the joy. There was something about Bea's furious expression that made Rosa feel instantly receptive to a large vodka tonic instead. 'I wasn't expecting you back for a while. Is everything all right?'

Bea snorted. 'Dad is such a colossal twat,' she said melodramatically. 'I mean, I'm embarrassed we're even *related*. He's just so annoying and . . . *old* and . . . aargh!' This, with additional head-clutching and grimacing, as if words were quite beyond her.

So father and daughter time had gone fabulously, then. 'Er, less of the "old", thank you very much, he can't be all that much older than me,' Rosa said, rolling her eyes. 'Come in. Is there any news about your mum? Will she be home tomorrow, do you think?'

'That's where I've been,' Bea replied, scuffing a foot along the skirting board as she followed Rosa inside. 'She's not great really.' She bent her head and picked at the black varnish on her fingernails, tiny flakes scattering on the pale carpet. 'She's picked up some infection – I can't remember the name – but they said she's not responding very well to

147

the antibiotics, so . . .' She shrugged forlornly. 'I dunno. I dunno when she's going to be home.'

'Poor thing,' Rosa said, wondering what that would mean for Bea-duty as she kicked off her shoes and wiggled her tired feet. Her legs were killing her from standing up all day and then walking home again. The first week she'd worked there her ankles had puffed up like water balloons. 'Have you eaten anything? And does your dad know you're back here, by the way?'

Bea made a scoffing noise at the mention of Gareth. 'Does this face look like I care?' she asked.

'Frankly, no, but . . .' Rosa made a jug of elderflower cordial with a whole tray of ice cubes, and felt very much like sloshing in a load of gin with it. She wasn't sure if she had the energy to cope with Bea in this mood. 'But that's not the point, is it? He'll want to know you're all right.'

'Ha. Yeah. If you say so.'

Rosa sighed, feeling as if she wasn't getting anywhere. 'Look, there's no need to be arsey with me about it, okay?' she asked, feeling her patience shredding. 'What's so bad about him anyway?'

Bea's chin went all pointy and for a moment Rosa thought she might storm out of her place as well. But then she looked down and mumbled that she was sorry. 'I'm not being arsey with you, it's just . . .' She slurped at her drink before remembering to say thank you for it. 'He just doesn't want me around. I tried to talk to him but he's not interested in me. All he wants is to hang out in the pub with his stupid mates or *Candy*, who's just like *the* most annoying bimbo *ever*.' The girlfriend, presumably, Rosa thought, remembering the breathy female voice that had floated out behind Gareth when they were at his door. *Who is it, Gar?* 'I mean, you saw him yesterday,' Bea went on darkly. 'I think he'd even forgotten I was meant to be *coming*, you know. *That's* how bothered he is. Well, I'm not bothered either.' She folded her arms across her chest. 'I knew going there was a crap idea in the first place. I did *say*.'

Washing a punnet of strawberries at the sink, Rosa listened while Bea poured out her grievances. Reading between the lines, it sounded as if a vicious circle had sprung up, of Bea feeling hurt and saying she didn't want to see Gareth, and her dad taking this at face value and saying okay – which only led to Bea feeling even more rejected.

'Well, you're here now,' Rosa said in the end, not wanting to take sides and start criticizing Gareth, even though Bea seemed convinced he was pretty much the worst human being ever to walk the planet. She could remember falling out with her own parents as a teenager, how every hurt had seemed magnified, and softened towards the girl. 'And I'll let your dad know that you can stay here tonight, although we'll have to sort something out for tomorrow, I guess. Maybe you could go to a friend's instead, if it's all right with your mum?'

Bea curled her lip. 'Right. Cos I'm so popular,' she muttered under her breath.

Rosa eyed her, wondering what that was all about. 'You can talk to *me* about stuff if you want,' she added, leaving a pause although nothing was forthcoming. Maybe not then. She tipped the strawberries into a bowl and wiped her wet hands. 'I guess it's up to both you and your dad to keep trying with the relationship, if that's what you want.'

'Not really.' Bea snaked a hand over to the bowl and stole a strawberry, biting into it. 'I'd rather send him an anonymous shit sandwich.' A smirk twisted her mouth as she chewed. 'Did you know there's this revenge service on the internet where you can actually pay them money and they'll send someone a *real* shit sandwich, like two slices of bread with a genuine human turd in the middle. I'm not kidding!'

'Is that right,' Rosa said, selecting a plump scarlet strawberry for herself. 'The wonders of the twenty-first century, eh?'

'So if there's ever anyone you want to do the dirty on . . .' Bea said. '*Literally!*'

'I'll bear that in mind,' Rosa replied. She could think of one person anyway. 'So,' she went on, deciding to change the subject. 'Didn't we say something about having a roast dinner tonight? I'd better make a shopping list.'

Chapter Ten

Curled up in bed on Saturday night, Georgie glanced tenderly – actually rather drunkenly – at her handsome yet stressed boyfriend, who was lying on his back staring up at the ceiling. A patch of moonlight was falling through a gap in the curtains onto his forehead, lighting it up like a landing signal. It made him look kind of ridiculous, which in turn left Georgie feeling disloyally giggly. Simon was not normally someone who allowed himself to look ridiculous.

Rolling over towards him in a sudden rush of affection, she knocked gently on his forehead. 'Knock knock,' she said.

He turned slightly, the patch of moonlight falling briefly across his eye like a pirate patch. 'Who's there?'

She pressed herself against him. 'Forehead,' she said, or rather all the wine she'd drunk earlier did.

'Forehead who?'

Ahh. This was the problem with accidentally starting a joke to which you had no punchline. She thought quickly. 'Fore-heddan's sake, Si, you'd better not snore tonight.' She grinned at her own lightning wit. 'Forehead-an's. For heaven's. Get it?'

He rolled over and slung a heavy thigh over hers. 'That was terrible, Georgie. Really bad,' he said, but she could hear he was smiling. 'If you have to explain a joke, it generally means it doesn't work.'

Affronted, she elbowed him in the ribs. 'You do one, then,' she told him.

'Knock knock,' he said after a moment, knocking on her forearm.

'Who's there?'

'Arm.'

'Arm who?'

'Ah, my lovely girl, go to sleep. Get it? ARM my lovely—'

'Si, if you have to explain a joke, it generally means—'

'Oh, shush. Good night, Georgie.'

'Good night, Simon.'

They were getting there, thought Georgie optimistically, as they lay together in the darkness and she heard his breathing lengthen and slow. Navigating their way in this new place, recalibrating their relationship in its changed setting. They'd had a good laugh together that day, mucking about on the funfair at the end of the pier, screaming on the roller coaster (her), winning a stuffed gorilla on the hook-a-duck (him) and people-watching in general. Then they'd sauntered back to the flat via a pub for a cheeky half, and had enjoyed really good sex on the living-room floor with the windows open. Yeah! That was one advantage of living high above street level at least. If they'd tried that back in Stonefield, they'd have had Mrs Huggins from next door knocking anxiously after two minutes, calling through the letterbox to see if they were okay, only she thought she'd heard a bird trapped in the chimney or something.

We'll be okay, she thought, remembering how they'd lain there afterwards, breathless and feeling naughty, buck naked on the living-room floor. Five and a half months to go and they'd be back home in Stonefield anyway. They could get through it.

On Monday, Georgie put off attempting any actual writing work for a while as she uploaded photos to Facebook: her and Simon with their faces in one of those funny cut-out boards on the pier (him as busty Baywatch-style lifesaver, her as a half-drowned swimmer wearing a rubber ring). 'HILARIOUS!!!' she typed underneath, trying to recapture the laughter of the moment.

Just as she'd posted the update, her phone chirped notifying her that she'd had an email and she flipped to her inbox to see that – at last – she'd had a reply from Viv, the magazine editor. Not only that but the subject line read *New edition now live!*

Oh my goodness. Today was the day! The magazine was

out – and presumably so was her very first *Hey Em* column. Who said Mondays were rubbish? Imagine her friends' faces when she posted the link on her Facebook page. Or maybe she should go into town once she'd read the online version, grab a bunch of printed copies and post them off to her parents and her mates as a surprise. They would be so impressed!

Without bothering to read what Viv had actually written in her email, Georgie clicked through to the link, fingers turning to thumbs in her haste, hardly able to believe that she was about to see her name there on her very own inaugural problem page. How cool was that? The first of many too, she hoped. Give it a few months from now and she'd probably be really blasé about being in print, but today it felt thrillingly momentous.

The magazine opened in a new window and she scrolled through hurriedly to find her contribution – title page, contents, some feature about this local actor blah blah, whatever, she could read all of that later. Then she reached a spread headed *Hey Em* in big writing, and her heart beat faster with pride. Here it was!

Viv had written a little intro at the top of the page. *Problems? You're in the right place. Meet Em, our new agony adviser. She's cool, she's witty – and she tells it like it is!*

Amen to that, sister, Georgie thought joyfully. Cool and witty, that was her. Even better, it was right there in black and white, somebody had actually said that she was cool and witty. She couldn't *wait* for her friends to see this. Amazing! Although . . . ah. No mention of her name, unfortunately. No big letters announcing that Georgie Taylor was the talent behind cool, witty Em. Which was a tiny bit gutting, if she was honest.

Hey Em, she read, feeling her sense of satisfaction return as she scrolled down the page. There it was, the real-life problem from the waitress in her café that she'd written up and then replied to. She held her breath as she went through the paragraphs, but Viv had hardly changed a thing. Pride swelled within her. Well, would you look at that? There were *her* words in print, sentences she had written, for the city to see. She, Georgie Taylor, had brought Em to life!

But then she noticed there was further text following Em's reply and scrolled down the screen to read on.

> *Em's had her say – now it's over to you. Here's*
> *another problem which we want you, our readers, to*
> *advise on. Tell us what you think!*

Georgie frowned. Another problem? That was odd. She'd only sent in one. Had Viv written a second letter to fill up space on the page or something?

> *Hey Em*, she read,
> *Do you know what, my boyfriend is being a real*
> *arse. He's got this hot-shot new job and now—*

Whoa there. Her blood seemed to freeze in her veins. She almost stopped breathing. Wait just a cotton-picking minute. What?

> *– and now thinks he's like this super-amazing professional. We've moved down all the way from Yorkshire so that he can indulge his wet dream, I mean, take up this wowzers job—*

Oh my God. Oh Christ, no. She thought she might throw up. How had this . . . ? *No.* She hadn't sent the wrong document to Viv, had she? The wrong document with her rant about Simon in it? She stared at the screen, horror drumming through her.

> *– and I feel a bit insignificant to him all of a sudden. I'm trying my best – I've gone out and found my own new job – but it's like everything's changed in our relationship.*

Shit. She had as well. She must have done. Her hand rose silently to cover her mouth as she was filled by the sudden urge to scream. She had actually been that stupid, that unprofessional, that bloody dim. Fuck! What a total total bellend. How incompetent could you get?

He acts like he's the important one, while I'm just tagging along for the ride, she read on miserably, her own words tormenting her. *Maybe I am just tagging along for the ride?*

Viv had added '*Help, Em, what should I do?*' and signed the letter 'Yorkshire Lass'. Georgie's heart sank even further and she stared aghast at the screen. Well, there was no way she could show her column to Simon now. Absolutely no way. She couldn't show it to her mates either, never in a million years. She'd be the laughing stock of Stonefield! She'd never live it down! *But you said you were having an amazing time!* her friends would frown, confused. *All those sunset photos you kept posting! That funny lifeguard one – HILARIOUS!!! you wrote just this morning!*

The thought of their reactions – their pity! – was so horrendous that she put her hands over her face and shuddered. Well, she told herself, trying to rally her spirits, they would never know about it, end of story. Her terrible secret was going to stay right here on the south coast and that was that.

Wait – there was more, though. Underneath the letter . . . oh, *no*. Kill me now, she thought dismally. Underneath the letter was the online poll she'd written, supposedly for Freckles, the subject of her proper problem.

> *So, it's over to you guys. What do you think Yorkshire Lass should do in this situation? Take part in our online poll and have your say!*
>   *Yorkshire Lass should:*

DUMP HIM? He's no good! Steer clear!

LUMP HIM? Put up with him in the hope it'll get better.

HUMP HIM? Sod it, he sounds hot, shag him anyway!

Click to vote . . . and see what others think.

Georgie's eyes felt as if they were on stalks. Worse and worse. Just worse and effing worse! She was going to wake up in a minute. Please, let her wake up in a minute!

She pinched herself in case she was in the midst of some godawful nightmare but unfortunately she was already awake and it was all really happening. So not only had the magazine printed her whinge about Simon – her private whinge that no other human was meant to see! – but now everyone in Brighton had been invited to speculate on her relationship, to vote on its outcome!

Oh, help. This was so bad. This was beyond silver linings and bright sides. In fact the only tiny remote glimmer of not-badness that she could think of was the fact that her name *wasn't* anywhere on the page.

Click to vote . . . and see what others think the text urged her. 'Sod off,' she growled. It was like finding herself in an episode of a tacky reality TV show. *What happens next for Georgie and Simon? YOU decide!*

But then again, what *did* others think? she couldn't help

wondering. What did the wider Brighton population reckon she ought to do in this situation?

Hating herself for it, she loyally clicked the 'Lump Him' option. (Viv must have added that one, she thought.) She wasn't 'lumping' Simon, anyway, she reasoned defensively. She loved him! He was her one true love! Her one true love who was a bit work-obsessed and irritable, sure, but didn't everyone get like that sometimes?

A new window had popped up on screen.

THANK YOU! Voting so far:
DUMP HIM: 76%
LUMP HIM: 4%
HUMP HIM: 20%

Georgie's mouth fell open in outrage. Only four per cent of voters thought she should stick with him? That was ridiculous. How shallow were these people? She wondered in the next moment how many readers had actually voted and whether that four per cent actually represented her one single click.

She closed down the page, feeling trembly. What an absolute disaster. How could Viv *do* that to her? She must have known that Georgie had sent the wrong version, she could have guessed that Georgie was the subject of the Simon letter, too. Was she deliberately trying to make her look an idiot?

Belatedly, her mind still fogged up with the awfulness of it all, Georgie remembered that Viv had written an accompanying email when sending through the link of doom. Oh joy. This was sure to be even more embarrassing.

Hi Georgie, the email read,

Thanks for the letters – great stuff! We thought your voice as Em was spot on, although I decided that the poll was better suited to the unanswered question – was that what you intended? It wasn't quite clear in your email. Fab idea to ask for reader feedback though, love it.

Re your other ideas, I like the suggestion for a 'You Send Me' feature where readers suggest activities for you to try out around the city. You're on! I'll kick-start things by sending you to the Roller Disco in Saltdean – there are two free passes available for either Tuesday or Wednesday evening so you can take along a friend (mention the magazine when you arrive). If you could write this up and get it to me by Friday, we can put a note up on our Facebook page asking for suggestions for next time.

Cool! And obviously another 'Hey Em' problem or two for Friday as well. Let's try one of each again,

answered and unanswered so that readers can join in;
the juicier the better! Finally, do let me have your bank
details so that I can pay you.
   Cheers
   Viv

Georgie slumped back against the pillows, trying to take all of this in. Well, there was her silver lining, at least: payment, although it felt more like blood money now that she'd unwittingly aired her and Simon's dirty laundry in public. And Viv liked her idea about Georgie trying out all sorts of unusual things around the city, so that was good too, although she was fairly certain already that Simon would refuse point-blank to go with her if she asked him to go to a roller disco. ('You're kidding me, right?' he said scathingly in her head.)

Still, it was progress of a kind. A commission. With that and the new problem letters to write, she might even be able to pay off that expensive dinner for two she'd put on her credit card last week. *Hey Em*, she thought to herself, rolling her eyes, *I'm trying my best down here in the south but it's not that easy . . .*

Chapter Eleven

MEMO
To: All staff
From: Anthony Gillespie
RE: Sunset Years Befriending Project

Please ensure all forms have been completed and returned to ME by the end of the week. Remember to include full details of your 'befriendee' for our records. If you don't have a suitable candidate, please make that clear on your form and we will assign you one accordingly.

Come on, people! It's for the community! It's going to be a beautiful thing!

A beautiful thing, indeed, give me strength, thought Charlotte, pulling a face as she read the email. She hadn't filled in her form yet, though, having been too shy to broach the subject with Margot over tea on Saturday afternoon. She still wasn't convinced her older neighbour needed befriending anyway, when her social life seemed way more active than Charlotte's. Plus Margot was definitely not helpless and feeble. Once she'd finished talking about dying, she'd proceeded to grill Charlotte with all sorts of questions about her job and her upbringing, with unnervingly keen interest. 'And there is no husband? No handsome lover keeping you warm in the night, *non*?' Margot had asked, with a twitch of her perfectly plucked eyebrows.

'Um . . . *non*, I mean no,' Charlotte had mumbled. 'Not any more, anyway.' That was the moment she had drained her teacup hastily, swallowed back the last crumbs of her lilac macaron and got up to leave before Margot could lean forward and delve any deeper. 'Well, it's been lovely,' she'd said, feeling her cheeks turn pink. Margot must think her terribly drab, she fretted, when the older woman's favoured conversational topics consisted of love, death and passion. Meanwhile Charlotte was as dry as an old stick with nothing to say for herself, other than boring on about the intricacies of life in a conveyancing department, if only to avoid the subject turning back to more personal matters.

Her hostess had excellent manners, though, kissing her on both cheeks as she left and then doing that odd, rather embarrassing thing of foraging in her purse for a pound coin again, which she presented to Charlotte, in the manner of a generous benefactress. 'There's really no need,' Charlotte said weakly.

'Please, I insist,' Margot said. 'It has been delightful to speak with you. Now, what was it you tell me last time? That you would spend the money wisely?'

Charlotte blushed again. 'It's what my grandmother always used to say when she gave me money at Christmas,' she explained.

Margot's eyes had twinkled. 'I see. Very sensible,' she said. 'Well, I am glad to make a wise new friend. You are welcome here any time.'

Welcome any time, Charlotte thought now, spinning a paperclip around between her finger and thumb as she read the email again. Margot *had* said it. And maybe her neighbour was merely being polite but if Charlotte had to befriend an elderly person for the company community project, then didn't they say that charity began at home? Where better than her own apartment block?

With this in mind, Charlotte made a detour to Julien Plumart, the patisserie favoured by Margot, after work that day. Having deliberated for some time over the pastel-streaked meringues in the window, she decided to buy a selection of dainty lemon and raspberry tartlets packaged carefully in a white cardboard box, and knocked on Margot's door with them once back in Dukes Square.

Margot answered the door wearing a charcoal woollen

dress with a scarlet scarf knotted around her throat, and reading glasses perched on her nose. 'But what a surprise!' she exclaimed, seeing Charlotte with the patisserie box. 'You must come in. I was just pouring a martini and about to have a cigarette out of the window. Please, do not tell that awful Angela woman. But is there anything nicer than a cigarette with a martini on a Monday evening?'

Charlotte hesitated. 'Um . . . No?' she hazarded.

Margot laughed. 'Is okay. You do not need to pretend. I am a bad old lady, you are a good young girl. Do not let me correct you.'

'Corrupt me? I'll try not to,' Charlotte said. 'Hello, any-way,' she went on shyly. 'These are for you, to say thank you for Saturday. It was lovely to chat.'

'My favourite!' Margot said, accepting the box. 'That is so kind. Are you sure I cannot mix you a martini? Or I have some very fine absinthe . . .'

'Thanks, but no, I . . . I have things to do,' Charlotte said. Yeah, a microwave bolognaise to heat up and a crazy schedule on the housework front. It's all go round my place, you know! 'But . . . Well . . . I was wondering.' *Spit it out*, she ordered her-self. 'The company I work for, they're starting a community project. Befriending the—' She stopped just in time before she said the word 'elderly'. Margot Favager might refer to herself as an old lady but that didn't necessarily mean anyone else was permitted to. '– the community,' she said after a small pause, 'where we sign up to visit people, help with chores, whatever they might need doing . . .'

Margot's nose wrinkled delicately in a frown. 'Chores?'

'Chores – like running errands. Going shopping for you, or helping with the cleaning. Well. That is, if you want to be my . . . person. Befriendee.' Charlotte blushed, hoping she hadn't just insulted the woman. She had made it sound so formal, so *un*friendly, in fact. Besides, Margot's flat had been pristine the other day, she clearly had no trouble keeping the place clean. 'Or we could just drink tea and chat, of course,' she added in a rush.

'Ahh,' said Margot, her face clearing, 'it is a charity thing for lonely people? Helping unhappy old ladies?' She pursed her lips. 'But I am not lonely. Or unhappy.'

'No. Of course you're not.' Of the two of them, Margot was definitely not the lonely one. 'And I didn't mean to suggest for a second that . . .'

'You are taking pity on a dying old woman who drinks too much, that is it? Holding my hand across the street – you think I need this help?' Margot's voice rose with each question and Charlotte's face flamed.

''No! Not at all!' she cried wretchedly, wishing she'd never asked. Why had she even *thought* it was a good idea? She was so clumsy, so blundering! And now Margot, the one person in Brighton who'd been kind to her, who'd welcomed her into her home, was annoyed, her feelings hurt. 'Listen, it doesn't matter, it was just a thought,' she babbled, stricken. 'Really, I'm sorry I even men—'

But Margot was patting her arm and roaring with laughter all of a sudden. 'Ahh, Charlotte, I am teasing you. I am joking you,' she said. *Oh, thank goodness, thank goodness, thank goodness.* 'That would be very nice. I will send you on a chore every week to buy us more pastries and some gin, *hein*? And then we will talk and enjoy yourselves. Yes?'

'Yes.' Charlotte bit her lip, feeling chastened. Well, that had put her in her place. That had told her. 'Thank you, that would be lovely,' she said quietly. 'Does Friday afternoon suit you? You could come to my flat if you'd rather, or—'

'I would love you to be my guest. Friday afternoon. It will be like our club. And we can make the world right.'

'Yes,' Charlotte said again. She didn't bother to correct the idiom. 'We can make the world right.'

Monday night meant window cleaning, hoovering and laundry sorting. A busy way to start the week. After the bolognaise dinner (very good, thank you, Waitrose), she got stuck into the hoovering. The flat was so small, it never took her that long unfortunately. (Occasionally, if she was having a really bad day, she might go over it twice, just to eat into the empty evening.) Often as she pushed the nozzle around, she found herself wishing she had endless rooms, several flights of stairs, a hallway that was longer than two whole metres to get stuck into. It was the same with the laundry – the meagre load of washing never took much time to sort through. She thought of her friends with kids who would moan unthinkingly about all their domestic chores. *The laundry!* they would sigh, comically clapping a hand to their heads as if it was just too much to bear. *The mess!* Like they knew what it was to suffer. Like they had a clue! Charlotte would have willingly scaled mountains of stinking laundry every night for the rest of her life without a single complaint if it meant she could have kept Kate. If she could be hanging clean wet sleepsuits on a radiator right now, shaking out tiny pairs of striped tights and baby vests.

Don't think about it. Keep busy. Keep going.

She had kept just one little sleepsuit, a soft white one with a sweet hedgehog print on the chest. It had been too big for Kate, her legs only reaching halfway down the insides, the sleeves needing to be bunched up and rolled over at the cuffs in order to let the baby's tiny pink starfish hands emerge. *Don't think about her, Charlotte. Don't go there.*

With one last savage sweep of the hallway, she switched off the Hoover and it sighed into silence. Only seven-thirty and there were hours of evening left; she'd have to spin out the window cleaning, she decided. Scrub them with soapy water and then polish with vinegar for extra sparkle. Wasn't scrunched-up newspaper meant to be good for cleaning windows? Maybe she would give that a try, kill some extra time.

Oh, but who cared, though? she thought in a sudden rush of anguish, her hands tightly curled into fists. Who cared? Why was she even bothering about her bloody windows, what was the point?

She ran into her bedroom, unable to hold out any longer, wrenching open her wardrobe doors and pulling out all the clean jumpers and hoodies she kept there, to find buried underneath her precious treasures, the only mementos of Kate. The sleepsuit, the photographs, the white plastic nameband she'd worn around her tiny wrist at the hospital . . . She tried to ration looking at these things as if too much exposure would somehow lessen them of their worth, reduce their specialness. But sometimes, like now, she just wanted to pore over the photographs, to press the soft hedgehog sleepsuit against her face, and . . .

Her hands were lifting off the lid of the box – *I can't bear it, I can't bear it* – when she heard a knock at her front door. 'Charlotte?' came a voice, followed by a second knock.

Charlotte jumped at the interruption. She had barely had a single visitor in the time that she'd been here, other than the postman now and then, or someone ringing the buzzer wanting Jo downstairs. With a last look at the box, she replaced it and gulped in a few calming breaths, before going out to the hall. 'Um . . . yes?' she called. The voice didn't sound like Margot, so it couldn't be her. And yet she didn't know anybody else in Brighton, other than people at work, and they didn't have her address. Well, the HR department did, she supposed, her mind racing ahead frenziedly. Was she in trouble for something? Maybe they had noticed that she never seemed to sign up for staff karaoke evenings or the bowling night that some keen person in Accounts had organized. What if it was the boss, Stella, come to have a little *Buck your ideas up, love* kind of chat in private?

'It's me, Georgie. From next door? Have you got a mo?'

Georgie. From next door. The twenty-something girl with the red skirt and northern accent who'd complimented Charlotte on her shoes. 'Oh,' she said dumbly, then gathered her wits and unlatched the security chain. 'Hi,' she said, answering the door and hoping she didn't look too crazed. *Hey, don't mind me, I was just about to start sobbing over a shoebox. Like you do!*

'Hello again.' Georgie was in jeans today with a pink halter-neck top and dangly gold earrings, her blonde hair up in a messy ponytail. 'Sorry to bother you. It's just . . . Well, the thing is, I've been given these tickets for a roller disco night in Saltdean. I've got to write about it for this local magazine.'

Charlotte blinked. As conversational openers went, this was a new one on her. 'That's . . . nice?' she ventured, unsure what else to say.

'And I was hoping Simon would come with me – my boyfriend.' A fleeting expression of exasperation crossed

Georgie's face. 'But he's not keen. Or rather, he said "Over my dead body will I put on a pair of flaming roller skates."' She spoke in a gruff overly northern accent to make her point.

Charlotte said nothing but had a horrible feeling that she knew where the conversation might be heading.

'So I was wondering,' Georgie went on hopefully, 'if you might like to come along instead. Neighbours' night out? It could be a laugh.'

'Oh,' said Charlotte again. Roller skating? She hadn't strapped on a pair of skates since she was a teenager. She thought of whirling around the old roller rink in Newbury, hand in hand with her best friend Shelley, their hair streaming out behind them. Then she thought of her unfit thirty-eight-year-old self and the unworn new trainers still virgin white, and how lately she'd started making little 'Oof' noises whenever she got up from a chair. 'Well, I'm not sure . . .'

Georgie bit her lip. 'Right, I'm going to be honest with you, cards on the table now, because the thing is, I don't actually *know* anyone else in Brighton,' she confessed. 'We've only just moved in and my mates are all miles away. I just thought . . . I mean, it would be good to get to know each other, wouldn't it? And . . .'

She had such wide blue eyes, Georgie, and there was such hope shining from them. Charlotte had to look away. She did not want to go to a roller disco, she reminded herself. She was an adult woman and it was perfectly acceptable to say no. Anyway, she still had the windows to clean yet, didn't she? 'I'm a bit busy right now,' she said weakly in the end.

'Oh, I don't mean *now*,' Georgie said at once. 'I've got free tickets either tomorrow or Wednesday, whichever suits you best. I can drive us there and back. And if it's shit we can always sneak off and just go to the pub instead. What do you say?'

Charlotte could feel her resistance crumbling. She was rubbish at saying no to people, that was the problem, especially when they were standing right in front of her wheedling and pleading and giving her full puppy-dog eyes. It was probably why charity fundraisers always made a beeline for her in the street because they could tell she was a soft touch.

'I . . .' she said. Again came that memory of how it had felt as a teenager to whizz along on eight spinning wheels, fast and free. And then Margot's voice was echoing in her head: *A new friend, how delightful!* 'I suppose I could do tomorrow,' she found herself saying faintly. Tuesday was always a bit light on the housework front anyway, she often ended up watching natural history documentaries or doing the Sudoku in the newspaper to avoid the tempting siren of the shoebox of Kate photos. Look at the way she'd fallen apart tonight, on the verge of losing it completely before Georgie's knock on the door. Whereas if she was out of the flat altogether . . .

'Tomorrow would be brilliant,' Georgie said, pouncing on her capitulation. 'Oh, thanks, Charlotte, that would be fab, I really appreciate it. Shall I knock for you around seven?'

'Okay,' Charlotte said, wondering what the hell she had just agreed to. A roller disco, with her neighbour who must be ten years younger than her? Had that actually just *happened*? She must have lost the plot, she thought as they said goodbye and she shut the door. Then she leaned against the wall for a few moments, feeling as if her common sense had just been hijacked. Maybe she would have to come down with some terrible food poisoning tomorrow, she thought worriedly. Maybe she would just silently lock her front door and pretend to be dead.

Still, looking on the bright side – her recent moment of utter despair had now slipped noiselessly away, a small pebble sinking down to the depths of the ocean. Returning to her wardrobe, she piled the jumpers and hoodies back in the place above the shoebox and closed the doors, will-power restored once more. There, she thought, her hands lingering for a moment on the wooden panels. All at rest.

Now then. Windows.

And so it was that not twenty-four hours later, Charlotte found herself snapping down the catches on a pair of hired roller boots at the side of a chalk-smelling leisure centre hall, while speakers overhead boomed out 'Boogie Wonderland'

and lights flashed red, green, blue around her. She still wasn't quite able to believe she was actually there. Work had been a bit crap earlier – she was wrangling with an over-zealous solicitor who wanted her clients to take out indemnity insurance about the use of a shared alleyway behind their hundred-year-old house (ridiculous!) and then she'd spent forty minutes on the phone to a particularly needy client who had insisted on Charlotte's help as she filled in her property information form, line by line. Charlotte, increasingly impatient, had found herself absent-mindedly doodling skates on the corner of her notepad. Then – the weirdest thing – she had finished the call and refreshed her emails to see that her long-lost friend Shelley, she of the teenage roller rink days, had sent Charlotte a friend request on a social networking site out of the blue. It was as if Fate was giving her a big old nudge and telling her what to do.

Thanks to Fate – and the pleading face of her neighbour – here she was anyway, freckled with flecks of coloured light from the spinning disco ball suspended from the centre of the ceiling, and several scary miles from her comfort zone. She hoped this wasn't about to be an enormous mistake that she'd live to regret. She hoped that she would actually live long enough to regret anything. She'd seen Casualty enough times to know that a terrible accident could happen anywhere, especially if each of your feet was strapped to a set of spinning wheels.

'Wooo!' bellowed a DJ, punching the air in time to the music, as the skaters twirled and gyrated below, and Charlotte and Georgie finished fastening their boots. 'Let me hear you singing along!'

'Oh my God,' Georgie laughed, dumping her coat and bag on a plastic seat and levering herself up on the skates. 'This is nuts. Some people are taking this way too seriously. Look at that guy in the white jeans and trilby! He's so getting a mention in my write-up.'

Charlotte gingerly stood, clinging to the back of another seat while she found her centre of gravity, then gazed out at the mass of skaters. Ahh, *him*: white jeans, burgundy trilby and a glittering silver waistcoat . . . with his bare muscled chest and shoulders proudly on display. His skin was already glistening with sweat, or maybe he had oiled it especially for the occasion. Other skaters were working an Eighties look in neon headbands, black mesh vests and legwarmers. There were quite a few pairs of hot-pants too, especially on the men. Oh Lord. Why had she allowed herself to be talked into this?

'I can't help feeling a bit under-dressed,' she murmured, gazing down at her jeans and the long-sleeved blue Gap top she had on. Nobody was wearing helmets either, although some people had wrist and knee-guards. Weren't these people worried about head injuries? Had they never watched a hospital drama series on TV? 'Blimey, look at him, old Adonis over there, skimming about with all that hair.'

They both stared as a tall, handsome man skated past, his hair like a luxuriant lion's mane around his face, his body toned perfection in Lycra cycling shorts and a designer T-shirt. Then they made simultaneous 'Ewww' noises as they saw him skate directly behind three women in succession, pinching one's bum, grabbing another by the waist, and then twerking horribly around the third. 'Grim. Definitely stay away from that creep,' Georgie said. Like Charlotte, she was also wearing jeans but with a turquoise T-shirt that had silver appliqué stars, and she'd put her blonde hair up in bunches so she looked slightly more the part, at least. 'Shall we join the throng?' she went on. 'I might need to hold hands for the first spin round, if that's okay. Last time I had a pair of these on, I was about fourteen, and loads fitter.'

'Same,' Charlotte confessed. Clinging to each other, they inched forward and onto the smooth polished floor with little squeals of trepidation. 'I can't believe I'm doing this,' she gasped over the pounding beat of Lady Marmalade. The ping of her microwave and the comforting rumble of a David Attenborough narrated documentary seemed very far away, practically on another planet all of a sudden.

'Nor me,' Georgie giggled, her free arm windmilling as they set off. 'Whooaaaa! Shit, man. This is *hard*.'

Georgie was right, it *was* hard, but already the technique was starting to come back to Charlotte. Once upon a time, she and Shelley had gone every week to the roller rink, with too much blusher and their hair coated in copious amounts of sticky spray, strawberry bubblegum nonchalantly chomped as they whizzed around, eyeing up the boys. Concentrating fiercely now, teeth gritted, her body seemed to remember what to do: sliding her feet forward and slightly out like a duck, knees bent, hips building a rhythm as she glided slowly along on her left foot then her right. Within minutes she was experiencing a cautious sense of gathering euphoria; the dizzy light-headed conviction, as they spun around a corner together, hands still tightly locked, that she might not be about to die after all.

'So tell me about the magazine,' she said breathlessly as they completed their first circuit and high-fived in triumph. Then they set off again, a smidge faster this time. 'You're a journalist, are you?'

'A novice journalist,' Georgie replied, skidding a little as a more experienced skater sailed by them, pelvis twisting fluidly to the music. 'Whoa,' she yelped again, struggling to regain her balance before tumbling to the ground, where she sat, rubbing her elbow and laughing, until Charlotte pulled her back up. 'Ow. As much a novice writer as I am a skater,' she said. 'Thanks.'

Off they went again, gingerly at first and then lengthening their strides with increasing confidence. 'This is good,' Charlotte said as they picked up speed. She could feel a joyful emotion rising inside her. *Hey, Shelley, you'll never guess what I'm doing. Hey, Mum, I went out the other night. To an actual roller disco!* 'We're not bad, are we?' she asked as they navigated a corner with aplomb. Some might even say flair.

'We have totally nailed this,' Georgie agreed, just as she swerved to avoid a man in a diamanté-adorned Stetson and promptly clattered over again. 'Whoops. Ow. Pride goes before a broken wrist, as they say.'

'You okay, love?' asked the man, reaching down to haul her up. He was wearing a neon pink vest and mirror shades and shorts so tiny they were practically indecent.

'Thanks,' said Georgie. 'We're new here. As you can probably tell from my pratfalls.'

He clapped her on the back. 'Welcome to the gang. Oh, TUNE!' he cried, speeding off, bum wiggling as the song changed to 'Yes Sir, I Can Boogie'.

Georgie grinned at Charlotte. 'Do you know what, I'm a bit in love with Brighton,' she said. 'I mean . . . Look at that guy. Look at this whole place. There's no way anything like this would happen in Stonefield, where I grew up. No way. And it's ace!' She gripped Charlotte's hand a little tighter as they swirled around the bend. 'No doubt I'll be back in my old life by Christmas and this will all seem like a weird dream.'

Charlotte laughed. There *was* something vaguely dream-like about being here, she agreed: the rushing neon-dressed skaters around them, the thumping disco beat, the spinning of wheels underfoot, building up speed, their hair flying out behind them. 'The weirdest,' she agreed. 'And do you know what's really weird? I'm actually quite enjoying myself too.'

By nine-thirty, their legs had turned to jelly and the two of them limped to the side and removed their skates, fingers trembling from the exertion. Before this, Charlotte could have counted on one hand the number of times she had done any form of exercise since Kate was born – scrub that, she could have counted on a closed fist. None. No times. No exercise. Until tonight when she'd used all sorts of muscles she'd completely forgotten about. And . . . whoa. Here came the endorphins, bustling through her bloodstream like a parade of cheerleaders shaking pom-poms. It felt good. Really bloody good. Actually, she'd go as far as to say that it felt *epic*.

As well as burning all those calories – she had *so* earned her next box of chocolate eclairs, she realized happily – she and Georgie had chatted and laughed the whole evening and it had been fine. Fun, actually. Spinning around a roller disco dancefloor meant there was never any danger of the conversation turning heavy or sombre: Georgie had told Charlotte about being here for six months with her boyfriend and writing for the magazine, and Charlotte . . . Well, Charlotte had mainly listened, to be fair, and hadn't really said much about herself, but she'd ventured the odd titbit of information in return: how she'd met Margot upstairs in the flats and how her old skating buddy had contacted her out of the blue just that day. Nothing major. Easy-going chat. But even that was a novelty, she realized. Georgie was like the naughty little sister she'd never had.

Once back in their ordinary shoes – goodness, it felt so strange to walk again, after all that skating – Georgie suggested driving back into town and going for a drink before they called it a night. Charlotte was now feeling so uncharacteristically upbeat and – yes, she would go as far as to use the word 'kick-ass' – that she agreed immediately. And so it was that twenty minutes later, they were settling down in a corner of the Hare and Lion, a rather dingy old boozer that didn't care how sweaty-faced its clients were, with a gin and tonic each, and after a single sip, Charlotte could feel herself getting pleasantly swimmy. 'Thank you,' she said shyly to Georgie. 'Thanks for asking me along this evening. It's ages since I went out. I really enjoyed it.'

'Oh, Charlotte, thanks for *coming!*' Georgie exclaimed. 'I would have been bricking it, going there on my own, you did me a massive favour. And I could tell you didn't really want to at first and were just being kind to me, so double thanks. You rock.'

Charlotte blushed. 'Well . . .'

'Don't argue!' Georgie ordered, holding up a finger, then took a long slurp of her drink. 'God, I needed that. I'm knackered! It was fun though, wasn't it, in a slightly mad sort of way.'

'It was great,' Charlotte said, surprising herself. She wasn't even being polite, for once. While whizzing around the roller rink, she had felt young again, free, happy. How often did that happen? 'You'll have to let me know when your write-up comes out so I can read it. Are you going to mention the conga at the end?'

'Too right I am. And the limbo bit. Oh, and wasn't it brilliant when those two women did their dance-off? I loved them! Didn't you just want to become their new best friend and hang out with them forever?'

'They were fab,' Charlotte agreed.

'I'm worried already that I won't have enough space to fit everything in,' Georgie said happily, 'which is the best kind of problem to have.' She raised her glass. 'Cheers, anyway. To roller discos and all who sparkle there. To us!'

'Cheers!' They toasted one another. 'Where do you think you'll go next week?' Charlotte asked. 'People make suggestions, is that right, and then what? Is there a vote, or will your editor just pick somewhere?'

'I reckon she'll pick,' Georgie said, fishing the lemon slice from her drink and sucking it. 'Knowing her, she'll go with the wildest suggestion of all, so . . .' She held up crossed fingers and pulled a face. 'I could be heading off anywhere. To any mad Brightonian thing – and after tonight, I get the feeling that there are some pretty wild ones around. What have I let myself in for?'

Charlotte smiled. There was something immensely like-able about Georgie, she thought – she was just straightfor-ward and nice and upfront. No side. No corners either. And she was brave, as well, putting herself out there for the pub-lic's entertainment in such a way. Charlotte would never have had the bottle. 'Maybe I should flood the office with ideas of things that you might actually want to do,' she sug-gested now. 'Like wine-tastings and spa-testings and dinner at fabulous new restaurants . . .'

'*Yes!*' cried Georgie, with a laugh. 'Charlotte, you're a bloody genius, that's a great idea.' She grinned. 'And I tell you what, you get first dibs on any of the good ones, as my partner in crime. Do we have a deal?'

'We have a deal,' Charlotte heard herself say.

Chapter Twelve

SeaView House Noticeboard:

POLITE REMINDER
To All Residents

*PLEASE may I remind you that this is a
NO SMOKING house. Smoking is strictly forbidden
AT ALL TIMES in both the flats and the communal areas.*

*Angela Morrison-Hulme
Property Manager*

'Did you really not know?' Rosa's friends had asked, wide-eyed with incredulity, when she told them she and Max had split up, and the reason why. 'Did you really have no *idea*?'

No, she'd had to reply dismally, head down. She'd really had no idea whatsoever. Because she had loved him! She'd trusted him! She'd thought this was it, jackpot, proceed straight to Smug-Coupledom for the rest of her time on earth!

Sometimes in the middle of the night, she lay awake wondering miserably if it was somehow her fault that things had spiralled so wildly out of control. Had she been so desperate to fall in love that she'd been gullible to the point of being blind; that she'd deliberately ignored the warning signs that everyone else seemed to think she must have missed?

In hindsight, his flat alone should have been a giveaway; its sleek, minimalist feel more reminiscent of a hotel suite than a homely feet-up pad. 'Where's all your stuff?' she'd laughed once, opening a kitchen drawer and finding it empty. He'd looked disconcerted for a moment and she remembered worrying that she'd hurt his feelings – oh, the irony! 'Travel light, that's me,' he'd said after a second, before changing the subject. Then, of course, she'd remembered that his parents had both been in the Forces and he'd moved around a lot as a child, and so, using her own cack-handed sixth-form psychology, had assumed that this was the explanation for his apparent rootlessness. She'd moved in a short while later, renting out her small terraced house in Walthamstow, her heart full of wanting to create a home for them both; the home he'd never really had. More irony! You had to laugh, really. Laugh or padlock your own chastity belt, anyway.

Then there had been Catherine's innocent question about whether or not she could have seen Max on the King's Road. At the time Rosa had discounted the query without a second thought – of course it hadn't been Max! His job was based in Amsterdam, so he split the week, half with her in London, half in a small quirky flat just off Prinsengracht in the centre of the city. (She had spent a few days there with him in the past and been charmed by everything from the wide wooden staircase to the gable windows, with their views of canalboats and stoned cyclists. Stoned cyclists actually toppling into the canal and clambering out dripping wet – that was even more entertaining.) This was why Catherine had to be wrong about seeing Max in London because it was a Wednesday and Rosa knew full well he'd be in his office just off Dam Square, no doubt berating Henrik, the hapless intern, about whose dim-wittedness there was many a story. He couldn't possibly be in the King's Road, so that was that.

Another missed clue came when she suggested going on holiday together, somewhere really luxurious. Rosa had just got her end of year bonus and was feeling extravagant. 'My treat,' she told him, thinking palm trees, white sand and sparkling crystal seas. Tan lines and sandy feet and languid sex on a big wide bed. 'Five-star all the way. Give me your passport and I'll book us somewhere amazing.' To her surprise, though, he had come up with excuse after excuse. A conference on the horizon that he had to go to, he wasn't sure when. A problem with getting time off work. His sudden suggestion of a holiday down in Cornwall instead – or in the Lake District, even. Then it was him wanting to book everything, wanting to treat *her.* 'Christ almighty, is your passport photo really *that* embarrassing that you can't just let me do it?' she had joked, and there had been a flash of something – panic? – in his eyes that made her feel confused. 'I only want to treat you,' he had said, and then she'd felt like she was making a fuss about nothing, especially when he sorted out the best holiday she'd ever been on, in the Maldives; a week of utter bliss. It didn't matter so much, who paid and who arranged things, did it? Her friends thought she was mad for even thinking twice about it. (See? she reminded herself afterwards. *They* hadn't suspected either, had they?)

Then there was the gradual realization that, after eight months of being together, she had met hardly any of his friends and none of his family. He'd met everyone in her life, of course, she had paraded him in front of them with almost indecent glee, practically as soon as they'd been on a second date. *Look! Look at him! Isn't he gorgeous? And he's my boyfriend! Mine!* 'I never stayed anywhere long enough to make friends as a kid,' he'd said, shrugging. 'And now all my colleagues are Dutch, so it's not like I can hang out with them at the weekends, is it?' No, she'd agreed. It wasn't. But still, it was odd the way they moved almost exclusively within her social circles, going to dinner and to the pub and weddings with her friends. Almost as if he was ashamed of her in some way. Or even as if he had something to hide. But no! she kept telling herself. He loved her! Wasn't he always telling her how much?

Even the post that arrived sporadically for a certain David Chandler was explained away – the former owner of the property, Max said, bundling up the letters to forward on to him. No, Rosa had not suspected a thing.

At last, in the first week of December, when the whole of London seemed festooned with tinsel and fairy lights, and the dark streets were awash with cheap drunks wearing reindeer antlers, there came the big one. The clue that wasn't so much a clue as a slap round the face, impossible to ignore. She and Max were having drinks in a bar near Liverpool Street, just around the corner from Rosa's office – only a quick one, because he was due to fly back to Amsterdam that evening, or so he'd said. The bar was rammed, with Christmas music pounding from the speakers – Girls Aloud in tiny dresses, crooning to Santa on the TV above their heads – and Rosa and Max were squeezed in a corner, a glass of red wine each. It was to be their first Christmas together, and Rosa was already excited, determined to make it the most magical day ever spent. 'Are we going to do each other stockings?' she asked, with an almost unbearable thrill of excitement as she imagined waking up beside him on Christmas morning.

'You bet,' he said. 'Satsuma and a walnut, that'll do you, won't it?'

She'd punched him, laughing. 'Just try it and see.'

'Go on, then, I'll throw in a lump of coal as well, isn't that what you're meant to give someone in their stocking?'

'A lump of coal? That's at New Year, you idiot.' He was such a wind-up merchant, she thought fondly, pushing her leg against his under the table.

He leaned forward. 'Ahh, well, you can have one for Christmas *too*, seeing as you're so special. Don't say I never treat you! Maybe even two pieces of coal if you're *really* good . . .'

They were both laughing when the voice cut through and interrupted. 'David! Hey, David! Long time no see, mate! How are you doing?'

Rosa assumed the male, rather plummy voice, was aimed at somebody else, somebody called David, clearly, rather than her boyfriend, but then that strange clenched look of panic had appeared on Max's face again, just for a second, before his features were wiped clean of expression. 'Oh God. This tool. I'll explain in a minute,' he said, rising smoothly to his feet and taking a few brisk strides out to the man who'd spoken. The man was middle-aged, with floppy blonde hair and a rather nasty pale blue suit that was too tight on the shoulders. 'Jeremy!' cried Max, clapping him on the back with such enthusiasm that Rosa feared for the already strain-ing seams. 'Good to see you. Can I buy you a drink?'

And then he was steering blonde Jeremy away, one arm around him, but not before Rosa heard the man saying, 'How are Ann-Marie and the kiddies? Two, is it, you've got now?'

It was like being in a weird dream. A dream where noth-ing made sense. She thought for a moment her ears were playing tricks on her. Ann-Marie and the *kiddies*? David? Her heart thudded, her mind skidded wildly around, unable to make sense of what had just happened. Blonde Jeremy must have got the wrong person, she told herself eventually. He must be one of those people who was terrible with names, who went around getting others muddled up, wrongly assigning them random partners and children, that was all. Perhaps he had early-onset Alzheimer's and Max was just being kind, humouring him. *I'll explain in a minute*, he'd assured her, and there he was now, head quickly turning to check on her, giving her a look that said, *Don't worry. There is a perfectly rational explanation to all of this.*

Yeah, thought Rosa, her breath catching in her throat, looking from her gorgeous, wonderful boyfriend to the space where he'd been sitting not thirty seconds earlier, laughing with her about Christmas stockings and lumps of coal. She glanced back over at Max, who appeared to be buying Jeremy a drink, one arm still chummily draped around him

– and even that was odd, she thought uneasily. Why hadn't he introduced them? Why hadn't he said, Jeremy, mate, this is my girlfriend Rosa, come and join us, it's about time she met some of my old muckers. That would have been the normal thing to do, wouldn't it? The normal boyfriend thing to do.

She remembered the post that arrived for 'David' occasionally, the business with the passport. And then she realized that down by her feet was the suitcase Max was taking to Amsterdam, and the small carry-on bag he'd packed, which would contain his passport, there for the checking. She could unzip it in a single second, peer inside, just for her peace of mind, just to banish the questions and the doubts that were starting to circle like buzzards.

Her mind made up, she bent down, fingers on the zip and tugged . . . just as she heard Max's voice – 'God, sorry about that' – as he returned, and she had to sit up again quickly and pretend she had dropped a tissue on the floor. Mariah Carey was warbling in the background now and a couple of women were screeching along at the next table.

Rosa couldn't look at Max as he sat down. In fact, all of a sudden, she had forgotten how to sit naturally in the company of her own boyfriend and her leg started to jiggle as he eased himself along the seat next to her. 'Old school pal,' he said with a little laugh in his voice. A fake laugh? Rosa thought suspiciously, her senses on full alert now. 'His stupid joke, liked to call everyone in the rugby team David. Can't remember why, one of those lame school things.'

Her heart still thumping, she watched his mouth moving as he spoke, his eyes smiling into hers, but it was as if something had already shifted, as if a chasm had opened up between where they were now and their happy old carefree life together. *Who are you?* she thought, panic taking hold of her. *Who are you, really? And what about Ann-Marie and these kids I've just heard Jeremy mention? Why aren't you telling me about Ann-Marie and these bloody kids?*

'Hurry up over there, Butternut, I don't have time for slackers on this ship,' snapped Brendan. His mood was positively glowering on this particular Wednesday morning, his face unshaven and pasty. *Does somebody need a hug?* thought Rosa sarcastically, battling through the pile of butternut squash she was peeling and chopping for a soup. 'Do you hear me?' he growled.

'Yes, chef,' she replied through gritted teeth, peeling the thick skin of the squash in strips. Butternut, was she today? After almost three months spent slaving for this imbecile? How hard was it to learn the names of the people you worked with, day in, day out? Beside her Natalya was hacking beetroot, hands already purple, while Liam, the trainee pastry chef, had his pimply face bowed in concentration over the delicate spun-sugar lattices he was making as adornments for that day's desserts. None of them were slackers. All of them deserved a bit of respect. Oh God, she thought wearily, maybe she wasn't cut out for this job any more. Maybe her mum had been right, that she'd only ping-ponged into the catering world because she was having a mad midlife crisis, and that she should just quit already, hawk her wares around some temp agency and get some sensible office work instead.

But then again, she only had to think of the salted caramel muffins she'd made the day before (so delicious she was having to ration herself extremely strictly) and the roast chicken, which had completely turned around Bea's bad mood the other evening, and actually yes, all those millions of dinner parties and mates' brunches she'd thrown when they'd told her en masse, salivating, that she was definitely their favourite friend ever and an utter goddess and, hey, she really should go in for *Masterchef* or the *Bake-Off*, she'd win it, hands down! It was those moments, the flushed pride and the warm hum of satisfaction, that reminded her that cooking *was* what she enjoyed. Cooking, especially for other people, was what she *loved*. It was just working with Brendan the oaf which was less appealing.

'No offence but your job sounds kind of shit,' Bea had said bluntly on Sunday night, as they made short work of their succulent bronzed roast chicken. The conversation had moved on, thankfully, from discussing the failings of Gareth and shit sandwiches, and Rosa had been telling her teenage neighbour about working at the hotel. 'I mean . . . is that really what you want to *do*, for*ever*? Peel stuff and get bossed around? Not gonna lie, I would be like, no *way*. Sorry, but forget it. Don't you throw no ladles at *me*.'

'Well, it's a new thing for me, really, I'm just starting out. I used to work in advertising for a company in London, but—'

Bea had almost dropped her fork. 'What, like in *Mad Men*? Oh my God, and you *left*, to come here and peel carrots at the frigging *Zanzibar*?' Her eyes were uncomprehending, but then her expression flickered into doubt. 'Oh, wait – unless you got sacked or something . . . Shit. Awkward. Um.'

'I didn't get sacked. It was a . . . life change,' Rosa said, deciding not to go down the whole Max story. 'I wanted to do something different, something I enjoyed. So that was my decision.'

'Riiiight,' Bea said, clearly unconvinced. And although Rosa seized the chance to start talking about something else, the girl must have been wrestling with the information for a while because later on, tucking into the cinnamon-spiced apple crumble, she brought up the subject again. 'But, I mean . . . Can't you just be a *chef* somewhere instead of, like, a skivvy? Because you're really bloody good at it.' She pointed at the steaming, custard-laked crumble in front of her as if citing evidence in court. 'Like, *really*, properly good.'

Rosa had felt quite touched by the praise. She knew Bea well enough by now to know that her teenage neighbour was not one to mince her words about anything. 'Thanks, but it's not that easy,' she'd replied. 'I can't just walk into a chef's job when I've hardly got any experience. Things are tough, restaurants are closing down all the time and there are people way more qualified than I am.'

'Yeah, but . . . Can't you just start your own place then?'

'Hmm, maybe, if I had a spare half a million quid.' And the rest. Rosa had some savings salted away still and the rent coming in from her Walthamstow house, but that was her emergency fund; back-up should things go wrong here. 'It's fine, honestly. I'm learning stuff every day, I get to see amazing chefs at work . . .'

Bea didn't sound convinced. 'I bet you'd rather be cooking nice food, though, rather than all that peeling and chopping.'

Rosa didn't reply immediately. Truth be told, she had sometimes fantasized about opening her own little restaurant; it was a particularly lovely daydream that she liked to indulge in now and then. Just a tiny restaurant, a bistro really, with ten or so tables and a small, beautifully curated menu; a friendly sort of place where she knew her customers and would come out to share a brandy with them at the end of the evening, basking in the warm glow of their compliments about her food, of course. 'Well, obviously, but . . .'

'*Butternut!*' Brendan yelled just then, interrupting her little reverie and her hand shook on the cleaver. 'Jesus wept, woman! Are you with us today, or are you away with the fecking fairies? Get on with that godforsaken squash before I come over there and shove it somewhere unpleasant!' he bawled, spit showering from his mouth.

Enough dreaming. Rosa snapped guiltily back to attention, the kitchen jerking into focus once more as she mumbled, 'Yes, chef' and turned her attention to the squash mountain. Hack, hack, chop, chop. If nothing else, it was doing wonders for her biceps.

Having started work at six that Wednesday morning, Rosa finished her shift at three in the afternoon and headed home, hurrying when she got caught in a sudden April shower with no umbrella. *Max*, she thought ruefully, as she always did, whenever it rained. Was it raining where he was? she wondered, pulling her jacket up around her neck and ducking under a shop awning. Or was he in bed with some other gullible woman and completely oblivious of the weather outside?

It had been so simple, in the end, for her to unravel his lies. After the Jeremy incident in the pub, they'd said goodbye outside Liverpool Street station because he was getting the train to Stansted airport as usual, while she was going to get a bus home. Only she didn't stick to this plan. And nor, as it turned out, did he.

After assuring him there was no need for him to wait with her at the bus stop – it was going to take forever! He'd miss his flight! – she watched him walk away before slipping from the queue herself and stalking him through the station with exaggerated stealth. It would have been quite exciting, all the dodging into shops and café entrances, if it hadn't been so devastating at the same time. The Stansted Express left from platform 4, according to the noticeboards, but he walked straight past it without so much as a flicker and hurried down into the Tube instead, where he got on the Hammersmith and City Line, heading west. *Liar*, she thought, tears springing to her eyes as she slid into the next carriage along, hiding herself behind a group of rugby fans, and peering out to check on him each time the train stopped.

King's Cross. Euston Square. Baker Street. It was like a knife in the stomach, a physical blow, as they rattled along further and further away from Stansted. He wasn't even going to Amsterdam, was he? Did he even work there at all? He had taken her to the little Prinsengracht flat, though, hadn't he, so he must do! Some of it had to be true, surely?

On they went, to Edgware Road and then Paddington, where he got off the train and headed briskly into the main train station. *Liar. Liar.* She watched him board a train bound for Oxford – off to see the mysterious Ann-Marie and those kiddies? – and then her energy ran out, like air whooshing from a punctured tyre, and she had to lean limply against a coffee stand, watching the train as it chugged slowly out of the station. Goodbye, Max. David, whatever the hell your name is. You go off to Oxford and whatever other life you've clearly got waiting for you up there.

Me, I'm going back to our flat – your flat – and I'm going to get to the bottom of this, once and for all.

It was still pouring as she reached Dukes Square and in her mad haste to get inside and under cover, she almost tripped over the woman sitting on the front steps looking hopefully up at her. 'Hello!' the woman said in a breathless, northern-sounding voice. She had blonde hair twisted up in Princess Leia-style buns either side of her head and enormous gold dangly earrings shaped like fish. 'Do you live here? Only I've locked myself out, like a massive plum. Oh,' she went on, jumping to her feet and sticking out a hand, 'I'm Georgie, by the way. Flat 3. Hi.'

It was the same voice Rosa had heard floating down the stairs now and then, she realized; the same voice she'd heard singing all those power ballads so tunelessly above. The woman with the very loud laugh, who seemed to enjoy an astonishing amount of noisy sex. 'Rosa,' she said, taking Georgie's hand and shaking it. 'God, that was a very British introduction. Hello. Here, I've got some keys.'

'Thanks so much. I've been sat there half an hour and my arse has been getting number and number. All I could think about was my mum telling me I'd get piles if I sat on cold walls. I hope it's not the same for cold steps.'

In they went, Georgie shaking the raindrops from her polka-dot umbrella. She was wearing a dark denim jacket over a navy blue and white striped dress; bare legs, silver ballet flats and Rosa felt suddenly grubby and scruffy after her stint in a hot kitchen all morning. She hoped she didn't smell too strongly of onions.

'Christ knows what I've done with my keys, I thought they were in here,' Georgie went on, patting the small red bag on her shoulder. She pulled a comical face, her blue eyes mischievous. 'God help me if I've lost them and I have to tell Terrifying Ange the bad news. If you hear the sound of someone being murdered with a zebra-print stiletto later on, that'll be me.'

Rosa's lips twitched at the nickname for their landlady. 'She is pretty scary, isn't she? Although apparently her son's a bit of all right, or so she told me. *If you're looking for a man, Rosa, I'll send him round, he's gorgeous, though I say so myself.*'

Georgie burst out laughing. 'No! She said the same to me too! *And* to Charlotte as well, we had a laugh about it the other night. Paul, I think he's called. So gorgeous he needs his own mum to sort his love life out for him – mmm, sounds a right catch to me.'

'It's almost worth pretending to have a blocked sink or

something just to get the guy round so we can all see—'
Rosa said, just as Georgie's phone started ringing.

'Absolutely – we so should do that,' she agreed, plunging
a hand into her bag. 'Sorry, I should get this, it's Simon, my
boyfriend, 'scuse me.' She swiped the screen. '*Hi!*' she said,
perching on the stairs, elbows on her knees. 'I've left so
many messages for you! Were you . . . ? Oh, right.'

Rosa hovered at her own door, feeling torn as to what she
should do. She didn't want to seem like an eavesdropper but
if Georgie was locked out, it seemed churlish to leave her
stranded on the stairs until her boyfriend came back. She put
a hand surreptitiously to her nose while she was dithering
and sniffed. Onions. Great.

'So did you get my messages?' Georgie was saying. 'Yeah.
I know, I'm an idiot. No, I'm in the building now but can't
get in the actual flat. You couldn't pop back and let me in,
could you?'

Rosa put her key in the door and was pushing it open
when Georgie's voice rose in dismay.

'Oh, you're kidding! Can I go to the office then and get
them there?' Rosa turned to see her clap a hand to her head,
then pull a face. 'Shit. Well, what am I supposed to? . . .
Yeah, I know but . . .' She sighed. 'Never mind. No worries.
You just . . . carry on. I'll sort something out.' She stabbed
a finger at the screen to end the call and made a muffled
screaming sound. 'Bollocks.'

Rosa held her door open. 'Do you want to come in here while you wait? I've got salted caramel muffins and you'd be doing me a huge favour if you stopped me eating them all myself.'

Georgie grinned and jumped to her feet. 'That's my kind of favour. Yes, please.'

Chapter Thirteen

As they left the motorway and the traffic melted away, Georgie gave a contented wriggle in her seat. It was the bank holiday weekend and like hordes of other people, she and Simon were getting away for a few days, in their instance heading back north to Stonefield to catch up with friends and family. She'd only been down south for three weeks but her heart had quickened with true gladness as they passed the Welcome to Yorkshire sign. Oh *yes*. Brighton was fabulous, and she had just enjoyed her best week there yet (meeting not one but two fabulous women in SeaView House, one who could roller skate like a demon, the other who could bake like an angel. Those muffins!). At the end of the day, though, home was home. Home was *best*. Just look at those gorgeous rolling hills. Just look at the sheep and the farms and the dry-stone walls; all of that great green emptiness. It was even quite sunny, to make the scene properly idyllic. Well, all right, so nobody would be parading around in their bikinis yet, obviously, but it wasn't raining at least. Same difference.

'This is more like it,' she said happily, winding down her window and putting her bare feet up on the dashboard. 'Breathe it in, Si, the air of Yorkshire. Ahh . . . delicious!'

'It's freezing,' he grumbled, but he was smiling nonetheless. 'And it smells of shit.'

'I can't imagine *why* the Tourist Board haven't been after you for some inspirational marketing copy yet,' she replied before affecting a gruff imitation of his voice. 'Yorkshire: It's freezing and it smells of shit.'

He snorted. 'You're the writer, not me,' he reminded her. 'Still, you'll be a dead cert for the Tourist Board job if this journalism lark goes pear-shaped, anyway.'

'If the journalism goes pear-shaped?' she repeated indignantly. 'I'll have you know my editor *loved* my roller disco write-up. *And* she's forwarded loads more problems for the problem page.'

'Cool,' he said, reaching over and squeezing her knee. 'So when am I going to read this magazine, then?'

'Um . . .' Well, she definitely wasn't going to let him read the current issue, that was for sure. 'The next one's out on Monday,' she told him. 'You can read that and then realize what a talented, awesome, amazing girlfriend you have. I'll let you bask in my reflected glory, if you like. I'm generous that way, see.'

'Ah, you're too good to me,' he said, indicating without warning to turn off the road and then heading down a winding lane.

'Er . . . What are you doing?' Georgie asked as he pulled over in a deserted layby.

'I'm appreciating this talented, awesome girlfriend of mine, that's what,' he said, shooting his seat backwards and hauling her onto his lap in one slick move. 'Hello, glorious. Fancy some basking?'

'Ooh, hello,' she said, feeling giggly. 'Simon!' she yelped in surprise as he started nuzzling her neck. Within moments she was powerless to resist, though. 'Yorkshire: Freezing, Smells of Shit, and Gives You the Horn,' she murmured, peeling her shirt over her head and leaning in to kiss him.

'Hell, yeah,' he agreed, unbuttoning his jeans.

'Now that's what I call a deviation,' Georgie said, a while later once they were just about decent again and she was sliding back into her own seat. She hoped the tractor driver who'd passed them minutes earlier and given them a cheery wave was short-sighted and hadn't actually glimpsed her bare bum. Maybe they were all at it around here, though.

'Excellent deviant behaviour,' Simon agreed, doing a U-turn and heading back to the main road. 'I feel at home already.'

'It's good to be back,' Georgie said, gazing out in contentment at the wide sky. Even without the impromptu roadside shenanigans, they were going to have a great time. Tonight they'd be down the Shepherd's Crook with everyone, tomorrow she was taking a trip into Leeds with Amelia and Jade before dinner out with Simon somewhere romantic, and then a big old hike on Sunday before – obviously – a massive trouser-busting roast at her mum's. Oh joy. It was shaping up to be the best weekend ever and they'd barely even started.

Half an hour later, Simon was slowing to a reverential twenty miles per hour as they passed the old village sign with its carved oak leaves still visible on the weathered stone. His shoulders seemed to drop the moment they crossed onto hallowed Stonefield soil. (Tarmac, then. Whatever.) There was the pub. The village shop. The primary school. Amelia's parents' house where Georgie had stayed for several million sleepovers as a teenager. The gate she'd fallen off the second time she'd kissed Simon. (It had been that good a kiss.) The stop where they used to wait together for the school bus, holding hands and sometimes having a cheeky snog. (The bus driver had honked them once during one particularly passionate clinch. 'I'm not having any of that on my bus, you two, do you hear?') It was all there, so familiar, so normal, so right. Just as she'd left it.

'Everything's exactly the same,' she sighed in satisfaction and Simon shot her an amused glance.

'George . . . you were only here a few weeks ago. Of course it's the same. Stonefield's always the same.'

'You say that like it's a bad thing,' she remarked in surprise.

'No, but . . . Anyway. Here we are.' He pulled into his parents' driveway and turned off the engine. 'Home.'

Ahh yes. His parents' place. In her excitement at returning, Georgie had somehow managed to overlook this salient fact, that they would be staying with Christine and Harry, rather than in their own lovely little house. Their own lovely little house was now temporarily rented out to another couple, of course, both teachers, the perfect tenants, according to the lettings agent, and therefore out of bounds. It was kind of odd, though, thinking of other people being there. She wondered if she'd be able to walk past without pressing her face against the window and peering inside.

In Stoney!! she texted Amelia and Jade quickly as she saw the curtains twitch at the in-laws' living-room window. That would be Christine, Simon's mum, a woman who had her finger so firmly on the pulse of village goings-on she could probably tell you with precision timing who had last farted in the locality as well as what they'd had for their lunch. *What time will you be in the pub? Can't wait to see you!!! xxxxx* she typed quickly before pressing Send.

'Are you coming or what?' Simon was already round at the boot, hauling out their overnight bags plus the bunch of sunflowers and wine Georgie had insisted they bought at the last service station. She was regretting splashing out now when she knew already that Janet would make some comment about imported flowers and Harry, Simon's dad, would purse his lips as he read the wine label, before cracking a 'joke' about it coming in handy next time they ran out of vinegar.

'I'm coming,' she said, trying not to be so mean. Christine and Harry were very nice, she reminded herself, and it was good of them to have her and Simon for the weekend.

Her phone bleeped just then: Amelia. *Yay! About 8? Everyone coming – inc Chloe and Daz! Xxx*

Georgie frowned. Chloe and Daz? Who the hell were Chloe and Daz?

'Hurry up!' Simon called, as the front door opened and Christine appeared, her arms folded underneath her matronly bosom.

'*There* you are!' she said, with her usual martyred air. The world was totally out to get Christine, the poor woman; everyone conspiring to make her life that bit more punishing. 'We expected you *hours* ago! Dinner's ruined but never mind. Come in!'

'Hi, Mum,' Simon said, his arms full as he went over. 'Good to see you. Sorry we're late. Here.' He presented her with the flowers. 'These are for you.'

'Oh, darling! Aren't they beautiful! You shouldn't have,' she cooed, reaching up to hug him.

'Georgie chose them,' he said, as Georgie heaved down the boot with a clunk.

'Oh.' Christine's face fell immediately and Georgie saw her squinting at the sticker on the cellophane bouquet. 'From Kenya, I see. Ahh. You know, another time, some good old English lily of the valley would have done me just fine.'

Georgie made a valiant attempt at a smile. 'Hello, Christine,' she said, her voice sounding rather strangled. She tried not to think about strangling Simon's ungrateful mother. 'Thanks for having us.'

'Oh, not at all. It's always delightful to have my son back. Goodness, I've missed you!'

Christine was just being motherly and not deliberately leaving her out, Georgie reminded herself through gritted teeth, but still, she didn't have to talk about having her son 'back' like that, as if she'd had to wrestle him from the clutches of awful Georgie. She took a deep breath as they went inside and did her best to keep that smile firmly in place.

'Hi, Dad,' she heard Simon say as he reached the kitchen before her. 'Here – we brought some wine for dinner.'

'Wine, eh? Let's see. Good grief! Where did you pick this up, did it fall off the back of some Polish lorry or something? Ha ha. Still – if we ever run out of vinegar . . .' He was slapping his own thigh with mirth as Georgie walked in on this touching reunion scene. 'Only kidding, son. Let's have a look at you. Eh, you're a sight for sore eyes, you are.' Harry clapped him on the shoulder, the nearest he ever came to an actual embrace with another male human being. 'Welcome home.'

Georgie had never been so happy to walk into a pub when it reached eight o'clock that evening. Forget Christine. Forget Harry. Here she was in her nicest bootcut jeans, that hoisted her bum up and actually made it look reasonably perky, as well as a pretty silky blouse, charcoal grey with a pink flower sprig design and a bow at the top, that she'd found in a second-hand shop in the Lanes. Her hair was loose around her shoulders, she had (for once) achieved really good smoky eye make-up and added some bold red lipstick, which always made her feel great. Nobody, but nobody, could say she'd 'let herself go' since leaving Stonefield, that was for sure.

The Shepherd's Crook was one of the oldest buildings in the village. Built of stone, it had a cosy, cottagey feel inside with low ceilings and small windows, horse brasses nailed up on the rough plaster walls, as well as framed sepia photographs of Stonefield in years gone by, back when it was mostly farmland. It smelled, as ever, of chips and beer, and Georgie was pleased to see that Big Bill, the landlord, was there behind the bar, greasy curls glistening as he pulled old Barney Wheelwright a pint of Tetley. Everything was right in the world.

Georgie found herself reaching for Simon's hand as they

went in, a show of unity. How many Friday nights had they spent in this place with the old gang? Hundreds and hundreds. Too many to count. Pints on the table. Meatloaf and Bonnie Tyler on the jukebox (Big Bill was stuck in the Eighties and proud). Chat and laughter and private gossips in the draughty loos with the girls as they touched up their make-up. *He didn't! He did, you know.*

'There they are,' she said, waving as she saw Amelia and Jason at one of the big tables in the back, along with Jade and Sam, Lois and her sister Mel, plus a few of the lads, Steve, Rob and Ed. Her heart swelled at the sight. Amelia had had her hair done in a sweet ringlety style that really suited her face and Jade wore a navy sleeveless top Georgie didn't recognize but they both had their heads back in a simultaneous cackle which she *did* obviously recognize. 'Hey, guys!' she called, beaming. She dimly registered Simon saying something behind her about buying drinks as she rushed over to her friends, too excited to answer him.

'Georgie!'

'She's back!'

'Oh, come here!'

There was much hugging and exclaiming and complimenting as the five women were reunited whereas the men barely looked up from their conversation about fell-running routes, other than to give Georgie a brief nod and smile.

'I love that top, is it new?' Amelia said. 'You look fab.'

'Thanks! It's from this little boutique in Brighton,' Georgie said, feeling very cosmopolitan. She wouldn't mention that it was second-hand, she decided. 'I love your *hair*! It looks really cool.'

'Oh, cheers, Chloe did it actually,' Amelia said, touching it with her fingertips. 'She'll be here in a minute. You should get her to give you some tips, she's brilliant with the old tongs.'

'She's going to do my wedding hair,' Jade put in proudly, twiddling a chestnut lock around her index finger. 'I'll have to show you the photos, George, we've had a little practice session already. Where is she, by the way? I thought she was going to come early.'

'Who's—' Georgie began, confused by mention of this Chloe person again but Amelia was already in full flow.

'She was popping a pie round to Mrs Huggins, I bet she got stuck listening to her going on about that mangy old cat of hers again.' Amelia rolled her eyes. 'She'll chew your ear off, that one. Mrs Huggins, I mean, not the cat!'

Georgie was feeling rather nonplussed as the others fell about laughing. Mrs Huggins was her former neighbour in Orchard Road, who was as creakily arthritic as she was gossipy. 'Um . . . Who are you talking about?'

They stared at her. '*Chloe!* Chloe Phillips. She lives in your house, you daft pillock,' Amelia said. Her ringlets fell around her face as she laughed again.

'Oh,' said Georgie, taken aback. Had Amelia always

laughed in such a loud honking way, her head thrown back in hilarity? New hair, new laugh, new *friend* . . . What was it Simon had said earlier, that Stonefield never changed? She was starting to think there were a few too *many* changes around here already; too many for Georgie's liking. 'Right. The lettings agent did everything, I never actually met—'

'Here she is. Chloe! Over here!' And then Georgie was momentarily forgotten as Amelia, Jade, Lois and Mel all turned to greet the new arrival.

'Hey!'

'About time!'

'What kept you?'

What had *kept* her? Georgie thought, glancing up at the brass-edged clock on the wall. It was only five past eight. What was the big deal? And why were her oldest mates all seemingly in such thrall to this other woman, when – hello? – Georgie, their real friend, was back again following a three-week absence. It was the longest she had been away in years! She put her hands in her lap, feeling uncomfortable all of a sudden. Hurry up, Simon. How long did it take a man to buy a few drinks, for heaven's sake?

Chloe was small and busty in a tight black cleavage-revealing dress and spindly heels, the sort that Georgie would catch in a broken paving slab within about two minutes of squeezing her foot inside. She had coppery hair pulled up in a chignon with a few artfully tousled tendrils loose at the front, green eyes and pale freckled skin, and Georgie felt underdressed immediately as Chloe tottered over. Since when had anyone come to this pub in a little black dress, she wanted to ask, other than on New Year's Eve?

'Dudes!' called Chloe as she approached. She even had a swagger on her, Georgie noted, feeling rather sour. A swagger, and she had only been in the village five minutes. Who did she think she was? 'Hiya. Sorry I'm late. Mrs H was telling me about her son – he was out in Afghan, you know, and she's that proud of him. The big news is, he's going to be a dad, anyway, and she's well happy.' She tapped her watch and pulled a funny face. 'Twenty solid minutes' worth of being happy, mind, where I couldn't get a word in edgeways, but what can you do?'

'Aww.' This was Jade, head tilted on one side, expression sappy. 'Bless. She just loves you, Chlo. Nice for her to have someone to talk to.'

Georgie stiffened. The way Jade said it made it sound as if Georgie had always shunned her elderly neighbour when she so *hadn't*. You could hardly step foot in the back garden without Mrs Huggins hurrying out in order to buttonhole Georgie for a chat. And how many times had she sat in her neighbour's musty-smelling living room, legs itching on the prickly velvet chair, listening to her spout on about her cat, her son, her sadly deceased husband . . . ? Many times, thank you. Certainly many more than this Chloe interloper had.

'Come and sit here, I've saved you a place,' Amelia said, shuffling up and patting the banquette with great eagerness. And then *everyone* was moving up, rearranging themselves so that Chloe could take centre stage, while Georgie found herself shunted to the edge of the table beside shy Mel, who only tagged along with Lois because she didn't have any friends of her own. Effectively she'd been edged out into the wilderness, she thought, trying not to look hurt. Edged out, by her own mates, in her own local pub, thank you very much. This was not exactly the welcome home she'd been anticipating.

'Cheers, babe,' said Chloe, wedging her bum into the gap with a wiggle.

Babe! If there was one thing Amelia hated it was being called pet names. Babe. Sweetie. Hon. Crimes against vocabulary, she'd said before. Cheesy words for cheesy people. Georgie hid a tiny smirk waiting for her friend's usual waspish response but Amelia said nothing, just patted her stupid ringlets and smiled goofily at the vocabulary criminal.

'Hello, hello.' Chloe had noticed her now. 'Who's this? A new member of the gang?'

Georgie's hackles rose. 'New? I don't think so, love,' she scoffed with a little laugh. She'd intended to sound jokey but it came out sounding rather aggressive. 'I should be asking, who are you?'

'It's Chloe, you muppet, we told you that a minute ago,'

said Amelia disloyally, pantomiming slapping a hand to her head as if Georgie was the thickest person in the room. 'And Chloe, this is Georgie, our mate who's been down in Brighton. She's your landlady, so watch what you say!'

Was it Georgie's imagination or did Chloe's green eyes sparkle with mischief at this news? 'Ooh God, nobody tell her about the party last night, then!' she cried, clapping a hand to her mouth. 'Don't worry. I'm kidding. We haven't broken that much yet although we did paint the front room purple, I hope that's okay.'

'Purple?' Georgie echoed uncertainly.

'Kidding again! Of course we haven't. We've been very well behaved, honest. If you don't mind us having shagged all over the place, ha ha!' She gave a meaningful wink. 'Nice bed, by the way. Oh, we've christened that bed all right.'

'Here you go. Sorry it took ages.' Simon was back, plonking drinks on the table – and thank goodness, thought Georgie, because she was in sore need of a distraction from this utterly repellent Chloe person. Shagging all over the place indeed. In her house! On her super-comfortable memory-foam bed! She was so going to borrow her mum's steam-cleaner before she moved back in. The mattress could go on a bonfire too; there was no way she wanted it back now it had been forever ruined by horrible Chloe cavorting all over it.

'Thanks,' she said gratefully, taking a massive swig of

her pint. She wasn't enjoying tonight as much as she had expected. In fact, if Chloe could kindly sling her hook now and butt out of Georgie's circle of friends forever, that would be very much appreciated. She watched rather dolefully as Simon wandered down to the far end of the table where the other blokes were gathered and greeted him with an enthusiastically slappy round of man-hugs. *Don't leave me*, she suddenly felt like calling after him but that was ridiculous. Barring Chloe, these were her best and oldest friends, the women she loved more than any others. Normally she couldn't wait for him to leave her and her mates to it, so that they could get down to a proper meaty gossip.

Dragging her attention away from Simon and the men, she feigned polite listening as Chloe blah-ed on at length about some incident at work that day. Yes, that was right, she was a teacher, Georgie remembered now, as was her tall, rugged partner, currently being served by Big Bill at the bar. Somehow she'd pictured the two as sensible tweedy types, who would be respectful with her soft furnishings and sit quietly marking their homework books every evening, rather than this pint-sized loudmouth who seemed to have muscled in on her mates in Georgie's absence. That would teach her to go around making lazy assumptions, she supposed.

Talk turned – inevitably – to Amelia and Jade's wedding plans, and to Georgie's annoyance, Chloe insisted on hearing the last tiny detail of everything. Even when Amelia and Jade started looking embarrassed and saying things like 'Oh God, I'm getting boring now, aren't I?' and 'Sorry, am I going on?' to which the answers were obviously, Yes and HELL, YES, Chloe waved them aside, and said 'No way! If it's important to you, it's important to us. Right, girls?'

'Right,' the others chorused dutifully, apart from Georgie who pretended she had just seen something really urgent on her phone.

'How are things in Bournemouth?' asked shy Mel just then.

'It's Brighton,' Georgie replied, thankful that they might actually be changing the subject at last. 'And yeah, it's great. Different from here, obviously. It's a bit . . . wilder. And outrageous. Loads of bohemian types.'

Lois pouted. 'She's saying we're not wild enough for her any more,' she joked.

'Of course I'm not!' Georgie laughed. 'Don't forget, Lois, I was there at your twenty-first when there was the stripper and cucumber incident. That's all the wild I will ever need in my life, thanks.'

Amelia immediately began humming the Stripper tune, batting her eyelashes coquettishly and pushing her top slightly off her shoulders in a suggestive sort of manner, and everyone burst out laughing. Then they laughed even harder when Lois accidentally sprayed a mouthful of vodka and tonic through her nose.

Chloe looked a bit put out not to be sharing the joke and turned her eyes, like laser beams, on Georgie. 'So what are you up to down beside the seaside?' she asked. 'I heard you followed your boyfriend down there. Sweet!'

Georgie bristled at the implicit criticism. 'Actually I'm writing for a magazine,' she said loftily. So shove that one in your hole, Chloe. 'It's really cool. I'm their agony aunt, and I've got this column where—'

'Ooh, what's it called?' Chloe said, whipping out a tablet and opening her browser.

'I . . .' All of a sudden, Georgie didn't want to tell her. She was sure that Chloe would only try to belittle her work somehow, make a joke about it. 'You won't have heard of it, it's a local thing,' she said, waving a hand. 'But yeah, it's really fun living by the sea. There are loads of arty people and famous actors and the shops are ace . . .' Her voice trailed away. The others weren't listening. They were all poring over Chloe's tablet as she typed into a search engine.

'Brighton . . . local . . . magazine,' she said. 'Let's see. BN1 . . . *Regency Magazine* . . . *Brighton Rocks* . . .'

Georgie gave a guilty start and unfortunately for her, Jade noticed. 'Try *Brighton Rocks*,' she said. The traitor.

'No, don't, my stuff isn't on there yet,' Georgie said, feeling a flutter of panic. Shit. The first thing they would see if they tracked down her *Hey Em* page was that awful whinging letter about Simon. He was still blissfully ignorant of the whole thing, and that was most definitely how she wanted him to stay. 'Anyone want another drink?'

Chloe stared her down. 'Georgie! Chill!' she instructed. 'Anyone would think you were embarrassed about your new journalistic career. Or even that you'd made the whole thing up!' She elbowed Amelia. 'I'm dying to read this agony aunt page now, I'm telling you. Gagging to!' She clicked a link and began scrolling. 'Aha – this looks promising. *Hey Em*! That you, is it?' She sniggered. 'Did they not think your name was cool enough for them or something?'

'No, I—' Georgie thought for a moment about snatching the tablet out of Chloe's hands – she was like the worst kind of school bully, sensing prey and going in for the kill. Then she heard Amelia's sharp intake of breath and knew her fate was already sealed. Too late.

'Wait,' Amelia said, who had always been a fast reader and was ahead of the others. 'Is this about—?' And then, bless her for her loyalty, because she did try to close the page down before anyone else could see it, shooting Georgie an aghast look. *Yikes*, said the look. *Really?*

Yep, said Georgie's unhappy face in reply. *Really*. Unfortunately, Chloe had wrestled the tablet away from reach and was already reading out the second letter in a sing-song voice.

'"Hey Em, Do you know what, my boyfriend is being a real arse. He's got this hot-shot new job and now thinks he's like this super-amazing professional."' She raised an eyebrow and read on. '"We've moved down all the way from Yorkshire so that he can indulge his wet dream, I mean, take up this wow-zers job" –' Her eye fell upon Georgie as she, too, realized the unfortunate predicament for the new writer. 'Oh dear,' she said with slow relish in her voice. Gotcha. 'No wonder you didn't want us to read it. Trouble in paradise, eh?'

'Bloody hell, Georgie, does Simon know you've written this?' Jade said, craning her neck to read to the bottom. 'Oh my God, there's even a vote thing at the bottom. You can choose whether to . . .' She stifled a snort – 'lump him, dump him or hump him!'

'Look, it was just a joke, it's not even—' Georgie gabbled but then there came the worst question she'd ever heard in her life.

'Does Simon know about what?' Right on cue, there was the man himself. He'd always had bat-ears, worst luck. He caught her eye and winked but she was unable to do any-thing but slide her gaze unhappily away. *Oh shit. Oh, Simon, I'm sorry. I'm really sorry but I cocked up big-time.*

'Nothing,' she mumbled but Chloe, sensing mischief, spoke louder.

'Awkward!' she sang, then held the tablet aloft. 'So are you going to tell him, George, or shall I?'

Chapter Fourteen

As the senior management team had previously decreed, the office of Dunwoody and Harbottle closed promptly at three-thirty on Friday afternoon, ensuring the staff could troop out into the city and spread some brightness and cheer amidst the elderly community. That was the theory, anyway, although Charlotte had heard quite a bit of grumbling and muttering from her colleagues about the endeavour being a waste of everyone's time, and that they had way better things they'd rather be doing. It was the bank holiday weekend and some of them were clearly planning to make their befriending visit as brief as possible, the length of a gulped-back cup of coffee by the sound of it, in order to make a break for the motorway and weekend plans elsewhere.

Charlotte had completely forgotten it was a bank holiday. It was only when her boss called out, 'See you all on Tuesday' before whizzing out of the building in a perfumed dash, that Charlotte clicked why everyone had been discussing their weekend activities in a way that they didn't usually.

Camping trips (ambitious, she thought, having seen the drizzly forecast), a spa weekend, an exclusive gourmet supper club night, visits to in-laws and siblings . . . everyone, it seemed, had lots to keep them busy over the next few days. Apart from Charlotte, obviously.

She pondered on this as she went home, picking up a bunch of velvety white roses (for Margot) and a microwave curry meal (for her), plus a bottle of New Zealand sauvignon blanc that was on special offer (definitely for her). Weekends were lonely enough anyway when you lived by yourself and didn't have any local friends, but when that weekend was increased by a whopping fifty per cent to become three whole days of emptiness . . . frankly, there wasn't enough cleaning in the world to fill that time. Not when you had a flat the size of hers, anyway. And look what had happened last weekend when she had braved it onto the pier only to end up in such an embarrassing situation with the man and his lost daughter!

Once back at SeaView House that afternoon, she slung her curry and wine in the fridge, thinking distractedly as she did so how her ex-husband Jim would have told her off for that particular combo. 'You're meant to have *beer* with curry, not wine!' he'd have said, shaking his head at her poor etiquette. Bit of a booze snob, Jim, really, now that she thought about it, whereas Charlotte was happy to have wine with anything, pretty much. She'd have wine with a plate of chips and beans if she felt like it, actually. She'd have wine with a nice sandwich and packet of crisps, even. And yes, okay, so when Kate had died and her breasts had swollen to beachball proportions, ginormous and tender and still hopefully producing milk that was no longer required, Charlotte had poured herself a glass of wine at breakfast one morning and proceeded to polish off most of a bottle by the time the postman arrived with yet more condolence cards.

They had been terrible days. The worst. Days she really shouldn't be dwelling on now either, when she was due to see Margot Favager again in five minutes. Come on, Charlotte. Pull yourself together. Onwards we trudge.

Spritzing on some perfume she peered into the mirror to reapply her lipstick – Margot was the sort of person who made you feel you should take care of these things – and caught her own gaze. Jim had fallen in love with her eyes, he'd always said. Big and brown and trusting; 'Don't give me those cow eyes now,' her mum had warned whenever Charlotte had gone begging for something as a child. It had been a while since she'd actually stared into them herself, she realized, her breath gently misting the mirror. She had avoided looking at her unhappy reflection after Kate had died because it had seemed as if there was nothing there behind her eyes any more. Now she practised a smile, realizing in the next moment that she had lipstick on her teeth. There –

see? Maybe smiling was good for something after all, she thought, wiping it off with a square of loo roll.

Deep breaths, she told herself as she headed up to the top floor a few minutes later. Everything would be okay. If you kept on saying it to yourself, you eventually believed it, according to the self-help articles her mum still emailed her.

'Ahh, Charlotte, it is marvellous to see you again. A sight for old eyes. Come in, come in,' said Margot when she answered the door. Today she was wearing a soft grey cashmere jumper with a boat neckline and mannish charcoal-grey trousers, as well as an eye-catching necklace of large round beads, like polished marbles, in ox-blood red. 'And what lovely flowers, that is so kind. Thank you. Now – actually . . .' Her eyes glittered but Charlotte couldn't read her expression. 'I will make us some tea, but I was wondering if you could help me a little. Like you said you could? A chore – is that the word?' She pronounced it 'shore' and it took Charlotte a second to register before she nodded. 'A very very small shore. Would you mind? I am sorry to be a trouble but . . .' She gave one of her elegant shrugs. 'You know, I am a dying old woman. And . . .'

'I don't mind at all – of course,' Charlotte said and then, feeling alarmed, asked, 'Are you feeling ill, though?' It was unnerving, just how much Margot went on about dying, in such a matter of fact way. When her grandmothers had died, she remembered them being very stoic and British about it, neither of them letting on that they were ill, practically until their last breaths were gasped. Margot, on the other hand . . . It was probably wrong to say that the woman was *milking* it but all the same, she couldn't help detecting a certain amount of relish in the drama of the situation. 'Should I call someone? A doctor, or – ?'

A certain haughtiness appeared on Margot's face at the mention of doctors. 'I am not dying *now*,' she corrected herself. 'And doctors know nothing, anyway. They are no good to me.'

'Okay.' Charlotte's heartrate subsided. 'So . . . what do you want me to do?'

Several minutes later, Charlotte was walking back up towards town with a very strange list. In Margot's sloping, curlicued handwriting were the following instructions.

1, Grey and Green – Figuier candle (ask for Johann)
2, Madame Chocolatier – 12 rose cremes (ask for Marc)
3, Cheese shop Western Road – Ami du Chambertin (ask for Emile)
4, Wine and Dine – bottle of Cornas Premices (ask for David) . . .

And on it went. Wine and chocolate and cheese, fancy toiletries and stationery – and with every shop, a person that she needed to deal with specifically. Funny how all of them were men, Charlotte thought to herself, frowning a little at the list and wondering if any of her fellow befrienders were having to run errands half so glamorous as these.

The first port of call was a posh homewares shop, everything tasteful and contemporary, soft music playing, hipster-looking assistants standing a respectful distance away while shoppers browsed. It was rather like doing the shopping challenge on *The Apprentice*, Charlotte thought, as she sought out Johann, and found him to be an incredibly beautiful young man of about twenty with eyelashes to die for, as well as extremely tight trousers. Trust Margot to have made a note of *his* name. With his help, they found the candle that had been requested, a Diptyque one, no less, that smelled utterly divine, and Johann assured her in his low sexy voice that he would add it to Madame Favager's account. Goodness. The whole thing felt extremely luxurious to Charlotte, who would never dream of spending so much money on something like a candle. *Money to burn?* her dad quipped sarcastically in her head, and a part of her couldn't help agreeing.

After thanking Johann, and trying not to gaze too impertinently at those extremely tight trousers, Charlotte tucked the tissue-wrapped purchase carefully into her bag and moved on to the next shop.

So this was how it felt to be Margot, Charlotte thought in amusement as she traversed the city, picking up one gorgeous item after another, being served by one dashing young man after the next. One item on her list wasn't even to buy anything, it was to pop into a flower shop in the Lanes and give Margot's best wishes to someone called Eric who – of course – turned out to be yet another model-type hottie. At the mention of Margot's name, he smiled in delight and pressed a small posy of violets into Charlotte's hand, from him to Margot. How the other half lived!

The last item on the list was a large cappuccino from Sea Blue Sky, the café nearest Dukes Square, 'and get yourself whatever you would like too, darling,' Margot had added. 'We are living dangerously today, eh? We are being the *most* extravagant.' She had winked. 'But for you, I will *make* a drink if you prefer. Of course.'

Charlotte shifted her bags onto one arm as she pushed open the door to the café. She had only walked past it before but it was very nice inside, with stylish decor and the pleasing smell of good coffee. There was a man with pink hair wearing a very smart pin-striped suit sitting at the first table, and on the next a young woman with a huge peroxide beehive hairdo and a lime-green mini-dress. Yes, Charlotte could see why Margot liked coming in here.

'Hi, what can I get you?' asked the man behind the counter when Charlotte went over.

'I'm looking for Ned, I've been sent here by Margot Favager . . .' she began but then her voice faltered as she realized she recognized him from somewhere. Rumpled hair, glasses, brown eyes – yes, she had seen that face before. But where had she met him? Then the penny dropped with an audible clang. It was the man from the pier. Shit! The actual same man from the pier, the one she'd screeched at like a deranged harpy, the poor dad she'd basically accused of neglecting his little daughters. ('I fort you was Mrs *Johnson*,' the girl said in her head, the memory still vivid of her tiny hand clasping Charlotte's.) Every cell in Charlotte's body urged her to bolt from the café, the way she'd bolted along the pier, barging through passers-by in her haste to escape. But her feet seemed locked to the floor, immovable, as a deep scarlet blush swept through her skin.

He was looking quizzically at her and then she saw a similar light of recognition dawn in his eyes. *Hey, aren't you that crazy woman?* 'Oh,' he said. 'Hello again.'

'Er . . .' she stammered, face burning. 'Um . . . Actually I've got to go,' she said, desperate to escape before another word could be said. 'Bye.' And she turned and hotfooted it out of there, heart pumping, adrenalin whizzing around her body, barely able to breathe until she was safely round the corner and out of sight.

'Charlotte! My goodness, you look exhausted, it was too many shores for you, I think,' exclaimed Margot when Charlotte returned to the flat a short while later, still flustered and pink in the face. 'I am sorry. I am selfish, *hein*? Too lazy. And now you suffer!'

Charlotte could take Margot's melodrama with a pinch of salt now at least and gave a smile. 'I'm fine, I'm not suffering at all,' she replied. 'Sorry I took so long,' she went on, holding the shopping bags aloft. 'I picked up the coffees from a different café to the one you said, I hope that's okay.' Now she was blushing wildly, hotter than ever as she followed Margot into the living room. *Don't ask me about it. Don't ask.* 'Where would you like me to put everything?'

Margot peered at her. 'You do not like my café?'

'Oh! I'm sure it's lovely, but . . .' Charlotte set the bags down, allowing her hair to swing forward, hiding her face. 'Well . . . It's a long story,' she said eventually when Margot showed no signs of letting her off the hook. She put the cardboard tray containing their cappuccinos on the table. 'It's complicated.'

'Ahh, a mystery!' Charlotte could feel Margot's gaze sharpening, interest piqued. 'But I can see it is not my business. It is fine. Did you enjoy . . . the other views I gave you, though?'

Charlotte laughed uncertainly. Did Margot mean what she thought she meant? 'What, the . . . um . . . the shop assistants?'

'Yes,' Margot replied. 'My God, they are nice, yes? Sexy. No, no,' she said, as Charlotte began unpacking the purchases. 'They are in fact for you. My treat. And now you know where I keep all my boyfriends also. Ha! I am joking. Unfortunately. Now, let me put our drinks into nice cups, and then we can talk.'

'You . . .' Charlotte couldn't quite get past what Margot had said several sentences ago. 'These things . . . seriously? They are for me?' The candle alone had been almost forty pounds and the bottle of wine just short of twenty. In all, there was almost one hundred pounds' worth of goods there. 'N-no,' she stuttered. 'I couldn't.'

'But of course you can. And you must! They are my gifts to you. I hope you like them.'

Charlotte's mouth was hanging open. 'But . . . Really? They are all lovely. And it's so incredibly generous. But . . .'

Margot wagged a finger. 'You always say you will spend money wisely, *hein*? But sometimes it is nice to be *unwise* with the money. To be reckless. And extravagant.' She patted Charlotte's arm. 'And don't forget the men. They are my favourites and now I have shared with you. That means we are friends, yes? Come.'

'Thank you,' Charlotte said, still finding it hard to summon the right words as she followed Margot into the living room. But why? she wanted to add but didn't quite dare. Why me? Why all of this? '*Thank you*,' was all she said again, though.

Margot waved away Charlotte's thanks. 'You are welcome,'

she said, and gestured for Charlotte to sit down. 'And here we are. Make yourself at home.'

Contrary to the pessimistic doom-laden forecast earlier that week, Saturday dawned bright and sunny, perfect for a bank holiday and the local radio presenters seemed able to burble on excitedly about nothing else as Charlotte sat down to eat her breakfast. Through her window she could see the syrupy morning light glinting from car windows below, and noticed how it scattered golden sparkles across the sea like confetti. The water looked bluer than she'd ever seen it; the rides on the pier were in full swing, the cafés were open for business and there were already hordes of people wrangling with deckchairs on the beach, setting up for a relaxing day ahead.

Last night, following her visit to Margot's, Charlotte had enjoyed the very good cheese after her dinner, had lit her beautiful scented candle and nibbled her expensive chocolate, and she'd felt . . . cheered. Tentatively better. She'd picked up a historical romance novel for the first time in ages and lost herself in its pages, letting the story pick her up and carry her far away to an era where men galloped around on horseback and rescued ailing damsels. (It was the sort of book that Jim – a reader of non-fiction and broadsheet newspapers – would have scoffed at but somehow that made it all the more enjoyable.) Then she'd gone to bed and slept deeply all night, and her first waking thought hadn't, for once, been despair. What was more, here she was now, looking out at the sunny world through her window and feeling as if maybe, just maybe, it was good to be alive on such a day.

Delicious cheese and a romantic hero and a cloudless sky, a kind neighbour making a fuss of her, reaching out to haul her out of her sadness . . . was that really all it took to make a woman feel vaguely human again? Grief had overwhelmed Charlotte for so long now; it had caused the unhappy unravelling of her marriage, it had stubbornly resisted the counselling and the pills, and she'd started to accept it as her default setting as if this was how life would be from now on. And yet . . . This morning she felt as if she could look the world in the eye without turning away. This morning she was thinking to herself that perhaps everything was bearable after all, that she might actually get through this period in her life if she just kept on looking straight ahead.

She drained her coffee and then grabbed her phone. No, she would *not* spend her weekend doing chores alone in the flat, she decided, typing a quick message. Yes, she *would* make the most of this unexpected shift in mood.

Hi Mum, sorry for the short notice. Don't suppose you're around today, are you? X

'Let me look at you. Oh! You look so *well*, darling. Doesn't she, Tony? And what a lovely surprise to hear from you. You're lucky because we'd been up Fenley Hill earlier where there's no reception, but we'd made a pit-stop in the village because there's that sweet little shop that sells home-made jam, do you remember? And I said to your dad, I'll just pop in, we're clean out of gooseberry, and then he said, was that your phone? And of course, it *was*, and it was you, and I was so pleased to get your text. Sit down anyway, take the weight off – Tony, why don't you get Charlotte a drink? What are you having? Look at me, on the cider – I said to your dad, *you're* driving us back, it's so warm I couldn't resist. Oh, it's good to see you, darling. How *are* you? I picked up some jam for you, by the way. Bramble jelly. I hope that's still your favourite.'

Never ones to stay indoors when the sun was shining, Charlotte's parents were already out and in their hiking boots when she had called earlier but thanks to the wonders of modern technology – and the jam-selling shop in Fenley village with good phone reception – here they were now, having arranged to meet in a pub for lunch and sitting at a weathered wooden table in the beer garden. Her mum might even pause for breath any second, you never could tell. 'I'm fine,' Charlotte said quickly, spotting her chance. 'Just a Diet Coke, please, Dad. Thanks.'

Her mum hugged her again as the two of them were left alone, and Charlotte breathed in the comforting scents of VO5 shampoo and Pears soap; her mum's unique signature fragrance. All of a sudden she was six years old and they were walking back from primary school together, hand in hand, while Charlotte's big brothers ran ahead. *Just us girls together*, her mum would say conspiratorially, and it had always made Charlotte feel special.

'It's good to see you too,' she said as they eventually drew apart. They had always been close, the two of them, and she knew her mum had been confused by Charlotte's abrupt decision to leave Reading, to unstitch her whole life there and start again. At moments like this, when she was back with her parents and felt so safe, so loved – the smiles on their faces when they had seen her walk into the pub! The rapturous way they'd fallen upon her! – she couldn't help feeling kind of confused by her decision too.

'What a treat, meeting up like this,' her mum replied, clasping a hand to her heart. 'Every time I drive past your old house I find myself slowing down and looking for you in there. You'd think I'd be over it by now, but no. Every time!'

Charlotte felt her smile slip. That house with the Winnie the Pooh decorations up in the nursery, she thought. The house she and Jim had bought as newly-weds, where she'd got pregnant and thrilled at her own expanding waistline. The place where she'd lain on the bed for days after the worst had happened, immobile, drowning in misery. She never wanted to see that house again, to be honest.

'And of course, the boys are around, and it's nice to see them but it's not as good as a daughter, obviously. It's nowhere near as—' She broke off hurriedly, realizing her mistake. *Don't mention daughters.* 'Well, it's lovely to see you,' she said again, squeezing Charlotte's hand for good measure.

'One Diet Coke, ice and a slice,' said Charlotte's dad Tony, reappearing at the table and setting a tall glass carefully on a coaster in front of her. (He had a thing about coasters and place mats. Every table, large or small, in their house was awash with them, even plastic tables where a cup of tea couldn't do any damage, however hard it tried. Even *outdoors*, in a pub garden, with a picnic table so old the wood had turned grey, he couldn't bear the thought of a water-ring.) 'And three menus.'

'Thanks, Dad.' This was the right decision, Charlotte thought, sipping her drink while a warm breeze ruffled her hair. This was *nice*. The pub garden was spacious, the grass a thick luxuriant green, a bird was cheeping nearby and the atmosphere was pleasantly somnolent as if nothing bad could ever happen here. They would have lunch and a good old chat and then drive back in convoy to her parents' cosy semi where the cats would roll on their backs like purring apostrophes at the sight of the prodigal daughter's return.

Tony cleared his throat and looked meaningfully at his wife. 'So have you . . . er . . . ?'

'No,' she said quickly, flashing him a look that Charlotte had seen many times before; a look that said quite plainly

Shut up and *Don't put your foot in it* and *For heaven's sake, man, think before you open that mouth of yours.*

'Ahh,' he said, lowering his gaze. He took a menu and began browsing studiously, as did Charlotte's mum.

Charlotte looked at them both and sighed, her feelings of contentment evaporating like a puddle in the sunshine. 'Go on, then. What is it?' One of her sisters-in-law was pregnant, at a guess. She had been dreading it; having the memory of Kate, her parents' first grandchild, usurped by another, healthier baby. As for having to be *happy* for them, play the doting aunty, attend the christening, first birthday party, first Christmas . . . she could feel a tightening in her throat at the thought. All those special occasions she had never got to enjoy with Kate. It was so unfair. How would she be able to stand it?

'It's nothing,' her mum said firmly. 'What are you going to have, then? The chicken and ham pie sounds good, doesn't it? I'd want chips with it, mind, not the sweet potato mash. I don't know about you, but I find it a bit poncey the way every pub seems to—'

'Mum. Don't. What is it that you're avoiding telling me?' Charlotte asked, trying to see past the dark lenses of her mum's sunglasses in order to meet her eye. 'Please. I'm not an idiot. I'm not a kid any more either. I can take it, whatever it is.'

'Well . . .' Her mum faltered. A hesitation, a loss for

words: this didn't happen very often. The pause was enough to immediately set alarm bells ringing in Charlotte's head.

'It's Jim,' her dad said, taking pity on his daughter.

'Jim?' Charlotte's head swivelled round. 'Is he all right?' She hadn't spoken to her ex for a while, she realized suddenly. Once she'd forced herself to finish with the drunk maudlin phone calls, he hadn't been in touch at all. Was he struggling to cope, like her? Trauma caught up with people at different rates, she knew. He'd been the strong one when it all happened; he'd propped Charlotte up like a crutch when she kept collapsing, an absolute rock at the funeral. Maybe the loss was only just hitting home now?

'He's met someone else,' her mum blurted out in a rush. 'I bumped into Sheila in Morrisons and she told me.' Her mouth buckled and she reached out for Charlotte's hand again, gripping it in her own. 'I'm sorry, darling. It's not what you expect to hear in the tinned goods aisle. I didn't know whether I should say anything or not.'

The words crashed against Charlotte like a wave against a sea wall. Jim had met someone else. Her husband – ex-husband – was now with another woman. Not struggling to cope at all, then – in fact quite the opposite; he had moved on, forgotten her, forgotten *them*.

Charlotte moistened her lips, trying to process the information, trying to gauge how she felt. Numb, mostly.

Stunned. She managed a shrug. 'It's okay,' she said even though she wasn't sure this was true.

Her parents exchanged a look. A look that told Charlotte there was more to come. *Are you going to break it to her or shall I?* that look asked. Oh no. What else? He hadn't gone and shacked up with one of Charlotte's friends, had he? He'd always had a not-so-secret soft spot for her friend Ruth – Charlotte had teased him about it in the past, back when things were still rock-solid between them, back when they were an ordinary couple and still laughed about silly stuff. Come to think of it, hadn't she just seen Ruth posting something on Facebook about a new bloke? 'Is it someone I know?' she asked before she could stop herself. Jim's mum Sheila would be over the moon if it *was* Ruth, she thought. Everyone loved pretty, clever Ruth. She could already see the wedding photos – second time lucky! – with Charlotte discreetly left off the guest list. *Sorry, but . . . you know. We didn't want to make you feel uncomfortable.* 'It's not . . . It's not Ruth, is it?' she blurted out.

'Ruth Collins? No!' her mum cried. 'She's dating some bigshot from London, according to Janice. I saw *her* in the Co-op.'

'Hotbeds of gossip, the supermarkets round our way,' Charlotte's dad joked nervously. He put down his menu and harrumphed. 'I'm going to have the shepherd's pie myself. Charlie, have you decided what you'd like, love?'

Her parents were so bad at pretending everything was

okay. Now Dad was saying something about the golf tourna-
ment he'd played in recently and Mum had taken off her
sunglasses and was polishing them on her sleeve. Charlotte
knew she had two choices – either to play along and remain
in blissful ignorance as to the full gory details around her ex
and his love life, or to risk further pain by insisting on tearing the lid right off this particular can of worms. She sighed
again, knowing that ignorance would only lead to paranoia,
imagining every last worst-case scenario long into the night.
'Go on,' she muttered. 'I know there's something else. Let's
just get it over with, shall we? Please.'

Her mum's lip wobbled. She looked genuinely unhappy
as she twisted the menu around awkwardly in her hands.
And then before anyone could utter another word, Charlotte
knew, she just knew, and her heart was racing, her blood
turning cold. *No*. Not that. Not yet. She couldn't bear to hear
the words said out loud, she realized; she had changed her
mind and didn't want to know any more. 'Actually –' she
began, but her mum was already speaking.

'They're having a baby.' Four words, like four punches to
the head. Wallop. 'It's all a bit of a rush, obviously – a surprise to everyone, Sheila said, but they're going ahead with
it. Due in the autumn. So . . .' She was trying to catch Charlotte's eye but Charlotte was having to concentrate very hard
on not howling out loud and could no longer see straight.
'So now you know.'

Chapter Fifteen

All Rosa could think about as she walked home on Saturday night were her feet. Her poor, aching, tired feet. She had just worked a fourteen-hour shift which had included a seven-course wedding breakfast plus evening buffet for two hundred and fifty people. She'd barely sat down once in that time. It was nights like this when she missed having a bath, easing herself into a tub of hot scented water and letting her tired limbs relax. She wasn't sure she could stand up long enough to manage a shower.

The moon was hidden, the sky dark as she picked her way along the seafront, the salty breeze fresh and cooling. And then over the rushing of the waves, she heard the unmistakable sound of male voices ahead, catcalling and jeering. She tightened her grip on her shoulder bag and felt in her pocket for her key, holding it ready to use as a weapon if need be. You could never be too careful.

Approaching Dukes Square, she could see a group of people had spilled out of the pub on the corner, including a woman who was slumped over the back of a parked Land Rover. One of the men was behind her making obscene thrusting motions and his mates all roared their approval. Oh no. Was the woman okay? Should she be calling the police?

'Hey,' called Rosa, drawing nearer still and seeing that the woman seemed oblivious to the mob behind her. Her head was resting on the spare tyre as if it was a pillow, her long brown hair fanning around her shoulders. 'What's going on?'

The men turned towards her, their faces half lit from the street lamps and the pub behind them. There was something menacing about them all standing there with the woman so vulnerable in their sights. 'Lady's had a bit much to drink,' one of them offered, to a chorus of sniggering.

The woman, as if registering them at last, raised a hand in the air. 'Jush having a resh,' she slurred. 'Jush a liddle resh.'

Ignoring the men, Rosa went over to her. 'Are you okay?' she asked. 'Do you want me to help you get home?'

The woman stared unseeingly at her. There was mascara on her cheeks and even though the light was dim, Rosa could tell she'd been crying. 'My hushband,' she said haltingly, her breath sour as if she'd been sick, her voice small.

Rosa made shooing motions at the men then turned back. 'Your husband?' she repeated encouragingly. 'Do you want me to call him?'

The woman's mouth quivered and Rosa stepped back instinctively in case she was about to throw up again.

'Heesh . . .' she said, tears filling her wide brown eyes. 'Heesh met someone else. And . . .' One tear plopped onto the spare tyre where it glistened in the streetlight, then her gaze met Rosa's, anguished and broken. 'And they're having a *baby*.'

Oh God, the despair on the woman's face, the misery. 'They're having a *bay-bee*,' one of the men behind them mocked, and Rosa swung around, fists clenched, fierce with rage. 'Are you lot still here? You should be ashamed of yourselves,' she said, advancing on them. 'Go on, sod off. Leave her alone.'

To her relief they melted away into the pub, and she turned back to the sobbing woman. 'Come on,' she said, sliding an arm around her in order to peel her off the Land Rover. 'Let's get you home. Where do you live?'

Staggering a little as she found her balance, the woman pointed unsteadily up the hill. 'This way,' she said. Her hands were grazed as if she had fallen over and skinned them at some point in the evening. 'Number eleven.'

Rosa did a double-take. 'Eleven? Dukes Square? Same as me,' she said, and heaved the woman along in a slow, wavering stumble. 'I'm Rosa, Flat 1.'

'Oh fuck,' said the woman, stopping suddenly. 'Sorry.'

'It's all right,' Rosa said, misunderstanding. 'Look, we've all been there. I could tell you a few stories about my vile—'

'No,' the woman said urgently, struggling out of Rosa's grasp. 'I mean, I need to—'

And then she was sick all over the pavement.

Some time later, once they had finally made it up the hill to SeaView House, and they had agreed what complete bastards men could be, and when Rosa had managed to get Charlotte (as her name turned out to be) safely into her flat, leaving a pint glass of water and a sick bowl by the bed for good measure, she was able to sink under her own duvet at last. Honestly, a broken heart could do brutal things to a woman, she thought. It had reduced poor Charlotte to weeping and puking in the street, it had sent Rosa running from London with everything she owned in the back of her car. 'I don't even love him any more,' Charlotte had wailed tearfully, halfway up the road. 'I just feel *sad*.' Yes. Rosa got that. Feeling as if you were over an ex – as she did too, these days – didn't prevent you from being emotional about them. Look at her and her Ann-Marie-stalking, for example. What did that say about her?

Rolling over, she closed her eyes, remembering the steely resolve that had filled her as she saw the Oxford train pulling out of Paddington station, carrying Max – David – off to his wife and children. As soon as she'd arrived back at his flat, she'd got straight to work, determined to find out just what the hell was going on. Out came all of Max's clothes from the wardrobe and drawers, their pockets checked one by one. Out came his sports bag, his laptop case, the spare suitcase – all emptied and looked through in case they doubled up as hiding places. Out came the paperwork in their spare room-cum-office, dumped on the floor so that she could scan everything for evidence. David, David . . . where are you, David?

She tipped up a box of photos, turning her head away from all the smoochy coupley holiday shots of the two of them looking so happy together, she peered under his side of the bed and emptied the contents of his bedside cabinet. There must be something. Was she going mad? There had to be *something*!

There was only one drawer in his desk that she hadn't got into yet – the top one that he kept locked. She had never seen the key to it before, never thought to pay much attention, really. Until now, that was. And now she really, really wanted to see inside that locked drawer of the beautiful old oak desk he'd apparently inherited from his grandfather (another lie, probably). Having exhausted all other places to look, and not having a clue where the key might be, she had no other choice. She took a hammer to it and smashed through the lock. The wood made a satisfying splintering sound as it fractured, then she wrenched out the drawer. A pile of papers fluttered to the carpet, letters mostly, addressed to Mr David Chandler. Gotcha.

After that, it had been easy. She'd searched for David and Ann-Marie Chandler online and up had popped Ann-Marie's happy little Facebook page, unlocked, unguarded, with photo after photo of the four of them and their idyllic rural life. The kids helping with the Christmas decorations (adorable), the dog not helping with the Christmas decorations (also adorable), chit-chat about Josh's carol concert and little Mae's first wobbly tooth, and David, handsome, laughing David, cheering on Josh at some kids' football match, hoisting his little girl on his shoulders, one big strong arm around pretty doting Ann-Marie. And oh, it was just unbearable, it was impossible to see any more, because the tears were streaming down her face and her throat felt raw from wailing.

David bloody Chandler, and his whole other life. How she hated him!

'How are you doing? Here, I brought you some biscuits and magazines; this is the one that Georgie writes for, look. Have you met her? She's from one of the flats upstairs.' It was the bank holiday Monday and Rosa had come to visit Jo who was still languishing in hospital. Bea had texted that morning to say that Gareth was taking her out to see some cousins and would be gone ALL DAY and could she please, please pop in and say hello to her mum for her? It was the first time Rosa had seen her neighbour since staying in her flat, and it was hard to equate the pale woman in the bed with the exuberant hedonist she'd glimpsed in all her photos. 'Oh, and here's your post,' she added.

'Thank you,' said Jo, shuffling so that she was more upright in the bed. She still looked wan and wrung-out but there was more colour in her cheeks at least, just a tinge. It had been over ten days now since she'd first been rushed into the hospital and, according to the nurse, the infection she'd picked up had been pretty aggressive. Still, she was responding well to the antibiotics at last apparently, and hoping to come home before too much longer. 'Ooh, are those home-made?' she asked, perking up as she unwrapped the foil parcel Rosa had plopped into her lap and saw the chocolate-chip cookies inside. 'Bea's been telling me what a good cook you are. She seems to think you're opening your own restaurant any day soon.'

Rosa laughed. 'Um . . . Not quite,' she said. 'Learning the trade at the Zanzibar first. Lesson one, if the head chef throws a spatula at you, duck.'

'Shit, really? That sounds . . . kind of abusive,' Jo said, delving a hand into the cookies. 'Well, these look fabulous, thank you. Help yourself. How is Bea, anyway? Is she getting on any better with Gareth, do you know?'

Rosa hesitated before answering. During the week, Gareth and Bea were shuttling between his place and Jo's flat, to make things easier for Bea, and she'd heard a few arguments through the wall, and the occasional slamming of doors. That said, he'd also knocked at her place a couple of times, to ask (rather bashfully) if she could make some suggestions for Bea's food tech homework, and, on another occasion, about how to make porridge, because apparently Bea kept telling him his attempts were abysmal. 'He seems perfectly nice to me, but I'm not sure how well they're hitting it off,' she said diplomatically in the end.

'Hmm,' said Jo, chewing a mouthful of cookie. 'They've had a difficult few years really. I was hoping this might bring them back together but maybe not.'

It was on the tip of Rosa's tongue to ask what had happened but politeness got the better of her. 'She seems a great girl, Bea,' she said instead, her own words rather taking her aback. It was true though: these days she found Bea amusing and entertaining, a different character altogether from the hostile, angry person Rosa had first encountered. But then again, Rosa realized, she herself had changed too. No longer the same recluse she had been at the start of the year, no longer so determined to keep other people at bay. 'I love how passionate she gets about the injustices of the world,' she went on, 'how she sees everything in black and white.' *Why don't you . . . just be a chef?* Bea had asked, as if this solution was blindingly obvious.

Jo smiled faintly. 'I think that's part of the problem with Gareth,' she admitted. 'We fell out quite badly after I took

Bea to India against his will, and . . . well, things went a bit wrong. He was angry, I was defensive . . . and Bea basically took my side, Team Mum.'

'And because she was Team Mum, that meant she couldn't be Team Dad at the same time?'

'Exactly. Even though, actually, Gareth was well within his rights to be angry with me, because in hindsight I can see that what I did was selfish and impulsive and . . .' She grimaced, her voice trailing away, eyes downcast. 'Anyway. We all make mistakes.'

'We totally do,' Rosa said, with feeling. She'd certainly made enough of her own.

'I was all over the place at the time, that was the thing, I didn't realize . . . Anyway,' Jo said again, sighing. 'The ironic thing is that Gareth and I get on fine now, there's no friction any more. We split up because I realized – well, not to put too fine a point on it, that I preferred women. I can't imagine that would do much for any bloke's pride, but he got over it, we're mates, we've moved on. It's just Bea . . . It's like she made her mind up about him three years ago and won't budge. She thinks he doesn't care about her, so she rejects him, and then feels even worse when he doesn't come running after her. I don't know. It's tough, isn't it? Life, I mean. Families. Loving people.'

'Yeah,' said Rosa, remembering poor Charlotte on Saturday night, down there at rock bottom with her grazed hands and her tear-stained face. Remembering herself too, broken-hearted as she drove out of London, doing her best not to look back at what she was leaving behind. And Jo, and Bea, and Gareth . . . 'It's tough, all right.'

There was a golden wedding anniversary party at the hotel that night: cheesy music, endless canapés, a huge cake, and lots of people celebrating together in their best clothes. 'Thank God for the sound of laughter, I was starting to think everyone was miserable,' Rosa commented to Natalya as they took a break outside. They could hear the noise of the party floating through an open window, and then wild cheering. Perhaps the cake was being cut, or maybe the golden couple themselves had finally taken to the dancefloor. (Earlier there had been only one big-haired guy strutting about there, a handsome preening sort of man who was either already out of it, or had taken the song 'He's the Greatest Dancer' to be his personal theme tune.) 'At least there are still some happy people left in the world,' she added with a shrug.

'Tchah,' said Natayla scornfully. There was something generally glum about her colleague's disposition, Rosa thought. She had a sallow complexion, a great bush of brown hair that was messily tied back, and frown lines that seemed permanently etched into her forehead. 'They are happy *now* yes, because they have our food, and they are pissed and they are all together. But underneath they are miserable too. I tell you.'

Trust Natalya to bring a person back down to earth. Her words did make Rosa think, though. It was true, in a sense, that you could engineer some bonhomie and happiness, however fleeting, through food and wine and company. She thought how much she'd always enjoyed throwing dinner parties in the past, getting people together around a table. The world definitely seemed better when you were in a group, bellies as full as your wine glasses.

'What are you thinking?' Natalya asked, scrutinizing her. 'Your face is frowning.'

'Oh, nothing much,' Rosa said, draining her coffee and wincing. She really had to stop making it so head-bangingly strong. 'I was just thinking maybe I'd . . .'

'Oi! Are you two time-wasters ever going to finish yacking?' And there was Brendan, right on cue, yelling out of the door at them. 'Get a move on, there's work to do in here.'

'Work,' Natalya grumbled, stubbing her cigarette against the wall. 'Always the bloody work with that man.' She raised her voice. 'We are coming!'

I was just thinking maybe I'd throw a dinner party. Rosa finished her own sentence in her head, as she and her colleague made their way back inside. A dinner party for her neighbours. *Hark at you! a voice in her head scoffed. Getting sociable all of a sudden, aren't we, inviting the rest of the world in for a change!* But why not? It might be just what they all needed, her included. And while it was all very well being receptive to joy, as the fortune teller had advised, sometimes you had to try and share it around with others, too.

HELLO! My name is Rosa and I live in Flat 1. I've been here a few months now and have been working such unsociable hours I've hardly met any of you. But that's about to change! Would you like to come round for dinner? I am training as a chef and would love the chance to practise . . . you would be doing me a favour, really. If you are free this Friday evening at eight p.m., please come along, it would be great to get to know as many of you as possible.

Let me know either way by knocking on my door to say hello or by leaving me a note in reply. And do also let me know if you have any dietary restrictions to help me decide on a menu.

Hope to see you on Friday!

Love Rosa x

Chapter Sixteen

'You busy today, darling?' Viv's voice came down the phone. It was the morning after the ill-fated Stonefield trip and Georgie was still in bed, having slept through Simon's departure for work. This was probably just as well, seeing as he'd been in a thunderous mood ever since vile Chloe had gone and grassed her up in front of everyone. 'Um . . .' she said, wondering what Viv's question might be leading to. Maybe some feat of telepathy had compelled her editor to send her to try out a relationship counselling session. Frankly Georgie could do with all the help she could get right now, if she ever hoped to thaw the icy mood currently crackling around her boyfriend. *How could you do that to me?* he'd said on reading her problem page. It made her cringe even now.

'Only I was meant to be doing an interview but I've hurt my back,' Viv was saying in her ear. 'Can barely move. Anyway the job's yours if you want to earn some extra cash. Interested?'

Mere moments earlier, Georgie had been squinting at her

bank balance online and trying not to vomit in fear (she so shouldn't have bought all those clothes with the girls on Saturday) and therefore this could not have been a more welcome question. 'Of course,' she replied at once, then felt bad for sounding so eager. 'I mean – are you okay? Is someone looking after you?'

Viv barked a laugh. 'No. But I'm hoping to survive the day. All right, got a pen? It's the House of the Fallen Women – have you heard of it?'

'No,' Georgie admitted, frowning. 'Fallen Women? That sounds a bit archaic.'

'Yeah, it is. It's a big old Victorian house out along the coast that was an actual home for so-called fallen women, a hundred years or so ago. Unmarried mothers, women of the night, any destitute woman, down on her luck, basically,' Viv said. 'Oof. Ow. Jesus.'

'Are you all right?'

'Just the – ow – fucking sofa,' Viv said irritably. She must be one of those people who got very bad-tempered when they felt rough, Georgie decided. Simon was exactly the same. When he'd had the flu last winter, she'd come in to find him watching an old *Tom and Jerry* cartoon and calling Jerry an annoying little shit. 'What? I hate rodents,' he'd said defensively when she'd started laughing at him. 'Tom should rip his stupid smirking head off and be done with it.'

'So the house became derelict some time ago,' Viv went

on, 'back when women were no longer expected to feel shame for circumstances out of their control, and when better resources became available. In recent years, it's been squatted by a load of women who've used it as a refuge and drop-in centre; have you seriously never heard of it? They've got a good activist scene going on there. They call themselves the House of Women now – no longer "fallen", see.'

'Cool,' said Georgie, although the closest she'd ever come to being involved with any kind of activist scene was when she had started a petition about one of the libraries closing down, two towns away from where she worked. Things had been so cosy up in safe happy Stonefield, her social conscience had become rather dusty through its lack of use.

'Yeah. Well, it was, anyway. But now the site has been bought by some rich developer and they're all getting turfed out,' Viv said grimly. 'Only they're not going without a fight, of course. They're determined to stay and preserve a piece of the city's history, particularly in terms of women's history. And that's where you come in.'

'You want me to go and interview them?' Georgie's eyes lit up. This *did* sound like a good story, far more interesting than ordinary local news items. Proper journalism! She could go and stand in solidarity with these women, give them a voice in the magazine, maybe even help them make banners . . .

'You got it, kid. They want to spread word of their campaign out to the public, as well as to local historians and women's groups, anyone who might be able to help them. So I want you to go there and meet Tasha and Cleo, who are part of the collective, to find out more. I'm sending along a photographer too. Would you be able to do eleven o'clock this morning? The site is out in the Ovingdean direction.'

Georgie gulped. It was already half-past nine and she was still wearing her pyjamas, the laptop on her knee in bed. She needed to shower and blow-dry her hair and try to find some clothes that might make her look like a serious interviewer as well as find this house, wherever it might be. 'Absolutely,' she said with as much confidence as she could muster. She would do it for the women, she vowed, putting the phone down and leaping out of bed.

It was only as she was turning off the main road a short while later and up towards what looked like a building site that Georgie felt the first warning prickles of something being amiss, her sixth sense telling her that life might be playing a trick on her. Then, as she slowed to read some hoardings proclaiming the new development due to spring into life there by the new year, the horrible feeling of premonition grew stronger. *Macaulay Developments*, proclaimed the company name above the computer-generated image. *Coming soon: a luxury 5-star hotel with breathtaking views!*

She had seen that image before on Simon's laptop, on

print-outs spread across their kitchen table; she knew that name from the letters and contract that had plopped through their letterbox in Stonefield. Because, as bad luck and shit-stirring Fate would have it, this redevelopment was the very same one that Simon was working on; the hotel he had so painstakingly designed, whose progress he was overseeing. This place was why the two of them were in Brighton at all.

Oh knickers, she thought, braking to a complete stop, and remembering his comments the other week about pro-testors on site, whipping up opposition to the build. By send-ing her here to interview those same protestors, Viv had unwittingly given Georgie a whole new brick to lob against her increasingly fragile relationship. 'No more secrets,' Simon had said to her crossly after the excruciating *Hey Em* letter reveal. 'I promise!' she'd cried in reply. 'Cross my heart and hope to die!' But now what was she getting herself into?

As she took a right turn and went through some open gates onto the site itself, she saw the extent of the building work that was already taking place. Although the old Vic-torian house had been cleverly incorporated into the design, the main shell of the hotel was going up a short distance away; gigantic steels being manoeuvred into place by a team in hard hats and a yellow JCB, while an excavator was noisily flattening the land around it. A massive car park in the making, she thought, seeing it ripping up turf, soil speck-ling the air. There were two Portakabins at the side of the site and Georgie hunched low in the car as she drove past, wondering if her beloved was currently inside one of them. Imagine the look on Simon's face if he walked out and saw her on his territory – he'd probably assume she'd come to appease him by bringing something nice for his lunch. How his jaw would drop when he realized she was actually going in to meet with the women's group. *You traitor, George. What the hell . . . ?*

As she neared the Victorian house, she was able to read the banners swathing its exterior. SAVE THE HOUSE, SAVE THE WOMEN, read one. DON'T BULLDOZE HISTORY, pleaded another. The door and windowframes had been painted in purple, white and green – suffragette colours – and someone had stuck faces of women and children at each window, some wearing mobcaps, as if representing former residents gazing out. Carved into the stone above the front door were the words *IN THIS HOUSE YOU SHALL FIND MERCY*, and Georgie felt unexpectedly moved as she parked the car.

Outside, you could still hear the rumble of traffic from the main road below, the crash and rush of the sea beyond that further still, but there was birdsong up here too, wild flowers in the hedgerow, and a long lush lawn in front of the building. Georgie couldn't help thinking of all those women who'd come to this place before her – lonely, desperate women, perhaps with a child on one hip, a hand on a swelling belly, an ache in their hearts. The house must have been a beacon of hope for its broken, luckless residents all those years ago. The stories those walls could tell; the women and children who'd sheltered within, the kindness and comfort they must have hungered for, and hopefully found. Then she imagined the bulldozers coming in and knocking the whole thing down, the air thick with brick dust, a piece of history reduced to rubble. 'A bunch of sanctimonious twats with nothing better to do,' Simon had scathingly called the protestors. Was it sanctimonious to want to protect a building which had been important to so many people, though? she wondered, ringing the old-fashioned doorbell. Was it really so wrong to care?

Two women appeared at the door moments later: one slender and ethereal in a white column dress and bare feet, the other stockier with black jeans and a black T-shirt with some band logo Georgie had never heard of, hair in ginger bunches and her nose pierced. 'Georgie? Hi, I'm Tasha and this is Cleo,' said Ginger Bunches, her piercing glittering silver in a shaft of sunlight. 'Thanks for coming. We've set up in the library, it's along here. Follow us!'

Georgie hadn't been sure what to expect in terms of the women's centre when Viv had given her the brief that morning – she'd imagined it might have a studenty kind of vibe, perhaps, with posters and daubed slogans everywhere, the smell of mildew, an angry sort of militancy – but she was proved wrong almost immediately. Instead, she found herself stepping into an elegant hallway, painted a soft calm grey, with a central staircase sweeping up ahead. Light spilled through the generous-sized windows, and from distant rooms she could hear the sound of conversation, the burble of a radio, the occasional laugh. It was more country-house hotel than shoestring amateur-hour, she thought, gazing up at the high ceiling, and around at the colourful tapestries on the walls – one reading 'Welcome' in ten or so different languages – and arty black and white framed photographs of women and children. 'It's so peaceful in here,' she said. It was on the tip of her tongue to blurt out how much she'd love to come and stay until she realized how crass a comment that was. Like any woman ever *wanted* to go to a refuge.

'It's a sanctuary,' agreed Cleo, who had long dark hair and a soft sweet voice.

'So we've got the therapy rooms along here,' Tasha said, gesturing as she led them down a corridor past a series of doors. 'We have a couple of counsellors who help with emotional issues, and a lawyer who comes in one afternoon a week for more practical problems. The rooms can be used for meditation or group counselling too, whatever's needed.'

'And people can still stay here as temporary residents?' Georgie asked, scribbling a couple of notes as she followed. 'Or are you more of a drop-in centre now?'

'Women can stay,' Cleo said. 'Any woman, whatever her circumstances, if we have the space, she's welcome. The bedrooms are upstairs.'

They had paused in front of a door marked 'Library' but Tasha was pointing further down the corridor. 'Our kitchen is along there – plus the vegetable garden, what's left of it – and there's also a children's play room and an art room, all of which we can show you later. The library is a quiet area, where people can work or just sit and read any of the books in our collection. It's also where we keep our archive – come and have a look.'

An hour or so later, Georgie said her goodbyes and wandered back to the car, her mind buzzing with all that she'd seen, with the numerous women she'd met and spoken to. Some were victims of domestic violence who didn't want their photographs taken, some were volunteers who mucked in while their children were at school; there was one beautiful older woman she saw with long white hair in a plait and the kindest face who had been locked out of her house two days ago by her abusive husband and didn't have anywhere else to go. Maybe they'd felt themselves to have 'fallen' once upon a time – hadn't everyone – but these women had helped each other back up again, given one another their dignity back, and good on them.

The archive had been fascinating too – documents dating

from over one hundred and twenty years ago, listing the women who had come seeking shelter in the house, with their names, ages and occupations. Elsie Marks, housemaid; Martha Cartwright, governess; Florence Henry, seamstress; name after name, woman after woman, their arrivals charted in sloping black ink. There were some grateful letters stored in the archive, some from benefactors, who had originally been helped by the house and whose fortunes had greatly improved upon leaving. 'I was going to ask where your funding came from,' Georgie said, leafing through. 'Are you a registered charity, or do you rely on wealthy donors, or . . . ?'

'We ask the women to contribute if they can,' Cleo replied.

'Not everyone who suffers domestic abuse is poor,' Tasha said, arching an eyebrow. 'It can happen to anyone, even the richest person.'

This element of the house had been sobering – that there still had to be safe places set up for women, that abuse and cruelty were still going on – but the visit, overall, was incredibly inspiring. These women were tremendous! she kept thinking in awe. They were strong, tireless, compassionate. In fact, she was starting to feel bad about how little she did for others, how that very morning she'd been loafing around in her pyjamas, until Viv's call to action.

Neutral and professional, Georgie reminded herself, as she made her way back to the front door, visit over. Her job was to present the facts rather than take sides – but how would that even be possible when fundamentally she loved what the women were doing and was wholeheartedly behind them? She had seen for herself how the developers had carved into their beautiful kitchen garden. 'Out of spite,' Cleo had said, voice trembling, 'when they're not even planning to do anything in this area.' She had heard, too, the builders' catcalls and derogatory remarks when one of the residents went out to peg up some washing. 'And this used to be the one place women could feel protected from wankers like that,' Tasha said, bristling with rage as she defiantly gave the builders the Vs, to a round of jeering in return. 'The one refuge they could come to, and be healed. Now we have to put up with these dickheads, trying to bully us out, and they don't seem to care.'

'I'll tell your story, I'll do what I can,' Georgie promised them, as they said goodbye. Then she had to walk right past Simon's car in the car park and immediately felt like the most double-dealing girlfriend in the world. But she cared about this place now, that was the problem; she agreed with these women rather than Simon's hotel. Plus, she was itching to write up a proper piece like this, a serious campaigning story rich with history and injustice, rather than an agony column.

No more secrets, warned Simon in her head as she unlocked the car and she sighed. No more secrets, she had promised.

But if she told him what she wanted to do, it might be the end of them. Was any story worth that?

'This is what you call a no-win situation,' she complained to the green-haired gonk as she clambered into the driver's seat. 'Wouldn't you say?'

As usual, the gonk didn't deign to reply, merely smiling its mysterious beatific smile back at her in response. Its bloody useless and unhelpful smile, frankly. 'Fat load of good you are,' Georgie muttered, releasing the handbrake and turning the car around. 'I'll just deal with this myself then, shall I?'

Chapter Seventeen

The day Charlotte met Jim, she'd recently moved into a damp basement flat in west Reading which had a tiny court-yard garden. Charlotte had been much more of an optimist back then, a romantic even, capable of projecting visions of domestic beauty and wonder onto the most tired cold rooms and cat-shit-decorated flowerbeds – hence she'd slaved tire-lessly, slapping paint onto the walls, running up curtains for the windows and buying a load of bargain cushions and throws to brighten up the living room and bedroom. It was a veritable transformation, though she said so herself.

Now for the garden, she'd thought, driving to the nearest garden centre, imagining the small narrow flowerbeds a riot of colour come the summer months: sunflowers as tall as she was, scented roses and hollyhocks and carnations bring-ing in bees and butterflies from miles around. No matter that she'd never planted so much as a cress seed in her life, by the time she'd finished with it, the tiny outdoor space would be a wildlife *haven*, just wait, she thought, as she parked the car. And definitely not just a haven for all the shitting cats in the neighbourhood either.

All this home and garden improvement, it did really make you feel like a grown-up. A proper job-and-mortgage grown-up, who took control of their own life, who made things happen, who paid bills and stripped wallpaper and owned their own new drill bits and garden tools. Well . . . so she thought anyway, but then she'd hauled her trolley back to the car and realized she couldn't actually lift all the heavy compost bags she'd just bought into the boot. Er . . . Ahh. Now what? A strapping male assistant had lumped them onto the trolley in the first place but it had somehow slipped her mind that she would have to then a) heave them into her own car and also b) heave them out again when she got home, not to mention down the side alley and into her actual garden. Oh dear. And now she felt really stupid and feeble, and if there was one thing positive-thinking Charlotte hated, it was feeling stupid and feeble.

'Do you want a hand, there?' A tall man with a round smiling face who was loading what appeared to be a small tree into his own boot, two cars along, took pity on her thankfully.

'Um . . . Yes, please.' Charlotte blushed, embarrassed by her own weediness. She would drive straight home and do twenty arm-trembling press-ups in her newly decorated living room so that this never happened again, she vowed.

'Thank you so much,' she said as he lugged everything off her trolley, even the plant pots and packets of seeds (she could manage to lift *them* up, fine! she wanted to exclaim), and slotted them all neatly into her boot. 'That's really kind.'

'Not a problem,' he said, wiping his hands on his jeans and smiling at her. 'And you've got someone at home who can lift them all out again, I take it?'

'Um . . .' she said again, hesitating for a second. Of course there was nobody but her, unless she asked the rather grumpy guy from upstairs to help, she supposed. It was him or the athletic woman next door who was always coming back from a run when Charlotte left the house for work in the morning – she could probably heave up a bag on each shoulder, she seemed so fit. 'Not really,' she confessed. 'I can get my dad to come over and help though, so it's not a big deal.'

'Or I could follow you back and unload them for you too?' he asked. He had chestnut-brown hair and a boyish sort of face, she noticed; one of those men where you could see exactly how they must have looked as an eight-year-old, with freckles across the bridge of the nose and ears just verging on being a bit juggy. He was actually kind of cute, now that she thought about it. 'I promise I'm not a weirdo or anything. And obviously if you live in Glasgow or some other faraway place then I realize that's not exactly practical . . .'

'I'm just round the corner,' she told him, suddenly

breathless. There was something so competent and . . . well, *manly* about him, she felt fluttery, as if she had been flung straight into her very own romance novel (even if it *was* only in the rather unsexy setting of the garden centre car park). 'Would you mind? I could make you a coffee to say thank you . . .'

'A coffee? Now you're talking,' he said and stuck out his lovely big manly hand. 'I'm Jim.'

'Charlotte,' she said, blushing wildly.

'Wagons roll!' he said, with a grin.

The news about Jim, his new girlfriend and their even newer *baby* had quite knocked Charlotte for six. She'd done her best to keep up appearances with her parents after their bomb-shell but the moment she'd been in her car, driving back to Brighton, she had cried and cried, hot anguished tears pouring down her face. It wasn't fair. It just wasn't *fair*. She kept imagining Jim with his hand proudly on another woman's tummy, the two of them going to ante-natal classes together and making plans. She remembered how, back in the day, she and Jim had transformed their spare room into the baby's room one rainy weekend, how optimistic they had felt with their paint rollers and newspaper on the floor, how excited and joyful. For a wild moment, she had considered swinging the car around and heading back to Reading in order to stake out the happy couple, to park in front of their house to

watch Jim with his new girlfriend, whilst digging her fingernails into her palm and crying. Then she imagined their pitying looks if they noticed her – *Oh dear. Is that your ex, the one
who went off the rails? Not taking it well, is she? Poor Charlotte.
If only she could find someone and be happy, like us!* – and her
heart hardened. No. She would not wear her pain like a
badge. Not in front of them anyway.

Although, in hindsight, she probably shouldn't have gone
out and got paralytic, puking-in-the-street drunk, either. Nor
had to be helped up the street by the woman from the flat
downstairs for that matter.

Poor Charlotte. She really is taking it hard, isn't she?

Taking it hard and still making a fool of herself, yep. One
step forward, two steps back. She had ventured down to
clear the air with the agonizingly kind woman from Flat 1 –
Rosa – several times, but her downstairs neighbour always
seemed to be out, and so she'd had to leave a bunch of apology flowers outside her door in the hope that it would do
in the meantime. Perhaps she was avoiding her, peering
through the spyhole and deliberately not answering. Or so
Charlotte might have thought, had a dinner invitation not
been slid under her door a few days later. She didn't know
whether to laugh or cry when she read it. So now she had to
face this woman across a dinner table and make polite conversation! Was Fate ever going to give her a break?

★

Before she could gear herself up for the dinner party on Friday night, there was her weekly afternoon call on Margot upstairs to catch up on, though. With a box of her neighbour's favourite perfumed tea in her handbag as she climbed the stairs, Charlotte wondered if the older woman would have any chores lined up for her this afternoon. Another hotties' tour around town, perhaps? Or tea and cakes, with Margot's inimitable conversation swinging rapidly from the possibility of her death to Charlotte's personal life. *Only one way to find out*, she thought, knocking at the door.

Margot answered in a black silk dressing gown, rubbing her eyes and looking pale.

'Oh gosh, are you not well? Can I do anything to help?' Charlotte asked in concern.

'It is just a migraine,' Margot replied, wincing. 'Stupid migraine. They come sometimes and *pouf* – then I must sleep. So I am sorry. No tea and talking today. No shores. But wait –' She padded along the hall, her small white bare feet making her look surprisingly vulnerable. 'I have actually one shore. One small shore.' She returned with her old-fashioned clasp purse and opened it, her fingers struggling a little with the stiff fastening. 'Here,' she said, drawing out a five-pound note. 'Today's shore – you must go to the café, remember the nice café I like from last week? Go there and have a coffee. Ask for Ned.'

Charlotte felt her shoulders sink. 'Oh. But . . .' she said, not taking the note. 'I mean . . . That's very nice of you, but I'm not sure—'

'Because he has been *asking* about you. He say, who is that girl who came in for you? What is her name? I think he likes you. Do you like him?'

Whoa. Even when she was in the midst of a paralysing migraine, Margot still managed to catch Charlotte off-guard with her rapid-fire line of questioning. 'Well . . .' she said, then sighed. Time to put this one firmly to bed, she decided, and not in the way Margot was hoping either. 'I'm sure he's very nice but, actually, I'm not sure he *does* like me. I made a bit of a fool of myself in front of him. Twice now. It was kind of awkward.'

Margot raised a shoulder, shrugging off Charlotte's feebleness. 'He *does* like you,' she insisted. 'He had that look in his eye. And I know that look of a man.'

Charlotte didn't doubt the latter for a minute but was determined to set her neighbour straight on the former. 'Look or no look, I think he might already be with someone anyway. He definitely has a couple of kids. He was probably just being polite.'

Margot shook her head a fraction, wincing at the movement. 'No. Not with someone. He tell me, very sad, his wife die three years ago. They ran the café together, you see. Now it is only him. So.' She nodded meaningfully and placed the five-pound note into Charlotte's hand, and then wrapped

Charlotte's fingers around it before she could protest. 'You go. That is your shore. He is waiting for you. And have a very nice time.'

Charlotte's mouth dropped open. Her eighty-something-year-old neighbour was totally setting her up here, with the very man she wanted to avoid. What was the world coming to, when eighty-something-year-old neighbours set you up? 'Right,' she said weakly, wondering if there was any point in trying to get out of this. She was starting to wonder if Margot's 'migraine' even existed, or if it was all part of some devious matchmaking plan.

'And now, I must sleep. My poor head,' Margot said, as if reading Charlotte's suspicious thoughts. 'I am sorry not to be going to the dinner tonight. And I am sorry not to chat today, darling. I enjoy our chats.'

'Me too,' Charlotte said. Despite her misgivings at being manipulated into a potentially humiliating situation she found herself leaning forward impulsively and gave the other woman a hug. It was like hugging a small bird, one that you could break if you squeezed too hard. Then she handed over the packet of tea. 'This is for you anyway. I hope you feel better soon. And just knock if you want anything.'

So this was all horrifically awkward, she thought, trudging back down the stairs and wondering what she should do. She could just not go to the café, of course, make up some excuse to Margot next time she saw her – a sudden bout of food poisoning perhaps or a blinding headache of her own that rendered her incapable of leaving the building. But Margot wasn't daft. And Charlotte was pretty sure she wasn't the sort of person who would give up on a pet project either, once she'd got an idea in her head.

Sod it, she was just going to have to go and cringe her way through a coffee with Ned of the café and two daughters, wasn't she? And then she would most definitely have to make it abundantly clear to Margot that such a 'shore' was a one-off, never to be repeated, and, moreover, that Charlotte's definition of chores for her befriendee did not include going on blind coffee dates with the men of her choosing, thank you very much. (Although even as she decided this, she knew already that Margot wouldn't take any notice of this kind of foot-putting-down.)

Pausing to dab on some confidence-boosting perfume in her own flat, Charlotte practised smiling again in the mirror. At least she could apologize to him for the scene on the pier, she thought. Clear the air. Maybe the two of them would even laugh about the awkwardness of the situation, of being set up by the elegant, mischief-making Margot and what a terrible old stirrer she was. Then Charlotte would drink her coffee, apologize for wasting the man's time, and leave, never to set foot in the café again. Whatever her neighbour might be hoping.

'Right then,' she said to her nervous-looking reflection. 'Let's get this the hell over with then.'

He was serving behind the counter when she went in, a pencil tucked behind one ear, his glasses slightly lopsided on his nose. As before, he was wearing a white T-shirt and jeans underneath a navy blue serving apron, and even though Charlotte was braced for the humiliation of seeing him again, she hadn't anticipated quite what a hot blush would come to her face as Ned looked up from his blue-rinsed customer and smiled at her. *He likes you*, Margot had insisted. *I know that look.*

Yeah, well. Charlotte would be the judge of that. For all Cupid upstairs knew, he might have got her here under false pretences, to complain about her terrible behaviour. Any minute now he could hand her a restraining order, or call the police.

'Hi,' she said apprehensively, once the woman in front of her had paid and was making a slow careful walk away with her full cup of coffee.

'Hi,' he replied, straightening his glasses with the end of his forefinger. He had nice eyes, she thought distractedly. Chocolate-brown and properly twinkly. 'Good to see you again.'

Was it? She couldn't tell if he was being sarcastic or not. 'Listen,' she said, wanting to pre-empt him, 'I need to apologize. For that day. For what I said. I totally over-reacted, I was so out of order. And I'm sorry. I promise I'm not always a maniac.'

He waved a hand as if to say *Oh, that*. 'God, don't worry. I'd forgotten all about it until you came in the other week. And anyway I was so grateful that you'd found Lily in the first place that you could have said anything and I wouldn't have minded,' he told her, which was both very gallant of him and almost certainly untrue. She distinctly remembered how he'd flinched when she'd gone on the attack and called him negligent or whatever awful fishwife-esque thing she'd come out with.

She bowed her head. 'That's very nice of you,' she said cautiously and then there was a small excruciating pause which they both rushed to fill.

'I'm also sorry if Margot—' she began, the words tripping over themselves to get out, just as he started with, 'I hope you didn't mind me—'

They both stopped and looked at each other, then laughed. 'Go on, you first,' he said.

'I just wanted to say, I'm sorry if Margot put you up to this,' she repeated, biting her lip. Honesty was the best policy, she decided. 'She seems to have made it her mission to reinvigorate my love life by introducing me to every eligible man around the city, and quite a few others besides. Which, while well-meaning, I'm sure, can make things a bit embarrassing at times. Especially if the men in question are not even interested.'

There – the perfect get-out clause for him, if he wanted it. The chance right there on a plate for him to admit that, yes, okay, Margot *had* twisted his arm, persuading him in that charming-bulldozer way of hers to go along with this ridiculous whim out of pity for poor lonely old maid Charlotte.

But instead, he was shaking his head, his shaggy hair bouncing. 'God, no, there's no need to apologize. In fact, I was going to say I hope you didn't mind *me* asking about *you*. I didn't want to come across as pushy or creepy, only – well . . . when I saw you again and you mentioned knowing Margot, I was interested. Curious. I couldn't resist asking her about you.' He hesitated as if worried he might have revealed too much of himself. 'But she didn't "put me up" to anything, honestly. It was the other way round.'

'Oh.' Charlotte's cheeks flamed. He was *curious* about her, she repeated to herself, feeling startled – and flattered too. She had never seen herself as the sort of person that other people – particularly men – thought twice about. Blend into the wallpaper, that was her. Quiet and plain and ordinary, just getting on with her life as best she could. Apart from the mad-lady screaming on the pier incident, obviously. (She hoped that wasn't what he'd found so 'interesting' about her. This wasn't all an elaborate stunt to get her committed to the nearest psychiatric ward, was it?)

'So, anyway . . . have you got time for a coffee? It's quiet in here so I could slip out for a bit,' he said, oblivious to her sudden internal panic. 'We could go down to the beach, maybe, have a chat?'

Gosh. This was all kind of unexpected. *He* does *like you* said Margot in her head again, and then the next thing she knew, a prickle of nervous excitement was skittering through her. 'That sounds nice,' she said. 'Yes, please.'

The sun had been shining all day, a hot yellow stud in the pale denim sky, and the pebbles had soaked up the heat, feeling pleasantly warm through Charlotte's linen skirt as she and Ned found a place to sit on the beach a few minutes later. She had taken off her flats so as best to navigate down there and wiggled her toes through her nude opaques, wishing she had the nerve to whip them off too and free her bare legs. 'Do you know, I've never actually sat here on the beach,' she confessed, shifting into a more comfortable position as he set down the cardboard tray of drinks between them. 'I've lived here four months, just around the corner from your café, and it's taken me this long to come and actually –' She gestured at the undulating pebbly expanse around them. 'You know. Hang out.'

Ugh, she thought, in the next moment, 'hang out' made

her sound really old and uncool. And why had she even said that anyway, about not coming to the beach, when *that* made her sound like some weird hermit? 'I mean,' she went on, as he extracted her cappuccino from where it was wedged into the moulded cardboard tray and handed it over, 'it's not that I don't *like* the beach, it's more that I would feel self-conscious sitting here on my own. When everyone else in Brighton seems to be part of this massive posse, you know, with a whole gang of really cool and beautiful mates.'

Worse and worse. Why was she saying all of these things? Now she sounded even more of a loser. To her great relief, he was nodding, though.

'I know what you mean,' he said. 'But it's one of the things I love most about this place, that people don't judge you if you want to sit on the beach alone, or . . . I don't know, go skinny-dipping, or chain yourself to a railing for some cause or other. Nobody would bat an eyelid, honestly. Far more outrageous things go on for anyone to care.'

'There is that,' Charlotte admitted.

'Seriously, don't worry about it. I come out to have my lunch break here all alone most days and nobody's ever looked twice.' Then he looked thoughtful for a moment, raising one eyebrow comically. 'Unless I've got it wrong, of course, and the whole city has been pitying me all this time, but I've been too thick to notice.'

She smiled shyly. 'Well, I didn't like to say . . .' she joked, 'but there has been a fundraising campaign for you.'

He pantomimed shock. 'No!'

'Yeah, and this . . . this petition. Solidarity with the Solo Luncher. It was on the news and everything; mournful footage of you here alone with your sandwich with wistful music in the background.'

'Really?'

'Did you seriously not know?' She was warming up now. She was actually *making a joke*. 'There's this whole support group trying to find you some friends to have lunch with . . . There are posters, T-shirts with your face on . . .'

He threw his head back in laughter and the sound was so infectious that she joined in. And of course, what he'd said earlier was true: no way was this a place with small-town attitudes and small-town judgements, where people would gossip about what you got up to. It was a place where you could go roller skating in tiny hot pants and nobody gave a damn, after all. Why would anyone turn a hair at a woman enjoying the sea-view on her own? 'Anyway, you're right, I should be a bit braver about these things,' she said. 'Stop caring so much. You wait, I'll be here all the time from now on, brazenly not giving a damn. I'll become part of the Brighton scenery.'

'You'll be appearing on all the postcards,' he agreed. 'People will avoid sitting here because they'll know it's your spot.' He ripped open the paper bag of pastries he'd brought down as he spoke and spread it out between them. 'Here, help yourself. Better watch out for the seagulls, though.'

She took a chocolate custard twist, and he went for the almond croissant. 'So, tell me about your girls,' she said, biting the end off. Let's get the subject out there, she thought boldly. It was like poking a scab. Tell me about your beautiful children and I'll try not to choke on this extremely delicious pastry.

'Lily and Amber? They're . . . a handful,' he replied, his face softening as if enjoying a private thought. 'Lily's six and Amber's three, they're both great. Lovely girls. Full-on, mind you, but yeah. They keep me on my toes.'

'They looked gorgeous,' Charlotte said truthfully, the image of the small blonde poppets bundled up in puffy coats and mittens returning to her instantly. 'Do they have similar personalities, or . . . ?'

'They're wildly different,' he replied. 'Lily's really confident and outgoing, she's got lots of friends and is just all-singing, all-dancing, walks into a room and lets you know she's there.' His nose crinkled. 'Amber's more dreamy. She's away with the fairies half the time, has umpteen imaginary friends, a million teddy bears . . . They're chalk and cheese. Just as I think I've got one of them sussed, the other does something new to surprise me.'

She'd been wrong about him, Charlotte realized, sipping

her frothy cappuccino as he talked. Far from being the negligent weekend dad she'd assumed at their first meeting, you could tell from his eyes that he just adored those girls. 'Margot said . . .' she began then faltered, trying to come up with the right words. 'Margot said that it's just the three of you now,' she eventually got out.

He nodded, eyes clouding momentarily. 'Yeah, that's right. My wife – Tara – died just after Amber was born. So it's not been the easiest ride, to be honest, but we muddle along. My sister's only up the road from us so she's been an absolute godsend in terms of help, and it's definitely becoming easier, the older they get.' He ventured a small smile. 'We only have the very occasional getting-lost incident on the Palace Pier, I promise. I'm not that inept all the time, honestly.'

'Oh gosh, no, I'm sure you're not,' she said hurriedly. She turned a warm pebble in her hand and gazed out at the sea for a moment, noisy and bustling as it rushed up the shore. Damn it, she was going to have to explain now, she was going to have to lay some cards on the table too herself so that he understood. 'I'm sorry about your wife,' she said. 'That must have been so hard. And I do know what it's like, trying to pick up the pieces when the worst happens, because . . .' She was shredding the edge of her flaky pastry, she realized, stilling her hand and forcing out the rest of the sentence. 'Well, it happened to me, too. Only it was my daughter. So I've been a bit funny about other people and their kids ever since. Hence acting like a madwoman that first time we met.' She dared look up at his face to see him looking stricken. 'I *am* sorry,' she said, her voice a croak.

'Oh, Charlotte, how awful,' he said. 'Do you want to talk about it?' His eyes were so kind behind the glasses it gave her a lump in her throat. Other people's compassion, however well-intended, always set her off.

'It's okay,' she replied, looking down at her toes. 'I'm sort of muddling through too, steering my way around it.' She pictured herself at the helm of a heavy ocean liner, forcing a path through icy waters. 'It's coming up to a year and a half now, so I'm definitely over the worst, but it's taken me this long, really, to start feeling vaguely normal again. If you'd seen me last year . . .' She shook her head, remembering that moment in the park in Reading and tried to repress her shudder.

'It does take a while,' he agreed. 'Because it's a big ter-rible thing to get over. It's the worst. And even now, at Lily's school, it's like I'm this tragic figure to the other parents. I'm the one whose wife died, I can see it in their eyes. The mums are always telling me what a good job I'm doing, what a brilliant dad they think I am . . .' He spread his hands, eyes rolling. 'I mean, *really*? Just because my wife died, this makes me some kind of hero? If anyone's a hero, it's my sister, Debbie, who picked up the pieces and kept me sane. I'm just like anyone else, trying to keep all those plates spinning, and hoping that we all get to bed safe and sound every night.'

'I got sick of the pitying looks too,' Charlotte confessed. 'All my friends with healthy babies back home in Reading, they couldn't quite bring themselves to look my way. And when they did, it was like . . .' She cocked her head on one side, pushed her lower lip upwards and slanted her eyebrows in the worst kind of 'Poor you' face. 'My mum kept going on at me to plant a tree for my daughter, to start a memory book, to go to therapy . . . But in the end, I just decided the best thing to do was to get right away, to start again in a new city where nobody knew my "tragic secret".' She made little quotation marks with her fingers then took another bite of the pastry. 'This is amazing, by the way.'

'Good,' he said, and held up his coffee cup. 'Well, here's to new starts and no more horrendous pitying looks.' He pulled an exaggerated version of the face she'd just done, which made her smile. 'And it's working out, is it? Coming here?'

She thought about herself sobbing and puking in the street on Saturday night and being helped home by Rosa. Maybe not. But then she remembered whizzing around the roller rink with Georgie the week before, tea and macarons upstairs with Margot, the fact that she was going out to dinner that night . . . 'I'm getting there,' she said eventually. 'Thanks,' she added with a shy smile. 'You're actually the first person here that I've told about Kate. My daughter.' She stirred a hand through the pebbles. 'Even saying her name out loud feels kind of momentous. Like I've . . . I dunno, let a genie out of a bottle. Broken a spell. If that makes sense.'

'That totally makes sense,' he replied. They sat for a few moments in silence, both watching the sea rolling in and out, back and forth. There was something reassuring about the timelessness of the repeated motion, knowing that it was part of an endless loop, destined forever to foam up the shore and then suck back down again, hour after hour, day after day, for as long as the earth was turning. When events knocked you off your feet, you needed to know that other things could be relied upon, to continue being exactly the same.

He finished his coffee and pushed the plastic lid into the empty cup. 'I guess life just chucks these shitty things at you now and then, and all you can do is try your hardest to be an unshitty person in response,' he said eventually. 'Do your best not to go on being angry or resentful or bitter for too long.'

She drained her cup too and looked over at him. 'Well, I think you're an unshitty person,' she said shyly, then laughed at herself. 'Worst compliment ever.'

His eyes crinkled at the corners as he grinned. 'You're pretty unshitty yourself,' he replied magnanimously, and they laughed again. 'Listen, I'll have to get back to work soon before I go and pick up the girls, but it's been good talking to you. Looks like I owe Margot an espresso for the favour.'

'Looks like we both do,' she agreed, and hauled herself upright, the stones shifting beneath her feet. What now? she wondered, not sure where this left them. 'Thanks, Ned. For the coffee . . . and this.'

'My pleasure,' he said, standing up and dusting off his jeans. 'So . . . um . . . maybe we could . . . do it again? Or go for a drink one evening. What do you think?'

The sun was hot on her face and she had to put a hand up to her eyes to look at him. He was smiling but seemed a bit nervous, too, as if he was uncertain how she would answer.

She smiled back at him. 'Yes,' she said, her heart thumping. 'Yes, that's a great idea. I'd really like that.'

Chapter Eighteen

Some gorgeous pink gerberas had been left outside Rosa's door on Tuesday when she got back from work, as well as a card. *THANK YOU for getting me home*, it said, in beautiful loopy handwriting. *I'm so embarrassed about my behaviour and have tried knocking several times to apologize but must keep missing you. It won't happen again! Thanks also for the invitation to dinner. I'd love to come along. Charlotte x*

Feeling touched – anyone would have done the same under the circumstances – Rosa put the flowers in water. It was hardly surprising Charlotte hadn't been able to get hold of her in person, seeing as she'd just worked three insane shifts back to back, with the blisters and cracked hands to show for it. Sometimes she wondered if she really had what it took to work full-time in a large kitchen after all. While she loved the cooking and satisfaction of a job well done, the stamina required was something else. Still, looking on the bright side, at least a small, neighbourly dinner party would seem a complete doddle afterwards. She hoped.

However, even a small neighbourly dinner party was not without its problems, as she discovered over the next few days. First there was the fact that poor Jo took a slight turn for the worse again in hospital. 'Delightful news: there is now a pus-filled abscess in my abdominal cavity,' she told Rosa over the phone, sounding utterly fed-up. 'It's quite common after an appendectomy, apparently, which makes me feel a bit less special. So that little bastard needs to be surgically drained before I can go home. Where's bloody Dyno-Rod when you need them, eh?' (Rosa had had an even glummer text from Bea, moaning about how badly she and Gareth were getting on, and please PLEASE could she come over for the evening again soon, especially if Rosa was planning on baking any more cakes HINT HINT.)

Then there was the fact that Georgie and her boyfriend had had a series of very shouty rows that Rosa hadn't been able to avoid hearing through her ceiling. She had humiliated him, apparently. She was sorry, but do you know what, he was making way too much of a big deal about this. How many times was she going to have to apologize before he let it go? – and on it went. Rosa thought she might have heard them having some loud make-up sex more recently (it was hard to tell with a pillow over her head and fingers in her ears) but she was half expecting one or both of them to drop right out of the dinner arrangements.

Finally, on the day itself, the older lady from Flat 5 who

had previously accepted the invitation with a perfumed note of thanks, knocked on the door. 'I am sorry, it is so rude of me to cancel late, I know,' she said, pressing two fat champagne bottles into Rosa's hands. 'But this migraine, I know him, he come and I can do nothing.' She did look wan as she shrugged ruefully. 'But I bring you this champagne for your evening. I hope you enjoy.'

'Mrs Favager, that's so kind,' Rosa had said. 'I hope you feel better soon. Maybe some other time.'

'Margot – please. Mrs Favager, it sounds so old. And I am not *so* old.' Despite her headache, her eyes twinkled. 'And now –' Margot gingerly touched the tips of her fingers to her temple – 'I will go to my bed. I hope your party is a great success. Have fun. Be naughty!'

They were dropping like flies, six reduced to four, and possibly even three, if things continued to be rocky between Georgie and Simon, but the show must go on, Rosa told herself, setting up the table in her living room. She had borrowed a white linen tablecloth, china plates, posh cutlery and wine glasses from the hotel, and set some squat church candles in the centre. Then she wrote herself an exhaustive shopping list and went out to buy ingredients.

Charlotte was the first to arrive that evening, looking anxious as she clutched a chilled bottle of a very nice-looking Marlborough sauvignon blanc as well as a bunch of pale yellow roses that smelled heavenly. 'Hello again,' she said, biting her lip and getting lipstick on her teeth. 'It's me, the drunken disgrace from Saturday night.' She managed a shaky laugh but her gaze remained wary, uncertain, and Rosa couldn't help flashing back to the pain on her face the first time they'd met, that naked misery there for the world to see. When she wasn't sobbing and four sheets to the wind, she was actually very pretty with her wavy brown hair and those dark chocolate eyes. 'Are you sure I'm welcome across the threshold after what happened?' she asked.

'Of course you're welcome, come in,' Rosa said warmly. 'God, my girlfriends have had to scrape me up in far worse states than that over the years, trust me. Are you okay now?'

Charlotte nodded. 'Yes. It was just a blip. A massively over-reacting blip but I got it out of my system at least.'

'Good,' said Rosa. 'What gorgeous roses, let me put them in a vase. There's only four of us tonight,' she went on, leading the way into the living room. 'Georgie and her boyfriend, plus us two. Margot upstairs isn't feeling great and Jo next door is still in hospital, unfortunately. Have a seat. What would you like to drink?'

She was just pouring them a glass each of wine when there was a second knock on the door and it was Georgie, resplendent in a Pucci-print dress and matching hairband, although *sans* boyfriend and looking rather red in the face about it. 'I'm *so* sorry, Rosa, he's such an utter twat, and I told him a million times it was tonight, I know I did, but now he's saying he's had this work thing on all along and I must have told him the wrong evening – which I so *didn't* . . .' She made an exasperated face and brandished a misted bottle of prosecco in the air. 'Sod it, we'll have a better laugh without him anyway. But I hope this hasn't buggered up your cooking plans. Feel free to dump a plateful in his laptop bag if you're *really* livid with him.'

Rosa laughed at the comedic way Georgie was rolling her eyes up to the ceiling. 'I'm not livid,' she said. She was relieved that they were still together and that Georgie merely seemed irritated rather than delivering news of a painful break-up, frankly. 'And it just means there's more for us anyway. Ladies' night!' She took away the extra set of cutlery and poured Georgie a large drink. So there you had it: her dreams of a big jolly dinner party had shrunk even further but never mind. 'Right then, are you ready to eat? I'll serve up the starters.'

'Thank you so much,' Charlotte said, sniffing the air appreciatively, as Rosa brought through the first course. She'd been planning halloumi-stuffed peppers to cater for vegetarian Jo but with her neighbour's prolonged stay in hospital, had changed her mind, plumping instead for an old favourite: crostini with seared beef, plus Stilton, rocket and a herbed crème fraiche.

'It's a bit of a build-it-yourself job, I hope that's all right,'

Rosa said, plopping a teaspoon into the crème fraiche. 'This has chives and horseradish in, by the way. Tuck in!'

As the three of them got started, Georgie launched into tales from some outrageous art club she'd been along to the night before for one of the columns she wrote. 'My editor gave me the brief, and I thought, Hmm, art club, people in smocks painting watercolours, sounds a bit dull. But no. We're in Brighton, aren't we? This is an *alternative* art club.'

'What does that mean?' asked Charlotte, wiping crème fraiche from the side of her mouth.

'It means using whatever you like to paint with – includ-ing *bodily fluids*,' Georgie said, eyes wide.

'No!' cried Rosa.

'Oh yes, and using your body parts to *print* stuff, if that floats your boat.' She giggled. 'Honestly, people round here love getting their kit off, don't they?'

'It sounds terrifying,' Charlotte said. 'You didn't have to . . . get *your* kit off, did you? Was there some wild orgy by the end of the night?'

'No, not at all,' Georgie said. 'In fact, they were all amaz-ing. Coffee, this one woman used to paint with, and her pic-ture was absolutely brilliant. One guy used this sort of greeny mush he'd got from liquidizing plants – he actually painted with it and then used bits of coloured petals to pick out details here and there. It was so good! And another woman used tape – black tape, that was all, cut into different-sized strips – and yet, somehow, she managed to create this stunning picture. I couldn't believe it.'

'What did you use?' Rosa asked, her mind boggling.

Georgie looked a bit bashful. 'Well, don't laugh – this will show you what a total amateur I am – but I turned up there with a packet of felt-tip pens in my bag. I know!' she cried as the other two fell about laughing. 'What a plum; I didn't dare confess. Especially when all the rest of them were so outlandishly artistic. The guy next to me had even made his own paint from egg and weird pigments, can you believe . . . ?' She rolled her eyes.

'So did you whip your felt-tips out?' Charlotte asked, giggling.

'No way,' Georgie replied. 'I suddenly remembered I had loads of make-up in my bag: mascara, eyeshadow palette, lippy, eyeliner. . . So that's what I used. It looked completely shit, still – I mean, I can't draw for toffee and I'm not just being modest. But what cracked me up was that the teacher came over and she sort of stared at my really crap piece of art for a while and then said, in this dead posh voice, *I take it this is a comment on the artificial nature of beauty versus the naked human form?* and I was like, *Yeah, definitely,* all deadpan.'

The other two cracked up again. 'Wait a minute,' Rosa gurgled. 'Did you just say "the naked human form"? Do you mean . . . ?'

'Yep,' said Georgie. 'Did I not mention that? Nude model.

Not only that, but nude model who – and I'm not kidding – had the weirdest-looking penis of any man I've ever seen. I'm serious!' she yelped as the other two collapsed in giggles again. 'I mean – I just kept thinking liver sausage, that's all I'm saying. It was *hideous*.' She clapped a hand over her face. 'Oh God, yeah, and the funniest thing of *all* – the nude model, Charlotte, you'll never guess: it was the guy from the roller disco, the creepy one who really loved himself. Him!'

'No! The one who was twerking and touching up all the women? Ugh!'

'Yeah! *And* he's a right one, apparently. A total slapper. The woman I was sitting next to – her friend slept with him, she told me, and had the worst case of crabs afterwards.'

'Wait,' Rosa said, trying to keep up. Had she missed something? 'Hang on. You two go *roller skating*?'

'Just the once,' Georgie said, 'although I wouldn't mind going again some other time. It was a right laugh, wasn't it, Charlotte?'

'It was excellent,' Charlotte replied, who seemed to be getting a bit squiffy already. (Good, thought Rosa.) 'Terrifying but excellent. You should come too next time, Rosa, if we go. Girls' night out!'

'We *should* go for a girls' night out anyway,' Georgie said, seizing upon the idea. 'And – what was her name? Jo, too, when she's better.'

'And Margot!' Charlotte cried. 'She's *brilliant*. Have you

met her yet? She is the most glamorous, cool woman . . . I was a bit scared of her at first but she's ace.' She giggled again. 'Do you know, I asked her if she wanted me to run any chores for her the other week and she sent me off on this little tour of Brighton – basically to all her favourite shops, where I had to ask to be served by all these gorgeous men she's . . . well, *curated*. And they all love her! How bad-ass is that? For a woman in her eighties!'

'No way,' laughed Rosa. 'Love her. So – what, she has this sort of harem of men around the city, her favoured team of shop assistants?'

'Exactly. It was a real eye-opener,' Charlotte replied. 'I was sent to buy posh candles, wine, fancy cheese, all these really lovely shops, and then down to the café to get us cappuccinos. "Make sure you ask for Ned",' she said at the end in a terrible French accent and for some reason her cheeks turned pink as she mentioned the man's name.

'Oh, *Ned*, I know him – Sea Blue Sky?' Georgie said in surprise. 'He's lovely, isn't he?' She posted the last bit of crostini into her mouth and licked the crème fraiche from her fingers. 'So do you think she was trying to fix you up with these men? And did you like any of them?' Her eyes widened and she leaned forward without waiting for an answer. 'Go for Ned. He's so nice. Do you know him, Rosa? Sort of earnest and funny and speccy . . . He runs the café just down from us on the front. Makes a mean coffee too.'

'I don't know him but I'm definitely going to check him out now. *And* his coffee,' Rosa joked, arching an eyebrow as she got up to collect their empty plates. 'Hmm, and I can't help noticing that Charlotte's gone very quiet in answer to your questions, Georgie,' she added teasingly.

'She has,' Georgie agreed. 'Come on, Char. Fess up. Which one was the sexiest, just for future reference? Just so that we can casually drop by and introduce ourselves to Margot's top man-god.' She winked. 'Sounds like a TV show to me. Who goes through to the next round of Margot's Top Man-God? *You* decide!'

Charlotte looked flustered. 'Well . . . Oh, I don't know.' She drained her wine glass with a gulp and Rosa suddenly remembered the drama about the ex-husband from the weekend before. Maybe the conversation had taken a path Charlotte would rather avoid. 'Um . . . as Rosa knows I've been a bit of a mess recently . . .' Her face flamed as she met Rosa's eye. 'But then, saying that . . . Well, I did actually have a coffee with Ned the other day, so . . .'

'Ooh!'

'Get in!'

Charlotte's face was now tomato-coloured and she squirmed at the excited faces of the other two. 'He said maybe we could do it again, so . . .' She shrugged but there was a tiny smile now visible, Rosa noticed. 'He seems really lovely.'

'He *is* really lovely!' Georgie cried. 'Oh, this is brilliant news. Cheers to you!'

'That *is* good news,' Rosa agreed. Charlotte's whole face looked softer and happier all of a sudden. 'I think that's my cue to open another bottle of fizz.'

'So,' said Georgie as Rosa brought in the next course a short while later. 'We've covered my dodgy art class. We've nosied into Charlotte's blossoming love life. But I don't really know much about you, Rosa. You're a chef, are you?'

'Well, not yet but that's the dream. I think, anyway,' Rosa said, putting a dish of buttered new potatoes on the table. For the main course, she'd cooked salmon en croute, adding pak choi, coriander, ginger, lime, lemongrass and chilli to the salmon inside its pastry casing so that it had a bit of a kick. Phew, the pastry was flaking perfectly as she cut it into thick slices.

'You sound unsure,' Charlotte ventured as Rosa set a plateful in front of her. 'Although, looking at this, I can't imagine why. I'd come and eat in your restaurant any day.'

'God, yeah, and me, absolutely,' Georgie said enthusiastically.

Rosa smiled. 'Aww, shucks,' she said. 'Thank you. I do love cooking, but the shifts at the hotel where I work are pretty brutal. And my boss is not really one for career advancement, if you know what I mean. I think he'd have me peeling potatoes and chopping onions forever.'

'When you can make things like this? That's just *criminal*,' said Charlotte, doling potatoes and salad onto her plate. 'And I'm saying that as someone who eats a ready-meal every night.'

'It's a bit of a new thing for me,' Rosa explained. 'I only started working there this year. I was in advertising before, living in London. Packed up and came here for a new start, when . . . Well, things went pear-shaped, basically.' She glanced at Charlotte. 'Man trouble, in other words.'

'I hear you,' Charlotte replied. 'So none of us have been here that long, then. I moved here in the new year myself. Another fresh start.'

'And we came down a month ago,' Georgie said, taking a photo of the dish and typing something into her phone. 'Sorry, I'm just sending this to Simon to make him jealous, serves him right for being so ignorant. You're missing out, mate!' She jabbed a button and then put her phone back in her bag. 'Well, here's to new beginnings, anyway. New careers too – *and* new neighbours. And double cheers to a bloody lovely dinner!'

'Cheers!' they chorused, holding up their glasses.

'I'm having such a lovely time,' Charlotte added, eyes shining with the candlelight. 'Thank you, Rosa, this is all brilliant.'

'Me too,' Georgie agreed, mouth full. 'Do you know, when I moved here, my friend Amelia – she's madly into astrology – got all excited about me living at number eleven. The eleventh astrological house is all about friends, hopes and wishes, she said to me. And I was like, yeah whatever, at the time. But . . .' She grinned, clinking her glass against Charlotte's and then Rosa's. 'But maybe this is what she meant. Here we are, new friends, hoping Charlotte will go for it with lovely Ned, wishing that Rosa will ask us round like this again . . .'

Rosa laughed. 'You're both welcome any time,' she said, scooping salad onto her plate. And she meant it. Having the neighbours round for dinner – and such nice, friendly neighbours they were too – was *fun*. This was easily the most enjoyable evening she'd had since moving out of London. She'd cut herself off from her old friends, moving down here, wanting to be alone, stewing in her own heartbreak, but having dinner with Georgie and Charlotte had made her realize just how much she missed female camaraderie. She must organize a get-together with the old gang, and soon.

As they dug into their food, the conversation turned again, this time back to Georgie's burgeoning new journalistic career, and in particular to the dilemma she was currently facing, with the so-called 'House of Women' who were opposing the hotel development designed by her boyfriend.

'Does Simon know you did the interview?' Charlotte breathed, leaning forward.

'No, he bloody doesn't – and that's just between me, you guys and the gatepost, all right? We've not exactly been getting on lately. What happens at Rosa's table stays at Rosa's table, okay?' They chorused their agreement at once. 'The thing is, the deadline for the piece is tomorrow and I'm still in two minds. I mean, it's the best bit of writing I've ever done, you know, it's proper journalism rather than silly pieces about a roller disco or a weird art club. But then again . . . it's Simon's career too. His big break. How can I pit myself against him?' She pulled a face. 'I can't, can I? I shouldn't. He would kill me.'

Just at that moment, there was a knock on the door, and Georgie's phone bleeped simultaneously with a text. 'Oh Christ, it's him,' she yelped. 'It's Simon at the door, Rosa. Of all the moments! Nobody say anything, will you? Shit!'

None of them could keep a straight face when Simon came in moments later, a bottle of champagne in hand, apologizing to Rosa for his late arrival and to Georgie for 'being a bit of a dick lately. What's so funny?' he frowned, when she couldn't hide her guilty laughter.

'Nothing, nothing,' Georgie spluttered, not entirely convincingly. 'Charlotte had just told us a brilliant joke when you got here, that's all. Anyway.'

'Really?' He looked at Charlotte, who blushed and squirmed.

'You kind of had to be there,' she told him, kicking Georgie under the table.

For dessert, Rosa had baked a good old apple and blackberry pie, but she'd scented it delicately with ginger and made custard flecked with real vanilla. Simon, meanwhile, polished off the massive leftover portion of the salmon en croute, and told Rosa that she was a goddess, and that it was the best dinner he'd had since he'd left Yorkshire. 'A proper dinner, that's what it was. I'd pay good money for this, I'm telling you.'

'And he's a Yorkshireman, remember, so he's tight as a gnat's chuff,' Georgie said, ducking as he tried to swat her.

'I'd pay too,' Charlotte echoed. 'Hey – you could do one of those supper clubs,' she added suddenly. 'Someone at work went to one at the weekend, said it was brilliant. It's like a dinner party in your home but people actually cough up for the privilege. Basically this, but with us shelling out twenty quid or something.'

'Get ten or so people together,' Simon said, nodding. 'Cover your costs, everyone brings their own booze . . . You'll be laughing.'

'There was something about supper clubs in the magazine the other day,' Georgie remembered, chipping in. 'I'll dig it out and find it for you. But, yeah, you could totally do it, Rosa.'

Rosa glanced from face to face, as if expecting them to be teasing her, but they seemed deadly serious. Her skin prickled with a rush of sudden excitement. 'Really? You think people would pay to have dinner here in my flat?'

'Definitely!' they all said as one. 'What have you got to lose?' Georgie added, waving her empty spoon in enthusiasm.

'Think about it anyway,' Charlotte urged.

'I will,' Rosa said. Her heart was pounding a tattoo all of a sudden, her head was whirling. A supper club, she repeated to herself. Her own miniature restaurant right here. She could do it, couldn't she? And why not?

Chapter Nineteen

SeaView House Noticeboard:

POLITE NOTICE TO ALL TENANTS

Please could you endeavour to keep all noise DOWN
after ten o'clock at night. I have had complaints
from the neighbours and would like to remind you
that this is a respectable house NOT a DISCO.

Angela Morrison-Hulme
Property Manager

Georgie tossed a pebble into the sea with a plop and sighed. The new edition of *Brighton Rocks* magazine was out and she had three whole pieces in it this week, but the pleasure and pride that she might normally have felt at such an achievement was tainted by the conviction that she was probably the worst girlfriend in the world. Yes, she had submitted the women's refuge interview, written under a pseudonym. Yes, she knew this would only add to the opposition Simon was facing at work. Yes, it was probably pretty unforgivable of her.

'You're taking over the magazine!' Viv had emailed cheerfully when she sent over the link to the digital edition. As well as her interview, there was also the write-up of the Alternative Art Club which Viv had loved, and the *Hey Em* column, which was getting more hits than ever, as well as a whole inbox of new problems. The interview itself had had a lot of feedback online, and someone had even started a petition to save the house, which had gathered almost a thousand signatures already.

There was no way she could tell Simon of her writerly success, though. It had been bad enough him finding out about the whinging agony letter she'd written and accidentally got into print, but this was far worse. He was not easily prone to forgiveness either, being the kind of man who liked to have at least one grudge simmering away at any given time. In the past he'd had it in for the binmen, former colleagues, the manager of Leeds United, the Prime Minister . . . the list went on. The last thing Georgie wanted was to go straight to the top of his chart.

Anyway, the magazine was *tiny*, she reminded herself. Petition or not, hardly anyone read it; it wasn't like she'd stitched Simon up in the national press, or on television. He never had to find out. Maybe in years to come, she'd confess and they'd roar with laughter about it, she thought optimistically, lobbing another pebble overarm into the waves. Maybe they'd even show their grandchildren. Yeah.

Her phone was ringing in her pocket, she realized, and she pulled it out to see her editor's name on the screen. 'Hi,' Georgie said, turning her back on the roaring sea, and cupping her other ear in the hope of better hearing. A gale was whipping up around her, snatching at tendrils of her hair, and she bowed her head against it and began clambering back up the pebbly bank in the hope of finding shelter.

'Hey, George, you okay?' Viv asked. 'Got any plans for tonight?'

'Well . . .' There was *Silent Witness* on later, and a steak and ale pie in the fridge (Simon's favourite), but that was about the extent of it. 'Not really,' she admitted.

'Great, because I've got the next challenge for the You Send Me column, and it's a *doozy*.' Viv was smiling in a very pleased-with-herself sort of way; you could hear it behind her words. 'Get your best frock on, girl, because . . .'

A seagull overhead chose that moment to let out a screech and Georgie, back up by the arches now, ducked into a small trendy gallery selling hand-painted cards and crackle-glazed earthenware bowls, where silence reigned. 'Sorry, I missed that,' she had to say into the phone. 'Could you tell me again? I can hear you now.' *Get your best frock on*, she was thinking. It must be somewhere posh. The theatre, maybe.

The opera. Ballet, perhaps! She hoped it would be something romantic so that she could drag Simon along with her. She pictured them holding hands in the audience, maybe sharing a tentative smile and reconnecting once again.

'Are you there?' Viv yelled, so loudly Georgie had to hold the phone away from her ear. 'I said, we're sending you *speed dating*. Only it's speed dating with a difference. Have you got a pen? I'll give you the details.'

'Well, I . . .' Georgie found herself meeting the eye of the woman behind the counter in the gallery, a woman with hennaed hair and a pierced nose who looked a bit too interested in the speed dating conversation for Georgie's liking. She turned away and lowered her voice, pretending to be browsing through a rack of birthday cards. Bloody hell, six quid each, she noticed. No chance, mate. 'The thing is . . . I've got a boyfriend, and . . .' She could just imagine the gallery assistant's ears now flapping with nosiness and cringed. 'Look, I've got a boyfriend,' she repeated, more firmly this time. 'So . . .'

'So you don't have to *do* anything, Jesus, I'm not asking you to shag around. Come on, Georgie. You don't have to tell anyone there that you're boringly hooked up. You don't have to tell your bloke either. Just go along, have an open mind and report back. That's all I'm saying.'

Georgie hesitated. 'But . . .' It was all very well saying 'You don't have to tell your bloke' but if her name was printed alongside the speed dating piece, it was going to be pretty easy for him to find out, wasn't it?

A snap of impatience had entered Viv's voice, the smile abruptly dropped. 'Look, love, this *was* your idea. *Send me anywhere, I'll do it, I'm up for anything,* that's what you told me. And now you're wussing out?'

'I'm not wussing out! It's just that—'

'Right, well, I'll give you the address, then. Have you got that pen ready? First rule of journalism, always have a pen ready.'

Georgie sighed. She didn't have a pen ready, obviously, because she was not that organized, so there was the journalism test failed. Cursing herself – and Viv too, for her stupid bloody ideas – she eyed up the gallery's selection of pens displayed in a small pot nearby, for five pounds each apparently. They could bog off and all, she thought crossly, rummaging in her bag for her lipstick and a crumpled old receipt. 'Ready when you are,' she said through gritted teeth.

Just another secret from her poor mistreated boyfriend, then, Georgie thought glumly as she loitered outside the Olive Grove cocktail bar that night, wishing she still smoked so she could light one up in order to kill some time. She wished too that she had put her foot down more vehemently with Viv, told her in no uncertain terms that she wouldn't cooperate. Did she have the nerve, she wondered, to file copy for a completely different 'You Send Me' night, one that she actually wanted to do? She could write the column about a new comedy place that had opened in Hove, or the samba group she'd seen advertised, for instance. The readers would be interested in both those things, let's face it, way more than they'd want to read about someone who already had a boyfriend going speed dating.

Glancing through the steamed-up windows of the bar, she could see that there was already a big crowd of people inside. Women in little black dresses with their hair up in gravity-defying dos. Men in jeans and pastel-coloured shirts, a couple in suits as if they'd just stepped off the London train. She bet it stank in there, of bad aftershave and nervous sweat. Shit. And she was meant to join them and go along with it all, flirting and bantering and listening to chat-up lines flying about, while there was poor unsuspecting Simon, grafting away at work. This was all wrong. This was not ideal girlfriend behaviour, was it? Yet again.

Georgie looked down at her own outfit – a rather tired plum-coloured dress bought in the Hobbs sale about three years ago and a pair of court shoes that were scuffed at the toe. Her hair was decidedly undone – and could do with a cut, moreover – and she had grudgingly slapped on some make-up as a token effort, without really caring how she looked. Bloody Viv, she thought, scowling and wondering what to do. Was the woman deliberately trying to sabotage

Georgie's relationship, or something? Speed dating, indeed. And not just that – this was *silent* speed dating, where you couldn't even have a laugh about how awful it was but instead were meant to communicate through your eyes alone. Georgie had googled the event details earlier and it sounded absolutely excruciating.

Sod it, she decided; she'd had enough of secrets. There was no way she'd be able to relax tonight and go along with any of this tosh if the whole time she was feeling racked with guilt about Simon. Sorry, Viv, it's not going to happen. She would call her unsuspecting boyfriend who was working late *again*, the poor thing, tell him about this cringeworthy new stunt and – *yes*, that was it, she thought as an idea came to her. Instead of slinking in there alone and going through the whole naff pantomime, she would persuade Simon to come along too. Genius! They could both pretend not to know one another and then catch each other's eye across the room. It could actually be quite sexy!

A smile spread across her face as she pictured the scene; her beckoning him over in a sultry come-to-bed sort of way, undressing each other with their eyes, desire building to fever pitch as perhaps she licked her lips suggestively, leaned forward, pressing her knee against his under the table . . .

She dialled at once. Viv never had to know that Georgie was sneakily bending the rules, did she? As far as her boss was concerned, Georgie was merely doing what she'd been asked; she would write up the evening, accidentally on purpose leaving out the bit where she snogged the face off her boyfriend and then went home and had wild electrifying sex with him all round the flat.

After ringing about six times, a woman finally answered. 'Hello, Simon's phone?' she said.

Georgie stiffened at the unexpected voice down the line. 'Oh. Er . . . Where is he?' she asked, hearing the frostiness of her own reply. There was music playing in the background, which was strange, she thought, remembering the rather basic Portakabins she'd seen on the site. It must be someone's radio.

'He's at the bar,' the woman said, her words slightly muffled by a gale of laughter in the background. 'Do you want me to give him a message?'

Georgie's jaw dropped. 'He's at the bar?' she echoed, her eyebrows twitching in a frown. That was weird. Simon hadn't mentioned anything about going drinking after work.

'Yeah, he's getting the drinks in, and about time and all,' the woman replied. 'We were starting to think his wallet had been surgically attached to his trouser pocket.'

'Right,' Georgie said as another roar of laughter went up. She could feel herself bristling at the way the woman was joking about her boyfriend. Who the hell even *was* this person anyway? And how dare she be so rude about Simon like that? After a suitably disapproving pause, she said, rather coldly, 'This is Georgie. Please could you let him know that I called. And ask him to ring me back as soon as possible.'

'As soon as possible,' echoed the woman – and maybe it was Georgie's paranoia, or the line was crackly, but she could have sworn that the woman was mimicking her York-shire accent. 'Right you are, chuck,' she said – yes, she defi-nitely was – and then the line went dead. No doubt there were further peals of laughter across the pub table at her expense right now.

Georgie stood there fuming for a moment, wondering about calling straight back and demanding to know where this pub was, so she could march in and have a word with the cheeky cow who'd answered the phone so cockily just now. But then she imagined how irritated Simon would be as a consequence, how he'd tell her, probably quite shirtily, that he didn't need any battles fighting on his behalf, thanks all the same, and, Christ, couldn't she take a joke?

A couple of women tottered up just then, arm in arm, their voices already high-pitched and shrieky as they laughed together. 'Here we go, the Olive Grove,' said one. 'Ready to find Mr Fabulous?'

'Fuck, yeah, babe,' replied the other. 'Where is he? Let me get my hands on him!'

And in they went, their laughter hanging in the air for a moment like a smoke trail after the door had swung shut behind them.

'Come on, Simon,' Georgie muttered, turning the phone over in her hand, but it remained smooth and silent, seemingly in no hurry to announce an incoming reply call. What should she do? Her fingers itched to send him a text, just in case old Cocky McGobby in the pub hadn't passed on her message – but then if Simon had the kind of colleagues who thought nothing of answering his phone when left on the pub table, what would stop them from nosily picking it up again when her text made its appearance? They'd be all over it like a rash, she bet, remembering the cackles of laughter heard down the line.

Ooh, look, it's her again, she doesn't trust me, the mouthy one would crow, seeing Georgie's name on the screen. *What's this, then? She's asking him to join her on a speed dating evening? Whoa, kinky! Look out, here he comes – oi, Si, over here, your girlfriend's been in touch. Open relationship is this, then, eh? You dark horse, you . . .*

Bloody hell. *Rock, meet hard place*, Georgie thought grimly. *Can I just say, it's really crap being between you guys right now?* Then came a sudden patter of rain on the pavement which forced the decision. She would go into the speed dating bar, she vowed, but only until she heard from Simon. And in the meantime, she'd have a large drink and keep dry.

Trying not to look as if she was walking to her certain

doom, she pushed her phone back in her bag and went up to the door.

'Okaaaay, beautiful people, so let's start off with a few ice-breakers before we get all silent and intimate on each other,' said a woman in a tasselled red dress, with a neckline so plunging it was probably a deep-sea diver in its spare time. This woman, their self-appointed host for the evening, had introduced herself to the gathered throng as Dominique, although Georgie could have sworn she heard one of the bar staff calling her 'Dawn'. Whatever her real name, Dominique had a mane of tousled black hair, sunbed-orange skin, half a ton of smoky eye make-up and cherry-red lips that seemed glued into a permanent pout. 'Could everyone make their way over to this side of the room, please?'

Off they shuffled, Georgie draining the rest of her Throbbing Orgasm in one apprehensive gulp (the cocktail list consisted of one ridiculously sexualized name after another, so that merely by asking for a drink, you were effectively demanding some X-rated performance from the staff). She was yet to speak to another person here, because she'd been checking her phone every ten seconds to see if Simon was calling back. So far, she'd heard nothing.

There were about thirty of them gathered at the far end of the room now, all covertly checking each other out as they awaited their next instruction. 'First time?' asked a florid-faced man leaning too close into Georgie's personal space.

'Sorry, what?' He was wearing a striped shirt and his gut ballooned over the waistband of his too-tight jeans. His low husky voice and strong Belfast accent meant that it took Georgie a moment to decipher his words. 'Oh, right. Yes, first time,' she replied, trying to edge discreetly away.

'Right then, my darlings! Let's get to know each other a little better, shall we?' Dominique asked coquettishly, rubbing her hands together so that her cleavage wobbled, bronzed and fleshy, beneath the spotlight, momentarily distracting Striped Shirt man. 'Or maybe quite a *lot* better, who knows?' More pouting and a wink. 'We'll begin with a few naughty home truths to warm things up and then move on to the speed-dating part of the evening. But first, it's confession time!'

There was a round of nervous titters, while the man next to Georgie closed in on her again. 'You should really put your phone away, sweetheart,' he murmured, his breath hot and repellent in her ear as he bent towards her. 'It's all about animal attraction in here.' And then – no word of a lie – he made a low growling noise in the back of his throat, which presumably was meant to sound sexy, although it just made Georgie think of the choking sounds emitted by Mrs Huggins's cat back in Stonefield whenever it was about to cough up a furball in the garden.

It was on the tip of Georgie's tongue to primly inform him that she already had a boyfriend, and that even if she didn't, overweight sleazeballs had never been her type but she managed to restrain herself. It wouldn't do to be outed as someone coupled up right now for one thing; the other prospective daters might drive her out with pitchforks or, worse, take it as some kind of challenge. 'Excuse me,' she muttered, 'I just need to . . .' And then she squeezed through the crowd, so that she didn't have to listen to him any more. Now wedged between a woman in a leopard-print catsuit and chandelier earrings, and a man in a rugby top who had nuclear-strength BO, she did her best to concentrate on what Dominique was saying, while the phone remained resolutely silent in her hand. Hurry up, Simon. Hurry *up*!

'So, tell me,' Dominique purred, looking across at the throng through her mascara-heavy eyelashes, 'has anyone here ever had sex outside, in broad daylight? All those who have –' She beckoned a scarlet-nailed finger. '– cross to my side of the room.'

There were a few red faces and another ripple of giggles as everyone glanced at their neighbours and wondered who would respond first. Georgie looked down at her uncomfortable shoes, remembering the summer when she and Simon had been eighteen, in that gorgeous post-A-levels lull when they had spent long lovely afternoons in beer gardens with friends for much of the time. He'd borrowed his mum's car one hot day at the beginning of July, and they'd driven out into the Dales, taking a picnic blanket and iPod speakers with them. The sun had been so warm on her bare skin, she could remember it now, as they fell, laughing into the prickly dry grass. 'Someone will see us!' she'd squeaked, suddenly fearful, as he began peeling away her clothes, but he'd muttered, 'Who cares?' and kissed her so passionately that she had stopped caring too.

Back in the room, a cheer went up as a man in tight white jeans and a black silk shirt brazenly stepped out from the crowd and strode over towards Dominique. A pair of grinning women followed suit, and then other people braved the walk of confession, some rather pink in the cheeks, while others seized the chance to show off their naughtiness with a sexy insouciance. Georgie sighed. If Simon was here with her, they could have caught each other's eyes right now, maybe squeezed one another's hands, remembering together. Instead, she felt as if she was somehow tarnishing her golden summer's day memory by admitting it under these circumstances, and joining the walkers. But it was either that or be left behind and look like a total stiff, she reasoned. So, eyes straight ahead, so as not to meet anyone's gaze, she quickly crossed the room, dying a little inside.

'Cool, there we go. That wasn't so bad, was it? Next I'm wondering how many of you have ever had a *threesome*?' Dominique asked, arching an eyebrow. 'If so, stay on the naughty side of the room with me. If not, slink your butts back over there.' To the boring side, in other words, Georgie thought, gritting her teeth and smiling fixedly as she and about half of her group returned across the room once more. 'Okay, so we're building up a bit of a picture here, aren't we? Keep an eye on anyone you fancy . . . you might discover you've got things in common, if you know what I'm saying!' She pouted, just in case anyone was stupid enough not to get her meaning. 'Next question! Who's had sex on a beach? Magaluf, Margate, any beach will do. Walk that walk!'

On it went, and on. Who liked to dress up, who had ever had a one-night stand, who was into spanking . . . Georgie could feel herself becoming primmer and primmer about the whole affair, and definitely not drunk enough. She was no prude but compared to this lot she was starting to feel distinctly vanilla; an old maid who'd been out of the singles market for too long. (Thank goodness; a cuddle on the sofa with Simon in front of *Emmerdale* had never been so appealing before.) God help anyone who had come along with lovehearts in their eyes, hoping for a romantic encounter tonight. This event seemed to be more about washing your dirty (post-coital) linen in front of a host of complete strangers. Rubbing it in their faces, more like (and having been here for half an hour now, she got the feeling that some of the people here would probably quite enjoy that).

Finally, just as Dominique was asking about whipping,

Georgie's phone went and she was able to escape with it to the loo. *Simon.* 'Oh, hi, thank goodness,' she said, leaning against the cool tiled wall, the noise of the pub receding as the door closed behind her. 'Are you okay? I was hoping you'd ring, I'm stuck at this—'

'Sorry I'm late,' he said. His voice was thick and slurring, as if his batteries were running down. 'Got caught up at work. Busy day.'

'Oh. I thought you were in the pub?' she asked. He wasn't seriously trying to kid her that he was still slaving away at his desk, was he?

'Yeah. In the pub *now*,' he confirmed, like it needed any confirming, when she could hear for herself the thud of music and raised voices behind him. 'You okay?'

'Yeah, I'm . . .' She shut her eyes briefly, wondering what to say. She had a feeling that he was already drunk enough that she wouldn't be able to explain her whereabouts without him getting the wrong end of the stick. If she tried to tell him about the speed dating, and how she hoped he'd join her, he just wouldn't get it, he'd leap furiously to the wrong conclusion. 'I'm out too,' she said eventually, lacking the energy to go any further.

'Cool. Think it's gonna be a late one here – Maz's birthday,' he told her, then she heard laughter and a clamour of voices in the background with Simon replying, 'Yeah right! No, I didn't!'

Some laddish argy-bargy was going on by the sound of things, whooping and shouting. Georgie caught sight of her reflection in the dingy loo mirror and felt her spirits sink. Her eye make-up had all but melted into her skin with the warmth of the bar, and a blob of mascara had smudged on her cheek. And had her dress really been that wrinkled when she left the flat? It looked as if she'd slept in it. 'Are you still there?' she asked plaintively after a moment when Simon showed no signs of tearing himself away from the conversation with his mates.

'Sorry, love. There's talk of going on to some other place, I'm just trying to . . . Yeah, in a minute!' he called.

Sensing his attention waning once more, she made one last try to pull him back. 'Listen, why don't I join you? It's a bit crap here actually, so . . .'

'Hang on, I can't hear you – ahh, sod off, you bloody knobhead. Listen, I'd better go, this lot are going mental. Don't wait up, all right? I'll see you tomorrow.' And then he was gone, and she was left staring at her blotchy-faced reflection in defeat. Oh Christ. Now what? She didn't feel like going back into Dominique's humiliation zone, she couldn't bring herself to listen to any more shagging exploits, and she certainly didn't feel as if she could fake any kind of flirtatious speed dating, silent or not. Yet if she went back to the flat now, she would be pacing around, wondering where Simon was and lying in bed wide awake until he eventually crashed back in there.

The door banged open just then and two women came in, both laughing and talking about some bloke they had their eye on, a blast of sweet perfume and hairspray in their wake. Georgie pretended to be rummaging in her bag for a lipstick so as to hide her face, feeling her heart boom-boom-boom in her chest. This was all wrong, she thought, her hand trembling as she searched. What was happening to them? Simon was off boozing with all these new mates – and that rude woman – apparently not giving a toss for whatever she had to say. Meanwhile, here was Georgie deceitfully taking part in a speed dating night elsewhere in town, having recently admitted to a room full of utter strangers all sorts of candid truths about her sex life. She had another rapid flashback to that gorgeous June day – them as teenagers stretched out on their picnic blanket in the middle of nowhere – and remembered with a pang how madly in love they had been at that time, how the whole world had shrunk gloriously to contain just the two of them, Georgie and Simon Forever. Thinking about it made her clutch hold of the sink all of a sudden because, for a horrible moment, she thought she might cry. What had they become? How had things gone so wrong?

'You all right there, darling?' One of the women – the older blonde, with a voice that bore witness to thousands of Marlboros – had just come out of the cubicle and eyed Georgie in concern. 'Bit full-on in there, isn't it? More sharks than the bloody ocean, if you ask me.'

Georgie smiled weakly. 'I'm fine,' she managed to say though she didn't feel fine at all. She wasn't even sure who she was any more. The Stonefield Georgie would never have come in here, never in a million years. Yet this new Brighton Georgie kept getting herself into scrape after scrape. 'Thanks.'

She had two choices, she realized dimly, as she found a couple of lipsticks at the bottom of her bag – one a traffic-stopping red, one a softer caramel – and stared unseeingly at them both. She could dredge up some enthusiasm, remind herself that this was part of her Dream Job and didn't mean anything, and join in with the silent speed dating. Or she could trudge back home, put this whole sorry evening behind her, and instead spend her time thinking up ways to repair her relationship before the last thread of it snapped clean through.

'Red,' advised the woman beside her at the sinks, now dusting blusher on her cheekbones. 'Your lippy, I mean. Go for the red one, every time. Makes you feel a million dollars. And all the men love it, don't they?'

Georgie attempted another smile in response. *Red for danger, red for love*, she thought but duly rolled it on anyway. Not because the men loved a red lipsticked mouth, mind, but because she needed all the million-dollar help she could get right now. Then she stared hard at her reflection, took a deep breath, and made her decision.

Chapter Twenty

Facebook: Ann-Marie Chandler

Recent updates

Finger painting with my little princess this morning! A future Picasso!!!

Joshie came top in his spelling test at school. Definitely takes after his Daddy!!!

Whoops . . . been shopping with the girls and accidentally bought a few goodies. Naughty Mummy. Nobody let on to my hubby!! #shoes #Iloveshoes

Anyone for cocktails? Celebrating our new conservatory being finished at last. Cheers! #tipsyalready

Good news . . . clever David's got this amazing new job! So proud!!! Less good news . . . he'll be away more than ever now. What can I say . . . everybody wants him. Who can blame them?? #blessed

Rosa had been feeling so much more chipper since her lovely

dinner party – actually *joyful*, Madame Zara, yes, joyful, so stick that one in your charlatan's pipe – that there was a part of her that felt kind of sordid to still be grubbing around, lurking on Ann-Marie's Facebook page, unable to resist poring over every single gushing update and beaming photo. The perfect nuclear family, just look at them, so attractive and wholesome – and yet she knew full well that it was a pack of lies, completely hollow at the centre. She could knock the whole careful structure down with one little shove.

At the end of the day, you had to feel sorry for Ann-Marie, really: sorry for poor, pretty, enthusiastic Ann-Marie who was just so gullible and trusting. As Rosa had been, of course. She of all people knew how credible Max – David – could be when he gazed into your eyes, how a woman wanted to believe every damn thing he had told her.

This mention of a 'new job', though, and being away more than ever – that didn't sound good for Ann-Marie, did it? Wake up, Ann-Marie, and smell that freshly made cappuccino you've just conjured up from your flashy new coffee machine! He's got someone else again, he's playing you for a fool! And what had he called himself this time? Rosa wondered. Was he Max again, or would he have a different name now? You'd think it would get confusing after a while, all these identities. Exhausting, really. Obviously the effort was worth it, in his eyes; the game too irresistible to stop playing just yet. *It got out of hand, I do love you,* he'd said pleadingly on the phone to her that last time, and he'd sounded genuinely sorry. Not sorry enough to stop himself moving straight on to someone else, though, clearly.

If you were to read right back through Ann-Marie's time-line, as Rosa had done before (yes, all of it, because she was masochistic like that), the evidence was there, quite plain for anyone of a suspicious mind to piece together into a bigger picture. David's sales job that meant he had to travel so much, and attend so many conferences – especially at week-ends! The kids did miss him so, but they were grateful too, for clever hard-working Daddy, who was just doing his best for the family. Even when poor David had to miss Joshie's birthday that time because he was in New York, and Ann-Marie had had to email a video of little Mae's first steps because he was away again, this time in Boston, and oh, so many other times, actually, where Rosa could read between the lines and see that for all the posturing and mugging up to camera, David was very much a part-time father, a shad-owy figure on the outskirts of his kids' lives. He'd been with *her* each time, of course, in London, in Amsterdam, in the Maldives, not in New York, or Boston, not at any confer-ences. And yet Ann-Marie seemed to have accepted each absence uncomplainingly, the poor deluded cow.

Anyway. Whatever. She had better things to do this after-noon, like printing off a poster to put in the hall, advertising her inaugural supper club. Yes! She was going to trial it, just a small one at first, for people she already knew, basically, but you had to start somewhere. Her neighbours had been so encouraging, and even Natalya had nodded her approval. 'People will pay you for cooking dinner in your *flat*? Is good,' she had pronounced. 'Is right.'

The buzzer at Rosa's front door went just as she was saving her first stab at a poster, making her jump. 'Hello?' she said into the intercom.

'Hi, Rosa, it's Gareth,' came the response and she was still so immersed in the Facebook page that, for a moment, she found herself stupidly thinking it must be a Gareth she'd seen on Ann-Marie's timeline, her friend Miranda's husband. Get a grip, Rosa! 'Is Bea at your place?' he went on, before she could say anything. 'Have you seen her?' He sounded breathless, as if he'd just been running, anxious too. 'I don't know where she is.'

The words were pouring from his mouth so fast they were tripping over each other and Rosa felt taken aback. It was gone five; school had long since finished. 'I've been at work most of the day,' she said, pressing the button to let him in and going out to meet him in the hall. 'She might be in the flat, I suppose, but I haven't heard her. Should I have done? I mean, aren't you supposed to be . . . ?'

Barely listening, Gareth ran past her to pound on Jo's door. 'Bea? Are you in there? I'm sorry, all right? Bea?' No answer came and his fist dropped to his side, his expression one of defeat. 'Damn it.'

'What's happened? I take it you've tried ringing her?' Rosa gestured back at her own open front door. 'Why don't you come in for a minute? I could try phoning if she's got the hump with you, or—'

'That's part of the problem,' he said, following her into the flat. He sank into the sofa, his long legs bending like an anglepoise lamp, and pulled a small purple smartphone from his pocket, holding it up with a grim expression. 'I've got her phone. I confiscated it again from her last night when we had this big bust-up. The worst one yet.' He rubbed his eyes, his body language signalling defeat. 'God, I'm shit at this,' he confessed ruefully. 'I'm just . . . I don't know what I'm doing. I thought it was hard when she was a baby and screaming all night with colic, but this . . . this not knowing . . . The two of us locking horns about everything, arguing constantly . . .' He spread his hands and looked up at Rosa, humility in his eyes. 'I'm making a right pig's ear of things, basically. And now I don't have a clue where she is. My own daughter!'

Rosa tried to think in practical terms. 'Have you phoned the school to see if she went in today?'

'Yep,' he replied. 'They said she was in her lessons all day and doesn't have any after-school clubs. She's not been in to see Jo either, I checked with the hospital. I've drawn a total blank.'

'What about mates? Do you know any of their names, where they hang out?'

'That's the other thing,' he said. 'I looked at her phone for that reason, to see if there were any old conversations about meeting up or going to particular places and . . .' He grimaced.

'What?'

'Well, she's been getting these horrible messages. Like, properly horrible. Nasty, bullying stuff.' She noticed his hands curl into fists again. 'I had no idea,' he went on gruffly. 'I'm her dad and I had no bloody idea.'

Right. Cos I'm so popular, Rosa remembered Bea muttering sarcastically that time. Oh God, who would be a teenage girl again? 'What do you mean horrible messages?' she asked worriedly. 'From who? Someone at school, or . . . ?'

'It's all anonymous.' He bent over the phone and swiped the screen. 'It's like "Why don't you just die, bitch?" "Nobody likes you, bitch." "Ever thought of drowning yourself, bitch?"' He shook his head. 'And so on.'

Rosa turned cold, hearing the hateful words. 'Oh no. Poor thing.' She thought of Bea's wary scowl that some-times – if you were lucky – became a crooked smile; the hurt she must have been carrying around all this time. People were so fragile at the end of the day. Everyone covered up, constructing public faces for themselves, but imagine getting messages like that, drip drip drip, every day, wondering who had sent them, wondering who else knew. 'What did the school say, did they know about this?'

'They said she'd been rather "volatile" lately. Arguing back in class. One teacher had noticed her spending a lot of time on her own,' he said flatly. 'I wish she'd told me. Said something. I might have been able to help, but . . .' He got to his feet in a sudden movement. 'Anyway, I should get out there and look for her. *Shit*. I was so sure she'd be here as well. If I give you my number, will you ring me if she comes back? I've got to find her and put this right, not least because Jo would . . .' He broke off, anguish in his eyes. 'I've got to put it right,' he said again.

'I've got a better idea,' Rosa said, getting to her feet. 'I'll come with you.'

Having left a note for Bea along with both Rosa's and Gareth's phone numbers, they headed off in Gareth's car. 'She'll call us from Jo's landline if she gets back before us,' Rosa said, clipping in her seatbelt. 'Where shall we look in the meantime? Where might she have gone?'

'She doesn't have much money,' Gareth said, 'not enough to get the train anywhere, so hopefully she hasn't gone far. Unless she's hitched, of course.' He hit the steering wheel as they crawled to a stop in the rush-hour traffic snaking along the seafront. 'Oh God. Please let her be more sensible than that.'

'She *is* sensible,' Rosa said firmly, although she knew from her own experiences that even the most outwardly seeming sensible person could act irrationally when they'd been badly hurt. 'Let's think about places around here first. She's obviously unhappy, she's had a horrible time. Is there anywhere special to her that she might have gone to, for comfort? Any favourite place where she might be hiding out?'

'There's the pier, I suppose,' he said. 'There are always tons of kids hanging around there. And she loved Hove Lagoon when she was younger, we used to go there a lot together, back when I first became a weekend dad.' He groaned. 'God, I can't believe this is happening. I can't believe it's come to this. I shouldn't have been so hard on her, she's only a kid.'

Rosa tried to steer the conversation back to practicalities. 'Does she have any favourite cafés, or shops? Have you looked on the beach at all?' She gazed out at the calm blue sea and the words of the horrible text messages came back to her. *Ever thought of drowning yourself, bitch?* Rosa shuddered despite the warmth of the car. She wasn't even going to mention that particular possibility. Not until they'd combed every inch of the city, anyway.

'No,' he admitted, 'but you're right, we should. Sod it,' he said, swinging the wheel round to the left, swerving up the next side street and parking the first chance he got, even though there were double yellow lines and the city traffic wardens were notoriously generous with their parking tickets. 'It'll be quicker to walk. Let's just start looking.' He locked the car. 'Come on.'

They tramped along the beach, scouring the horizon for Bea but she was not to be found anywhere on the pier, nor in any of the cafés they put their heads into along the way. Neither was she outside the big shopping mall with other KFC-eating teenagers, or down by the skateboarding ramps. The sun was sliding into the sea now, the sky becoming gauzy with the dusk. Any beach-going families had packed up and gone home for the day, the sea was empty of all hardy swimmers and paddlers; the deckchairs folded back up in the beach hut where they were kept. Meanwhile, the beachside restaurants and bars were filling up for the evening, while groups of teenagers and twenty-somethings lingered on the pebbles with cigarettes and bottles of beer and music. *Where are you, Bea?* thought Rosa as she mentally checked and discarded one girl's face after another. *Where are you?*

Gareth bought them a bag of salted chips to eat while they continued back along the beach towards Hove. The lights were all coming on along the seafront as they walked, strings of golden bulbs festooned between the lamp posts like bunting. Before long, the sky would be deepening into a school-ink blue and if Bea was down on the beach, it would be doubly hard to see her. At what point did you start really panicking about a missing child? Rosa wondered uncertainly. At what point did you get the police involved?

Gareth had his head down. 'This is all my fault,' he said wretchedly. 'It's been difficult with Candy staying, I should have known it wouldn't end well.'

'Candy – that's your girlfriend?' Rosa asked, remembering the sleepy female voice she'd heard at Gareth's house.

'No, my sister,' he said. 'She's in between flats so I said she could stay for a while but Bea's never really got on with her. I think she blames Candy for my breaking up with Jo.'

Rosa frowned, not understanding immediately.

'Because Candy was the one Jo went off with? Yeah, my sister and my wife,' he confirmed, seeing Rosa's shocked face. 'Talk about a double whammer.'

'Bloody hell,' said Rosa, glancing sideways at him. 'That must have hurt.'

'Yep. All shades of awkwardness have been experienced,' he said, with a half-laugh, peering into the distance. 'But, you know. We're all adults. And there's Bea to think about too, in the middle of everything. Saying that, I'm not sure any of us behaved brilliantly throughout, though.' He grimaced, his features leaping into a sharper focus as they went under a lamp post, and Rosa remembered what Jo had said, about Gareth taking their split particularly hard, his manly pride being dented. Men could tie themselves in such knots, couldn't they, trying to live up to these stereotypes, every bit as much as women did, she thought sympathetically. Perfect people, perfect parents. Did anyone ever achieve it, really? She bet even Ann-Marie Chandler, uber-goddess of parenting, screeched at her kids sometimes, made mistakes, had a gin and tonic at five o'clock once in a while because she'd had a pig of a day. Didn't every human being feel the same way, now and then?

Before she could speak, Gareth had stiffened suddenly beside her. 'Hey. Is that her, look? On the wall down there?' And before Rosa could reply, he was running, waving a hand above his head. 'Bea! Hey, Bea!'

They had reached a beachside playground, silent and shadowy now, a stark contrast to how it must be in the daytime, swarming with shrieking children and their parents. Rosa couldn't see anyone at first and strained her eyes in the dim light, then saw the still figure, taking up the smallest space possible on a low wall, hugging her knees, her long hair dangling over her legs. Bea – at last – in a kids' playground where once upon a time she must have spent happy times, presumably happier than in more recent weeks.

Rosa held back a little, not wanting to interfere in the moment between father and daughter. She watched as Gareth rushed over, relief palpable in his voice as he called his daughter's name again, then felt a lump in her throat as he sat beside her, both arms curling protectively around her in an embrace, and Bea leaned against him, for once not pulling away. *Dad's here. Dad's got you.* She remembered with a lump in her throat all those times her own dad had rescued her, from a fall, from a fight with her sister, from a bad day at school.

'I'm sorry,' she heard Bea sobbing. 'I'm sorry, Dad.'

His voice was low and murmuring, his arms still locked around her, but Rosa could guess what he was saying in return. *I'm sorry, too, love. Come on, it's going to be all right. Let's go home, eh?*

Rosa was all for slipping away and leaving them to it, but Gareth insisted that she join him and Bea for dinner in a pub not far from the square, the Regency Arms. 'Go on, let me buy you a drink and something to eat other than chips,' he urged when she hesitated. 'Between me and my daughter, we did just drag you out on a very long beach walk. A restorative glass of wine and some food is the least I can offer in return.'

'Sorry, Rosa,' Bea said, looking up at her from beneath her clumpy, tear-sodden eyelashes. Her nails were bitten down to the quick, Rosa noticed, and she gave the girl a hug.

'Don't worry about it,' she said. 'I'm sorry too, that things have been tough for you. But we can sort it out between us, I'm sure.'

'Starting with those weasels who've been texting you stupid messages,' Gareth said. 'I've already sent them back a little message of my own.' And he held up Bea's phone, which she snatched from him immediately.

'Dad! You didn't! Oh my God. DAD! What did you *say*?'

Gareth winked over his daughter's head at Rosa while the girl clicked frantically at her phone. Then she gave a spluttering sort of laugh. 'Oh my *God*. I can't believe you did that.'

'Is it okay? Too much? I was a bit cross, to be honest,' Gareth said. 'Might have gone a touch overboard.'

'What did you put?' Rosa couldn't help asking.

Bea passed her the phone so that she could read the message for herself in the streetlight as they walked along.

THIS IS BEA'S FATHER. I'LL BE SHOWING THE POLICE AND THE SCHOOL THESE MESSAGES. IF MY DAUGHTER HAS TO PUT UP WITH ANY MORE OF YOUR SHIT YOU'LL HAVE ME TO DEAL WITH.

'Whoa,' said Rosa.

'I *know*,' said Bea, but you could tell she was pleased. 'No reply either. They must be bricking it.' She giggled. 'Well . . . that is unless they've actually *seen* you, Dad, of course.'

'Oi, watch it,' Gareth said, but he was grinning. 'By the way, you should really work on a better password, Bea. Took me all of two minutes to guess yours and get into your messages. At least make it a *challenge* for anyone who nicks your phone.'

Bea rolled her eyes. 'Dad's a hacker,' she told Rosa.

'Er, I write software, you mean,' he corrected her. 'I'm not a criminal mastermind. Although . . .' He tapped his nose. 'I have learned a few tricks along the way.'

They had reached the pub now and Gareth pushed the door open for them both. Inside, the place was decorated with pink brocade wallpaper, with a glitterball twinkling from the ceiling and velvety leopard-print sofas. Very Brighton, thought Rosa with a smile as they headed for the bar. Gareth ordered a round of drinks and bid them sit down, then, as he came back with a tray of clinking glasses and a sheaf of menus, Bea moved up so that he could sit down next to her. It was the tiniest of gestures, an olive branch so small it might have been missed by an onlooker, but Rosa noticed and was gladdened by it, and Gareth immediately slung an arm around his daughter and ruffled her hair, which made her laugh and push him away. Affectionately, though. Like a proper dad and daughter.

He came good, Rosa thought, feeling unexpectedly fond of Gareth as she picked up the menu. Dad to the rescue, just when he'd been needed most. When disaster had struck, Gareth had been there to catch his daughter, to save her from the fall. That would teach Rosa to write off all handsome men as untrustworthy. Maybe he was one of the good guys, after all.

The waitress had just set down their plates of food and

was bustling away again when Bea's phone started ringing in her pocket. The three of them immediately looked at each other, clearly all thinking the same thing: that it was the school bully once more, weighing in for another attack. 'Do you want me to take it?' Gareth asked, already reaching out a hand.

'No, I'll . . .' Bea swallowed. 'I've got it.' She pulled out the phone and then her expression changed. 'Oh, it's Mum!' she said, hurriedly swiping the screen. 'Hello?'

You could have heard a pin drop as both Rosa and Gareth leaned forward. '*Really?*' said Bea and her eyes were suddenly shining with tears. 'Oh, Mum, that's so brilliant. Let me just tell the others – she can come home tomorrow!' she cried. 'Yeah, everything's fine here,' she said into the phone, smiling shyly at both Gareth and then Rosa. 'We're in the pub, actually. No, I'm not drinking. Dad's only had three bottles of wine so far.' She stuck her tongue out at him as he made a yelp of outrage. 'I'm joking, Mum. No, it's been fine. Dad's all right really, I suppose. Yeah, me too. Bye, Mum. See you tomorrow.'

Chapter Twenty-One

SeaView House Noticeboard:

PRACTICE SUPPER CLUB
FRIDAY 20th MAY!

Three courses at Rosa's flat.
Bring whatever you'd like to drink.
Ten quid – special introductory price!

Everyone had been so delighted when Charlotte and Jim got together. 'He's so right for you,' her mum had gushed after that first Sunday dinner. 'Seems like a good bloke,' her dad had commented, when Jim helped him put a fence up. Even her difficult Aunty Irene, who never liked *anybody*, grudgingly decreed him 'better than the last few, anyway'; high praise indeed. The perfect couple, friends had sighed on their wedding day. But nothing lasted forever. Even so-called perfection could twist and buckle, especially when you were forced to watch your own baby die together. Locked in their parallel worlds of sadness, they had no longer been able to reach one another after the funeral, no longer able to find a connection. Not so perfect after all, then.

Goodness only knew why she was thinking of Jim again, when she was meant to be getting ready for her first date with *Ned*, Charlotte chastised herself, trying to put her mascara on but blinking at the wrong moment so that she jabbed her eye with the wand. *Ow*. There, that was karma, telling her to focus and step away from the past. Now she was going to turn up to her date with a bloodshot eye and bad make-up, and she'd only have herself to blame.

Her *date*, she marvelled, trying to wipe away the black smears on her eyelid with little success. She was actually going on a date again. So there, Jim, you're not the only one who can move on. The past was the past. She was all about the future these days.

'A date!' her mum had exclaimed when she mentioned it on the phone. 'Gosh! Are you sure this isn't just . . .' She had trailed off diplomatically but Charlotte knew her mum well enough to hear the unsaid '. . . because of the news about Jim?' there in the ensuing silence.

'It's only one date, Mum,' she said firmly. 'Dinner with a man. I'm dipping a toe back in, that's all, okay? Testing the waters.'

Margot had been more enthusiastic at least when Charlotte went up to tell her about it. She still looked pale and unwell, wrapped in a dressing gown, her speech punctuated by a lung-wrenching cough, but assured Charlotte that she was on the mend, and that this news was just what she needed to help her recover. 'Have fun,' she said. 'And be brave. And *bad!*'

Bad, indeed. Like Charlotte was that sort of person. But she could be brave, all right. She could go out there and try again, wear her experience like armour and take that leap of faith. He knew the worst thing that had ever happened to her, after all, and he hadn't flinched. If anything, his kindness and understanding were what made her feel she could trust him.

She started again with the mascara, taking care not to stab herself or muck it up this time. She'd gone out clothes-shopping in her lunch hour the day before, finding a really flattering mint-green top whose silky fabric fell softly against her skin, somehow disguising all the ready-meals and chocolate eclairs she'd put away recently. That would do with a nice pair of jeans and maybe some wedge sandals, wouldn't it? She had finished the outfit with a gold circlet that looked understated yet a bit classy too; a look, all in all, which said, in her opinion, I've made an effort but I'm not trying *too* hard. Staring at herself in the mirror, she brushed her hair and arranged it around her shoulders, suddenly feeling a bolt of nerves. God. Would he expect to *kiss* her, she wondered, pulling a face at her reflection. It had been so long since she'd kissed anyone, really snogged them properly in a cor-fancy-*you* kind of way. What if she had forgotten how to do it? What if she somehow got it wrong?

Her phone rang just then and it was him. 'Um . . . Charlotte?' he said, sounding worried. 'About tonight. There's a slight problem.'

'I'm so sorry about this,' he said, as he answered the door to her half an hour later. Grabbing a bottle of wine from the fridge, she'd taken a cab over to his place in Hanover, a Victorian terrace on a steep hill, with pink flower shapes Blu-tacked into one of the upstairs windows. 'Daisy – the babysitter – is normally really reliable but she double-booked and only realized at the last minute. I tried my sister but she's hosting twelve drunk women at her book club tonight, apparently. Her words, not mine.' He looked flustered, raking a hand through his shaggy hair so that it stuck up at the front. 'Come in, anyway. Dinner is a bit . . . random, I'm afraid, but I've got tons of wine at least.'

She stepped into the narrow hall, past dinky purple and red children's wellies, a half-collapsed buggy with a plastic necklace draped around one handle, and almost tripped over what appeared to be a ride-on ladybird with deranged googly eyes lurking beneath the coat rack. A proper family home, she thought to herself, feeling a twist of envy inside, mingled with the familiar sadness of something that had been denied to her. Living right in the city centre, as she did, it was easy to forget about neighbourhoods like this one, with bikes propped outside, cats draped along windowsills, glimpses of dinners being served in brightly lit kitchens, curtains being drawn upstairs. Of course, she'd deliberately chosen to live away from happy families in streets like these, but coming here, seeing the ordinariness of so many lives carrying on around her, she realized she'd missed it too in a strange way.

'Here, add this to your collection,' she said to him now, holding out the bottle she'd brought. 'And it's fine, honestly, about the restaurant and everything, don't worry about it.' She shrugged off her jacket and hung it on an empty peg on the wall alongside a Snow White cape, a small shiny yellow mackintosh, and a battered denim jacket. There were some little trainers on the floor too, messily kicked off. Weren't small shoes the sweetest things ever? She had kept a single pair of knitted white bootees that Kate had worn in intensive care and, even now, could remember how those tiny feet had felt in her hands. *Oh, Kate.* She hoped she could keep it together, being here, surrounded by the regalia of two other little girls. What if her emotions got the better of her, what if being here stirred up all her feelings of loss again?

Don't go there, she ordered herself, taking a deep breath as she turned back. *Keep your cool.*

'Hello,' came a high, interested voice just then, and Charlotte glanced up to see that a small, curious face had appeared at the top of the stairs, peering down; the girl from the pier who'd held her hand. Lily, was she called?

'Hello,' she replied, swallowing uncertainly and trying to smile. *Please don't remember that I screamed at your dad that day.*

Ned groaned at the sight of his daughter. 'You're meant to be in bed,' he reminded her.

'I'm not tired.' The girl sat down on the top step, stretching a pale pink nightie down over her knees. 'Not even a very *bit*.' She opened her eyes wide as if demonstrating how extremely awake she was. 'Look.'

'Lils, come on. It's bedtime and you've got school in the morning.' A timer started beeping further into the house and he glanced over his shoulder helplessly at it. 'And that's the lasagne. Go on, hop it. Quick! Right now! Good girl.' He pulled a funny face as his daughter reluctantly got to her feet. 'Sorry, Charlotte, come through. Let me get you a drink.'

Charlotte followed Ned down the hall and into a long narrow kitchen, whose walls were decorated with various paintings and collages. A face made of pasta shapes. Some animal – a dog perhaps? a cow? – constructed of scraps of fabric with black buttons for eyes. There was a stuffed monkey dangling from the curtain rail, and a tableau of Sylvanian Family animals having a tea-party with a small plastic dragon down by the back door. Charlotte had to blink quickly and look away. *He's allowed to have a family,* she reminded herself, her fingers curling into her palms. *They're allowed to be happy. This is real life, Charlotte. That's just how it is.*

'Smells delicious,' she said, noticing the pile of saucepans stacked up in the sink and feeling touched that he'd gone to so much effort on her behalf when she'd have been perfectly happy with a fish and chip takeaway. 'Thank you. This is lovely of you, especially at such short notice.' (If he could whip up a lasagne at the drop of a hat, she must never let him see the woeful emptiness of her fridge, she thought in the next moment.)

'It's vegetarian, I hope that's okay,' he said, his voice slightly muffled as he bent to check inside the oven. 'I didn't think to ask if you ate meat, when I . . . Oh, *Lily.*' His voice became stern at the sound of pattering footsteps. 'What are you doing down here? I thought you'd gone to bed!'

Charlotte turned to see the little girl standing in the doorway, hopping from foot to foot. 'Hello again,' she said.

Encouraged by this, Lily danced into the room, her white-blonde hair flying out around her head as she pointed her toes. 'I like your shirt,' she said winningly to Charlotte, who felt pathetically flattered. 'Green is my best colour.' Then she came to a stop by the freezer and gazed up at her dad. 'Are you going to have ice cream?' she asked him in a

way that left no room for misunderstanding where this particular conversation might be going.

'Maybe later but—'

'I *love* ice cream,' Lily told Charlotte confidingly, as if he
hadn't spoken. 'It's my *best*. Specially chocolate. Aunty
Debbie lets us have *sprinkles* and—'

'Lily. You can have some ice cream tomorrow if you go
back to bed right now,' Ned said, folding his arms across his
chest. 'But if you don't go this minute, then Charlotte and I
will eat *all* of it tonight, without you. *And* we'll have all the
sprinkles.'

Lily's jaw dropped in outrage. 'But—'

'This *minute*, I said.'

Eyes blazing, Lily whirled around crossly and stamped
upstairs. Then they heard a door bang, shortly followed by a
pitiful wail. 'Oh, great,' sighed Ned. 'Now she's woken her
sister up. I'm sorry about this, Charlotte.' He took down two
wine glasses and held them up, looking rather helpless. 'Red
or white? Or should I just put you out of your misery and
order you a cab home?'

'No! Don't worry about it,' she told him. He was looking
really frazzled by now, taking off his glasses and rubbing the
lenses on his shirt. She noticed the ironing board propped up
in the corner of the room just then too, the iron still cooling
on the side, and realized he must have ironed his shirt on her
behalf. He was trying hard, you had to give him that. 'Red

would be lovely,' she said. 'I can pour if you need to get on with dinner.'

'Would you? Thanks.' He passed her the bottle, corkscrew and glasses. 'Right. Let me chuck together a salad, and then we can eat.'

It took approximately half a glass of wine, several mouthfuls of (excellent) lasagne and a slightly stilted conversation about his work running the café and her unloved job, before they had their first bonding moment when they realized they had both been to university in Birmingham. This was pretty much the exact point where Ned stopped looking quite so harassed and Charlotte started to relax. It took a second glass of wine, their scraped-clean plates and the joyful realization that they had friends of friends in common ('No! You were in halls with Eleanor *Gray*? She went out with my flatmate Neil!') to have them clinking glasses like old mates, exclaiming what a small world it was, and reminiscing about their favourite pubs and gigs they'd been to around the city.

But just then there came the sound of small footsteps again, and in came Lily, this time holding hands with Amber, both in their nighties with messed-up bed hair. Amber's nightie was patterned with dinosaurs, and a ragged brown teddy dangled from one hand. Lily, for some reason, had donned a pair of fairy wings and some stripy socks. Charlotte's breath caught in her throat at the vision. Oh, these girls. They were simply adorable.

Lily put her arm around Amber. 'You was making too much noise laughing,' she said disapprovingly, 'and you woked us *up*.'

'And now we want ice *cweam*,' Amber said, a determined set to her jaw.

'I told her you had ice cream,' Lily explained smugly, 'and now she wants it.' She shrugged as if the adults only had themselves to blame for the situation.

'Is that so?' Ned said, raising an eyebrow then catching Charlotte's eye. He was pulling such a severe Dad expression she found herself wanting to giggle.

'I had a bad dweam,' Amber said in a piteous and not altogether convincing way, cocking her head up at her father. 'Because you was *laughing*.' She looked at Charlotte from under long dark eyelashes. 'And what is *your* name?' she asked, sliding a thumb into her mouth.

They were so unbelievably cute, standing there together in bare feet, naughty little partners in ice-cream wangling. Maybe it was the wine, maybe it was that she'd had such a nice time with Ned, but Charlotte no longer felt cramped up inside with envy or pain. Goodness, if she had tiny sweet daughters like these two, she'd probably let them have ice cream all day. Look at them! How could anyone refuse them anything? 'I'm Charlotte,' she replied. 'I'm sorry we woke you up. I'm not sure but I think your dad *might* have some ice cream,' she went on, hoping the cheering and leaping up and down this prompted from both girls wouldn't incur her host's wrath. She couldn't bear for Ned to send them back up to bed immediately, she realized. Also, and this was even more shallow, she wanted them to like her. Talk about a pushover. 'Sorry,' she said, turning to him. 'I couldn't resist. They're so gorgeous.'

Lily stopped leaping and cheering in order to beam graciously at Charlotte and then twirl around on the spot so that her wings fluttered. 'I am a beautiful fairy,' she agreed.

'Can we have ice cweam now?' asked Amber, just in case anyone had forgotten why they were there.

'Oh, go on, then,' Ned said, caving in and rolling his eyes at Charlotte. 'One small bowl each and then it's straight back up to bed, all right? Just this once.'

By the end of the evening, everyone had eaten and drunk their fill, and Charlotte had a sleeping Amber on her lap, nestled into her like a small warm bear-cub. Lily had already been carted back up to bed, fast asleep, over her father's shoulder, but Charlotte had shaken her head when Ned offered to peel his youngest daughter away similarly. 'She's fine,' she told him. It was more than fine, actually, having a soft little person sleeping on you while you drank another glass of wine and flirted daringly with their father. Every time she felt Amber breathe or sigh or murmur, every time she glanced down and saw that tiny pink ear whorl, the flutter of those long dark eyelashes against a rounded cheek, the tangle of long brown hair slippery against her arm, it was like the best kind of balm on an old hurt. The most comforting feeling in the world. *You're not Kate*, she thought, *but you're lovely. And you're here.*

'Thank you, I've had a brilliant evening,' she said when they'd finally called it a night. Amber had been taken up to bed, Charlotte had put her jacket back on, and a taxi was waiting outside, engine purring beneath the streetlights.

'Me too,' he replied. 'And I promise that next time, all babysitting arrangements will be firmly in place so we don't have to eat with an entourage,' he added with a rueful face.

Next time, she thought, hugging the phrase to herself. 'I didn't mind,' she told him truthfully, then hesitated in the doorway, wishing she could stop thinking about kissing quite so much. Should she lunge at him, make the first move? she wondered, biting her lip. *Be brave*, urged Margot in her head but Charlotte remained frozen to the spot. It was all right for Margot to say such a thing; she was perfectly shameless and didn't seem to care what anyone else thought. Charlotte, on the other hand . . .

'Well,' she said, reluctantly. 'Good night, then. And thanks again.'

'Good night, Charlotte,' he said, and then, before she could even panic that she might have garlic breath or have turned into an incompetent kisser, he was looming towards her and his lips were on hers. Goodness, yes, and now his arms were around her, all firm and muscular, and the two of them were locked in the most fantastically passionate kiss that made her legs feel quite weak and her body just want to press herself against him, and . . .

And the taxi was beeping from the road, and then they were laughing at what an unromantic killjoy the driver must be, and disentangling themselves. 'That was an excellent kiss,' she heard herself saying recklessly before leaning over and giving him a last quick goodbye on the lips. Then she turned and hurried down the steps, her face one gigantic smile.

'Let's have another soon,' he called after her.

'You bet,' she called back, clambering into the taxi. She could see Ned still standing there leaning against his door frame, and he put one hand up in a wave, as the driver pulled away. Charlotte waved back, grinning like an idiot, her heart pounding at what had just happened. *I kissed him*, she thought wonderingly, her fingers reaching up to touch her own lips. Her skin was tingling all over. *I kissed Ned!*

The driver caught her eye in the rear-view mirror. He was about the same age as her dad and had a kind face, for all that he'd beeped them a minute ago and interrupted the best kiss she'd had in ages. 'Had a good evening?' he asked, as he swung round a corner and headed towards the glittering dark sea.

'Yeah,' she replied dreamily, leaning back against the vinyl seat and smiling to herself. 'Yeah, I had a really good evening, thanks.'

Chapter Twenty-Two

You Send Me . . . Silent Speed Dating!
By Georgie Taylor

So this week, I've been sent to check out the mysterious world of speed dating – with a twist. Those clever people at Forever Yours matchmaking agency reckon that a silent encounter with a potential partner can be intimate, romantic and very sexy, and that gazing into a person's eyes is often every bit as revealing as listening to them boring on about their job and love of Arsenal – perhaps more appealing, too!

That's the theory – but how does it stack up, in real life? As your fearless reporter, I went along to find out for myself.

Tonight's event was held in the Olive Tree on Grosvenor Street – and as soon as I walked in, I was hit by a wall of aftershave, perfume and the scent of thirty nervous people, most of whom looked as if they'd already taken advantage of the evening's free cocktail and perhaps a few more besides, in the name of Dutch courage. Who can blame them? I went straight to the bar myself and ordered a Throbbing Orgasm (no sniggering at the back, please), conscious that this was not going to be a straightforward night out down the boozer.

There is something quite liberating about being in a room full of singletons, there for the sole purpose of finding someone to love. People were openly checking each other out, there was a lot of meaningful eye contact, and I could hear several sneaky chatting-up attempts taking place as punters tried to get ahead of the game before the actual silent part of the evening got underway (or before they became too drunk to be coherent, perhaps).

The dating event began with a series of warm-up exercises . . .

Georgie groaned and put her face down in the bed. Dating schmating. What a load of bollocks it had all been. It was half-past one on Friday afternoon now, and she had three hours left before she was supposed to file her speed dating copy. If she didn't, she was pretty sure Viv might tell her to stick her column. But what on earth should she write?

Just as she was idly wondering about going foraging in the kitchen for Brie and crackers and maybe one of those pecan cookies Rosa had dropped round, the door of the flat suddenly crashed open, and her heart almost stopped in shock. Oh my God, she thought, eyes widening in alarm.

This was it – she was going to be burgled. Assaulted. All the warnings on the dangers of city life from her mum rang uselessly around her head as she rolled off the bed – a proper stunt roll, thank you – and grabbed the nearest thing to hand as a weapon. 'Hello?' she yelled, trying to make herself sound forceful and menacing, before looking down and realizing that she was holding a fluffy slipper in her hand. Brilliant.

'Hi,' came the reply and Georgie instantly sagged with relief, adrenalin draining away as she recognized the voice. It was not, thankfully, the voice of some crazed crackhead hellbent on ransacking the place for valuables after all, but the weary, dejected-sounding voice of her boyfriend instead. 'Only me.'

God, he sounded weird, Georgie thought, the slipper dropping from her hand as she quickly shut the laptop then hurried out to see why he'd come home so early. He sounded terrible, actually. Was he ill? Had one of the massive steel joists of the new hotel dropped on his head or something? 'What's up? How come you're back already?' she asked, finding him in the sitting room. He was slumped on the sofa with his head in his hands and she knew that something really bad must have happened. 'What . . . What's going on?' she asked fearfully, wishing belatedly that she wasn't still in her pyjamas and had got around to brushing her hair.

'It's over,' he said, and for a terrible moment she thought he meant that the two of them were over, that he was dumping her right here, right now. Did he somehow know about the speed dating evening?

'Wh—' She gulped, breath seizing in her lungs. *No.* This could not be happening. Not when she was still in her jammies and had a massive looming-period zit in the middle of her forehead, *please*, she found herself thinking, which just went to show what a dreadful, shallow person she really was. 'What do you mean, over?'

'The hotel. It's all off. The developer's pulled out.'

Oh, she thought, knees buckling as her brain caught up. The *hotel* was over. Not them. Thank goodness. 'Shit,' she said, trying to sound suitably devastated. Actually, this *was* pretty devastating. 'How come? Was it money, or . . . ?'

'It was those bloody women,' he said bitterly, looking up at her for the first time since she'd entered the room. 'Jesus, George, are you not even *dressed* yet? Fucksake!'

'I'm . . .' She found herself putting her arms around herself as if that was any kind of disguise. 'I just got carried away,' she mumbled. 'Writing this new . . .' She trailed off again. The last thing she wanted to talk to him about was her column. 'What do you mean, those women?' she asked him instead. Then the penny dropped, as hard and painfully as any steel joist on the head. Clunk. *No*, she thought in horror. Did he mean the women at the refuge and their campaign? Their campaign which she'd helped kick-start with her interview?

'It's the women on site,' he replied darkly. 'They've got a refuge there and have refused to leave. This campaign started up and now the national press have picked up the story and things have gone berserk. The Historical Building people have got involved and are calling for the house to be listed. The council have withdrawn planning permission—'

'Can they even *do* that?'

'Yeah. If details come to light of which they were previously unaware . . .' He sighed, deflating into the sofa as if his last atoms of energy had deserted him. 'So we've had to down tools while they decide what they're doing. It could take months, to be honest. So . . .' He spread his hands, grim-faced. 'So that's that, then. My big chance – come to nothing.'

'Oh, Si.' She went over and put her arms around him, feeling terrible for him. She knew how hard he'd worked on the original tender, she knew how delighted he'd been to get the commission. 'God, what an absolute bummer.' Her mind was in turmoil. All she could think about was her interview, and how passionately she'd written in support of the women's centre. *This house of women should not fall*, she'd typed, regardless of how it might affect Simon's career. This was all her fault, she thought, a cold sweat breaking out on her skin. 'I'm sure something else will come up,' she said weakly. 'There'll be loads of architect firms around here, I bet.'

He shrugged. 'Not where I've got contacts, there aren't,' he said. 'I might as well go back home.'

'Back to Stonefield? But . . .' Whoa, this had all come out of the blue. Just when she was starting to feel at home down here in Brighton, too. She didn't feel ready to go back yet! 'But . . . Well . . .' She thought frantically, unable to quite believe what she was hearing. What had she done? 'Our place is rented for another four months, remember. We can't exactly chuck the tenants out.' However horrible they might be. (Although now that she thought about it, it *would* be incredibly satisfying to evict that awful Chloe, once and for all. *Get out and stay out!*)

'We can stay with my parents,' he said, shrugging. 'Or give the tenants notice, tell them we've changed our minds.' He turned to look at her, eyes narrowing. 'I thought you wanted to go back anyway?'

'Yeah, I did, but . . .' She bit her lip. But that was before she made a few friends, before she discovered her favourite café and shops, before she found herself loving her brand-new writing career, moreover. And she absolutely did not want to stay with Simon's parents longer than a single night either. 'We probably shouldn't rush into anything. The hotel might be back on again soon, mightn't it? You could have some time off instead.' She found herself gabbling in her desperation to lift his spirits. 'Do some fun stuff. We could have a holiday, maybe!'

'A holiday? When I've just lost my job?' He looked at her as if she was mad. Then he heaved a sigh and got to his feet. 'I'm going to the pub,' he said. 'I need a drink. The day I've had, I need a few.'

'I'll come with you,' Georgie said. Buying the man a drink was the least she could do, she figured. Hell, she was guilt-tripped enough right now that she'd shout him lunch too. 'Give me two minutes to get some clothes on and I'll come with you.' Somehow or other she had to make this right, she thought as she hurried into the bedroom, fingers trembling as she yanked her pyjama top over her head. But how?

A few days went by where, when he wasn't packing up boxes of his possessions, Simon was on the phone to his old contacts in the north, still seemingly insistent on the idea of returning to Yorkshire as soon as possible. Meanwhile Georgie was carrying around her guilty secret like a lead weight in her stomach, feeling like the most disloyal girlfriend ever. She had managed to beg a few days' grace on the delivery of the speed dating write-up by pretending to Viv she'd been struck down by violent food poisoning, but her editor had not been happy about being left with empty column space at such short notice.

To make matters worse, Cleo, one of the women from the refuge, had emailed her to thank her for writing the interview in the first place. *If it hadn't been for you presenting our case so sympathetically, we could still be fighting,* she'd written; every word like a dagger to Georgie. *But as soon as your article was out there, the petition went viral and we were able to use the momentum to get the national press and council onside. It's been amazing – we can't thank you enough!*

Oh, it was just so killingly ironic! If the email had been from anyone else, under any other circumstances, she'd have been cheering from the rooftops and totally claiming all the credit. As it was, Cleo's words just felt like another massive helping of guilt to add to the already considerable portion festering away inside her. On top of which, Georgie had undertaken some secretive googling and seen that the *Guardian*, *Times* and *Telegraph* had all quoted lines from her original interview in their pieces, which was, again, both gratifying and mortifying. *If it hadn't been for you!* Cleo kept saying in her head, eyes shining with delight. Yeah, Cleo. If it hadn't been for me, my boyfriend would still be in his job and there would be none of this box-packing and talk of going home. Good one, Georgie!

It was almost enough to make her want to contact her own fictional alter ego for advice. *Hey Em, I basically shafted my boyfriend with this article I wrote which has effectively meant him losing his job. Should I confess to him or bear the guilt in silence for evermore? Oh yeah, and I also went speed dating behind his back, but that was for an article too. What can I say, it's complicated!*

Em's disdainful reply came to her in a flash. *The poor bastard. Sounds like one toxic relationship to me. What do you love more – him or your work? Whichever, it might be time to set the guy free and tell him the truth – I reckon he deserves better than you anyway!*

Even for an imaginary agony aunt, artificially constructed for a magazine column and existing only in Georgie's head, Em had a point, you had to admit.

'Do *you* think I should say anything?' she asked Charlotte on Tuesday evening. Unable to bear the oppressive sound of Simon bundling shirts into a suitcase, she had slunk next door where she had made her guilty confession – whispering of her terrible misdeeds because she couldn't risk any chances of being overheard, even separated as they were by a brick wall. 'What would you do?'

There was something different about Charlotte, Georgie realized belatedly, peering at her suspiciously. She'd opened the door with this goofy sort of smile, and her whole being just seemed . . . relaxed. Carefree. Having spent a couple of excellent nights out together, Georgie had come to feel very fond of her neighbour but, with the best will in the world, Charlotte had struck her previously as on edge. Nervy. She'd looked positively terrified that first time Georgie had badgered her into going roller skating. And now here she was, bare feet tucked up beneath her on the sofa, pouring wine, music on in the background, that Mona Lisa-ish secretive smile on her face . . . Something had happened. All of a sudden, Georgie was a bit less keen on talking about her own problems, she wanted to know what had changed so drastically in Charlotte's world.

'. . . I mean, trust is really important,' Charlotte was saying. 'Me, I'm terrible at keeping things to myself anyway, I've never had a good poker face. Keeping a secret like that would kill me.'

'Mmm,' said Georgie. Deep down, she'd known all along that Charlotte would advocate honesty; she seemed far too straightforward a person to choose the path of deceit, given the choice. But then again, it wasn't Charlotte whose relationship was in such precarious straits, was it?

'What do you think he would say? Is he the forgiving type?'

Georgie remembered the sulk Simon had plunged into the day she'd borrowed his car and managed to scrape it against a wall during an abysmal reverse-parking incident. He'd had the hump with her for an entire week. But then again, back in the good old Yorkshire days when he wasn't being stressed and bad-tempered the whole time, he'd laughed off other mishaps with good humour: the time she'd drunkenly attempted break-dancing in their old kitchen and managed to kick the Leeds United mug he'd owned since

childhood off the table (smashed to smithereens) for example, or that Valentine's Day when she'd managed to ruin her
own surprise by taking him to the wrong restaurant at the
wrong time. She'd been mortified, but he'd found it hilarious, and they'd ended up eating a Chinese takeaway and
laughing their heads off. He could be kind when he wanted
to. Gentle. Loving. That side of him had rather been swallowed up in stress recently, though.

'Yes and no,' she said after a moment's reflection. 'But
he's unhappy right now, and he's one of those brooders who
can't just snap out of a mood. It's much harder to forgive
someone and be gracious about their screw-ups when you're
feeling crap about your own life, isn't it?'

'It is,' Charlotte affirmed, just as her phone buzzed with a
text. 'Sorry, I'll just . . .' she said, glancing at the screen, and
then her face lit up as she read whatever message had just
come in.

Georgie's curiosity had reached peak capacity. She
couldn't bear not knowing any more. 'Enough about me and
my dramas,' she said. 'How about you? You seem very
smiley. Is there something I should know about?' Wait a
minute, she thought in the next second, remembering the
dinner party teasing the week before: the way Charlotte had
turned quite pink when they'd been discussing Ned from the
café. 'Hold on . . . Did you two see each other again? You
did, didn't you, I can tell by your face.' She topped up their

wine glasses and sat to attention, Simon temporarily forgotten. 'Tell me *everything*.'

Charlotte's happiness at her blossoming new relationship proved a welcome distraction but the very next day, Simon took things up a notch. Ever since he'd had news about the hotel project being shelved, Georgie had taken his talk of moving back home with a pinch of salt. He'd come round, she kept thinking; he'd get over himself, he'd find something else to do down in Brighton. All this packing and grumbling was just him letting off a bit of steam.

But no. Apparently not. Because there he was, jingling the car keys in his jeans pocket and looking shifty when he brought her a cup of tea first thing. He sat on the bed and she knew, just from gauging the set of his shoulders, that he was going to go through with it after all. 'So . . . I'm heading off this morning,' he announced gruffly. 'I could come back with a van for the rest of the stuff at the weekend, or . . .'

'Whoa,' she said in alarm. She struggled to sit upright, banged her head and spilled tea all over the duvet. 'You're really going? Today? But . . .' But what about me? she wanted to cry. Why hadn't they had a proper conversation about this, together? This was him leaving Stonefield all over again, she realized: taking the decision without so much as a glance her way. I'm off. Can't wait any longer. Stuff to do. Not hanging around.

He seemed surprised by her reaction. 'I did *say*,' he pointed out. 'I've said all along I was going back. Nothing's changed. It's you who can't make your mind up.' He put his hand on the duvet then removed it hurriedly, remembering it was soaked in tea. 'Look,' he said, 'if you want to come with me, I can—'

'No,' she blurted out. She couldn't quite believe this was happening. And she wasn't *ready* to leave. It was partly her fault for being in denial, for not confronting him about his plans, but then again, he hadn't come to her either, and said what shall we do about this? Let's sort this out together, the two of us, like a normal couple would. 'Can't we talk about it a bit more before you go? Do you have to even go *today*? It feels so sudden – like you've just decided without me. Like you're running away.' She closed her mouth before she tacked a 'from me' to the end of her sentence, knowing better than to start acting needy. If there was anything more guaranteed to send him, foot down, speeding up the M1, it was her being clingy.

'I'm not running away,' he told her. Damn it, now she'd wounded his male pride and he was looking all defensive. 'I'm just . . .' He shrugged. 'There's nothing left here for me, that's all. Well, apart from you, but you know what I mean.'

Apart from you. Well, at least she'd entered into his considerations, even if it was as an afterthought. Small mercies.

She took his hand, feeling as if they were skirting around something big and scary here, neither of them quite able to look the other in the eye. What did he want? Not this, clearly. And what did she want? She didn't want this either – the two of them tense and scratchy, unable to be themselves, be honest. Oh, she was tired of not being honest, all of a sudden. Ever since she'd followed him down to Brighton, she seemed to have been hiding all sorts of truths from him, her so-called beloved. It didn't make her feel like a good person. Maybe she *should* just sling her hook along with his, hop in the car, make some half-arsed apologies to Viv about the magazine, and then slip back into Stonefield life as if she'd never been away.

Her eye drifted to the photos she'd stuck on the bedroom wall: holiday and Christmas snaps, Jade's hen do, the village barbecue last summer . . . It would be so easy to pack up and go, wouldn't it? Admit defeat, scuttle back north, settle into the well-worn grooves of home. The delights of Brighton would come to feel like a strange dream whenever she looked back, a brief, glittering sequin-embellished detour from routine. And yet something was stopping her. Although a month ago she might have jumped for joy that Simon wanted to leave, there was a stubborn part of Georgie that hated to give up on anything. She liked it here now! She had her new friends, and work! And given the choice, she wanted to see the six months through, experience the city fully, rather than trot meekly along behind her boyfriend yet again, just because he happened to be in a hurry to get out of there. Why *should* she have to go along with whatever he wanted all the time?

'Simon . . . What's your dream scenario in, say, a year from now?' she asked, stroking the backs of his fingers. He had such nice hands, she'd always thought so – broad and strong, and just starting to tan now after the recent weeks of sunshine – but today it was like touching a stranger. 'I mean – magic wand, make a wish, what would be your perfect life? What do you hope happens next?'

He looked taken aback at the question as if he'd never considered such a thing. (Georgie, by contrast, would have been able to give you detailed one-year, five-year and ten-year dream scenarios at the drop of a hat ever since she was about fourteen.) 'Well . . . Living in Stonefield, great new job . . .' He scratched his chin while he paused to think. 'I'd love to build a house one day, buy a plot of land, you know, proper *Grand Designs* stuff. That's the dream, I guess. Why?'

And that, right there, was the difference between them, she thought glumly. His dream was about *him*, work, some stupid house he wanted to build, whereas her dreams had always been about the two of them, getting married, choosing their first rescue dog, starting a family, all that sort of happy-ever-after stuff. Was she even *part* of his dream scenario? Or was there just some shadowy generic 'girlfriend' slot, the details of whom bothered him less than the dimensions of his amazing house? Maybe she'd been kidding herself this whole time, she thought, a new tightness at the back of her throat. Maybe coming down here with him *had* been the worst sort of clingy-girlfriend behaviour.

She looked at him now, hunched over his phone, not even really waiting for her reply. Did he care about *her* dream scenario? She swallowed down a lump in her throat, remembering how happy Charlotte had looked the evening before, how her face had glowed when she talked about Ned and their romantic dinner, interrupted as it had been by his two cute daughters. When had she and Simon last looked at each other lovingly over a romantic dinner? When had they stopped having fun and feeling glow-y?

She sighed and poked her feet out of the duvet where they'd become too hot. He'd be fine without her, wouldn't he, in the rest of his life? He'd said so himself – she didn't even really factor into his dream scenario, for goodness' sake!

Well, then, she thought. Here goes nothing. 'I've got something to tell you,' she said. 'Actually, there are a few things.'

Once she had started, she couldn't stop. It was weirdly liberating, releasing one terrible secret after another, prising off their lids and setting them free into the room while he said nothing, just edged away from her on the bed with each new revelation, looking more and more aghast. And so out came the story about going to interview the women at the refuge and her part in his lost job ('It was *you?*'), and, yes, out came the confession about her speed dating experience too.

'But nothing *happened!*' she said quickly, seeing his face turn puce. 'In fact, I kept ringing you, trying to get you to come with me, but this *woman* answered your phone and was rude to me—'

'Oh, right, so you thought, sod it, I'll go on my own, I'll go *speed dating*—'

'No! Well, yes – but it wasn't like that. It was only a stupid work thing, it didn't *mean* anything. Just like you being in a pub with some woman after work didn't mean anything!'

'That was different. There were loads of us. And we weren't all flirting and trying to get off with each other either.'

His voice was so cold, she felt herself crumple. His jaw was set hard and furious; he wasn't even looking at her any more. 'Yeah, but . . . You've been out loads with them, haven't you? And that woman who answered your phone was really rude to me, and . . .'

Simon's jaw dropped. 'Wait a minute, how has this suddenly turned around to be about me? I'm not the one who went speed dating, George.'

'But it *is* about you too, it's about both of us.' She could hear her own voice getting higher and higher. Shrill, even; on the defensive. 'You never took my job seriously—'

'Where's all this coming from?'

'And you've been taking me for granted, ever since we moved down here—'

'Oh, for crying out loud!' Now he looked angry. 'No, I haven't.'

Georgie could feel the argument slipping away from her. 'Anyway, I went home early from the stupid dating thing because it was awful,' she said in a small voice.

'Really.' She could tell he didn't believe her.

'Yes, really. After I came off the phone to you, I went home and watched *Silent Witness* in my pyjamas and put a face pack on. *Really*.' Thank God Charlotte was out at work and wouldn't be able to hear her through the wall, she thought, wincing at her own rising volume. 'Look, I'm sorry, all right?' she went on, more humbly. He hated shrieking even more than clinging. 'I'm sorry things have been weird, I'm sorry we've not been totally honest with each other . . .'

'*We?* Don't bring me into this again, Georgie. I'm not the one who's been off bloody speed dating, am I?'

'No, but you've done things wrong too, you haven't exactly been a saint,' she retorted, unable to refrain from pointing this out. There were only so many times you could apologize, after all. 'You've kept me at arm's length the whole time we've been down here, it's all been about you and your stupid hotel. And even now, it's about you and your stupid "future house".' She made quotation marks with her fingers just in case he hadn't realized exactly how much she despised that wretched future house of his. 'Where do I come into the picture, then, eh? Am I even *in* your sodding picture?'

He stood up stiffly, not looking at her. 'I'm going,' he said, the door slamming behind him with an unmistakable finality.

She blinked very hard to stop herself from crying. 'I'll take that as a no, then,' she mumbled to the empty room.

Chapter Twenty-Three

SeaView House Noticeboard:

POLITE REMINDER
To All Residents

*PLEASE put your rubbish in the communal
dustbins outside. Do NOT leave rubbish bags tied
to the front railings. It is unsightly and a health hazard.*

Angela Morrison-Hulme
Property Manager

'So basically he was really really angry – I've never seen him
so angry – and he was like, I'm going, and then he just
l-l-left. He drove away without another word. And I've not
heard from him since!'

Rosa had been on an early shift that day, finishing at

three, and had been looking forward to vegging out with her feet up for the rest of the afternoon, fine-tuning the shopping list for her next dinner party – or rather her inaugural supper club as she supposed she should start thinking of it. As she was walking up the road, though, she'd spotted Georgie in the lawned square outside the flats, and had gone over to say hello, only to have her upstairs neighbour burst into tears on her and pour out a litany of Simon-related woes, her shoulders shaking with sobs.

'Oh no,' she said sympathetically. 'That doesn't sound good.'

'He was looking at me like he h-h-*hated* me.' Georgie scrubbed her wet pink eyes with a fist and hiccupped. She had no make-up on, which made her seem very little-girl-ish, and she was wearing a plain grey T-shirt and denim shorts, a far cry from her usual brightly coloured outfits. 'I can't believe it's o-o-over. Just like that. We've been together since we were *kids*. He's the only boyfriend I've ever had!'

'Oh, love,' Rosa said, her arms still around Georgie's narrow shoulders. 'I'm so sorry.'

'And it's all my f-f-fault,' Georgie wailed. 'I brought this about.' She blew her nose with a loud honk. 'He deserves better than me. A better girlfriend to live in his beautiful bloody house. We both came to that conclusion, basically.' Fresh tears sprang to her eyes and she wiped them away with the damp bit of tissue.

'Don't say that. You're lovely,' Rosa told her loyally. 'And it's not like he's been all sunshine and joy lately himself, has he? You said the other night he was grumpy and obsessed with work. So maybe it's you who deserves someone better than *him*.'

Georgie gave a wan smile but you could tell she wasn't buying it. Not quite ready for the *Yeah! Sisterhood!* part of breaking up with someone. Fair enough. It had taken Rosa long enough to get there herself after all.

'So what happens now?' Rosa asked. It was such a warm, sunny day, the sea a brilliant twinkly blue, it seemed doubly cruel to be unhappy somehow, when all around them were groups of students stretched out on the grass, children scampering about barefoot, dogs lolloping joyfully after tennis balls.

'He's probably back home in Yorkshire by now,' Georgie sighed. 'Oh God, his mum is going to love this, you know. She's always looked down her nose at me, like I'm not good enough for her precious man-child. He'll be waited on hand and foot, she'll be fussing over him and ripping me to shreds, I bet.' She drew her knees up to her chin and wrapped her arm around them. 'After that . . . he might give the tenants in our house notice so that he can move back in there, I guess. To our home.' She sniffled at the thought. 'Maybe he'll want to . . .' She swallowed. 'Sell the house. Our little house!' Her voice rose to a wail. 'Oh, this is so awful. I can't believe it's happening, Rosa. Me and Si . . . I thought we'd be together forever!'

She collapsed into sobs again and Rosa rubbed her back. 'See how things are when you've both cooled off,' she said comfortingly. 'This doesn't have to be the end. Maybe you both just need some thinking time apart, a chance to get to grips with whatever it is you each want. It'll be all right. Look at you – you're so vibrant and clever and sparkly – this is just a temporary setback, okay? With him or without him, you're still the same Georgie, just remember that.' And here *she* was, she thought, parroting all the things her friends had told her six months earlier, when she'd been the one devastated and feeling as if her life had juddered to an abrupt end. There was the circle of break-ups for you.

Nodding, Georgie blew her nose once more and pushed her hair off her face. 'Thanks,' she said in a small voice, twiddling a long blade of grass around her fingers. 'And I'm sorry for weeping all over you. I couldn't bear to be in that flat without him, the walls were closing in. I thought I'd come out and get some work done but I've just been crying and feeling shit the whole time.'

'Why don't we go back to mine?' Rosa said, getting up and holding out a hand. 'Change of scenery. I have coffee and flapjacks and loads of tissues . . .' They both looked at the very damp, very tatty, now totally useless piece of tissue that Georgie had been using, and Georgie did actually splutter a little laugh.

'Come on,' she urged, hauling Georgie up to her feet. 'Remind me to tell you some other time about *my* disastrous love life – that's sure to make you feel better about your own. But in the meantime . . . just hang out with me if you don't want to be alone. I was meaning to sort out my menu for Friday night, you can tell me what you think.'

'Friday . . . ? Oh, your supper club.' Georgie's face crumpled once more as they walked towards the house. 'I guess you'd better cross Simon off the guest-list. I'll have to sit on my own.'

'No, you will not,' Rosa said, seeing that Georgie looked as if she was about to start crying all over again. 'You can sit with my three oldest friends who are coming down from London for the occasion. And believe me, those girls are exactly who you want on your side when you're going through a break-up. If nothing else, they'll get you pissed and tell you all their dirty secrets. Or you can sit with Jo, if you'd rather? She's back home now, did you know? She's booked in, along with Bea and her ex, Gareth, Bea's dad, so . . .' Georgie was starting to look overwhelmed. 'Look, just see how you feel tomorrow anyway,' Rosa advised. They'd reached the front door and she unlocked it and held it open while Georgie trudged in. 'In the meantime, I'm going to force you to listen to my menu ideas, like it or not. You can make yourself useful and tell me what you think.'

*

Facebook update: Ann-Marie Chandler

Delighted to announce that David and I are expecting our third child!!! Had the 13-week scan yesterday and our baby is healthy and beautiful. We are so happy!!!! #blessed #happy #baby #family #love

Rosa closed the laptop and felt herself bristling all over. She had to stop looking at this page. She had to!

'So I was like, er, excuse me, I think *I* was here first – I was a bit pissed by this point – and then I did this double-take, like, holy *shit*, because I realized that the man next to me at the bar, the man I'd just been all hoity-toity to, was –'

'Oh God, *who*?'

'– Only bloody Harrison Ford.' Alexa threw her hands in the air. 'Han bloody Solo, my teenage crush! And me, getting all narky with the man. With Harrison frigging Ford! Mortified, I'm telling you. I was absolutely mortified!'

It was Friday evening and Rosa's practice supper club was underway. So far, so good, she thought, casting an eye around the room as she gathered together the scraped-clean starter plates and topped up a few wine glasses. There were eleven guests plus her, and earlier that day, she'd lugged her sofa and armchair into the bedroom so that there was space to arrange the tables in a long line in the centre of the room. (It was a bit of a squeeze, admittedly, but this only seemed to have led to greater camaraderie rather than any actual discomfort.) A few lamps and lit candles strategically placed around the place lent a soft glow, plus she'd bought some small terracotta pots of flowering thyme and rosemary which she clustered at intervals along the table, adding to the Mediterranean theme of her menu.

Her London friends had arrived just after six o'clock, laden with overnight bags and bunches of flowers and clinking carrier bags that seemed to contain gallons of booze, and the four of them had screamed so loudly on the doorstep that a passer-by had actually turned his head in alarm. She'd known these women for seventeen years now, almost half her life, and even though cutting herself off while she tried to get her life back on track had seemed like the right decision at the time, it was only now that she had them all back around her that she felt properly Rosa-ish again, as if she'd had a missing limb reattached.

Everyone seemed to be enjoying themselves at the dinner table, judging from the roars of laughter that greeted Alexa's latest showbiz tale. Working in PR for the TV and film industry, she always had a good story or two up her designer sleeve.

'Harrison Ford? No *way*!' cried Jo, who had dyed her hair aubergine for the occasion and actually had a bit of colour in her cheeks again too (perhaps it was the wine). 'I love that man. Oh, I'd willingly turn back for Harrison in a heartbeat, I'm not even joking.'

'Mum!' cried Bea, clapping her hands over her ears in horror. 'Don't *say* things like that in front of me!'

'Ex-husband klaxon,' Gareth announced drily, rolling his eyes. 'Cough. Awkward.'

Alexa, meanwhile, looked thrilled at Jo's comment and high-fived her across the table. 'Me too!' she screeched.

Was that a frisson Rosa detected between the two of them? she wondered in amusement, exchanging a raised eyebrow with Catherine next to her. 'Well, trust me, he's still got it anyway,' Alexa went on confidentially. 'Got it in spades. And he was really sweet and gracious too, once I'd apologized nine million times and offered to buy him a drink, out of sheer embarrassment.'

'So did he let you buy him a drink?' Georgie said, eyes goggling. She'd brought along her boss, Viv, and had been rather quiet up until this point, Rosa had noticed.

'Sadly not. He waved my offer aside, like this –' Alexa demonstrated – 'with his lovely beautiful hands.'

'Wrinkly old hands, you mean,' said Meg shuddering. 'He must be seventy by now, you pervert.'

'Which is, of course, still *young*, I would just like to say,' reprimanded Margot, with a beady glare at her. Rosa stifled a laugh at the mortified expression on Meg's face. She'd been thrilled that Margot had joined them that evening, arriving in an elegant black dress with her silvery hair coiffed to perfection, bearing champagne once more. ('Being ill, it is too dull,' she had declared rather majestically as she made her entrance. 'I decided – no! I will not miss another evening with my neighbours. Sometimes you just need to put on your dress and enjoy the world, no?')

'Seventy is *nothing* these days, darling,' Margot went on reprovingly now. 'You can still be a strong, proud man at seventy. A good lover, too. And I should know!'

Meg, who was never normally backward about coming forward, actually blushed. 'Yeah,' she said, chastened. 'Of course. I just meant—'

Margot's lips twitched. 'I am joking with you,' she confessed. 'Ahh – see! I might be an ancient old lady about to die but I can still joke!'

'Margot,' chided Charlotte fondly as Meg visibly blanched. Charlotte had curled her hair in soft waves that fell about her smiling face and looked positively radiant, Rosa thought. Being in love obviously suited her. 'Please don't talk about dying. You should see all the men she has lined up around Brighton,' she added to the others. 'Including this one,' she said, twinkling at Ned beside her. 'Although he's off-limits to you now, Margot, thank you very much.'

Margot looked delighted. 'But I saw him first!' she cried.

Rosa smiled to herself as she left for the kitchen. 'I'll be right back with the main courses,' she called.

'I'll help,' Catherine said, sliding out from her chair and following.

In the kitchen, everything was just about ready to be served. She had given the menu a Mediterranean theme, with a roasted vegetable and goat's cheese tart for the vegetarians, and herbed lamb cutlets for the meat-eaters, as well as three different salads. 'This all looks amazing,' Catherine said, piling plates into the dishwasher as Rosa cut the tart. 'It's going really well, isn't it? Well, from where I'm sitting, it is. Are you pleased? You must be! Everyone's raving about the food. And I love how most of us have never met and we're all just chatting away like old mates. Meg's face when Margot put her in her place just now! I've never seen her look so meek!'

Rosa laughed. 'I know! Margot's fab, isn't she? It's great to have her here. It's great to have *all* of you here.' She felt a rush of affection for the woman beside her, thinking about all the different kitchens they'd been in together over the years – through hangover breakfasts, and endless rounds of revision toast in the student days, countless drunken parties with dodgy punch and neighbours banging on the wall, all the way to hen parties, girly weekends away, diets, binges, New Year's Eve celebrations, her godchildren's birthdays . . .

and now here they were together again, in a new kitchen, Rosa's kitchen. It felt like a turning point, having the seal of approval from someone who really mattered.

Catherine hesitated as if she was about to say something and glanced across at Rosa, before seeming to think better of it, and picking up a couple of salad dishes. 'Shall I take these through for people to help themselves?'

'Yes, please. The more informal the better, I think. Thanks.'

Breathe, breathe, breathe, she reminded herself, sliding generous wedges of tart onto four plates, before Catherine bore them away for the vegetarians. Hosting her guests so far was like organizing a military operation – what with all the shopping and cooking and room-preparations to be worked out, the chairs and tables she'd had to borrow from her neighbours, the linen tablecloths she'd begged from the hotel. If she was going to do this seriously, she'd have to think about maybe asking Natalya to help her waitress another time, she thought, loading her arms up with serving plates heaped high with the fragrant lamb and setting them down at either end of the table. 'Help yourselves. I'll just grab some bread and butter, and a jug of tap water. Anyone ready for more wine? Okay, I'll get that as well. Now, please . . . dig in!'

By the end of the evening, Rosa was feeling stupendously happy. She was also stupendously drunk. The food had been a great success, with barely a crumb left of the vast white chocolate and berry cheesecake she'd made, and everyone had lingered pleasantly over coffee and final glasses of wine. Alexa had produced a bottle of ouzo from a recent holiday in Greece, which finished off several of the guests, with Margot, Charlotte, Ned and Viv all making rather stumbling exits for bed at around eleven o'clock. Next out of the door was Jo, who looked shattered. 'Just another half an hour, Bea, and then your dad's going to send you home too,' she warned.

'Yeah, yeah,' Bea replied in a not-very-convincing way.

'I think we should have a toast,' Catherine said, raising a mug of coffee in one hand and the ouzo bottle in the other. 'To our fabulous hostess with the mostest, a great cook and an even better friend. To Rosa!'

'To Rosa!' the others chorused, clinking glasses. 'Yeah!' added Georgie, who looked about as drunk as Rosa felt by now. Cheerful-drunk, thankfully, Rosa thought, catching her eye. Which was way better than maudlin just-got-dumped drunk, obviously.

'Thanks for being here and letting me practise on you,' she laughed, wrinkling her nose.

'Are you kidding me? Like we'd have stayed away when you finally got over yourself and invited us,' Meg huffed, but in a twinkly-eyed, only-joking sort of way.

'How come you guys haven't seen each other for so long?'

Gareth asked. He was a bit pissed as well; his words were sliding into each other like novice ice skaters, and his features looked as if their edges had blurred. Maybe that was just Rosa's own beer-goggles, though. 'I mean – London, Brighton, it's not that far. Have you all been insanely busy or something?'

'Dad! Personal!' Bea pointed out, rolling her eyes.

'Well . . .' Alexa glanced at Rosa then shrugged. 'Shit happens, right?'

'And we *are* insanely busy,' Catherine added, which was true. 'Or just busily insane, I'm not sure which.'

'It's not like we fell out or anything,' Meg put in.

They were all being so lovely and diplomatic, covering for Rosa, but the truth felt too big to keep back any longer. 'It was me,' she admitted. 'Just your typical midlife crisis kind of thing, you know, abandoning perfectly good job, running away to the seaside, going silent on best mates. *I vant to be alone.* Bosh.' She pulled a face, attempting to make a joke of it but then her voice went and shook at the last, completely giving away her real feelings. 'So . . . yeah.'

'But here we all are now, and you're over the worst,' said Catherine, who had three children under the age of five and was highly skilled at smoothing over emotional crises.

'Right,' said Gareth, looking a bit awkward. He was trying to give Rosa a searching look but she pretended she hadn't noticed and busied herself pouring more drinks for everyone. 'Well . . . good.'

Georgie knocked back her third glass of ouzo and winced. 'Is this anything to do with the love-life thing you mentioned the other day?' she asked, then cringed at her own bluntness. 'Sorry. You don't have to say. That was way too nosey a question. That was definitely the ouzo talking. What's *in* this stuff?'

'It says here, it's fifty-five per cent proof,' Bea said, peering at the label, then took the cap off the bottle and sniffed the contents. 'Bloody *hell*, proof of what? That you have to be mad to drink it?'

'Basically, yes,' Catherine told her, pulling a face as she took a sip.

Rosa twisted her glass around between her fingers. Then the next sentence fell out of her before she could stop it. 'His wife's having another baby, you know,' she said, and Catherine spluttered her drink everywhere.

'No!'

'The tosser,' Meg snarled.

'How do you know?' Alexa asked, her dark hair swinging as she leaned forward. 'Has he been in touch?' Then she glanced at Catherine and a look was exchanged. 'Did you—'

'No,' Catherine said quickly and put a finger to her lips but not before Rosa had seen it.

Oh great. Now what? Did she even want to *know* why her

friends had just looked at each other like that? Probably not. Definitely not. The room was swinging around her; she felt volatile, wild, all her emotions worryingly close to the surface. 'Sorry,' she said to Georgie, Bea and Gareth, as she realized too late that they were all sitting there, with not a clue what this was about. 'Just my tragic love life. Let's not go there. Moving on!'

'So how do you know she's pregnant?' Catherine said, ignoring Rosa's last words. 'Have you seen him again?'

'No! Of course I haven't seen him, I hate him,' Rosa replied. Then she sighed, knowing that her friends weren't about to let this one lie. 'I've been Facebook-stalking his wife,' she muttered. 'And tracking him down too. Turns out he never even worked in Amsterdam, can you believe. He's the marketing manager at some big tech firm in Old Street. Ha!'

'Um . . . Maybe this is our cue to leave,' Gareth said tactfully. 'Come on, Bea.'

'Yeah,' agreed Georgie, pushing her chair back. 'It's been such a good evening but if I drink any more of that ouzo I'll probably do something terrible like ring my boyfriend. Ex-boyfriend. Aargh. Maybe I should leave my phone here actually.'

'Oh, stay,' Rosa said. 'Don't feel you need to go on my behalf. We're going to change the subject from the torrid melodrama of my life now anyway. Aren't we? And I'm going to get us a jug of iced water in an attempt to dilute that ouzo.'

She'd risen from her chair, but Meg held up her hand – stop – like a police officer directing traffic. 'Hold your horses, lady. We'll change the subject and drink our iced water just as soon as we see that Facebook page,' she said, eyebrow raised. 'Go on. Give. You might as well.'

'We can all add poisonous comments underneath to the smug cow,' Alexa said.

'No!' Rosa cried. She had become oddly protective of poor gullible Ann-Marie, if that didn't sound too mad. 'It's not her fault her husband is a pig.' Grimacing, she briefly explained the situation to Gareth, Bea and Georgie who gave a full and rousing condemnation of Max's – David's – actions. 'I just need to forget him and leave him to his happy joyous blessed family,' she said sarcastically.

'Not that happy,' Catherine muttered.

'Cath saw him with another woman,' Alexa blurted out. 'What?' she added when Catherine made a hissing noise beside her. 'Look, she might as well know, just in case she's harbouring any mad ideas about getting back with the toerag.'

'I'm not!' Rosa cried. 'Really? You saw him, Cath?'

Catherine sighed. 'Yes. I saw him. But I was going to break it to you *sensitively*,' she said, glaring at Alexa. 'Like, maybe when you weren't steaming drunk and with new friends? Like, just the two of us with, say, a massive punch-bag to hand?'

'It's fine,' Rosa said dully. 'Whatever. I don't care.'

'It's not fine,' said Gareth. 'And if you ask me, he needs sorting out.'

Bea scoffed. 'What, you're going to go round and duff him up, are you?' she asked. 'This is a bit different to threatening a school bully, Dad.'

'I know but . . .' He shrugged. 'It just winds me up, how people can be so vile to each other. And then get off scot free.' He got to his feet and hauled his daughter up too. 'Right, young lady, we really had better go otherwise Jo's not going to be happy with either of us.' He hesitated, pulling on his jacket. 'Thanks, Rosa, I had a lovely evening. And . . . well, if you ever want to go in for a satisfying act of revenge to get your ex back . . .' He tapped his nose. 'You've got my number. Count me in.'

Chapter Twenty-Four

There were crumbs under Charlotte's toaster. A splodge of something brown and unidentifiable in the vegetable drawer of the fridge. She had run clean out of fabric conditioner and there was dust – yes, really, *dust* – on the black domed top of her beaming Henry Hoover. Standards, you could say, were slipping – and you'd be right. You would also be right in saying, however, that Charlotte couldn't have cared less.

She was *happy*, she had realized. She had remembered how it felt! A joyful little drumbeat in her blood, the giddy rush she experienced when a text or call came in from Ned, the way she woke up in the morning and felt glad. *Glad!* She had caught herself humming in the aisles of Waitrose the other day as she picked up various bits of food, adding a punnet of scarlet strawberries, some fancy grapefruit shower gel and a bunch of freesias just for the hell of it. Actually humming, out loud, in public!

It was as if she kept looking at herself and marvelling how far she'd come. There was no way she'd have been able to survive Rosa's dinner parties this time last year, for example: she had been too unhappy to eat, too inward-looking to chat, and too exhausted to even consider putting on a nice dress and some make-up and doing her hair. And yet she'd managed exactly that each time, all of it, and had thoroughly enjoyed herself into the bargain – getting to know her neighbours Rosa, Georgie, Bea and of course Jo, now, with whom she'd had a proper long conversation at last, and who seemed the coolest, sparkliest person.

Even work seemed okay these days. One of the solicitors in her team, Jacqui, who had golden hair and cat-green eyes had admired Charlotte's necklace one day over coffee, and they'd got chatting, and ended up having lunch together a few times since then. Another colleague, Shelley, had invited Charlotte out for her birthday drinks and it had been really fun, and she'd got to know lots of people in a shyly tipsy sort of way. There was talk of an office summer party and Charlotte found herself offering to help out . . . Charlotte was just saying yes to everything, in fact, these days. It was as if she were a daisy, opening her petals and offering them up to the sunshine. Hello, world. I'm back. I'm up for it.

'You're living again,' her mum had said down the phone. She sounded a bit choked up actually; either that or her hayfever was giving her grief. 'That's what it is – you've come out through the other side and you're living again. Rescued by love!'

Rescued by love? Charlotte had rolled her eyes at such a melodramatic response. 'I rescued *myself*,' she pointed out. 'And it's not "love" anyway, yet, I barely know him. We've only had three dates and one coffee on the beach.' Then, because she knew what an old romantic her mum was – and because it was true, moreover – she added, 'But he does make me happy.'

'He makes you *happy*,' her mum repeated with great satisfaction. 'Oh, darling, I'm so pleased. I'm so so pleased for you.'

'Me too,' Charlotte said. 'And actually – if this doesn't sound too mad – *I* make myself happy too nowadays. My life, the things in it, new friends . . . it's all sort of come together in one big lovely package. I can't explain it, but it's like the black clouds have moved on. Not that I'm ever going to forget Kate of course –'

'No, of course you won't. But it's learning to live alongside that grief, isn't it? It's not letting it shadow everything else in your world.'

'Yes. That's exactly it, Mum.' There was a lump in her throat. Losing Kate *had* cast a shadow, she realized: a massive shadow over everything, so dark that she couldn't see a way through it for a while. And although she was certain she'd always feel a tug inside at the sight of a new baby, probably for the rest of her life, that shadow had lifted, enabling daylight to come edging back in. Her days seemed fuller, she was sleeping better at night, she had stopped crying in the toilets at work for no reason. As for her cleaning schedule, that had all but been forgotten. Best of all, she hadn't pored tearfully over her Kate shoebox for at least two weeks.

'I really owe Margot one,' she said to Ned, a few days later. For all her talk of having rescued herself and creeping out from under the shadow, she would never forget quite how instrumental Margot had been as a catalyst for change. Margot, who'd questioned her so beadily, who'd listened to her, who'd made her feel human again, who'd reminded her that there were good things in life still to be enjoyed.

'Margot?' Ned repeated, turning on the burglar alarm inside the café and shutting the door behind them. He closed up at six o'clock each day, just as she was finishing work, and she'd come down to meet him a couple of times, ships passing in the night, a snatched kiss and hello, and perhaps a quick walk along the prom with him, as he headed back to pick up the girls from his sister's. Tonight she'd been invited back to have tea with them all – 'Hope you like fish fingers and pasta pesto,' he'd said, and she wasn't entirely sure if he was joking or not. Perhaps she was making too much of it, being silly, but it felt like a big deal to be allowed into the family's tea-time, admitted into the inner circle. She was flattered, excited and also racked with nerves. Was it shameless of her that she'd stuffed some jelly babies into her bag in a shallow attempt to win over those delicious little barefoot girls?

'Yeah. Not just for introducing the two of us – for the second time, I mean,' Charlotte added, a slight blush tinge-ing her cheeks. (She would probably never be able to think of their first fateful encounter without dying a little inside.) 'But because she's become . . . well, sort of a role model for me, I guess. Inspirational. I've never met a woman like her – who genuinely doesn't give a damn what others think, who is so charming and naughty and mischievous.'

'Who's such a terrible old flirt . . .' Ned said, pulling down the rattling metal shutters at the front of the café. 'She's not been in lately, actually. In fact . . .' He stooped down to click the padlock in place. 'I don't think I've seen her all week. She *is* all right, isn't she?'

The question slid under Charlotte's skin where it sat uneasily for a few seconds. 'Um . . . I think so,' she replied but now the doubts were starting to prickle. Margot had seemed so much her old self at Rosa's dinner party the week before that – to Charlotte's shame – she'd all but put the older woman out of her mind, in her own new zeal for living. She was due to pop round on Friday for their weekly chat as usual but, all of a sudden, Charlotte got the strong feeling she should go there sooner. Nothing specific she could put her finger on, just a sensation of urgency. *Hurry. Go.*

'Do you know, I might pop back and knock, actually,' she blurted out. 'Would you mind? I'm probably being silly but because she was so poorly before – and because she's always telling me that she's dying, too – I will just make sure.' She hesitated, conscious of his sister Debbie waiting for them to arrive and collect the girls – Debbie, who she hadn't met yet, but who was such an important part of her brother's life that Charlotte definitely wanted to make a good impression. It wouldn't be a great start, would it, if they rocked up later than expected, because she, Charlotte, got this fanciful notion in her head about her elderly neighbour. But now that the notion *was* in her head, there was no way she could ignore it.

'I'll come with you,' Ned said, giving the shutter one last heave to make sure it was secure before putting the keys in his pocket.

By the time they'd reached the house, having huffed and puffed her way up the hill in haste, Charlotte was beginning to feel self-conscious for letting her instincts have their way, for allowing her emotions and panic to have steered them off course and away from Debbie's house, thus delaying the fish finger teatime. It was going to be really embarrassing to knock on Margot's door and see the surprised expression on her neighbour's face when she answered it and saw them there. She would laugh, probably. She might even chide them for their interfering, over-anxious behaviour – 'Ahh, you think I am dying, *hein*? Not yet, my darling. Not today!'

Still. They were here now, right at the top of the house, they might as well just double check. 'Margot?' Charlotte called, knocking on the door. 'It's me. Are you there?'

To her surprise, the door slid noiselessly open. Her neighbour must have left it on the latch. 'Margot?' Charlotte called again, stepping inside. 'It's Charlotte. Are you okay?'

The flat was silent. 'Maybe she's gone out,' Ned said, hanging back. But Charlotte's heart was thumping. Something was wrong, she thought, walking down the hall. She just knew it: something was wrong.

'Margot?' Then she heard it: a faint answering whimper, and she was running, blood cold, into the living room, where – 'Oh my God. Margot! Margot! What happened?' – where her neighbour lay on the floor, face waxy, eyes almost closed, her hair a rat's nest of silver-grey tangles. Charlotte knelt on the floor and took the other woman's pulse – a feeble lagging beat as if her heart no longer had the energy for anything stronger.

'Shit,' cried Ned, bursting into the room a second behind her. He pulled out his phone. 'I'll call an ambulance.'

'No!' The passion in Margot's voice surprised them all, her eyes snapping wide open.

'Margot, we must, you're too poorly now,' Charlotte said, still holding her hand. She reached down and stroked

Margot's hair off her face. Her beautiful hair, usually so elegantly styled and sprayed – it now lay in thin hanks, betraying its owner's age and ill-health. The skin on her hands felt cold and papery, as if she'd been there some time. 'Oh gosh, you poor thing, did you fall? How long have you been lying here?'

Margot clutched at Charlotte, her eyes cloudy but imploring. 'Please. No. No ambulance,' she gasped. 'Please.'

'But—'

'*Please.*'

Charlotte gazed down at her helplessly, feeling conflicted. 'Can we at least call for a nurse, someone to look after you?' she asked, before remembering with a sudden bolt of clarity about Jo. 'Ned. Will you run down and get Jo? Flat 2. She's a nurse on a cancer ward, she'll know what to do. Oh, Margot,' she said, her voice a sob as he took off behind her. *Please don't go*, she wanted to wail. *Not yet! I've only just got to know you – and I love spending time with you.* 'I'm sorry I've not been round sooner. I should have thought to check. I've been a bad friend, I've been so wrapped up in myself.'

Margot's eyelids had closed, a tiny purple vein throbbing at one corner and her breath sighed out from her. For a terrible moment, Charlotte thought it was game over, that she'd just died, there and then, on her living-room floor, but then the older woman's lips parted. 'Good friend,' she said, her voice little more than a whisper. 'I am happy. For you.'

Ned ran back into the room in the next minute, followed by Jo, who knelt alongside Charlotte and spoke kindly and briskly to Margot. 'Hello, do you remember me? I'm Jo from downstairs, I'm a nurse at the hospital,' she said. 'We can have an ambulance here in two minutes, or I could drive you to the hospital myself if you'd rather,' she offered, but Margot merely shook her head. 'Are you sure you want to stay? Okay, well, let's get you a bit more comfortable, in that case, and if you change your mind at any point, just tell me.'

Tears ran down Charlotte's face as Jo took over, asking a series of questions before she and Ned carried Margot through to her bed. 'It's not looking good,' she said quietly to Charlotte. 'She's very weak and tired, I think we're approaching the end. Do you know of any relatives who might want to be here?'

'She has two sons in France,' Charlotte said, her voice catching. Oh goodness, this was all happening so quickly. Too quickly. She tried to pull herself together for Margot's sake. What were the sons called? She knew they hadn't always got on but they'd want to be with their mum at a time like this, wouldn't they? Hadn't they argued because they'd wanted her to die at home in France? She had visions of them arriving and hauling Margot away, tucked under one arm like a roll of carpet, and had to blink several times and swallow in order to think clearly. 'I'll try and get hold of them. She must have an address book or contact details somewhere.'

Ned was shifting from foot to foot, his expression uneasy. 'I'm really sorry, but I'm going to have to pick up the girls,' he said. 'I'd ask Deb to keep them a bit longer but I know she's got her Pilates tonight – it's the one evening of the week where I can't be late. I hate to leave you like this but—'

'It's fine. I understand,' Charlotte said helplessly. 'I'm going to stay here. Sorry. Can we rearrange for another time?'

'Of course! Don't apologize,' he said, with a long tight hug. 'Definitely another time.' He let go of her, his eyes concerned. 'Will you let me know . . . how things are, here? Keep me posted?'

'Sure,' she said, glancing over as Jo rummaged in a cupboard for an extra blanket, then laid it over Margot's body. 'I'd better go. See you soon.' They kissed and he gave her a last embrace before peeling himself away. As she heard his footsteps retreating down the stairs, she tried to dredge up some strength from inside. She had a feeling it was going to be a long night.

Margot died just after three o'clock the next morning, with Charlotte and Jo still by her side. The only other person Charlotte had ever seen die before had been her tiny baby daughter Kate in a sterile, brightly lit hospital room and it had been the most devastating, heartbreaking moment of her life. Margot's death, by contrast, felt oddly peaceful, almost imperceptible, a quiet slipping away by candlelight, the night outside respectfully silent, as if in hushed homage. Charlotte and Jo had been either side of her, holding a hand each throughout. There had been moments of conversation where Margot became lucid and could reply to them, interspersed by long periods of peace where the only sound was the ticking of a bedside clock and the laborious breathing of an old, tired pair of lungs. Charlotte had brushed Margot's hair for her, gently washed her face, rubbed a little handcream into her dry fingers. Small acts of kindness, each one saying, *I'm here. I'm grateful for what you did. I'm really going to miss you.*

Jo had telephoned the ward where she worked and spoken to the sister there, to tell her what was happening. According to their records, Margot had been suffering from blood cancer and, since early spring, had refused any more treatment. She'd last been seen by a doctor the Friday before, when it had been explained to her that she was now in the terminal stages of illness, and it was only a matter of time. In her notes it said that she'd been offered hospice care but had turned it down, preferring to stay at home. A tear trickled down Charlotte's cheek on hearing this. Of course Margot had turned it down. 'Die in a strange place with people I do not know? *Non*,' Charlotte could imagine her saying in that defiant way of hers.

'Friday was the day of Rosa's supper club,' she realized now, her throat tight with wanting to sob. 'When she looked so well, when she seemed so . . . so Margot-ish again. I thought . . . I assumed . . .'

Jo reached over and squeezed her hand. 'It often happens like that,' she said quietly. 'I've seen it many times. Sometimes there's actually a gladness to be told your time's almost up, especially if you've been in a lot of acute pain for a long time, as Margot has been. There is a relief in knowing the agony is coming to an end.' They both glanced over at the older woman lying there between them and Charlotte could hardly bear the welling sadness she felt, thinking of Margot putting on her lipstick each day, heroically covering up her pain. The strength of character that must have taken, the determination to face down her illness and go on alone . . . it was extraordinary.

'There's also this strange phenomenon where, soon before a person dies, they can often spend a day or two feeling quite well again,' Jo went on. 'It's like the calm before the storm, one last lull. Perhaps that was Margot's. Perhaps it was her last hurrah. And good for her.'

'Good for her,' Charlotte echoed. 'Good for you, Margot.' Tears pricked her eyes again as she thought for the hundredth time how glad she was that she'd followed her instincts, that some sixth sense had compelled her to check on her upstairs neighbour before it was too late. She still wasn't sure exactly how long Margot had lain there before Charlotte and Ned had burst in. How awful it would have been if they'd never made it, if she had gone on to Ned's house for tea with the girls. Margot might have died there, on her living-room floor, cold and alone. The thought was so awful it broke Charlotte's heart just to imagine.

In death, as in life, Margot had been organized and meticulous. As soon as Charlotte had started searching for contact details of the two sons, she had found a list of instructions in shaky handwriting, including phone numbers for Michel and Henri, orders for how she'd like her funeral (a cremation at Woodvale, with the ashes to be scattered in Auray, the French town where she'd grown up), along with details of her solicitor and the name of her doctor. At the bottom of the paper, she had written 'I enjoy my life' and then a simple 'MERCI' in capital letters, and it was that, the fact that even when very very ill and at the end of her existence, lights dimming, Margot had wanted to stamp her claim on the world with that bold, proud last sentence, that made Charlotte love her even more. *I enjoy my life.* Yes, you did, she thought, wiping her eyes as she prepared to telephone France. You bloody well did that, Margot.

When the end finally came and Margot stopped breathing, Jo checked her pulse to be quite sure, then recorded the time of death, gently pulled down her eyelids and tele-phoned the doctor. Meanwhile, Charlotte burst into tears and lay her head on the older woman's still chest like a child craving comfort. She thought of everything Margot had done for her – the confidence she'd given her, as well as the companionship, their weekly tea and pastries, her sense of adventure. Margot had reminded her of all the beautiful things in life worth celebrating, and she'd done so with such panache. Then she thought of Margot's sons, grimly heading towards Brighton, now too late for one final goodbye with their mother. Perhaps they were on the ferry right at this moment, looking up at the stars as they journeyed across the dark water, sending up prayers that she would still be there when they arrived. *I'm sorry*, she said to them in her head. *But she was not alone.*

She remained lying with her arm across Margot until Jo came back to say that the doctor would be round first thing to issue the death certificate, and that she should really get some sleep now. They pulled a sheet respectfully over Margot's inert cooling body, blew out the candles with soft smoky puffs, and then made their way back through the flat. 'Goodbye,' Charlotte said under her breath, lingering in the doorway. 'Goodbye, Margot. Sleep well.'

Chapter Twenty-Five

'"I am the resurrection and the life," says the Lord.' The vicar's voice rang out across the pews and Georgie, head bowed, reached along to grip Charlotte's hand. '"Those who believe in me, even though they die, will live, and everyone who lives and believes in me will never die."'

It was the following Monday and Margot's funeral was being held at the crematorium on Lewes Road. Georgie hadn't been to many funerals, but was pretty sure the turn-out for this one was out-of-the-ordinary, to say the least. The rows were all packed with mourners – and what a motley bunch they were too, ranging from silvery-haired ladies in neat twinsets, to a couple of luxuriantly bearded bikers, to bohemian types with colourful clothes and lots of beads, to . . . well, not that she was perving or anything, there at her former neighbour's funeral, but Georgie was pretty sure there were a few candidates from Margot's hotties' safari as well, heads lowered, come to pay their respects.

Everyone had loved Margot, by the looks of things – and

even though Georgie had only met her once, at Rosa's supper club the other night, she had taken to her immediately too, mentally filing her in the category 'Total broad'. She'd seemed so sharp and funny, and, according to Charlotte, had lived majestically up there in her attic flat, right until the end. That was the way to do it. Just as soon as Georgie could stop crying and feeling miserable about everything all the time, she fully intended to position Margot Favager as new role model number one. Catch Margot sighing and slumping about because a boyfriend had walked out on her? Hell, no. Catch Margot staring mournfully at photo after photo of Simon, rereading text after text, clicking on his Facebook page far too many times a day, and doing very little else? Never. Even after her brief time with the woman, Georgie was sure that Margot would have marched straight back out into the world, post-break-up, with her head held high, sending a gigantic two fingers to any ex-boyfriends in the process. If only it was so easy.

She'd still heard nothing from Simon up in Yorkshire. Not a word. It had been twelve whole days and nights now since he'd stormed out of the flat and driven home, and the radio silence had been at full volume despite all Georgie's apologetic texts. Amelia had glimpsed him apparently, looking 'miserable' as he walked the family's black Labrador around the village, but that was the sole piece of intelligence she'd managed to glean from her Stonefield spies so far. Either he was lying low with his parents, being well and truly cosseted, or he was out all hours having already steamed straight into some amazing new job, and forgotten about her. Neither scenario was much comfort.

Unfortunately, she couldn't even badger her two best friends into further spying forays – peering through Simon's parents' front window, loitering in the bushes outside with a pair of binoculars, that sort of harmless, innocent thing – because they both had enough on their plates right now. Jade's beloved granny had died and the whole family were in bits, whereas things had all kicked off for Amelia when horrible Chloe had brazenly made a move on Jason, Amelia's fiancé.

'Yeah! Actually grabbed him and tried to haul him out of the back of the pub for a snog,' Amelia had ranted down the phone, all high-pitched and squeaky with indignation. 'Can you believe the *cheek* of her? The nasty little snake. She daren't show her face near me again, I'm telling you. Not if she wants to live to see next Christmas, anyway.'

It made Georgie feel more helplessly cut adrift than ever, being so far from her friends when all three of them were undergoing their various crises. By rights, she'd have gone to pay her respects to Jade and the rest of the family, all of whom she'd known since she was four. And it went without saying that she should have been firmly by Amelia's side throughout the whole tawdry Chloe business, providing voodoo dolls for her friend to stab pins into, and thoroughly enjoying slagging the vile woman off over a bottle of wine or three. As for Georgie herself, needless to say, her two friends would have ordinarily been staunch pillars of support during her boyfriendless trauma. Although this did beg the question – would she have been in this situation at all had she never left Stonefield in the first place?

Best not to go there.

It had occurred to her, several times, that maybe she should just swallow her pride and drive back up to Yorkshire so that she could sort everything out. But then of course, Simon would probably get cross with her for following him again and . . . Oh, she just didn't know any more. Because she kind of *did* want to follow him, she did want to be back with him. Did that make her a very weak person who couldn't stand on her own two feet without a bloke? Or simply a woman who refused to give up on love?

One of Margot's sons was speaking now. He had piercing blue eyes and a hooked nose and dark hair that fell almost to his shoulders. Plus he spoke English in a deliciously sexy French accent. Not that she was eyeing up a bereaved son at his mother's funeral or anything so crass. Obviously.

'My mother, she love living here. We – my brother and I – we say, come home. We want you home with us. But she say, and leave England? No. I stay. *This* is my home. I have friends here, I am happy. And so I want to say thank you, to her many, many friends. Thank you from her family. You gave her a good life right until the end. She felt loved, by you. And for us, her family, we feel . . .' He thought for a moment to get the word, his bushy eyebrows colliding above his nose. 'We feel – grateful? Grateful – for this. That you welcomed her and loved her and called her your friend.'

Charlotte was weeping beside her and Georgie had tears in her eyes too, for wonderful Margot and her hook-nosed sons but also, if she was honest, because she was feeling so sad about her own mess of a life. If she died tomorrow, would Simon come to her funeral? Would anyone? Viv probably wouldn't, after Georgie had turned up snivelling in the office the week before, confessing that she couldn't write the speed dating piece after all, she just couldn't. Viv had been cross with her for two whole days before relenting and saying that perhaps Georgie could write a piece about 'Brighton Women Doing It Their Way' instead, and yes, all right, she could include Rosa and her supper club as one of the case studies, she supposed.

The first strains of Mozart's Requiem sounded, marking the end of the service and the congregation rose to their feet, dabbing eyes, blowing noses, putting their arms around each other. If Georgie took anything away from today, it was that Margot had been a spirited, passionate woman who had acted out of love, and followed her heart at all times. 'They just don't make 'em like that any more,' said a woman in the row behind.

When in doubt, have coffee. Preferably in a gorgeous beach-side setting with someone to make it for you, and – oh, go on, then – a massive fry-up as well. Georgie had come to Ned's café for solace and sustenance and a reminder that there were still some things in life to be enjoyed. It was only as she went to the counter and saw the freckled face of Shamira, the waitress, that she remembered her very first *Hey Em* problem, and the person behind it all. 'Hello,' she said, suddenly feeling awkward. She probably should have popped in earlier, she realized belatedly, just to make sure that Shamira wasn't pissed off with her kind-of-brash Em-ish response. 'How are you? How did it go with . . .' She had forgotten his name. 'The guy, and your sister?'

Shamira made her coffee, dimpling as she replied. 'John? It's going really well,' she said and gave a soppy sort of smile. 'I'm madly, stupidly happy. We both are.'

Georgie felt taken aback. 'What, so . . . ?' So you ignored my advice, she wanted to ask, me telling you to put your sister's feelings first? She couldn't quite get the words out. 'You . . . decided to make a go of it, with him?'

Shamira nodded. 'He's my true love,' she said simply. 'I always thought so. And my sister . . . she understands.'

'She *does*?' Whoa. Seriously? Would any woman be *that*

understanding? 'So . . . you've sorted everything out?' She couldn't get over quite how surprised she felt, she realized. Surprised and actually sort of disappointed that this woman had completely disregarded her advice, but somehow ended up living apparently happily ever after. It made Georgie feel – well, a bit stupid, if she was honest. Sort of redundant.

'Apparently, she knew things weren't right between them for ages,' Shamira went on blithely over the hiss of the milk-frother. 'She reckons the two of us are much better suited. We all sat down together and talked it through . . . we're cool. Everything's cool.'

'Cool,' Georgie echoed dumbly. 'I mean . . . Great. That's really great. I'm . . . pleased for you.' Was there anything she could do right? she wondered as she went to sit down, feeling unexpectedly glum at the waitress's beaming face. Anything at all?

'So she's left already, apparently. Moonlight flit. And good riddance, Chloe Phillips, is what I say. Don't bloody come back either!' Amelia's voice had a victorious ring to it but despite being separated by approximately two hundred and fifty miles, Georgie knew that her best friend would still be feeling deep hurt by the betrayal of this woman she'd considered a mate. She remembered the adoring way Amelia had gazed at her in the pub that night: there was 'girl crush' written all over her face. It was always worst when people you admired let you down.

'What an absolute cow,' Georgie said loyally, but then her thoughts turned to her house, now *sans* Chloe. 'Has he gone too, then, her fella? Is the house empty?' She was still wearing her black dress from the funeral but had hauled the duvet off the bed and was currently cocooned in it on the sofa along with a bottle of red wine, three cut-price and probably out of date Creme Eggs from the corner shop, as well as one of her favourite rom-coms on DVD. She paused the film in order to concentrate, realizing that this was potentially big news. If their house was now vacated, there was nothing to stop Simon moving back in, without her, and she felt a pang as she imagined him there again, sprawled out on their sofa alone. In their lovely cosy bed alone. A single glass, plate, knife and fork in the kitchen sink where he'd eaten alone. It was too weird. It was all wrong. What if he found himself loving the single life after all those years together? What if he changed the locks so that Georgie couldn't get back in?

'Daz? No, he's still there, mooching about with a face like death,' Amelia replied, mercifully interrupting this dismal train of thought. 'What with him and Simon, the village is practically overrun with unhappy men right now.'

Georgie's heart contracted with pain. 'You've seen him again?'

'Yeah, he was in the pub last night. Didn't stay long. I

heard him telling Jase something about wanting to keep a clear head for a job interview the next day. In Harrogate, I think he said.'

'Right.' Winded by this piece of news, Georgie took such a big gulp of her wine that she splashed some of it on the duvet. A *job interview*, she repeated to herself numbly. In *Harrogate*. Off he went cheerfully without her, getting on with the rest of his life, then. And how awful, how crushing to find this out through a friend rather than from Simon himself! Once upon a time she would have been the first person he'd told; they might have run through some practice questions the night before, she'd have helped him choose the right tie and wished him luck. She'd have crossed her fingers all day for him, dying to get a text or call about how it had gone. But now, in this strange new world, Simon did these things alone, he didn't need crossed fingers or tie-assistance. 'God,' she said dully.

'Yeah, I know. So that's the latest from the Stonefield News bulletin,' Amelia said before her voice softened. 'How do you feel about him, George? Are you okay?'

Georgie's throat was so thick for a moment she couldn't immediately reply. 'I miss him,' she said eventually. 'I can't get used to him not being here. I want to make it up to him but I don't know how; he was just so angry when he left, I feel like he's . . .' She swallowed down the lump in her throat. 'Like he's washed his hands of me. It's horrible.'

'Oh, love.' Amelia's sympathy was so sincere and warm, it made tears spring yet again to Georgie's eyes. (She was starting to think there might be something wrong with her tear ducts. They no longer seemed to have an off-switch.) 'Listen, I'll tell you what you need.'

'What?'

'You need your mates. You need a proper girls' night out. What are you up to over the weekend? It's about time I came to visit you, and I'll see if Jade is around too. Fancy a bit of company?'

'Yes,' gulped Georgie, feeling pathetically grateful. 'Yes, I do.'

Chapter Twenty-Six

Dear David Chandler,

Congratulations! You have been selected to join the prestigious Wankers Incorporated Alumni. Your womanizing, bullshitting and general wankerishness mean you are a prime candidate for our brotherhood. And poor Ann-Marie doesn't have a clue, does she? Amazing work there, fellow wanker. Welcome!

Here's how it works. We know you're a modest kind of guy who doesn't like to boast about all your many different conquests, affairs and – let's not put too fine a point on it – shags. Not you, David! But there's no need to be shy about being a wanker. No way! So we hope you'll allow us to blow your horn a little, if you'll pardon the expression. We'll be getting in touch with your colleagues, your boss and – of course! – your wife to inform them what a prize wanker you are. Oh yes, and you know that enormous billboard opposite your offices, right on Old Street roundabout? We're planning a special announcement there – a huge poster with your face on it and full details of your wankerish behaviour. Hey – we just want to celebrate our members! (So to speak. We know quite well how much you like to celebrate yours!)

Not only that, David, but we've done some research in your village as well and one of the local farmers is willing to rent us space in his field, enabling us to put up a huge sign there too, telling all your neighbours what a wanker you have been lately. No need to thank us, mate! We champion wankers have to look out for one another.

We're assuming you're happy for us to go ahead with all of this? Don't be shy now! To that effect, please find attached an image of our proposed poster – pretty eye-catching, I'm certain you'll agree. It's sure to get your colleagues and neighbours talking once they know what a prize wanker you are!

However, in the spirit of wanker brotherhood, if for any reason you would rather we didn't proceed with our Wanker Incorporated plans, then that's cool too. Whatever you say, pal! All you would need to do, in that case, is just stop being a wanker. Simples! That's really it! Just stop cheating on your wife, stop living a double life, stop sleeping with other women and lying to them . . . You know the sort of thing we mean. Oh, and with a third baby on the way – congratulations, by the way, dude! – you're probably going to want to 'resign' from that made-up 'job' that means you have to 'travel' so much during the week, too, aren't you? Spend a bit more time at home with your wife and kids. If you hear what we're saying.

In the meantime, we'll be keeping an eye on you, David, and waiting to see which way you choose. Cheers, mate!

All the best

The Board of Directors, Wankers Incorporated

PS Just a thought. Seeing as you love the ladies and all that (you legend!), how about putting your money where your mouth is and making a donation to this women's refuge project in Brighton? Prove what a real man you are, yeah?! Details are <u>here</u>.

'Do we send it?' said Gareth, his finger hovering above the mouse.

Rosa grinned at him. 'We send it,' she replied.

Gareth clicked the button with a flourish. *Your message has been sent*, a line at the top of the screen informed them. And then the two of them high-fived giddily and Rosa burst out laughing as she imagined her ex's face dropping as he read the damning email. *We're watching you. We know you. We're on to you.*

Ha. Revenge was *brilliant*. Forget getting over a man in quiet, miserable dignity, sniffling alone through the pain. Getting your own back and socking it to him was *way* more satisfying. 'You are a total genius,' she told her partner in crime and he raised his glass at her in salute. 'God, that feels good,' she sighed, leaning back against the sofa.

This was the second self-styled 'Revenge Meeting' the two of them had had now – the first had been in the Regency Arms where they'd come up with various ideas and settled on the Wankers Incorporated one as their favourite. Then Gareth had gone away and done all the hard work, setting up a complete site, with its own logo and email addresses, so that if Max – David – bothered clicking through to find out more, he'd soon realize the threat was genuine. Tonight, Rosa had cooked dinner for them and over platefuls of spaghetti carbonara and quite a lot of sauvignon plonk, they had concocted the killer email.

'Happy to be of service,' he replied, sloshing more wine into their glasses, and she caught a waft of his rather nice woody cologne as he leaned forward. He was wearing a smart dark red shirt too, ironed and everything, by the looks of it. Was he going on somewhere after hers? she wondered. 'Here's to giving David Chandler the fright of his life,' he added, sliding her glass over towards her.

'Hell, yeah,' she agreed, smiling at him. Far from being the worst person in the world as Bea had once said, Gareth was definitely one of the good guys, Rosa thought. He and Bea had totally sorted out their differences now, and were getting on much better, with Bea spending two nights a week at his place, and the pair of them recommending music and weird zombie films to each other with great eagerness. They were even going to see some obscure band next week together, apparently.

A strange sort of silence had fallen. Now that she and Gareth had finished what they'd set out to do, Rosa wasn't sure what else to say. 'Listen, can I give you some money for your time by the way?' she blurted out. 'It must have taken you ages to build that site.'

'You don't have to give me any money,' he said, sounding surprised. There was something very sincere about him, she'd come to realize. His dark eyes were soft as he looked at her. 'You've cooked me dinner, that's enough. Anyway, to be honest, I quite enjoyed it. A bloke mucking you around like that deserves everything he gets – it felt good to dish out a bit of justice. Proper men don't treat other people that way.'

She arched an eyebrow. 'And you're a "proper man", are you?' The words were meant to sound teasing but somehow came out sounding cheesy, as if she was trying to flirt with him in a really bad way.

'Yeah! Well, I wouldn't treat a woman like shit, anyway. I wouldn't treat *you* that way.'

It was quite late by now and Rosa was feeling swimmily drunk but there was something in Gareth's tone, a loud sort of earnestness, that made her sharpen up all of a sudden. He wasn't *flirting* with her, was he? she wondered, remembering the ironed shirt, the cologne. Then she dismissed the idea in the next second. No. Surely not. 'Mmm,' she said, noncommittally. 'Well, I think it's fair to say that most people don't go around inventing second lives for themselves in which to play two different partners off against each other. Unless I've wildly underestimated the rest of the human race, that is.'

'No, I mean . . .' He looked as drunk as she felt, his face flushed, his voice sliding about. His dark hair stuck up on end as he raked a hand through it. 'I mean, *I* wouldn't treat *you* that way. If we were dating.'

'Ahh. Hypothetically. Yes.' Good old 'hypothetically' and its depersonalizing qualities. Even if it was quite difficult to pronounce all those syllables in the right order when a person was three sheets to the proverbial.

'I didn't mean hypotheck – hypothetal –' Gareth wasn't letting her off the hook that easily, despite coming a cropper trying to get his tongue around the word. 'I didn't mean it in an *abstract* way,' he said, rolling his eyes. 'I meant. If. We. Were. Dating.'

Oh God. He really *was* flirting with her, even through her

squiffiness she could see that, and Rosa had absolutely no idea how she felt about such a development. What about Jo? she thought in a panic. What about Bea? 'Listen,' she said, thoughts scrambling, 'maybe this is not a conversation to be having when we're both r—'

But before she could finish her sentence, he had moved towards her and was kissing her in a wine-fumed, clumsy sort of way. Actually, even with the clumsiness, it was pretty good. His arm snaked around her back, and her insides went all trembly . . . 'Rat-arsed,' she said weakly when they came up for air.

'I've wanted to do that for ages,' he said, his voice low and husky. 'Rat-arsed or not.'

'Oh,' she said, gazing back at him, feeling conflicted, surprised and awkward all at once. Part of her wanted to carry on kissing him to see what happened. He was attractive, after all, and she'd come to like him very much. But another part of her – a more sober part – was holding back. Because it was Gareth! Ex-husband of her neighbour! And this could turn out to be a spectacularly bad idea. 'The thing is . . .' she began, inching away as she tried to find the right words.

He gave a rueful sort of laugh. 'It's all right. You don't have to say it. Just friends, right? Sorry. I shouldn't have done that. Couldn't help myself.' He put his glass down on the table. 'You are a lovely woman, that's all. Sorry if I overstepped the mark.'

'It's fine, don't worry about it,' she said, feeling awful now. She had enjoyed the kiss, that was the odd thing, but she hadn't thought of Gareth in a romantic way before then, and the moment had caught her off-guard. Plus, she had made enough mistakes with other people's husbands already. 'Um . . .'

'I'd better go,' he said, getting to his feet, face turned away. She'd embarrassed him, or he'd embarrassed himself, she wasn't quite sure which. Both.

'Well . . . If you're sure,' she said. Now she felt worse, as if she'd pushed him out. 'But thanks so much for everything. For the revenge plan. I love it.'

'No problem.' He was shrugging his jacket on, still not looking at her, feelings hurt. The joyousness of their joint efforts, the laughter and triumph, it was all gone, snuffed out in an instant.

'And do come along to the next supper club if you're free,' she went on. She couldn't stop prattling on all of a sudden, anything to fill the uncomfortable silences he kept leaving. 'I'm doing a French theme this time, in honour of Margot, so . . .'

'I think I'm busy,' he said, even though she hadn't actually specified which day it was. So that told her all she needed to know.

★

415

'You are okay? You are quiet, I think.'

It was the following morning and Rosa and Natalya were both taking a snatched coffee break, around the back of the hotel so that Natalya could smoke one of her evil Russian cigarettes.

Rosa reached up to touch her head and grimaced. It was the first day of June and the sunshine seemed painfully bright in her eyes. 'Headache,' she replied. 'Hangover. Too much wine last night.'

'Ahh. You should try vodka next time. Is better. Not so much pain.'

Rosa smiled weakly. 'I'll bear that in mind.' If there ever *was* a 'next time' with Gareth, of course. The way he'd left so hastily after she'd knocked him back, she wasn't holding her breath. Sipping her too-hot coffee, she leaned against the rough brick wall feeling tired of thinking about him, tired of replaying the awkward conversation. 'Natalya,' she said, almost before she knew she was going to. 'Have you ever been in love?'

Natalya arched one of her thick eyebrows. 'Love?' It sounded as if she was tasting the word in her mouth. But then she smiled, almost girlishly, and nodded. 'I have been in love,' she confirmed.

Rosa wasn't sure what to be more surprised about – the fact that she'd just seen Natalya smile and look bashful, or the words she'd heard from her lips. 'How could you tell?'

she asked. The question had been on her mind ever since Gareth had tried to kiss her. She was so wary of making the same mistake twice, of falling for another inappropriate man and being strung along all over again, that she no longer trusted her instincts. 'I mean, did you just know straight-away, or did it take a while before it dawned on you?'

'He was very handsome,' Natalya said, drawing hard on her cigarette and blowing out a long plume of foul-smelling smoke. 'Very big muscles,' she said, flexing her own bicep. 'Sexy. Strong face. You know? I like him.'

Okay. Lust, then, Rosa thought, nodding in reply. Which was not the same but never mind.

'It happen slowly, the love,' the younger woman went on. 'At first I think, he is a bit annoying. You know? He is pain in ass. Yes? But then one day . . .' And suddenly her whole face changed, becoming more animated, and Rosa could see past the frowning and gloom and unflattering kitchen-worker clothes to a younger sweeter Natalya, the Natalya who really *had* fallen for this guy. 'One night – Victory Day last year, last May, we are watching the fireworks together back home, big fireworks. And the sky is dark, and it is cold, we are in the crowd of people and I feel his body leaning against me. We have big coats on, hats on, and he is teasing me about my hat, we are laughing together, and I feel . . .' She paused, thinking, and then came that bashful smile again. 'I feel *warm* beside him. Not just my coat, not just my hat. I feel warm inside, like I never want to stop laughing, like I want to stay there with him forever, under the big sky and fireworks, like it is the best moment of my life.' It was the longest speech she had ever made to Rosa and her face was still soft from her memories as she delivered the punchline. 'And I think – I love him. I am surprised by that thought but it is so sudden, so sharp in my head. *I love him.* That is when I know.'

'Oh, Natalya.' Rosa felt touched by the story, imagining the crowd of people beneath the fireworks, the smell of gunpowder, the smoky trails in the dark sky. Natalya and her handsome young man in their coats and hats, standing close together. She hardly dare ask her next question. 'What happened?'

Natalya took a last drag on the cigarette and stubbed it hard against the wall, orange sparks showering to the ground. 'He went,' she said, shrugging. 'He vanish. He have some enemies – politics, you know? He said some stupid things. And then one day . . .' She turned her hands up in the air. 'He is gone. I do not know.' She rolled her eyes. 'So now I do not love. I work here. I forget about him.'

Rosa was sorry to have asked now. She felt as if she'd lifted a rock and seen all of Natalya's pain and hurt and secrets writhing underneath. She put out a hand to touch the younger woman in sorrow, in sympathy, but Natalya was already briskly turning to go back inside.

'Come. We work,' she said and tapped her watch. 'Is time.'

The French-themed supper club was a great success, and Rosa followed it with a summer-inspired menu the Friday afterwards. It was becoming her favourite few hours of the week, her supper club evenings, and ever since Georgie's glowing write-up in the *Brighton Rocks* magazine, she'd had a full house of diners each time, with a waiting list already underway. 'Get some of the foodie bloggers to come along too,' Georgie had advised, when Rosa told her this news. 'Hey, and there's this supper club app I've seen too – you need to get yourself on it. I bet that Gareth bloke would help, he's a techie, isn't he?'

'Mmm,' Rosa had replied, not wanting to mention the fact that she doubted Gareth would be doing her any more favours after the night of the kissing debacle. She had texted him twice since then, inviting him to the supper clubs, but he'd replied politely that he was busy each time, and she'd left it at that. 'I might even stretch to two nights a week, if I can work around the hotel rota,' she said instead. She was trying not to let her imagination run away with her but all the same, this was how businesses got started, wasn't it? This was how things took off: a serendipitous review, people telling their friends, loyal customers coming back for more . . . this could really be a thing, she kept thinking to herself. An actual, proper new thing. Bea had offered to type up menus for her each time, and Natalya was helping with the waitressing now, relieved to take on some extra work where nobody threw things at her. Rosa was already thinking ahead to future weeks and how she could put together different menus for evenings to come: Moroccan, Mexican, Italian . . . perhaps a Brazilian menu to mark the start of the Olympics. A barbecue one summer night, even . . . The possibilities seemed endless.

'You should definitely start charging more,' Ned had advised her the week before. 'Fifteen quid a head . . . Are you even covering your costs? You could definitely go to twenty if need be. I've seen supper clubs charging twenty-five pounds a head, which is still not exorbitant for a fantastic three-course meal.'

Rosa was loath to ramp up her prices just yet, though. She wanted to build her customer numbers first, get the business established before she started going all tycoon-like and strategizing about profits. Besides, for now, it was a sheer delight to be cooking dinner for people every week, a really enjoyable novelty, having her living room full of happy diners, seeing all those scraped-clean plates . . . the money almost seemed like an afterthought. Moments of joy, she thought to herself again. Life seemed full of them, these days.

This week, Ned and Charlotte were there, as usual, as was Georgie and a friend of hers from home, Amelia, plus ten other random strangers, all rather shy and quiet to begin with, as often proved the case, but livening up and chatting away once the wine was flowing. Jo was out on a blind date tonight apparently so couldn't make it, and Bea too, was out for once, at a friend's sleepover, both of which events sounded promising to Rosa.

The weather had been warm all week and with this in mind, Rosa had put together a light, summery menu, starting with a choice of salads for a starter, one with the most delicious cured trout, followed by an aromatic saffron chicken pilaf, with a vegetarian alternative. To finish, she was serving up individual lime and mascarpone soufflés, which had taken numerous practice attempts to perfect but which she'd finally got the hang of and were deliciously tangy and more-ish. That said, she was personally steering clear of any alcohol until she'd served up all fifteen of the fluffy little fellas, at which point, she would be treating herself to a very large glass of wine and a sit-down.

The evening had started well. It turned out that two of the guests already knew each other, and so the group was soon buzzing with conversation, and everyone seemed to be getting along. This was another nice thing about the supper clubs – the number of new Brightonians she was meeting. No longer did Rosa feel completely alone in the city, she had been plugged into this whole social scene – right in her own front room. She felt like someone again, as if she had a place in the community. *Dinner At Rosa's*, she imagined her website saying. *Come in, all welcome!*

Enough daydreaming for now, though! She had a pilaf or two to serve up, pistachios and parsley to chop and sprinkle, and the jug of iced water needed refilling. She was just setting down the main course dishes onto the table, though, to a gratifying chorus of 'Ooh's, when there was a loud knocking on the door, and a rather cross-sounding female voice. 'Hello? Are you there?'

Frowning, Rosa wiped her hands on a tea towel and hurried to answer it, trying to think if she was expecting anyone else to arrive. The person knocking was obviously someone with a key to the front door of the building but the voice hadn't sounded like Bea or Jo, and, as far as she knew, Margot's flat upstairs was still vacant, after her sons had cleared out her possessions. 'ROSA!' came the voice again, sounding very impatient now, as she rushed along the hall. The voice – female – was familiar somehow, and reminded her of the way her mother would scream up the stairs at her in Rosa's teenage years for playing her music too loudly.

She opened the door – but it was not her mother standing there. Instead it was her landlady, Angela Morrison-Hulme, in a tight-fitting black dress and heels, arms folded across her chest, her fuchsia-pink lips pursed in a most forbidding sort of way. 'Oh,' gulped Rosa, instantly aware that this was not a social call. Aware also, and far too late, that perhaps she should possibly have floated the supper club idea past her landlady in the first place. 'Hi, Angela,' she croaked, feeling her skin flare red. 'How are you?'

'How am I? Well, *thrilled*, naturally, to discover that one of my tenants has set up a business within the building, without bothering to ask my permission first,' Mrs Morrison-Hulme snapped, eyes flinty. Oh God. She was practically hissing with fury. 'How do you think I felt, discovering that you were running some kind of illegal restaurant here? Serving alcohol? On my property?'

'I'm not serving alcohol, and it's not a restaurant – nor illegal,' Rosa tried saying but her landlady seemed in no mood to listen.

'You can't do this, I'm afraid.' Her tone brooked no arguments. 'I've a good mind to serve you with an eviction notice, it's strictly against the terms of the contract. When I think how I treat you girls, how I look after you here – and you go behind my back like this. Did you think I wouldn't find out? Did you think I was so stupid?'

'No, of course not – and it really wasn't like that,' Rosa protested feebly, but she might as well have been talking to herself. From behind her floated the sound of laughter from her guests and Angela's eyes sharpened as they both heard it.

'They will have to leave,' she said. 'All of them. They will have to go.'

'But—' It was ridiculous but Rosa couldn't help thinking

of the dishes of pilaf she'd just served up, when she'd marinaded the chicken pieces in lemon juice and yoghurt so lovingly, when the vegetarian version was studded with pomegranate seeds, shining like rubies. She wasn't sure which would be more unbearable – for all that food to be wasted, or to have to suffer the humiliation of asking everyone to leave. 'Can't they just finish their dinner first? Please?' she begged.

Angela Morrison-Hulme clearly did not like to be crossed. She was also, apparently, in such a toweringly bad mood that she would not be backing down on anything she'd said. 'No,' she snapped. 'They cannot. They can go now, and you can consider this a verbal warning to you, as my tenant. Otherwise you will also have to go. You are lucky that I'm not telling you to pack your things and leave this very minute yourself, believe me.'

Natalya must have overhead the raised voices because she had appeared in the hall by now, cheeks pink. 'What is this?' she asked, looking from one woman to the other.

Rosa had to squeeze her hands very hard together to prevent herself from bursting into tears. 'It's over,' she said in a small strangled voice. 'The supper club. Everybody's got to leave.'

Chapter Twenty-Seven

Charlotte leaned back on the spade. 'Do you think that's big enough?' she asked, peering down into the hole she'd dug.

'Smashing,' her dad said, setting a bucket of compost at her feet. 'Chuck this lot in now, that's it, there she blows.' He clapped her on the back. 'Anyone would think you'd planted a tree before, kid. Nothing to it, right?'

Charlotte smiled sideways at him as she shook the last dark clods of compost into the hole. Having resisted her mother's tree-planting suggestions for this long, rejecting the idea as mawkish and clichéd, she had changed her mind recently. Perhaps it was her new habit of taking her lunch break out of the office on sunny days, in order to sit with a sandwich in the nearby Victoria Gardens, where she'd found herself admiring the spectacular elm trees, so majestically leafy and tall. Perhaps also it had been going out with Ned and the girls the previous Saturday for a woodland walk in Withdean and hearing the glorious shushing of branches, admiring the greenish light that fell through the leaves, and feeling the timelessness that the trees lent this place. She got it, all of a sudden, what her mum had been banging on about: the legacy of a sapling, the satisfaction to be gained from seeing it grow taller and broader month after month, year after year, changing with the seasons but with a comforting solidity.

And so, eating her words, along with a good old slice of humble pie, she had come to Reading for the day, meeting her parents at the local garden centre in order to choose a tree for Kate. After some deliberation, she'd decided on a small pear tree, which would have gorgeous white blossom every spring, and, with a bit of luck, a crop of pears each summer, once it had been in the ground long enough to become established. Reading was where Kate had been born and died, and so seemed the right place for her tree. More to the point, Charlotte's parents weren't planning on moving house any time soon. The tree would be safely nurtured in their back garden for years to come, and she could see its beauty every time she visited.

'In she goes, then,' her dad urged. 'Let's have her!'

Gripping the sapling's stem, Charlotte eased off the pot, a light shower of soil pattering over her boots, then her dad showed her how to tease out the rootball with her fingers, before lowering it ceremoniously into its new home. Then they filled in the soil around it, carefully trod the earth down and gave the base of the tree a thorough watering.

Her mum slid an arm around Charlotte and the three of them stood looking at it for some minutes: Kate's little sapling amidst the shrub roses and the camellias, the delphiniums shooting up nearby, and the first papery poppies. A bird was singing in the cherry tree behind them. One of the cats sunned itself on the patio, its fur warm and dusty. There was a cabbage white butterfly further up the garden, Charlotte noticed, flitting a wavering path through the flowers. She looked back at the little tree and imagined it hung with frothing blossom in years to come, golden pears weighting its branches. The thought made her feel happy. Happier than she'd expected.

Her mum gave Charlotte a squeeze. 'There. Didn't I say it would be a lovely thing to do?'

'You did, Mum. And you were right.' She hugged her back, feeling a rush of affection for both her parents, and laughed. 'If only I'd listened to you in the first place, eh?'

'Exactly,' her mum said, ruffling her hair as if she were eight years old again. 'Come on, let's go and have a cup of tea.'

The good feeling stayed with Charlotte for the rest of the day, all the way back to Brighton. She liked thinking of the tree, Kate's tree, slowly unfurling its root capillaries, stretching them tentatively into the new soil and drinking up the water. Was it too fanciful of her to admit that it reminded her of her own slow unfurling, sending out hesitant roots, shyly turning herself to the sun again? Perhaps. But her own new roots, here in Brighton, were definitely becoming more entrenched by the day. By the night, too, she thought with a secret grin as she let herself into the house.

'So is it serious, then, this new fella?' her mum had asked over tea and biscuits. She waggled her eyebrows in a jolly way but Charlotte knew it was only her way of covering up her anxiety.

'Well . . .' Charlotte didn't quite want to admit to him having stayed over for the first time the night before, but knowing her, it was written all over her blushing face anyway. Perhaps there was no need to spell it out. 'I like him,' she said demurely.

'And he's got two little girls, did you say? And that's okay?' Again, her mum asked the question as if it was of the utmost casualness but the fact that she'd accidentally added three spoonfuls of sugar to her tea rather than her ordinary two gave away her true feelings.

'Mum, it's fine. He's great. They're adorable. It's really – honestly – fine.'

Her words came back to her now as she grabbed the pile of post from the hall table and leapt up the main stairs in a sudden burst of energy. Her and Ned, it was way better than 'fine' and 'okay', frankly. Look at her, bounding up the stairs like a gazelle! He had done that to her. Look at her, singing in the shower that morning after she'd kissed him goodbye. He had done that as well. That twinkle in her eye? The song hummed under her breath? The joy bubbling through her veins? Him, all him. She hardly dare even say the word out loud in her head but it had been popping up in her mind all day, shining and bright, festooned with hearts and flowers and fairy lights. Love. LOVE. *Love.*

I'm falling in love with you, she kept imagining saying to him. *I'm falling in love.* Words she had never expected to say again, emotions she'd never expected to feel, but there they were, brimming to her surface once more, making her giddy with their rushing intensity. If grief had been like the initial stomach-churning plummet of a sky-dive, being in love was more like the immediate aftermath of the parachute opening: the sensation of floating, suspended like a bird in the blue, the adrenalin immediately turning to euphoria and breathless exhilaration. She wasn't sure she ever wanted to come back down to earth.

Everything about last night had been wonderful. The girls had been staying at his sister's for a sleepover with their cousins, and so, with the knowledge that she potentially had Ned to herself all night, once back from work that afternoon, Charlotte had cleaned her flat from top to bottom, smoothing on fresh bed linen and putting a box of condoms in the drawer of her bedside cabinet. (She had been a Girl Guide, Charlotte, and liked to be prepared, although she was pretty sure there wasn't actually a badge to be earned in Contraception Skills.) Then she had showered, plucked, moisturized and put on her best underwear, before spraying perfume liberally around the place. (Afterwards, coughing and spluttering, she'd opened the windows as wide as possible, fearing that the poor man would be asphyxiated on Jo Malone Red Roses the moment he walked through the door.)

She'd met Ned for a drink in the Regency Arms, around the corner, and then they'd gone on for dinner at Rosa's supper club – or rather, that had been the plan anyway, right up until Angela had turned up and ruined everything. Poor Rosa! In had marched the landlady, practically breathing fire, and proceeded to order everybody off the premises, while Rosa frantically made up foil parcels of food so that they could take something with them, simultaneously refunding half their money, pushing their half-drunk bottles of wine back into their hands and apologizing profusely, hands wringing.

'We are Rosa's guests and this is a dinner party; the tenancy agreement doesn't forbid us either of those things,' Charlotte had tried pointing out – quite bravely, she felt, given how terrifying she found Angela – but their landlady was having none of it, standing there with her hands on her hips until the last person had left. Of course, Charlotte and Ned, plus Georgie and her friend Amelia, had merely waited on the stairs above, like naughty children up past their bed-time, until Angela had flounced out of the building again, whereupon they'd crept back down to knock on Rosa's door and offer their condolences. The five of them had gone on to eat everything that was left, including all fifteen of the lime soufflés, whilst slagging off Angela with great vehemence.

Afterwards Charlotte and Ned had stumbled their way upstairs, Charlotte becoming increasingly apprehensive with every step. 'Come on in,' she said, as they reached her flat and she fumbled to open the door. Her heart was starting to accelerate. Here they were, just the two of them, with the whole night at their disposal. Would they have sex? Would she remember what to do? Would he notice her stretchmarks and comment on her lime-soufflé-engorged belly? (Oh, why had she eaten so much, tonight of all nights?) There was just so much to worry about. And what about the morning, too – would she be able to look him in the eye or would he be scurrying away from her as fast as humanly possible?

But then, before she could go into full panicking melt-down, he had his arms around her and was kissing her, and the questions melted away, her whole body responding to his kiss, as if she was Sleeping Beauty, woken from a long slumber. *Oh hello*, she thought as they manoeuvred along the hallway together, still kissing, and collapsed together onto her sofa. *I remember now. Yes, I remember this.*

With so much worrying beforehand, she had quite over-looked the possibility that she might actually enjoy the ex-perience, seeing it instead as a quagmire of humiliation and dread. What a surprise, then, to find herself throwing off her clothes with keen abandon! How unexpected to discover that lust still ran deep through her, a great forgotten spring of it that rushed up through her body as she peeled off his shirt and ran her fingers along his bare skin. The sensations that had erupted through her, the *noises* she had made, the tremendous spiralling joy she had felt afterwards, lying in the crook of his arm!

Charlotte the harlot, she thought to herself now, smiling at the memory as she dumped her bag and kicked off her shoes. Who would have thought it? Who ever would have imagined? She could hardly wait to get her hands on him again, frankly.

Waiting for the kettle to boil, she leafed through the post she'd picked up. Three pieces today: a Lakeland catalogue (they were probably panicking because she'd eased up on the cleaning products lately), something from her bank, and a thick cream envelope with the address written by hand. She was just ripping the latter open – it seemed to be from a local solicitors' firm, Tavener, Smith and Lloyd, which meant absolutely nothing to her – when her phone rang, and it was the man himself.

'Hi,' she said happily, smoothing out the pages of the

letter. Maybe she was being head-hunted, she thought distractedly, glancing again at the company logo. 'How are you?'

'Good, yeah. Been feeling magnificently cheerful all day,' he told her. 'Can't think why that could be. Oh yeah. Now I remember. Last night.'

She laughed. 'Me too,' she confessed shyly. 'I was just thinking about that myself. It was really . . .' She hesitated, unsure if there was a word big enough to capture all her feelings about the night. Lying with him afterwards staring up at the ceiling, feeling dazed, dazzled, her nerve-endings still quivering. Waking up to feel his heavy arm slung across her, feeling delighted as she smelled his skin, turned her head to see his sleeping face, noticing the faint freckles on his bare shoulder. She had held herself at a distance from closeness for so long, fearing this kind of intimacy with another human being, and now here he was, sleeping in her bed, like some kind of handsome miracle, benevolently hand-delivered by the Goddess of Bereaved Women. What was more, she felt completely thrilled to have him there. '. . . Great,' she said in the end. 'Really really great.'

'*Two* "really"s, I like it,' he teased. 'How did it go today, by the way? How was the tree-planting?'

'Surprisingly lovely. Actually very comforting.' She poured boiling water onto the teabag, remembering the peace and contentment she'd felt in her mum's back garden, the birdsong, the sunshine, the spade beneath her feet. 'I was wondering about doing something similar for Margot, you know. Now that I've broken my tree-planting duck.'

'No stopping you now,' he agreed. 'Good idea. Something elegant and beautiful, she'd have liked that. A stately willow, maybe. Or one of those gorgeous poplars you get lining the roadsides in France.'

'Yeah. Although God knows where I'd put it,' she replied, suddenly realizing the practical limitations of her idea. Imagining too the wrath of Angela if she put an enormous tree in the tiny courtyard garden at the back of the house. 'Maybe I'll have to settle for a sunflower in a pot for the time being.' Her eye fell back on the letter just then and she blinked, experiencing a déjà vu moment, seeing Margot's name there in print. What? Maybe this wasn't a head-hunting letter after all.

'Hello? Are you still there?'

'Hi. Yeah. I just . . .' But her concentration was fragmenting, her eye caught by words on the page.

Executors of the will . . .

Margot Favager . . .

My duty to inform you . . .

'Sorry, Ned,' she said, realizing he was speaking in her ear. 'I was just distracted by . . . Oh my God.'

'What? Is everything all right?'

My client made a bequest to you . . .

'Bloody hell. Whoa.'

'*What?*'

Charlotte blinked a few times and read the words again. And the numbers. Oh, Margot, she thought, tears pricking her eyes. You didn't! Seriously? 'Sorry.' She did her best to pull herself together. 'It's . . . It's something amazing actually. I've just found out . . .' She hesitated, feeling rude for admitting to reading a letter at the same time as being mid-conversation on the phone.

'What? God, will you just tell me?'

'Margot left me some money.' There was a lump in her throat, so big it was hard to get the words out past it. 'I've just this minute found out. She left me some money to . . . to "spend unwisely", apparently.' A little involuntary noise came from her, seeing the words there in print, and she couldn't be sure whether it was a sob or a laugh. 'It's what I always said to her,' she went on in explanation, 'that I'd spend the money she gave me wisely, and I could tell she thought that was very boringly sensible of me . . .' She made the noise again. A laugh, she told herself. A laugh, with a hint of sob.

'What an amazing thing to do,' Ned said and she could hear that he was smiling. 'Money to spend unwisely – that's pure Margot.'

'Isn't it just? Love her.' Charlotte kept looking again and again at the figure she'd been left – ten thousand pounds.

She couldn't quite believe it. Already her mind was whirling with 'unwise' ways to spend the money – on the holiday of a lifetime, a shopping spree in all Margot's favourite shops, a huge glorious piece of art, maybe even a pair of roller boots, just for fun . . . *Oh, Margot,* she thought again, with a surge of feelings. This fabulous woman, even in death, was opening new doors to Charlotte and pushing her through them. If only she could thank her in person, one last time!

She forced herself to put the letter down and switch her attention back to Ned. 'How are you, anyway? What have you been up to?'

'Well, that's why I called. Because aside from thinking about you pretty much every other second of the day . . .'

Warmth spread through her. 'Only every *other* second?' she teased. 'Rude.'

'I was trying to play it cool, but okay, yes, I admit it, every single second,' he replied. 'Miraculously I've been thinking about something else too, though. I've had an idea, actually, and wondered what you thought.'

'Go on,' she said. 'Enlighten me.'

'Well,' he began. 'It's like this . . .'

Chapter Twenty-Eight

'Oh wow,' said Amelia, laughing as she scrolled down the screen. 'She is totally going to *love* this. Yes!'

'Do you think so?' asked Georgie, pleased. 'I know it's all a bit rough at the moment, but—'

'I totally think so! Mate, she is going to be so chuffed. It's excellent!' Amelia elbowed her. 'Hey. Do you think you could do one for me, too? Please?'

'Too right I will,' she said, beaming at her best friend. 'You bet.' Oh, it had been so wonderful having Amelia to stay. They'd been shopping all day Saturday looking for wedding presents for Jade and her fiancé – well, in theory anyway, although to be fair they'd spent most of the time buying themselves new tops each in a North Laine boutique, before stuffing their faces with an enormous brunch. Then Amelia had insisted on visiting the pier and going on all the rides. 'I'm on holiday, humour me,' she'd said, as she forced Georgie to queue up for the roller coaster again. Saturday night, they'd ventured out in search of cocktails and ended up in some Seventies disco club where they had drunk all sorts of lurid concoctions and laughed themselves stupid, making up ridiculous dance moves together like they were seventeen again. It had been so much fun that, for a short while, she'd almost forgotten everything that had happened with Simon. Almost.

'It's great here,' Amelia had slurred, as they tottered back home, arm in arm, through the city streets once they'd finally called it a night. 'I can see why you like it so much. I'm dead jealous, you actually *living* here.'

'Yeah, it's brilliant,' Georgie agreed, then hesitated. 'Although without Simon, I'm not sure if—'

Up went Amelia's hand, shooting imperiously into the air. 'We're not talking about him, remember? He who shall not be named.'

Georgie lurched against a street sign, wobbling on her clonky heels. 'I thought that was Voldemort?'

'Him neither. They're both banned. And that's that!'

On Sunday, Georgie had woken early, and the moment her eyes opened, a genius idea had popped up in her brain like a slice of toast – the perfect thing for Jade's wedding present. Yes! Sure, she'd bought her a pretty lampshade yesterday, in a 'that would do' sort of attitude, in lieu of finding anything better, but the lampshade, while nice to look at, was not the sort of present that would blow any bride and groom away. It was not something Jade would snatch up from the living room if the house happened to be burning down, put it like that.

Her mind must have been working away at the problem the whole time she was deep in cocktail-induced slumber overnight, neatly presenting her with the solution – ta-dah! – as soon as she was vaguely conscious. And so, while Amelia slept on, pink eye-mask lopsided across her flushed face, Georgie tiptoed out of the bedroom and got to work. Opening up a desktop publishing program, she'd created a mock-up of *The Jade and Sam Gazette*, styled like a newspaper, with a big photo of the happy couple in the centre, and various headlines about them running down a sidebar. It wasn't a million miles away from the little newspapers she'd created as a child – *The Hemlington Road Gazette* and *The Stonefield Times* – she thought, smiling as she typed.

Wedding of the Year – Read All About It!

Ilkley Road Disco – Where the Romance Began!

Meet Molly – the Couple's Beloved Border Terrier!

'Oh, it's such an ace idea,' Amelia said, looking at the laptop screen again now, eye make-up still smudgy around her lashes. 'And Jade will love it. Genius! So will you make a print and frame it, or use the image for a card, or poster . . . ? Do you know, I'd quite like to commission some to have on the tables at our reception when we get hitched,' she went on eagerly, without waiting for an answer. 'Give everyone a bit of a laugh, wouldn't it, while they wait for their starters? Would you do some for me? I'd pay you, obviously.'

'You don't have to pay me, you nutter, of course I'll do them for you,' Georgie said. 'But yeah, I was thinking a framed print would be a nice present for Jade and Sam.' Her head was racing with ideas, suddenly. Mugs. Calendars. Coasters. There was probably scope for a whole range of this sort of wedding souvenir merchandise, now that she thought about it, feeling excited. Maybe this could be a new business venture for her!

'Cheers, doll,' Amelia said, then groaned. 'In the meantime, you don't have any Nurofen, do you? Last night is catching up on me all of a sudden. Did we really start a conga with all those disco divas?'

It was as the two of them were hugging goodbye at the train station later that afternoon that the second genius idea came to Georgie. This time it was about Simon. It had been over three weeks since he'd left Brighton and she still hadn't heard a word from him. Her texts to him had started off apologetic and grovelling, before becoming terse and then downright nasty, until she'd had to delete his number to stop her sending any more on impulse. Amelia hadn't had anything new to report about his doings either, no glimpses about the village, no overheard gossip in the pub, nothing. It was as if there was this wall of silence between them, getting taller and wider by the day. As if they'd never been a couple at all.

Well, bugger that, Georgie thought, waving as her friend went through the ticket barriers. The time had come to make a stand, to say her piece, to tear down that horrible wall of silence. And if Simon wouldn't take her calls or reply to her texts, then she had to try a new tack.

The whole time she'd been putting together her *Jade and Sam Gazette* that morning, there had been a voice inside Georgie: a sad, plaintive voice that kept wishing she could do something this lovely for her own relationship. And so she was going to. It would be her final gesture, one last attempt to salvage things and apologize before she admitted defeat and gave up on him forever.

'I do still really love him, that's the problem,' she had slurred to Amelia on Saturday night as they sat eating jammy toast in the kitchen, post-clubbing.

'I know you do, darling,' Amelia had sighed, butter shining on her chin. 'And I bet he still loves you too. You know what blokes are like. They can't admit when they've made a mistake. I reckon he feels terrible.'

Georgie had no idea how Simon felt, though; he could be doing anything for all she knew. He could have got this job in Harrogate, he could have fallen in love with someone else, he could have decided to pack everything in for a new life abroad in Hong Kong – and, for all Amelia's reassurances,

Georgie might very well be the last thing on his mind right now. So it was high time she reminded him, basically. To show him that her new passion for journalism didn't have to mean relationship destruction all the time. Maybe, just maybe, it could be an olive branch too.

The Dukes Square Bugle, she typed into her template screen once she was back at the flat, then pursed her lips and frowned. Was that okay? Would he care any more about what was going on down here in Brighton? He hadn't exactly given any indications that he might be missing the place, after all.

The Georgie and Simon Herald! she typed instead but even as she was pressing the keys, she was already shaking her head, knowing that that was also wrong; it was too hopeful and presumptuous a name when she wasn't even sure that there *was* a valid 'Georgie and Simon' thing left in the first place. Backspacing through the letters again, she racked her brain, trying to come up with the right words, the hook that this whole gesture represented. Finally it came to her and she typed one single word in the title area: *Sorry.*

The hours ticked by, interspersed by a chatty phone call from her mum, a text from Amelia saying that she was back home and thanking Georgie for a brilliant weekend, plus a quick plate of scrambled eggs on toast when she realized she hadn't eaten for five hours and her stomach was tying itself in knots. 'If a thing's worth doing, it's worth doing properly,' her mum had always been fond of saying, and Georgie was determined to do this, her apology, as properly as she was able. That was why, for her cover photo, she'd put on a pale blue top Simon had always liked, washed her hair and blow-dried it so that it fell loose and wavy about her shoulders, and taken about a hundred sad-face selfies, before settling on one in which she still looked quite pretty, yet also repentant. If you looked closely – which she hoped he would – you could see the bed in the background, and she hoped he'd notice it and remember happier times spent beneath those very covers. (Yes, all right, so perhaps it wasn't the subtlest of subliminal messages but sometimes a bloke needed a shove in the right direction, okay?)

As for the headlines for her *Sorry* magazine, she'd thought long and hard about those too. Upbeat was the key here, she decided: upbeat, positive, funny. I miss you, but not in a desperate, cringey way, was what she wanted to say. Sorry, and hey, if you want to try again, I would like that as well. She was not going to beg or boil bunnies, she was just going to put it out there, her heart and her hopes, in one big writerly act of love. And hell, if he ignored that too, then so be it. At least she would have tried.

Girl Misses Boy – I Screwed Up! she admits
Tenants' Shock at Dinner Disaster – Landlady from Hell
  Goes on Rampage

My Speed Dating Pain – Exclusive True Story
Plus! Ten Reasons Why You Should Give Georgie Another
  Chance

At the bottom of the front cover, she had typed in small letters: Sorry *magazine is brought to you in association with Apologetic Girlfriend Limited.*

That was just the start of it, of course. She didn't stop there. With her mum's words about 'doing something properly' still ringing in her ears, once completing the cover, she went on to create a number of pages inside the magazine: all the articles she'd listed in her mini headlines, plus lots of photos of the two of them, from back when they were school sweethearts in blazers, to the more recent snaps of them laughing and gurning on the Palace Pier. She even drew quite a bad cartoon of a new Knock Knock joke she'd thought of. (*Eyebrow who? Eyebrowt you flowers to say I'm sorry.*)

Some time later, when she had finished, she looked at the clock and realized with a jump that it was almost midnight. This was the point at which a sensible person would call it a night, sleep on the whole thing and read it through with fresh eyes in the morning, before sending it off. But now that Georgie had finished her big peace-making gesture, she just wanted him to see it – and besides, she'd never been a very sensible person to start with. And so she saved the document and wrote a quick explanatory email as an accompaniment. Then, after a deep breath, she pressed Send.

It was done, and there was no turning back. 'Over to you now, Simon,' she said aloud, closing down the laptop and going to bed.

She'd been sleeping late in the week, now that there was no boyfriend getting up early every morning around her, and after the busy weekend and her long stint at the laptop, she slept soundly right through until nine-thirty when the buzzing of her intercom finally woke her. Oh my God, she thought, leaping out of bed in an instant. It was *Simon*! He'd read her *Sorry* magazine at midnight and driven all the way down here to throw his arms around her, and . . .

'Parcel for you, love,' came the distinctly un-Simonish voice through the intercom. 'Needs signing for.'

Bollocks. It probably wasn't even for her, knowing Georgie's luck, and she would have dragged herself downstairs in her dressing gown, scaring the postman into the bargain, for nothing. *And* she'd been right in the middle of a really good dream, too. 'Just coming,' she muttered ungraciously, making sure she picked up her door keys before she went down.

It just went to show, you could be wrong about these things; far too pessimistic. Well, okay, so she hadn't been wrong about scaring the postman, who couldn't get her signature fast enough before scuttling away, but the mysterious tube-shaped parcel *was* for her. What was more, as she peered at the address label on her way back upstairs, she was pretty sure the handwriting was Simon's. And all of a sudden, she was wide awake and running to get into the flat as soon as possible, so that she could find out more.

Once inside, she scrabbled breathlessly to open the tube but Simon being Simon, he'd taped the ends down with brown tape so firmly that her nails were useless weapons in this instance and she had to pull out all the kitchen drawers in search of scissors. What had he sent her after weeks of silence? What on earth was in the tube? And oh help, how mortifying would it be, if it was something really horrible and fuck-off-ish when she'd just gone and sent her stupid *Sorry* magazine over to him the night before! Why had she been so impulsive? Why hadn't she been patient and measured enough to wait and send it today instead?

Once through the layers of tape, she wrenched the round plastic seal from one end of the tube and tipped the contents onto the kitchen worktop. A scroll of paper – some kind of architectural drawing, she saw, wrinkling her nose in confusion. For an awful moment, she wondered if he'd made some mistake, and accidentally sent her a job application or tender. But then she saw her name at the top of the sheet, the neat words in capitals: A HOUSE FOR US, GEORGIE

AND SIMON, and her heart thundered into top gear at once.

Smoothing the paper out and weighting it at each corner with two mugs, the bag of sugar, and her own elbow, she peered at the building he had drawn – a handsome, modern house – and read the notations he'd made.

> *Our bedroom – east-facing so that we get the sun in the morning. Big enough for all your books.*
>
> *Writing room – for Georgie, with an actual desk so you don't have to hunch over typing on the bed, plus loads of shelves to display all the magazines and books you're going to write.*
>
> *Huge kitchen – for dinner parties and Christmases. Definitely big enough for a dog's bed or two, as well.*
>
> *Living room – with open fireplace. For chestnut roasting? Maybe even sex. (Not at the same time.)*
>
> *Spare rooms – for friends staying over. Or children's bedrooms?*

His neat writing blurred suddenly as tears filled Georgie's eyes, because what he was describing, what he had created, was her perfect house. Her dream home, with all the things she'd ever wanted. And despite what she'd thought, he had loved her enough to notice each detail and record them in his mind.

Sniffing, she wiped her eyes and then blew her nose, before noticing a last neat note he'd written at the bottom of the paper.

> *One more thing to consider: location. I've been offered a new job in Reigate, about 40 miles from Brighton, so we could stay in the south, if you want to. Alternatively, my old firm in York is expanding, and they've asked me to come back so we could start over in Yorkshire, if you'd rather. Or, of course, we could go somewhere completely new together. I don't care about the geography, though, to be honest. I just want to be with you, George. You're my home. Sorry I lost the plot for a while. You were right – I haven't been a great boyfriend but I want to try again, if you'll let me.*
>
> *PS Sorry too if you've been trying to text. Managed to leave my phone behind in Trowell services like a plum. Have got a new phone – number below.*

Now she really was weeping. Proper, ugly crying, the sort that would have Simon running for the hills if he could see her now. She was his *home*, he'd said. He'd designed them a *house*. And after all her stressing about his interview in

Harrogate, it turned out he'd applied for a job down in *Reigate* instead. She couldn't take everything in.

Their olive branch messages had crossed, she realized, wondering if he would have seen her *Sorry* magazine yet. And actually, wasn't this how a relationship was supposed to be, both of them trying to put things right at the same time, both of them reaching out simultaneously, saying, Wait, can we talk? I made a mistake.

Feeling joy pirouetting inside her, she grabbed her phone and dialled his number immediately. He answered on the first ring, his voice hesitant. Nervous, even.

'Hey,' she said happily, still sitting there at the kitchen table in her pyjamas, the design of their house spread out before her. 'I got your house.'

'I got your magazine,' he said. 'I'm sorry, George. I've not handled this very well.'

'It's fine, I'm sorry too. I missed you.' She leaned back against the chair, feeling nothing but relief that they were having this conversation and that she was filled with certainty now that everything was going to be all right. 'We can sort this out. When can I see you?'

'I'm glad you asked,' he said. 'Because I was thinking . . . tonight?'

Chapter Twenty-Nine

Two months later

'Ready to roll, boss?' asked Natalya.

'Let's do it,' said Rosa, adding a last drizzle of olive oil to the final plate. 'Starters coming out!'

It was August, and a warm evening at Rosa's Supper Club, so the café doors were wide open to let the soft sea breeze blow in for her customers. She had a full house tonight, and forty hungry people were out there, chatting and drinking. There was nothing like the buzz of a supper club about to begin to give her tingles.

Back in June, after Angela had so forcefully closed down her tiny home-based dining operation, Rosa had been ready to quit, to forget the whole thing and resign herself to slaving at the Zanzibar hotel peeling carrots for the rest of her life. Right until Ned and Charlotte had knocked on her door with a proposition, that was.

'Ned's had an idea,' Charlotte had said, the words bubbling out of her as if she was fizzing inside.

'About the supper club,' he'd said. 'Why don't you run it from my café?'

It had been as easy as that one little question – to which there could only be one possible answer: *yes, please.* The arrangement suited Ned – who closed at six every evening anyway and could do with the extra income from renting out the space. The idea suited Rosa too – the café could hardly have been nearer her flat, for one thing, and the space was elegant and bright, and in a gorgeous seafront location. Big enough to fit in more diners, yet still small enough to maintain a cosy feel – plus, bonus detail, the café kitchen was way better equipped than her own one.

Once she'd contacted the people on her waiting list to alert them to the change of venue, she was off and running once more, the supper club making a seamless leap from home to café. In fact, the leap had been a fairly seismic one, with Ned advertising the evening on his chalk boards, which boosted her numbers immediately, so much so that he'd offered to lend her a second waitress, the keen-to-work-all-hours Shamira, for the first few weeks. (She was saving up for a flat with her boyfriend John, apparently.) Then, when the bookings reached thirty each week, Rosa had taken the plunge to hold the supper club on Thursday nights too.

By July, the supper club had become so popular that Rosa

had been able to hand in her notice at the Zanzibar. She'd learned a huge amount there and was grateful for the experience but she wouldn't miss the exhausting summer wedding shifts, nor her bellowing boss. To her great surprise, Brendan had taken the news well, without throwing a single thing at her, and had actually turned up for dinner there at the café one evening, with his charming and very beautiful wife, no less. Even more surprisingly, he'd been polite and quietly spoken the whole time, complimenting her on her dishes with every course. He had even left a tip. ('I think bodysnatchers are in town,' Natalya pronounced disbelievingly, biting down on one of the pound coins, to check it was real.)

Although this initial success was gratifying, Rosa was trying not to get too carried away. Running a supper club was always going to be easiest in the summer months when the hotels and guest-houses were full of tourists every week after all, and winter was sure to prove a much harder sell, when scouring winds came sweeping up from the sea. Still, with this in mind, she was already planning ways to keep her customers coming back week after week: some kind of loyalty scheme for local residents, perhaps, or doubling up to host wine tastings simultaneously or taking on private catering commissions . . . She'd figure it out, anyway.

To make ends meet in the meantime, she was working a couple of mornings cheffing for Ned in the café, and baking cakes for him on a regular basis. So it was all good, really. Better than good. She was relishing every minute.

'Good evening, everyone, I'm Rosa, your host, and here are the starters,' she said, as she and her team went out with loaded plates. Although she did all the cooking, she loved coming out like this and introducing the food, as well as herself. The more informal and friendly she could make the evening, the better it seemed to go. 'We have a sea-bass ceviche with pickled cucumber and lime, as well as a feta and beetroot salad for the vegetarians. There's more bread too, so just help yourselves. Hope you enjoy it.'

By day, the café was a space with lots of smaller tables for two or four, but for supper club evenings, Rosa arranged the tables into three long ones, each seating ten people. Out came the starched white tablecloths – she had bought a supply of second-hand ones from the Zanzibar – and out came the candles and flowers for decoration. She strung fairy lights around the walls and kept the doors open on warm evenings so that the sea breeze could waft in coolingly.

Tonight they had a full house, and she recognized at least half the people present, as friends and diners who'd come along before. 'Hello,' she said, setting plates down at the first table. Jo and Bea were sitting at this one, along with Jo's new girlfriend Izzy, and a friend of Bea's, India, whom she'd seen a lot recently. Bea seemed a different girl these days – smiling, giggly, relaxed. She'd had a cool new asymmetric haircut that really suited her face, the bullying at school had stopped, and she'd found herself in a nicer friendship group too, thank goodness.

As for Jo, she now sported a new tattoo on her ankle and was saving up for a winter holiday in Thailand. She'd carried on with her *Live for today!* motto, but, as she'd said to Rosa, she was also pursuing a *Look after yourself for tomorrow!* health kick as well following her hospital trauma, to which end, she'd persuaded Rosa to accompanying her to a seriously sweaty hot yoga session every Monday evening while Bea was at her dad's. 'The thing about nearly dying is it *totally* makes you want to live,' she had said more than once, and she and Bea had gone off on lots of spontaneous camping trips over the summer, even popping in to see her evangelical parents in an attempt to rebuild a few fallen bridges.

When it came to Gareth, his name had not really been mentioned by either Rosa or Jo since the attempted kiss, that drunken night back in June. She doubted Gareth was going to spill the beans on what had happened after she had rebuffed him, and she had decided, for the sake of her new friendship with Jo, that it was probably safest to say nothing either, to change the subject whenever his name popped up. But then the two of them had gone on for cocktails, post-yoga, earlier that week in a little bar on Western Road, and somehow the conversation had tumbled into Gareth's direction before Rosa could haul it back. They had been talking about kissing, of all things, because Jo was drunkenly telling Rosa what a fantastic kisser her new girlfriend was. 'On a par with Gareth, actually, who I'd always held up as this benchmark of excellent snogging,' she'd said, laughing. 'He is one hot pair of lips, that man, I'm telling you.'

It was almost as if she *wanted* Rosa to confess, really. And sure enough, Rosa had found herself blurting out, 'Yeah, I know,' before clapping a hand to her mouth and saying, 'Oh shit,' in the next breath.

Jo's double-take would have been hilarious if Rosa hadn't immediately been swamped with high-voltage guilt. 'You *know*? How come? Oh my God. How did I not know this? Are you two an *item*?' screeched Jo, gesticulating so dramatically that she almost sent her Sea Breeze sailing off the table. If anything, she looking thrilled, rather than toweringly angry, but all the same, Rosa still found herself cringing.

'Um . . . Well . . .'

'You dark horse! You sneaky so-and-so. How long has this been going on, then?' Jo demanded, then peered at her. 'Don't look so worried! Is that why you haven't said anything? God! *He's* just as bad, I was only speaking to him this morning and he didn't mention a *word*! Whoa. Wait till I tell Bea!'

'Jo – no – it's not like that. There's not anything to mention, that's the point: it was just a kiss. One kiss, and it was months ago now. We'd had a really good night and were quite pissed and . . . it happened. But I sort of . . . pushed him away, so . . .' She twisted her glass on the table, leaving wet circles. 'So that's it. End of story. I've not heard from him since then.'

Jo frowned, trying to process all of this. 'Oh,' she said. If anything, she seemed disappointed. 'Seriously? Shame. I actually think you two would be good together. So . . . what, you didn't fancy him, or . . . ?'

Rosa bit her lip. She had thought about Gareth a lot since that night, replayed the scene in her head umpteen times. 'I think you should go for it!' her friend Catherine had urged when Rosa had phoned to tell her all about it.

'Get over yourself! I thought he was quite fit!' Meg had agreed on Rosa's second agonizing phone call and Rosa hadn't been able to answer, couldn't quite put her finger on any problem that was holding her back. She'd only just come out of one bad relationship, after all, she reasoned to her friends. She wasn't sure if she was ready to throw herself into anything new so soon.

'Pffft,' Alexa had said scornfully, when she got to hear about it. 'You're thinking about it too much. Just hurl yourself in already; it's the best way.'

'I . . . I do really like him,' she said to Jo eventually, choosing her words with care. She remembered the glee of the website revenge mission with Gareth, how they'd laughed so much on those evenings, how she'd come to really enjoy his company, and trust him, too. 'I think he's a great guy. And it wasn't that I didn't fancy him, it just wasn't the right time for me, that's all. He took me by surprise.' She drained the last of her Cosmopolitan, feeling as if she'd drunk too much *and* said too much for one night. Why did those two things always go together? 'It's hard, though. I think I might have hurt his feelings, which was the last thing I wanted to do.' She spun her silver ring around her finger, an old nervous habit. 'Also, I was worried about what you and Bea would think,' she admitted. 'Because pissing you two off was the second to last thing I wanted to do.'

'Pissed off?' Jo cried, rolling her eyes. 'I'm not pissed off! I would have been delighted for you – and Bea the same. Honestly – look at me – it makes no odds to me, Rosa. I've been dying for him to meet someone else and be happy, rather than mooching about on his own forever. It might finally rid me of my hobbling guilt that I ruined his life, too.' Her green eyes were bloodshot from all the booze but still shone with sincerity. 'I mean it. Go for it!'

Four days later and Rosa still hadn't quite decided what to do about the situation. He'd probably met someone else by now, anyway, she told herself; forgotten all about her. Maybe he was embarrassed about the lunging kiss full stop, and hoping she'd have put it from her mind. Or else he'd written her off as frigid, a boring old prude. Maybe she *was* a boring old prude. Oh, whatever. Sometimes the timing was off and people missed one another. Paths crossing, but moving on to other destinations. Besides, she was so busy with her new foodie career taking off that she probably wouldn't have time for a relationship anyway.

'Thank you! Glad you enjoyed it!' The starters were all but finished now, and she could hear Natalya and Shamira busily collecting up plates out in the café area. Meanwhile, she was back in the kitchen, putting the finishing touches to a rather fabulous Spanish fish stew she'd adapted from a favourite Moro recipe, with monkfish and saffron and almonds. It smelled absolutely heavenly.

If romance wasn't in Rosa's life right now, it did seem to be springing up everywhere for other people, she found herself thinking, ladling portions of stew onto plates. Take Ann-Marie Chandler, for instance. Rosa didn't pay an awful lot of attention to Ann-Marie's Facebook timeline these days, granted, but even so, after she and Gareth had sent their little Wankers Incorporated bombshell to David, it was remarkable how quickly things had changed.

Amazing news! – Ann-Marie had typed, only days later – David's been promoted AGAIN! Even better, from now on, he won't have to do any travelling away from home! Family dinners every night again! Daddy home all weekends! We are so #happy #blessed #united.

Was that the distinct sound of a lesson learned, a wanker warned? It was definitely a line being scored underneath an episode in her life, that was for sure. Seeing Ann-Marie's guileless joy, the flurry of exclamations and hashtags, gave Rosa the strange feeling that she might just have saved her old enemy's marriage – so that was a large helping of irony for you. Still, she was over him now anyway. Was she bothered? No. Did she feel resentful any more? No. And had she enjoyed getting her own back? Yes, she bloody well had. They were quits, she had decided, and could leave it at that. Goodbye David, goodbye Max, hello rest of my life. And breathe.

'Is that all of them?' Natalya asked at that moment, and Rosa blinked at the plates of fish stew there in front of her, steaming and fragrant.

'Yes,' she said, closing the door in her mind to Ann-Marie and her husband. 'Yes, that's all of them.'

Out they went, she, Natalya and Shamira, delivering the main courses, plus bowls of a fennel and rocket salad, and some buttered Anya potatoes. 'Here we are, hope you enjoy it,' she said, setting plates down in front of Georgie and Simon, squeezed into a corner together, who were – yes – actually holding hands between courses. They had barely been apart since Simon's return to Brighton. (In fact, there had been so much joyful and noisy make-up sex that Rosa had had to buy some industrial-strength ear-plugs in the hope of ever managing to sleep again. Other people's love could be over-rated.)

'Thank you. This smells amazing,' said Georgie, smiling up at her now. Tonight she was wearing her blonde hair in plaits, fastened across her head, so that she looked like a milkmaid, albeit a milkmaid in a cerise mini-dress and big clumpy gold sandals, with clinking bangles halfway up one arm. 'God, we're going to miss this, aren't we, Si?'

'We are,' he said. 'We'll just have to come back to visit loads, that's all. Either that or you'll have to take some cookery lessons, George.'

'Er, what? You will, you mean,' she said, giving him a little shove. 'I'm not the one who nearly gave us salmonella with those raw poached eggs the other day, remember?'

'Definitely come and visit,' Rosa told them, simultaneously laughing and feeling a lump in her throat. She would really miss the two of them when they moved out at the end of the month. After much deliberating Georgie and Simon had decided to move back up to Yorkshire, where they were planning to buy some land so that Simon could build them a house. How romantic was that? Even better, they were getting married in the spring and inviting everyone who'd been part of their Brighton adventure.

'And I'll still be keeping *some* links with Brighton, even though we're leaving,' Georgie had told Rosa, 'because Viv says I can carry on with my *"Hey Em"* column from up north, special favour, she said. *And* she's got a mate who works at the *Yorkshire Post*, who she's going to put me in touch with. Plus there's my new business to crack on with. I'm really going for it – my friend Amelia's done me a website and everything, look, I'll show you on my phone. What do you think?'

Hold The Front Page! she'd called her new venture, and Rosa thought Georgie had actually hit on something pretty brilliant: mock newspaper and magazine covers, complete with personalized headlines pertinent to the subject, turned into prints, cards or posters for special birthday, wedding or anniversary gifts. 'I can see this really taking off,' she had told her truthfully, scrolling through the images on the website. 'Hey, and it's my sister's fortieth coming up, I'll definitely commission one for her.'

The other link – or perhaps even legacy – Georgie was leaving was with the House of Women, whose future now seemed secure thanks to a KickStarter funding campaign and talks of a government grant. Rosa couldn't help wondering if one of the hefty anonymous donations received had come from her ex – she sincerely hoped so. The women had reached an agreement with the council about staying in the building, too which they were all very happy about. Georgie had been volunteering every week there, starting up a book group; Charlotte had visited a few times, providing legal advice to the women; and Rosa too had begun helping out by giving basic cookery lessons once a fortnight. Every time she taught a recipe that included butternut squash as an ingredient, she thought of all she had learned this year, as well as all she could pass on to others.

'By the way,' said Georgie now, lowering her voice and leaning closer, as Rosa was about to hurry back to the kitchen. 'Is he here yet? Sexy Paul?'

'No! Not that I know of. He's teasing us, deliberately making a late entrance,' Rosa sighed, glancing over at the empty space next to her landlady, Angela, who was currently checking her watch and starting to look a bit miffed.

'He'd better bloody turn up!' Georgie said, rolling her eyes. 'After all this time! I'm desperate to see him. What if he really is as gorgeous and fabulous as Ange has always told us, and now I've got myself engaged to this one?' She elbowed Simon affectionately, and he elbowed her back.

'I know! Disaster!' Rosa joked. 'Well, I'm still single, anyway. I'll take care of him – if he ever shows, that is.'

Bustling back to the kitchen to get more food, she glanced again at Angela who was now calling someone on her phone. Sexy Paul, no doubt, to give him an earful. She could hardly believe that this legendary creature, unicorn-like in his mythical status, was actually going to turn up at her supper club and they would meet at last, after all of Angela's unsubtle matchmaking attempts with her various tenants. *You would love him, you know. I really must introduce* you. *He's just the perfect man, and I'm not saying that because I'm his mother. He is GORGEOUS. And still single! It's a crime, really it is. What are these women thinking, for heaven's sake?*

Mind you, a few months ago, Rosa would hardly have expected *Angela* to be here either, given the tongue-lashing she'd dished out that fateful night in June when her landlady had all but issued Rosa with her marching orders. It was amazing how being given a free pass to the supper club in its new surroundings had changed her mind. In fact, she'd even asked if Rosa might like to move upstairs, into Margot's old flat. 'It's much bigger than your current place, of course, and quieter up there too,' she'd said persuasively. 'Plus, it'll only cost you a tiny bit extra.'

A tiny bit extra in Angela's terms was no doubt double the price, but Rosa thanked her for the offer and said she'd think it over. Extra space and less noise was all well and good, but Rosa had become quite attached to her ground-floor flat, as it happened. Without wanting to sound like a cheesy greetings card, the place had been her new start, a cocoon into which she'd crawled at her lowest ebb, only to emerge, reborn and re-energized, all these months later. There was a lot to be said for a place that had handed you back your sanity, after all.

'Sorry about the wait, here you are,' she said now, delivering her final plates to the last table. This group of people included Ned and Charlotte, who looked thoroughly beautiful with her hair curled like a Fifties starlet, in a plunging neckline dress and red lipstick. Go, Charlotte! She'd seemed a new woman ever since she, Ned and his daughters had come back from a mega holiday in France, taking in sandy beaches, crumbling chateaux and a few days in Paris where they'd taken the girls to Disneyland. 'And all thanks to Margot,' Charlotte had sighed happily, showing Rosa the photos when she came back, tanned and bright-eyed from a fortnight in the sun. They had even gone out to Auray, the pretty little town where Margot had grown up and, having sought permission from a kind-faced chaplain in stuttering GCSE-level French, planted a white scented tea rose against a sunny wall in the churchyard in her memory. Afterwards, Charlotte told Rosa, Ned had taken the girls away in search of ice cream, while Charlotte sat for a while in the warm quiet sunshine of the churchyard and said her final goodbyes. 'And then we went and had really expensive gin and tonics in a bar, which I know Margot would have approved of way more than any old flowers,' she said, wrinkling her nose in a smile. 'So it was all good.'

Charlotte was still girlish and fluttery with love for Ned, even after spending two weeks away with him and his kids, which was surely an acid test of any relationship. Already they had met each other's parents (to mutual approval, apparently) and she was spending several nights a week at his place, as well as most weekends. During a recent SeaView House women's night out, she had opened up to the others, telling them about her daughter Kate who had died, before confiding in them that, although it was early days with Ned, she had already started thinking how lovely it would be to have a baby with him. 'I know you probably think I'm rushing madly into this but I feel good about the idea. Happy,' she had said. 'But in the meantime, I'm actually really loving being a step-mum. Did I tell you I'm taking the girls roller skating next week? I've bought us all matching skates!'

'Thanks, Rosa,' she said now, looking blissed out as she inhaled the scent of the fish stew. Then she craned her head to peer around the room. 'Hey, is he here, by the way? Paul? No offence, Ned, but I do want to at least get a *look* at this guy that Angela thinks is the perfect match for me, Georgie *and* you, Rosa. I mean, he must be some kind of Adonis, right? Some total hunk.'

'I'm amazed we haven't heard about him in the local press,' Ned said, deadpan. 'All those women that must swoon and faint every time he walks down the street . . .'

'Well, exactly! You'd think he'd be a public health hazard.' Charlotte fanned herself with the paper menu. 'I'm getting a hot flush just talking about the man, even before I'm in his godlike presence. I mean—'

'Wait a minute,' said Rosa, interrupting, as the door opened suddenly. 'This could be El Hunko right now . . .'

She, Charlotte and Ned all did their best not to stare as the latecomer walked in, gazing around as if looking for someone. He was tall and yes, as promised, extremely good-looking with what could only be described as a mane of shoulder-length brown hair which he shook back from his face as he strutted across the floor. Rosa frowned. She had seen him before somewhere, she thought. Where did she know him from?

'Oh my God,' Charlotte said, giggling. 'I don't believe it. It's *him*. I swear it's him. Where's Georgie?'

'Who?' Rosa asked, watching intrigued as Georgie and Charlotte pantomimed to each other across the room, both nodding vigorously, eyebrows raised. *I know!* their faces telegraphed with excitement. *It IS him, right?*

'Paul! Cooee! Over here!' Angela was shouting.

'Well, it's definitely lover-boy,' Ned said wryly, and they all watched as Paul strode over with an *Aren't-I-fabulous* sort of walk. That was where she'd seen him, of course! Rosa thought to herself, as the penny dropped. Preening on the Zanzibar dancefloor all alone, like he thought he was some kind of male god. So *this* was Paul!

'We saw him at the roller disco,' Charlotte hissed to them, her eyes wet from merriment. 'The twerking creep. The same one who was the nude model at Georgie's art class!'

'No!' Rosa said, spluttering with laughter. 'You mean . . . Liver sausage?'

'Liver sausage,' Charlotte confirmed. She leaned against Ned's shoulder, trying to compose herself. 'I think we had a lucky escape there, Rosa.'

'I think we did,' Rosa agreed, trying to keep a straight face as she went to greet the new arrival. *Lucky?* she thought, introducing herself, and vanishing into the kitchen to grab him a plate. Yes, she felt lucky. But there was such a thing as making one's own luck too, of course, with a pinch of bravery and a large chunk of determination thrown in for good measure. Look at her, for instance, running her own supper club these days. Look at Georgie too, setting up a new business and home – and Charlotte, taking the plunge with a whole new relationship and family. In fact, Rosa had had an inkling recently that, like Georgie, it might not be too long before Charlotte moved out of SeaView House herself, on to an even happier place.

Everything was changing at their big old house on Dukes Square, she thought; the house of hopes and wishes and friends, as Georgie had said over dinner that time. The house of new beginnings, too. Maybe it had always been like that, though: a staging post in people's lives, a temporary home where waifs and strays washed up, only to find themselves again eventually and move on. As she dished up Paul's stew, she reflected on how all three of them, her, Charlotte and Georgie, had moved in to their separate flats, feeling rather lost and unsure to begin with, fishes out of water all. It might have taken them a while, but these days it seemed they'd definitely all remembered how to swim.

'Anyone there?'

It was much later on, and Rosa was just about to close up for the night when she thought she heard a voice. The evening had been another successful one: the guests had all departed, leaving extremely pleasant compliments and even more pleasant tips in their wake, there was hardly any food left (always a good sign), and now the floor was mopped, the pots washed and the dishwasher busily taking care of all the crockery and cutlery. 'Hello? Anyone there?' came the voice again, followed by rapping at the door.

'Hello?' she called uncertainly, grabbing her denim jacket and bag from the side, her fingers reaching for her phone just in case she needed it. Very occasionally she'd had a drunk stumbling in as she was about to close – one guy had peed against the front door in the past – and she'd found another couple once practically naked and having sex around the bins. Natalya and Shamira knew to pull the door to behind them at least, but if there was some creep hanging around outside tonight, she might have to make an exit through the back. Oh God, she thought, and talking of creeps, what if it was Paul, come to chance his arm with her?

'Rosa? It's me, Gareth.'

His name was so unexpected that she stopped in her

tracks. 'Oh,' she said and, after a moment's hesitation, opened the door so that he could come in. Outside was shadowy dark, you could just about make out the sea, black and liquid, rushing and crashing in the background, with a few party-goers staggering past under the streetlight. In he came with a blast of cool night air, his hair a little longer than when she'd last seen him, his brown eyes kind of wary. 'Hi,' she said. 'I was just locking up.' She hesitated. 'How are you?'

'I'm very well,' he said. 'It's good to see you again.' There was a pause, and then he added, 'Actually, I was wondering if you fancied going on somewhere for a drink.'

Her heart thudded. 'What – now?' she asked. Jo had put him up to this, she thought in the next moment. She knew she shouldn't have had that last cocktail with her neighbour the other day, and blurted out the kissing confession.

'Yeah. If you want? I was just passing and wondered how you were.' He wrinkled his nose then shook his head. 'Well . . . No. I wasn't "just passing". That was me, trying to sound casual. I've been sitting in the pub round the corner for the last hour, wondering if coming here was a good idea or not.'

'Right,' she said cautiously. 'And you decided . . . that it was?'

'Yeah,' he said, although he still didn't sound very confident about it. 'Nice place you've got here, by the way,' he went on, gazing around. 'Bea's kept me up to date, obviously, with how business is booming, and how you're going to be the next Delia Smith, and—'

Rosa spluttered. 'Delia *Smith*? Is that the best you can do?'

'All right, Fanny Craddock, then, I don't know, but—'

'Fanny *Craddock*?' She started to laugh and the awkwardness she had felt at him being there ebbed away. 'God, Gareth, this drink you're going to buy me is getting more expensive by the second, mate.'

He grinned at her. 'Fine by me. I'll charge it to the Wankers Incorporated expense account. You can have whatever you like.'

She put her denim jacket on, turning her face for a moment so that she could think. 'Jo told you to do this, didn't she? This is Jo, sticking her nose in, I can tell.'

He opened his mouth as if he was about to deny it, then gave a reluctant nod. 'Well – she did ring me up and told me to pull my finger out,' he confessed, 'but she was only telling me what I already knew. And I'm not here just because of her, anyway. I'm here because . . . Because I missed you. And sometimes you have to go out and try again, don't you? Even if it is at the risk of making a dick of yourself twice over.'

His words resonated within her. *Sometimes you have to go out and try again, don't you?* It was true. Hadn't she just been thinking that earlier?

'You're not making a dick of yourself,' she told him

quietly, switching on the burglar alarm and then ushering him outside, where she locked the door.

'I'm not?' he asked hopefully. 'So . . . is that a yes? Are we about to stroll out into the night together in search of the most expensive drinking establishment Brighton can offer us?'

She laughed, pulling down the metal shutters and then attaching the padlock. 'It's a yes,' she agreed, turning to face him. Because sometimes it was worth trying again, wasn't it? Sometimes you had to pluck up the courage to take a chance on joy, be receptive to it, as the old fortune teller had advised. 'I'd love to let you buy me that expensive drink,' she said, smiling into his eyes.

Above them, the sky was freckled with silver stars, and the moon looked down, gleaming with a kindly light as the night wrapped itself around them. He slipped an arm through hers and they set off along the dark seafront together. It felt like the sort of evening where anything might happen, she thought, glancing sideways at his face and remembering the sensation of his lips against hers. Anything at all. What was more, she had an inkling that she was going to enjoy every last minute of it.